Chains and Anchors

Patricia Lock

Chains and Anchors

Single-handed sailor, Daisy, is used to looking after herself, but now, for the first time in her life, she's frightened and lonely. Her close friend, Floyd, has been killed whilst investigating suspicious activities at the marina where Daisy berths her yacht, Lady Louella.

Searching for clues to Floyd's murder, Daisy stumbles upon the human face of a trafficking racket and learns what life is like for an illegal immigrant without papers or money. At the same time, Daisy must meet her own challenges. Besides coping with Floyd's death, she is confronted with a chain of shocking revelations which links her family's prosperity with past iniquities and present crimes.

Author's note

I have drawn Daisy's passion for sailing from my minimal experience at sea and have devised Floyd's hinterland from original papers which came into my family in the early nineteen hundreds.

The documents were subsequently bequeathed to the William Wilberforce Museum and I wish to record my thanks to Vanessa Salter, Keeper of William Wilberforce House, Hull, who made them available to me and assisted me in my research.

I also wish to thank Hilary, Jane, Ailsa, Barbara and Annette, without whom Daisy would not have completed her voyage.

Cover photograph and design by Hilary Scudder

One

It's gone one a.m. when I cautiously ease open the door and peer out into the night. It's raining. Not a half-hearted drizzle, a full-blooded downpour capable of penetrating all but the most robust of city waterproofs. I guess I should be thankful for my offshore jacket, but somehow keeping dry doesn't seem that important. Not now.

I shake my head to clear my thoughts. I'm not going to think about Floyd, not at all. I've got to give my whole attention to getting away unseen. Even here, whilst I'm still sheltering in the doorway, I'm hoping - no, praying - I won't be spotted by some casual observer who happens to glance down from one of the darkened windows overlooking the yard: a somewhat unrealistic hope given the lurid fluorescent safety bands that illuminate my Musto.

Tears and rain mingle as I pull up the hood of my oilies and wipe my face with the tissue I've been using in my amateurish attempt to eliminate traces of my having been here with Floyd.

Floyd. No, no, not now, please, I need to concentrate.

Perhaps Floyd hears my plea, as, creeping and crawling through the yard like some monstrous glow-worm, I make my escape without falling over anything or colliding with the platoons of dustbins guarding the area.

At last I'm back on the street and I put on as much of a spurt as I my dodgy ankle allows as I pass the front of the barber shop and the Fast Tan Studio, the Party Place and the After Dark sex shop with its display of PVC corsetry, leather thongs and rubber masks, obviously intended for a different sort of party from those of the cake and jelly variety on offer next door.

The casual thought of food that the party shop provokes when Floyd is lying a few yards away with a hole in his head brings bile into my mouth and I lurch unsteadily to the kerb and throw up in the gutter.

Ducking into a shop doorway, I wipe my mouth and snatch a couple of deep breaths to steady myself. I emerge from my temporary refuge feeling guiltily conspicuous, but as the occasional car speeds past casting a curtain of spray between its cocooned passengers and me, it occurs to me that I needn't worry. Day-glow stripes or no, nobody will notice a solitary pedestrian in the rain, head down, hardly identifiable as female, scurrying away from the scene of a crime. Rain's like that - wet enough and you develop a shield of invisibility, concealed by mass misery from prying eyes.

Theorising on the particular qualities of rain gets me to the end of the parade but, as I'm waiting to cross the road, my blotting-out strategy fails me and the enormity of the crime I've left behind fills my head.

Crime: even the word's a fig leaf to my conscience: not crime, murder, and I'm running away from it - running away from Floyd. Leaving him there, alone, crumpled up and discarded, like an empty McDonald's box.

I can't leave him. I can't.

I turn round. Take a few paces. Falter. Stop.

I can't go back. How can I? Who knows what's going on there? I can't go back, and I can't go forward.

I'm hovering undecided on the pavement, caught on the horns of an immobilising dilemma, without the least idea of what I should do.

It's ages before the glaringly obvious occurs to me. The police. I must inform the police. But certainty changes instantly into doubt. How can I? Suppose they blame me for Floyd's death. Why wouldn't they? I blame myself. They'd have every right to lock me up and throw away the key. What's that expression they use? Impeding them in the execution of their duty. They'd say that, or worse, for causing Floyd's death. I'm pole-axed by the thought. They might charge me with his murder. The thought consumes me, surges through me in waves of panic. I need something to hold on to, to steady myself, but I can't move and the lamppost I'm groping for is swaying, toppling over...

The screech of car tyres saves me. I yank myself back from the brink. Dizzy and sweating, I force myself to start walking. I take a couple of steps and decide the thing to do is to report Floyd's death anonymously. A couple more strides and I know that's a stupid idea. So I keep walking. And I'm walking away from Floyd. I'm going home, back to Lady Lou where I'm safe. Still a nagging voice in my head's telling me that I'm not thinking straight; that if I were thinking clearly, I'd know that the only thing to do would be to get round to the nearest nick and drop the whole damn mess in their blue-serge laps, and take the consequences. But another voice is whispering about the horrors of solicitors and being interrogated and making statements, and the nightmare of trying to justify my efforts to remove my fingerprints doesn't bear thinking about.

So I'm tramping through the rain away from Floyd lying dead in the barber shop, and the further away I get, the fainter one voice becomes and the louder the other, and I'm nodding my head and whispering that I've a right to be irrational. I'm asking who wouldn't be, when they'd just discovered a dead body; the body of someone they were close to; someone they loved - though they never admitted it.

What I do admit is that I've been knocked off my perch and I'm reaching out trying to find something tangible to hold onto, but the only thing that's solid is that Floyd's dead and it's my fault. It's my fault for being obstinate, selfish and stupid. And having acknowledged that, the least I can do for him, the only thing I can do for him, is to try to carry on from where he left off, or rather from where he has been forcibly laid off, but without getting a bullet in my brains too.

As I cut across the road and hurry towards the alley where I chained my bike, I'm hanging on to that decision, trying to focus on what to do next, but a doubt about how I'm going to deal with the inevitable questions from friends at the marina when they read about Floyd's death in tomorrow's papers is creeping in. It's not until the doubt's a worry and the worry's bordering on panic that it occurs to me that it might never come to that; that even now, as I'm fleeing the scene, the perpetrator could well be spiriting Floyd's body away. I won't countenance the thought that I might even have interrupted him. And I definitely won't remember the noise.

A few miles out of town and my wretched ankle is really playing up; plus I'm already tired, wet and sweaty, cycling in my Musto being not unlike pedalling along in my own private sauna, but this seems preferable to stopping to take it off. Stopping, I think, wouldn't be a good idea. Stopping might lead to finding my legs turned to mush and an overwhelming desire to howl like the tormented heroine in a mawkish melodrama. So I go on, trying not to think about anything much, concentrating on the swish of the tyres as they eat up the miles, but every now and then I'm caught out when I see Floyd's face in the reflection from a headlight or hear his voice carried in the wind.

It takes what remains of the night to cycle back to where Lady Louella is bobbing on her moorings. Grey light is squeezing its way through the rain clouds when I arrive at the jetty, hoist the bike over the rail, release the catches to fold the frame and stow it in the aft locker.

Below, the cabin is warm and welcoming; the Irish whiskey even more so. One swig straight from the bottle and I'm peeling off my dripping jacket to hang it in the wet locker behind the companionway; two or three more before removing the rest of my kit. I tell myself I feel better already. And perhaps I do, but the tears spill out as I start the shower. Hardly worth turning on the tap, I'm crying so much. Floyd's dead and, for the first time in my life, I'm frightened and lonely.

Two

I'd been working as a temp in the government offices at the docks for the best part of eighteen months when I got the call.

'Telephone for you, Daisy,' a colleague called across the room to where I was engrossed in the never-ending search for missing files. 'Says it's personal.'

I knew it was Aunt Louise, or rather about Aunt Louise. She hadn't been in a position to make any 'phone calls for a year or two and it had been quite a time since we'd been able to have a sensible conversation. Recently, I'd just sat and held her hand, feeling the bones through her thin skin and seeing the purple blotches where other hands had gripped her too tightly, or she'd knocked herself against the furniture.

'Daisy,' she'd whisper, drawing my hand up to her mouth and kissing it. 'Daisy.' And that was all.

But before that, when she was still living at home, I'd sit opposite her, curled up in the wing armchair on the other side of the fireplace, and tell her my dreams. And sometimes she'd talk to me about the old days, when the house was filled with the babble and enthusiasms of three young girls.

Louise, my mother Ellen's sister, was older than her by a dozen years, and, since Mum had passed away, my only living relative. There'd been a younger sister too, called Victoria, but all Louise would ever say about her before she turned her head away and changed the subject, was that she'd drowned in the boating accident that had taken my grandparents' lives as well. And since I'm the world's worst at grasping the nettle myself, I never pressed her for the details.

We'd always been close, Mum, Louise and I, more so, I suppose, because Louise had taken charge of the household when my grandparents died, and there were no men around, my father having abandoned Ellen and me before I was out of nappies. That being the case, it didn't take a huge stretch of imagination to conclude that it was as a result of my father's behaviour that Aunt Louise would have no truck with men in general, and had seen off the oiks as she described the would-be suitors, who, she said, used to hover round the house like clouds of irritating

13

midges.

I suppose it's the result of being an only child that I don't find it that easy to unburden myself to others. My natural reserve in this area, combined with my succession of temporary jobs, has left me with a huge circle of what I think of as congenial acquaintances but few really close friends. And I can't pretend this has ever bothered me. The fact is there's a tradition of seafaring in the family - instead of relationships we have boats, sometimes on the river, but mostly by the sea – which may go some way to explaining why, after I left school, thoughts of boyfriends and romance were quickly eradicated by my love affair with sailing.

Hence Lady Louella, the love of my life, a 30 foot Bermudan sloop with a lifting keel, slab reefing, auto helm and a self-furling Genoa. She was moored at Mullion Quay and named in honour of my mum and my aunt, Ellen and Louise, who'd always been there for me. And she was where I spent my free time when I wasn't visiting the Nursing Home.

Anyway, a week or so after Aunt Louise died, I was sitting in the office of Mayhew and Robson, who had been the family solicitors, since, as they say, Nelson was a boy, and one, neither Mr Mayhew nor Mr Robson as it happens, but Mr Sedgeford, was telling me that the house was mine, lock, stock and barrel, which didn't come as a surprise as I knew there wasn't a mortgage and who else was there? What did come as a bolt out of the blue was the fact that I'd also inherited a very substantial sum of money; substantial enough to mean I certainly wouldn't have to worry about Louella's mooring fees anymore, or, come to that, any other financial affairs for the foreseeable future.

'Suffice it to say,' he reiterated carefully, in that pompous way solicitors adopt, 'that you are a direct descendant of William Callander who owned a number of lucrative shipping ventures in the late 1700's.'

I smiled politely and said that I had gathered from his exposition, (his face had twitched when I said 'exposition', but I couldn't decide whether that was because he hadn't thought I'd know any words of more than two syllables, or more likely because I hadn't used it correctly), the gist of what he was telling me was that money made from merchant shipping had been wisely invested through the generations. And he had nodded and, apart from a bit more legalese and signing a few forms, it was over and done with.

Thinking it over later, when the euphoria had subsided, I could see we'd always been comfortably off; for instance, as far as I could remember neither Mum nor Aunt Louise had ever gone out to work and I'd never been asked to contribute to any household expenses, which was why, I realised, I'd been able to afford to keep Lady Louella in the water. Come to that, how many young women get a yacht for their 21st birthday, albeit a second-hand one?

So there I was, approaching my thirty-first birthday, footloose and fancy free, and with enough money to take a year off work without worrying. More than a year in truth, but I thought twelve months about right for me to decide what I really wanted to do with my life. It was to be a year when Lady Louella and I might venture a little further abroad than Cherbourg or Caen, which were our normal ports of call whenever we could squeeze in the time.

The first thing was to hand in my notice. By comparison with some of the grotty jobs I'd had over the years, being a casual filing clerk in the offices at the docks wasn't that bad. The permanent members of staff were sociable, if somewhat harassed, and although the work in my lowly grade was basic and repetitive, I was surprised to find I meant it when I heard myself saying, at the boozy leaving-do they'd arranged for me in the pub, that I'd miss them, and it.

The next thing was to spend a week making the arrangements necessary for closing up the house for a year, and the last was to move the minimum of essentials onto Lady Louella.

I'd decided to lend my capacious, though somewhat battered, Nissan estate to Floyd, who had found himself between cars and temporarily out of funds having just sunk a not very small fortune on the down-payment of a flat, so the obvious solution was for him to come with me to the quay and drive the car back.

'Cor, luv a duck, Daiz,' he said, cranking up his South London accent into a parody of itself, as he checked out the minimum of essentials unloaded from the car and heaped up on the jetty, 'ow long yer going for?'

I could go on ad infinitum about Floyd's striking good looks, which I could best describe as Carlos Acosta come Denzil Washington, but I'll content myself with saying he was gorgeous. In fact, when I was first introduced to him, I had to make a conscious effort to stop my tongue hanging out.

'Daisy,' my manager had said, whilst I tried to stop myself blushing like some lovesick teenager, 'I'd like to introduce you to Floyd, who's here for a short spell to get a feel of life at the sharp end. Make sure you look after him.'

It turned out that Floyd was what is termed in the Civil Service a Fast Streamer, and he was working his way through the grades with some lofty position in view. He was currently on a whistle-stop tour of the outposts of the Home Office, which was how he came to have washed up on our shores, and why he'd followed me around for an hour or two, looking over my shoulder and making copious notes on his clipboard. I won't say it was anything earth shattering but I guess there was some sort of mutual spark because at lunchtime he'd murmured something about not knowing anyone and fancying a pint, and wondering if I'd care to join him. What's that question about the Pope being Catholic?

Floyd was, in my terms, a bit of a boffin. In anybody's terms, really. With some tactful probing on my part, I'd found out that he'd read Geology and related subjects at Cambridge, and after qualifying he'd taken his expertise out into the field, most recently to Africa. He hadn't said why he'd swapped his practical work in the Third World for the mundane administration of the British Civil Service, and there'd been a certain caginess about his reply when I'd applied a bit more of my tactful probing, which had discouraged me from pressing him further. That's not to say I didn't broach the subject again from time to time in my usual discreet manner, but I always met with the same evasiveness.

Actually, this nosiness on my part was pretty two-faced since I've never liked being questioned about my own life. But shortcomings and foibles aside, we definitely hit it off, and quickly got in the habit of slipping off for a beer or two after work. When his rapid induction into officialdom took him away to higher corridors, we'd meet up and grab a meal together whenever circumstances allowed. I liked him a lot and had gained more control over my tendency to drool, which didn't mean he was any less dishy, only that he was younger than me and destined for better things. Consequently I did my best to keep our friendship as just that, and much as I often bemoaned the distance between us, in a way I suppose it protected me from my baser desires, as irregular meetings in assorted locations weren't that conducive to romance.

'The quicker we get this lot on board,' I said, giving him a withering look, 'the longer I'll have to use it.'

For some minutes we worked in silence, apart from a degree of theatrical grunting and groaning as Floyd hefted the things over the rail to me and I stacked them in the cockpit. After that, it was just a matter of getting it all below and stowed away. I'd been up and down the companionway half a dozen times when it occurred to me that Floyd had disappeared. I poked my head out of the hatch and saw that he was standing idly on the pontoon.

'If you've got nothing better to do,' I said scathingly, 'you might pass some of the bags down, or are you just going to stand there looking decorative?'

Floyd had the grace to look embarrassed. 'Come on board, you mean?' he asked, glancing down at the gap between the fenders and dry land, 'well-'

'Have you dropped something in?' I asked as I stepped up onto the deck, 'I hope it wasn't the car keys.'

'It's not that, Daiz. It's-'

'It's what?'

'Water. I'm afraid of water.'

I was about to say something about not being so soft, when I noticed his expression, sort of stiff and drawn. Oh, oh. Serious stuff.

'Give me your hand,' I said, offering mine, 'and I'll steady you.'

He shook his head and turned away. 'I won't if you don't mind, Daiz,' he said, 'I like to have both feet on terra firma. Another time maybe.'

'It might not be for a while,' I said, as I scrambled off Lady Louella to join him, 'I'm hoping to be off on the first leg of my trip in the not too distant future.'

'It'll seem odd you not being around. I'll miss you,' he said, 'and worry about you. Are you sure you really want to do this? I mean, all that ocean; the Azores is a heck of a way away. And on your own?'

'No need to worry about me, I'm happy with my own company. Anyway it's not like I'm going round the world or anything, and I won't be by myself, I'll be with Lady Lou and we're like an old married couple that knows each other inside-out.'

Floyd sighed and stuck his hands in his pockets. 'Crazy,' was all he said.

'Just make sure you take good care of my car, or there'll be hell to pay,' I said, linking an arm through his. 'Shall I walk back to the car-park with you?'

'No, you get on with your chores, or you won't be organized before it gets dark.'

'It won't take long,' I said, and then suddenly not wanting him to go, added, 'Look, if you hang on, I'll get the rest of it below and then we can call in at The Salty Seadog for a drink and something to eat.'

He shook his head and pecked me lightly on the lips. 'I've never been any good at saying goodbye. So I'm off. Remember you've got my mobile number and you can always contact me at work. Be good and take care.'

I was up with the lark next morning, or at least I intended to be. As it was I didn't surface until after eight having been disturbed in the early hours by a bump and a shout, followed by a thump of feet on my deck that announced someone was about to tie up to the Lady Louella. Mullion Quay is only a small marina and it's not unusual to have boats rafted-up in the season, so this wasn't a total surprise, but it was a rude awakening. I briefly debated shrugging myself out of my sleeping bag to stumble up the companionway and poke a bare arm and thumbs-up through the gap above the hatch-board to signal I wasn't in a hurry to get away but couldn't summon up the energy.

A minute or two later as I was drifting back to sleep, I heard voices and activity above me and guessed the new arrivals were going ashore.

Some hours after that, clutching a mug of coffee, I emerged yawning from the warmth of the cabin into a chilly spring morning. A thin sun was doing its best but was being hopelessly outplayed by a brisk breeze, which was whistling through the marina, flapping emblems and pennants and anything else not securely tied down and chopping up the water to make it slap and slush between the yachts. There was a buzz in the air; the bustle of boats coming to life, the sight and sound of people coming and going and, from overhead, the constant discordant medley of wire halyards clinking against the masts. A flotilla of swans was moseying along the channel, now and then pausing to duck their elegant heads beneath the surface in search of grub, and everywhere the seagulls swooped and strutted and perched and preened, punctuating their activities with indignant cries. What was it Ratty had said in the Wind in the Willows? 'There is nothing - absolutely nothing - half so much worth doing as simply messing about in boats.' An understatement by my standards.

Sitting in the cockpit, sipping my coffee, I inspected the yacht that had tied onto me. She was a cutter-rigged ketch named Tiger Moth, longer than Lady Louella by several feet and certainly newer, but without her style. Or maybe that was just my prejudice talking. Perhaps it was because I'd spent so many hours scraping every trace of weed and algae and barnacles from Louella's hull and scrubbing her down inside and out that I thought she was sleeker and glossier than anything else in the marina.

There didn't seem to be anyone left onboard the Tiger Moth and it was obvious her crew had been eager to get ashore as they hadn't hung about long enough to flake the main, which was heaped over the boom and trailing on the deck. Tut, tut, I thought, what sloppy seamanship, I'd never leave Lady Lou half-dressed like that, however hungry I was. Which smug thought reminded me that my breakfast was overdue and drove me below, to rustle up eggs and bacon.

After breakfast I spent an hour or so checking Lady Lou out, tidying up and removing the splodges of birdlime, which are the downside to sharing a berth with the seagulls, and had just set off along the pontoon on my errands when I saw a youngish man coming towards me. I was still smiling and saying something about a lovely morning as he strode past with the barest acknowledgement and leaving only the whiff of a French cigarette hanging in the air.

I turned my head to watch him. He walked with a real seaman's roll, I suppose you might call it a swagger, and from the brief glimpse I'd caught of his face, I'd describe him as weather beaten and craggy. 'Please yourself,' I muttered under my breath. 'You might look like Steve Mc Queen in his heyday, but you certainly need to polish up your charisma.'

I stood and watched him until he drew level with Lady Louella, when I was somewhat mollified to see him flick his cigarette into the water before stepping over Lou's rail to reach the Tiger Moth. He didn't look back at me; so much for passing the time of day. For some reason I couldn't put my finger on, he'd quite spoilt my mood. I kicked at an inoffensive pebble and watched it spin away and drop between the boards of the pontoon into the water.

My good temper was restored in the chandler's. I pottered around for a while, and was sorting through a budget basket looking for a tap washer, when Megan, the manageress, spotted me.

'Daisy,' she said, 'the very person.'

'The very person for what?' I asked dubiously. Megan was a good friend and a saleswoman of no mean standing; a dangerous combination.

'Look, what d'you think of these? They only came in yesterday. Perfect for your trip.' She was steering me towards a rack of expensive looking fleeces.

'Very nice,' I said fingering a sleeve and turning over the price tag, 'but out of my price league. Plus I don't need one.'

'Don't be silly', she said. 'Of course you need one. You've been wearing that old thing for years. And anyway you're hardly broke. What about this one? It'll look brilliant with your colour hair. Try it on.'

'No,' I said firmly, as she slipped it off the hanger and held it out for me.

I was quite surprised when I looked in the mirror. It did suit me. I've got pale skin (in spite of all the hours I spend on the boat), and what I'm told is an unusual combination of red hair and blue eyes, and the intense blue of the fleece seemed to give me a definite something.

'There, I told you,' Megan said. 'I wish I had your colouring.'

Megan was very blonde and very tanned. It wasn't a genuine wish. 'Okay,' I said, 'no need to go over the top. I'll take it on condition you can get these fixed for me before my trip.' I handed over the pants of my Mustos, which I'd ripped on a cleat, to be repaired. She said they'd be ready in five days to a week, which tallied well enough with my plans. I could always wear my spares if I decided to make a short trip before they were back.

It didn't seem that long since breakfast but it was nearly two o'clock when I said goodbye to Megan and coasted into The Salty Seadog for a late lunch. I usually frequent the pub rather than the bar in the sailing club preferring the mix of people to the exclusively yachtie types in the club. The Salty Seadog's a post-war building, square, squat and ugly with nothing to recommend it except for its great atmosphere of warmth and hospitality, unlike the other pub down the road, a spit and sawdust sort of place where they don't take kindly to outsiders.

In summer there are lots of bare arms and brown legs in The Salty Seadog and in winter there's a mouth-watering smell of fish and chips and a roaring fire with a huge grate where you can dry as much of your clothing as it's decent to take off.

'Not long now then, Daisy,' Jeff, the barman, said as he brought my cheese ploughman's and another half of draught cider over to my table. 'I'll be thinking of you sailing the ocean blue whilst I've got my nose glued to the grindstone here.'

'As if you didn't get away once in a while yourself.'

Jeff grinned. 'You know what it's like. When you've been away a couple of months you can't wait to get home, and when you're home all you can think about is getting away.'

'What you mean is, the place gets too hot for you. Suzie finds out about Diane, Diane tells Ruth and it all gets back to Megan. Time you thought about settling down.'

'What is it they say about pots and kettles? I can't see any sign of you hanging up your oilskins.'

'The difference is I don't have an armada of admirers in every port.'

'Oh, you have them, Daisy. You have them. You just don't notice them floundering along in Louella's wake.'

I laughed. 'I wish,' I said. But I didn't really. A serious love life didn't figure in my plans at all. At least not for years and years.

When I got back to Lady Lou, I didn't feel like doing anything much. I put my new fleece away and fiddled around fitting the washer on the dripping tap in the galley, then went back on deck to catch what was left of the sun. Huddling myself up in the cockpit out of the wind with a flask of coffee laced with whiskey to hand, and a warp that needed splicing, I was soon dozing.

The smell of cigarette smoke woke me. People have different rules about smoking onboard, but since I'd kicked the habit I'd become obsessive about it and even resented folk smoking on their own boats if they were anywhere near Louella. Talk about over the top. Anyway, the culprit in this instance was a stocky dark-haired man who had one arm in a sling and a fag clamped between his lips. He was crossing my foredeck on his way to the Tiger Moth where the McQueen look-alike was lounging against the mizzen with a bad-tempered expression on his face. McQueen made no attempt to assist the hurt man as he climbed over the rail, but followed him down as he disappeared below. It crossed my mind that the man's injury could have been the reason for the crew's swift disembarkation that morning. On the other hand it could just as easily have had nothing whatever to do with it.

And that was the last I saw of them then, as by the time I got back from the pub that evening, the Tiger Moth had upped sails and gone.

I was planning to get away by the end of the month so when I wasn't getting my stocks on board and checking everything from the anchor to the yardarm, or poring over charts and tide tables and passage-planning check sheets, I was sticking rigorously to my daily cycling and fitness regime. Engaged in a constant whirl of activity meant that time sped by over the next few days.

It was only a little later in the day as when she'd tied up to me that first morning when I spotted the Tiger Moth again. Only this time I really had been up with the lark and had taken Lady Lou round to the quayside to fill up with water and diesel.

There weren't many people around as it was a dismal, wet dawn and it seemed to be taking ages to fill the tanks, so I was occupying myself watching the few yachts that were on the move - always a matter of great interest to us matelot types, a bit like plane spotters I suppose - when I saw Tiger Moth chugging up the channel. That's not to say I recognised her immediately, in fact she'd tied up and her crew were disembarking at a rate of knots when something half-clicked in my mind. Even then, it wasn't until I saw four people making their way along the pontoon towards the jetty, and was thinking how inadequately the women were dressed for any kind of sailing, let alone a night trip, that I finally recognised the men. Steve McQueen and A.N.Other complete with sling, all done up in their oilies, with two young women who, in marked contrast, were wearing skimpy jackets and unsuitable shoes, high-heels by the looks of them, and with hair that had escaped the confines of their flimsy headscarves, straggling wetly round their faces. A couple of birds the men had pulled the night before, I supposed, who were being returned to shore.

I was still watching them as one of the women caught the heel of her shoe between the planks on the pontoon and brought them all to a halt. After a brief struggle the shoe was wrenched free and the party set off again, the men visibly chivvying the women along.

At this moment the sound of water coming up the overflow pipe indicated the tank was full and by the time I'd turned off and disengaged the hose the Tiger Moth's crew were out of sight.

Three

I think it must have been three or four evenings later, because I know Louella and I had been over to France for a couple of days, as much for the change of scenery as to stock up on cheap booze, that I was going over the plans for my trip with Jeff, the barman in The Salty Seadog.

'Personally,' he remarked casually, 'I wouldn't undertake a single-handed voyage like the one you're proposing with a self-furling jib.'

Jeff has sailed more oceans than I've had hot dinners and to say I respect his seamanship would be a long way short of the truth. Consequently his remark was like being hit over the head with a sledgehammer, which was unfortunate since I'd just taken a generous slurp of cider.

'You wouldn't what?' I gabbled stupidly, as I mopped myself with the hanky he thrust into my hand.

'I wouldn't go with a huge mainsail and relying on roller reefing for the Genoa,' he said patiently. 'You'd be better off with a cutter rig in those seas, less canvas and more options. But I presume you've thought all this through.'

I hadn't, of course. I'd got so used to pottering around in local waters that I'd kind of forgotten the downside: the difficulties of dealing single-handed with that amount of sail in bad weather and the worrying prospect of managing without the jib if the gear conked out.

I was still mulling over his advice when he'd got up from my table and moved away to get on with his work and give Suzie, his latest conquest, who'd just breezed in, the benefit of his come-to-bed eyes, seafaring brawn and undisputed expertise.

It wasn't until much later when I was lying in my bunk on Lady Lou, listening to the waves slapping their insistent lullaby against the hull that I made up my mind.

I was in Sealine Rigging first thing the next morning.

Having outlined my needs, I was anxious to get on. 'The thing is,' I said, 'I was hoping to leave soon, so I need to know how long it will take, when you can start and whether you can do it in situ?'

'I dunno, Daisy,' Phil replied, 'I've got a lot on at the minute.'

'Oh,' was all I said, trying not to sound too disappointed, but I think maybe my expression said more, because he said,

'Okay, seeing as it's you, I'll see if I can come down later today and check her out, make sure it's straightforward. No promises mind.'

Walking back from the riggers, I was sauntering through the boat yard looking at the work in progress, when who did I bump into? Well, not exactly bump into but near enough; the crew of the Tiger Moth. They were coming along the walkway through the boatyard when I came out from behind a lugger; the same men, easy enough to recognise, what with the one's weather-beaten good looks and the other's sling, but with a couple of different women. True, I hadn't seen the first pair close up, but I was sure they weren't the same two. These seemed older for one thing, late twenties, I thought, and judging by their flat, lace-up shoes and dated coats, not too bothered about their appearance. They were clutching an assortment of bulging carrier bags and looked like a pair of hard-up 1950's housewives out of time and place.

'Morning,' I said brightly as they passed me, to which there was no response other than the barest nod of recognition from McQueen.

Odd, I thought as I ambled back to Lady Lou. Quite odd.

Of course, what I hadn't taken account of when I decided to change Louella's rig was that, although Phil from Sealine Rigging came through with flying colours and had the job done in a couple of days, the new sails were to take more than a week. By this time I was getting a bit fed up and had had my fill of The Salty Seadog's evening menu and suddenly another seven days of kicking my heels and eating jumbo sausage and mash seemed way too long.

I rang Floyd at work.

'Floyd,' I said, 'it's me, Daisy.'

'Blimey, girl,' he said, 'I was just thinking about you.'

'When you're supposed to be working,' I scolded him.

'I'm having lunch at my desk,' he said, 'and I think I'm entitled to think how much I miss you when I'm eating my sandwiches.'

'I'm flattered anyway,' I said. 'It seems ages since we had a session propping up the bar in the Red Lion.'

'I thought you'd be too busy to be missing me. 'Expect you're crossing the equator or some such as we speak.'

I laughed. 'Some such,' I said. 'Or a few times round the marina anyway.'

'You're still stuck in port?' he asked, suddenly serious. 'What's up? Lady Lou sprung a leak?'

'No, nothing like that, I decided to change my rigging, that's all. And these things take time.'

'I guess they would. So what you been doing with yourself?'

'Making sure Lou's shipshape, checking and counter-checking. You know the sort of thing.'

'Not really, Daiz, I've never set foot on a boat. Wouldn't know the port from the starboard and haven't got the least intention of discovering which is which.'

'You don't know what you're missing,' I said.

'I know I'm missing you,' he said. 'Look, if you're at a loose end, why don't I come down for a day or two? I could do with a few days' leave. We could have a few jars and you could show me round the area.'

'That'd be great,' I said.

I knocked a few miles off my daily cycling circuit to be there in time and was waiting for Floyd when he pulled into the quay car park next morning. I was pleased to see my car didn't have any new dents, but even more pleased to see Floyd.

'Daiz, it's great to see you,' he said as he scrambled out of the car and hugged me.

'You too,' I murmured, realising, from the confines of his hug, just how much I meant it.

'I've got until the end of the week,' he said. 'Need somewhere to stay.'

'There's loads of room on Lady Lou,' I reminded him hesitantly, not wanting to seem pushy. 'She could sleep six if you all knew each other very well.' I don't know if I was offended or relieved when he shook his head.

'I'd love to take you up, Daiz, but there's this little matter of her being on the water.'

Of course, I'd conveniently overlooked his hydrophobia. 'You're sure?'

'Sure.'

'It'll have to be a B & B or a pub then. Which d'you fancy?'

'Don't mind as long as it's near. What about that pub you hang out in?'

'The Salty Seadog doesn't have accommodation. We'll have to head into town and see what we can pick up.'

'D'you want to drive, or shall I?'

'You drive, I'm out of practice.'

He grinned. 'You're having me on,' he said.

Actually I wasn't kidding. For some reason I was feeling decidedly jittery and didn't fancy driving at all.

We found Floyd a reasonable B&B just outside the harbour area, dropped off his bag and the heavyish briefcase he'd brought with him, which turned out to be his laptop (a portable computer, he'd explained, in a voice that wondered what planet I was on) and bundled back into the car.

'Where to first?' he asked.

I checked my watch. 'I feel a pint of cider and a cheese ploughman's coming on. How about you?'

'Good thinking,' he said.

Over lunch he talked a bit about work. Since I'd left, he'd been assigned to a desk job in Immigration and I sensed he wasn't that happy about it.

'Why don't you like it?' I asked him. 'You said yourself it's only for three months to give you a feel for it.'

'I've got that all right,' he said, 'and maybe that's the problem.'

'Go on then,' I said, 'don't keep me in suspense.'

'Well, I've realised, you see, that no one on the front line actually makes policy, however high a rank he holds. Policy is made by politicians. Civil servants only serve that policy.'

'So that's why you joined the Civil Service,' I said, light dawning, 'and gave up your technical skills, to try to alter things.'

He nodded. 'When I got back from Africa I was burning to do something that I believed in; something I felt would really make a difference. I dunno, maybe I was deceiving myself, trying to cover up the hash I made of things while I was away.' He stopped abruptly.

'What hash?' I asked.

'I ... I'm not ready to talk about that yet,' he said. 'Still thinking it through.'

'My guess is you got too involved.'

He shrugged. 'You can see it straight away.'

'I know you've got a slow fuse,' I said lightly, 'but I think you'd find it extremely difficult to stand back if you saw something really iniquitous.'

'You've only known me since I came back from Africa. I wasn't so high-minded before.'

'I'm sure you were. I don't think that sort of characteristic suddenly comes on.'

'Who knows? The fact is that stint in Africa made me look at things differently and I've been trying to redress the balance ever since.'

'No wonder you're getting frustrated in the Civil Service. It's not exactly known for its progressiveness.'

'You're right.' He sighed. 'This is why I'm thinking about handing in my resignation.'

I was gob-smacked. 'Pardon?'

'I said, I'm thinking about resigning.'

'But what will you do? You've got the mortgage on your flat. Have you got something else lined up? You won't be moving away will you?'

He looked surprised. 'Why would you think that?'

'Oh, I don't know. Africa and everything.'

'Perhaps I should point out it's you that's hell bent on disappearing over the horizon.'

'Well,' I said, 'that's true, I suppose, but it's only a sailing trip for a few months.' He looked at me in such a penetrating way as I said this that I was quite unable to continue.

After a longish pause he said, 'Actually, I'm writing a book.'

That really took the wind out of my sails. It was quite some time before I spluttered something about him being a dark horse and when was I going to see it.

'Don't think it's your kind of thing, Daiz,' he said.

'D'you mean you think it's too literate for me, or perhaps too salacious?'

'Tetchy,' he observed. 'Let's change the subject.'

So I let it drop for the moment. There was plenty of time to change his mind for him.

After that we gossiped a bit about the affair between the po-faced deputy personnel officer and one of the pinstriped high-ups. Their liaison was generally believed to have started in the cleaners' cupboard at the Christmas party and the endless permutations of jokes relating to buckets and brooms and feather dusters were still sending gales of the laughter throughout the building, though Floyd guessed that it was only a matter of time before they were called to book. Most likely, we both agreed, it would be she of the po-face who got the chop, the Home Office being unlikely to sack the man in spite of its trumpeted equal opportunities policy.

In the afternoon we strolled through the old town taking in the rows of Tudor houses with their tiny mullioned windows, whitewashed walls and exposed beams.

'All very picturesque,' Floyd commented, as we gazed fascinated at one whose roof tilted at an alarming angle to its walls and whose windows slanted in an altogether different direction, 'but can you imagine trying to get your things in? I mean imagine a wardrobe or a fridge freezer. I doubt there's a flat wall in the place.'

'That's part of its charm, I suppose,' I said, 'and I expect you get furniture made to measure.'

'Hm,' Floyd said. 'Wouldn't do for me, anyway. I'm a modern-plumbing, purpose-built-property sort of bloke.'

'And there I was thinking you were a romantic.'

He gave me a quizzical look. 'You don't mean that?'

I laughed. 'Not really, you have traditional manners, but a modern outlook. On balance I'd say you were more of a realist than an idealist.'

'You don't think I have ideals?'

'I don't think that's the same as being idealistic,' I said. 'Being idealistic hints at an impractical dreamer; ideals are about principals and standards.' I paused for breath and glanced at him. He was grinning at me. 'Oh you,' I snapped, 'you're just winding me up. You know the difference perfectly well.'

'Shades of English,' he said, moving to the outside of the pavement and taking my arm, unconsciously exemplifying my point. 'What shall we do now?'

We glanced in the windows of a couple of the antique shops that were clustered in the square round the cathedral, but I could tell they weren't really Floyd's thing, and he didn't fancy the castle ruins, so we made our way back to the car.

'Where to?' he asked as he held the door open for me and I climbed in.

I reached round and picked up the driver's atlas that was lying on the back seat and began flicking through the pages. 'I don't really know what to suggest,' I said, 'I'm so used to just pottering around the harbour, or if I fancy a change of scene sloping off in Lady Lou. I wish you would come on board,' I said, without looking at him, 'I could show you the plan for my trip and -'

'Daiz,' he said taking the atlas away from me and dropping it back on the rear seat, 'I can't. I'm sorry.'

For a while we just sat there saying nothing. What was there to say? I loved the water and he hated it. It hadn't mattered a jot in the work environment but now it seemed like the most enormous problem. I couldn't invite him into my home.

Against my better judgement we ended up in the pub. I'd expected that Floyd's visit would have kept me away from its charms at least for a few nights and I wasn't overjoyed about it, but it worked out quite well. For one thing it meant that Floyd didn't have to worry about driving and for another there were enough people, especially women, all too pleased to engage him in conversation.

It was great, for a while, seeing Floyd being the centre of attention, but when May insinuated herself onto his lap and curled an arm round his shoulders, I suddenly decided enough was enough.

'We're going to eat now,' I said firmly, 'so I'll have to drag Floyd away.'

I usually eat in the bar, but The Salty Seadog does have a restaurant and it seemed a good time to try it out.

Floyd was looking very pleased with himself as we settled at our table.

'What's that smug expression in aid of?' I asked crossly.

'Nothing, Daiz, honest. I was just thinking how nice your friends are.'

I gave him my best withering look and we both laughed.

Starters and main courses behind us, we'd ordered our second bottle of wine and were chatting about nothing in particular when I decided to ask Floyd more about his potential writing career. 'What's the title of this book you're writing then? This book that's too highbrow for me to appreciate?' Uh-oh. The thought crossed my mind that I hadn't phrased that as tactfully as I might have.

Floyd's expression concurred.

'I meant,' I said hurriedly, 'that I thought we were friends and that being the case I'd have thought you might have trusted me with something you obviously care about.'

'As I said before, I don't think it's your kind of subject matter. Wouldn't want to bore you rigid.'

'I'm sure it wouldn't bore me. Anyway if you're serious about being a writer you've got to expect some criticism.'

'That's true.' He sighed and looked dejected and for a moment I thought he was going to clam up on me, but instead he said, 'I'll think about it, okay? He picked up the menu. 'Now let's change the subject. D'you fancy a sweet?'

'Only if you twist my arm,' I said.

'Oh,' he said, sounding disappointed and glancing back at the menu with a longing expression.

'Well, go on, twist it,' I said, 'I can't stand seeing strong men cry.'

We both chose *Death by Chocolate*. I didn't talk during this session. Couldn't. I just concentrated on every luxurious melting crumb and only looked up when I'd practically scoured the pattern off the plate. Floyd was leaning back in his chair a half smile on his face.

'Pudding was a good idea,' I said. 'Naughty -'

'But nice,' he concluded. He paused. 'That's part of what worries me, I suppose,' he said thoughtfully, his smile fading. 'We have so much and take it for granted. Yet we begrudge others a share in what we have.'

'No,' I said, 'I don't agree. I'm sure I've never...'

He interrupted. 'I don't mean individually, Daiz. Don't you see? We rely on our government to do it for us. Tough immigration laws; tougher measures about housing and benefits; holding centres; restricted rights to appeal, etc, etc, etc.'

I made a small movement with my head that might have been construed as a nod and waited for him to continue. I suppose the altruistic part of me wanted to agree wholeheartedly, but the selfish bit was saying something a good deal more pragmatic about having to have some barriers to prevent us being overrun. Overrun. As I thought the word I felt ashamed. Overcrowded, I corrected myself immediately, but there must have been something in my expression that gave me away, because I caught Floyd giving me a really sceptical look.

'Go on,' I said quickly, before he could say anything. 'I'm all ears.'

'No,' he said, 'now's not the time for a lecture on the inequable distribution of the world's wealth.'

'Just as well,' I said glibly, 'I'd be hopelessly out of my depth.'

He shook his head. 'That's it in a nutshell, Daiz,' he said, 'most of us don't have a clue about the injustices that come with a global economy. But think about it, how would you feel if you were starving whilst the fruits of your labours were literally being transported half way round the world for someone else's benefit?'

I shrugged and pulled a face. 'I take the point,' I said, 'but when it comes to this sort of issue, I tend to bury my head in the sand. What could I do about it, anyway?'

It was his turn to shrug. 'Lucky everybody doesn't think like that, or my family and hundreds of thousands of other people would still be enslaved.'

I started to say something about my not meaning that at all, but he shook his head again and said, 'All I'm trying to say is that, in my opinion, we should have a more humane policy towards refugees and economic migrants.'

It was a rebuke and probably justified, but it had been a good many years since anyone had chastised me and I didn't like it. 'Well, 'I began huffily, pushing back my chair and starting to stand up.

'No, Daiz,' he said reaching over and catching my wrist, 'I'm sorry. Didn't mean to have a go at you. Sensitive subject for me.'

I must say this whole conversation was something of a shock. Obviously I knew Floyd had suffered some pretty defining moment as a result of what he'd seen in Africa: what I had to get to grips with just how much it impinged on his thoughts. Not feeling well enough informed to keep up my end of the discussion with any degree of conviction I was casting around for a subject from within my sailing world to get the conversation going again, when Floyd beat me to it.

'So tell me, Daiz,' he said, looking at me searchingly, 'what you've been up to? Any husky sailor-boy swept you off your feet?'

I felt a frisson of alarm at the very idea. 'I wish,' I said.

'You always say that,' he said, 'even when you don't mean it.'

'Say what?'

''I wish.''

'Do I?'

Floyd didn't answer. I noticed he seemed to be studying a drip of wine on the tablecloth rather over-intently.

'Floyd,' I said hesitantly, and was unaccountably relieved when he looked up and gave me a lazy smile. It was strange, I thought, how stilted things had become between us and how near falling out we'd been all day. As if there was something we each expected the other to say. Or maybe -

The flash of insight that had been hovering on the brink of my consciousness nose-dived back into oblivion as Floyd asked, 'How have you been passing your time then? Don't tell me it's been in preparation for your trip - that must have been sewn up days ago.'

'I guess so although you can always find some job that needs doing. And -'

'And what?'

I was going to say something about never being bored on Lady Lou when I realised that wasn't quite true. Time had been hanging a bit heavy.

What had happened to our normal easy-going banter, I wondered, as after a longish pause Floyd asked, 'Keeping up your cycling?'

'Mm. And doing a bit extra.'

'That's good. What else you been up to?'

'Just pottering really. Watching the boats on the ebb and flow of the tide.'

'Sounds riveting.'

He sounded so indifferent, I felt quite cross and was about to say something sarcastic, when I thought of the comings and goings of the female passengers of the Tiger Moth. 'Well,' I said, as much to show that I wasn't a complete waste of space as anything, 'you'd be surprised at what I do notice. For instance -'

He raised an eyebrow.

'It concerns,' I said, in a voice laden with drama, 'the mystery of the Tiger Moth.'

Once I had his attention I dropped the silly voice and told him about the surly, though handsome, skipper, the mate with the injured arm and the two sets of females who had emerged from the boat and looked to be neither day-trippers nor crew.

'How could you tell that?' he said.

'Because of the way they were dressed, I suppose. I'd expect even occasional sailors to look a bit more yachty and visitors or day trippers less dowdy.'

'A couple of non-trendy women and you're making a mystery out of it.'

'Not two women,' I said patiently. 'Four. And it was the second pair that struck me as being so frumpy; I didn't think anything about the first two I saw, other than they weren't dressed for sailing.' I paused. 'Thinking about it now, I suppose it's a cumulative thing. I'd put the first two down as dolly birds on the pull and wouldn't have given them a second thought if it hadn't been for the others, who were so out of place.'

I'd gone on to tell him about the slapdash way they'd left the Tiger

Moth that first morning when I realised his attitude had changed. 'What's up?' I asked. 'You look funny.'

'I don't feel funny,' he said, 'the opposite if anything. Run all that past me again and don't spare the detail.'

And so I did, with him interrupting now and then to ask for times, and descriptions, and my impressions.

'Anything else you can think of?' he asked as I paused for breath.

I shook my head.

'Illegals,' he said. 'No question in my mind.'

'Illegals?' I repeated stupidly. 'Illegal what?'

'Immigrants. And for goodness sake keep your voice down.'

I flashed a look round the room. We were the only diners and the waitress had abandoned us once she'd loaded us up with coffee and liqueurs. 'Don't you think you're over-reacting slightly?' I asked sotto voce. 'This is The Salty Seadog and there's nobody here but us.'

Floyd glared at me. 'Daiz,' he said in a warning voice, 'just for once will you take me seriously. Can't you see how suitable the area is for bringing people in?'

'Not really, it seems to me that you're getting things a bit out of proportion,' I said as I reached for the coffee jug. 'A few minutes ago you're chastising me for making a mystery out of a couple of women inappropriately dressed for sailing and now you're conjuring up some international smuggling ring.'

'You forget where I work'

'*Precisely* what I haven't forgotten,' I said echoing his word. 'Don't you think it's because of where you work and how strongly you feel about the issue that you're getting up a head of steam?'

Floyd had started on an admonishing and eloquent discourse about my lack of insight when the waitress arrived at our table.

'Time's up,' she pronounced breezily, gazing at Floyd in what I could only describe as an openly lustful manner. 'The restaurant's closing now so I'm afraid you'll have to continue your tête-à-tête in the bar.'

It was gone eleven thirty when we left. We hovered for a minute or two on the pavement outside, but a spiteful wind seemed to be deliberately hurling the rain straight at us and it wasn't the place for a prolonged discussion.

'I'll say goodnight, then,' I said, pulling up the hood of my jacket and burying my hands deep in my pockets whilst trying to convince myself I didn't care how out of kilter we were.

'I'll walk back with you,' he said.

I looked at the rain dripping off his nose and soaking through the shoulders of his denim jacket. 'See you in the morning,' I said firmly, 'and wear something a bit more substantial.'

'Sure,' he said, 'I'll call for you about ten thirty.'

Four

Hurrying back along the jetty towards Lady Lou I spotted a crew disembarking along the left-hand pontoon. With my head down and most of the rest of me trying to disappear entirely into the protection of my Musto, it was amazing that I noticed them at all. I suppose it was because there was absolutely nobody else about that the movement attracted my attention. Even so, it wasn't until I caught a glimpse of white across one person's chest and registered the behaviour of the group that the penny dropped - McQueen's mate and four others, disembarking.

If you're not used to it, it's not that easy to cross the rails from one yacht to another, particularly if it's dark, windy and wet and the water's choppy, and three of the figures were obviously finding it difficult. Two were holding on to each other and lurching across the foredeck of the middle boat, the third was still cowering against the cockpit on the outer boat. The two others were moving between them, obviously urging them on.

Suddenly Floyd's hypothesis didn't seem so outlandish. My first thought was that I didn't want to be seeing this. The second was that in that case I should stop gawping and get the hell out of there. No sooner the thought than the deed. I scurried past the end of their pontoon and on towards the safety of Lady Lou, praying that they'd be too preoccupied to notice me.

Needless to say, I wasn't in the least sleepy when I got back on board. I poured myself a generous measure of Irish, pulled on a woolly hat and an extra sweater and settled myself in the cockpit. Rocking to and fro with the water, listening to the rain beating on the cover and the wind whistling round the rigging, I could easily have dismissed the difference of opinion with Floyd as being six of one and half a dozen of the other. But conscience wouldn't let me. The first point was that I'd been seriously out of order. Whether it was because I was miffed that things hadn't been going as well as I'd hoped between us, or because he'd had the effrontery to tell me off; or because it seemed likely that he'd been right and I'd been wrong about the Tiger Moth's activities, or, as I suspected, a combination of all three, what I absolutely definitely needed to do was to apologize first thing next morning.

I was going on to think something else profoundly meaningful when I heard something; something over and above the noise of water and weather and boats. I took another sip from my glass and listened attentively. There it was again - my name on the wind. I shook my head and downed my drink; time to turn in when you start hearing voices.

I got to my feet and was surprised to find how unsteady I felt. The deck was definitely vacillating and I didn't think it was all because of the broken water. Maybe, I conceded as I moved shakily forward to go below, the whiskey hadn't been my best idea on top of the wine and liqueurs.

At the precise moment that I leaned forward to step into the hatch, I lost my balance altogether. At least, in the seconds I had to draw any conclusion about what was happening as I found myself pitching forwards down the companionway with a high-pitched scream echoing in my ears, that's what I presumed.

When I opened my eyes, it took a moment or two to get my bearings. I was definitely on Lady Lou but seeing her from an angle not familiar to me. I squeezed my eyes tightly together and opened them again, but the view was just the same. Cautiously I turned my head to one side. A stabbing pain travelled from the top of my head to the tips of my toes. I winced and let out a curse that caused the pain to backtrack from toes to head and thrash around a bit before constricting itself like a scold's bridle to a band of agony above my eyes; all this to establish I was spread out on the cabin floor.

'Careful,' a voice said, 'you're not supposed to move. And that's not very nice language for a lady.'

Floyd's face hove into view. He was kneeling next to me and I realised belatedly, holding my hand. There was something under my head and a blanket over me.

'Blimey, Daiz,' he said, 'you had me worried there.'

'Floyd? Here?' I managed.

'You took a tumble,' he said.

I screwed up my face with the effort, 'I remember that, but how did you get here?'

'Later, Daiz,' he said, 'right now we have to deal with the practicalities. I've phoned 999 and the ambulance is on its way. I've got to keep you warm and quiet until they get here. Shouldn't be too long now.'

I felt a tear squish out and run down my cheek. Followed by one or two more. 'I'm fine,' I said.

'Sure,' he said, 'I can see that.'

They kept me on a trolley in casualty overnight, during which time an occasional medic passed my way, took tests, temperature and x-rays and eventually diagnosed a multitude of contusions, bruised ribs and a sprained ankle, not to mention what I thought was a hangover and they insisted was more than a touch of concussion. Throughout the whole sorry business Floyd hovered by my side like a guardian angel, filling in the hours by explaining what had happened.

'It's my fault,' he said holding my hand and gazing soulfully at me. 'I shouldn't have left you.'

I smiled wanly hoping I was looking brave and ethereal, but suspecting I looked ratty and washed-out. 'Don't be silly, of course it isn't. I had too much to drink and fell down the companionway. Serves me right.'

'No, I should have seen you back; made sure you were safe and sound before I left you. Not that -'

'Not that, what?' I asked.

'Sorry,' he said, 'I've lost my train of thought.'

I waited a minute to see if he was going to say anything else but he wasn't forthcoming. He just sat there looking glum and patting my hand.

'Tell me one thing,' I said. 'Did you call me; call out to me, a little while before I fell?'

He nodded.

'Well, that's a relief at least. I thought I was hearing voices.'

'All my fault,' he muttered.

'I'd have gone below at some point, you know,' I interrupted, 'and I'd had far too much to drink. I doubt your dulcet efforts to attract my attention made a hap'erth of difference. And what's more,' I continued before he could get a word in, 'if you hadn't come back I'd still be lying there.'

He shook his head, clearly unconvinced. 'I dunno -'

'There is one thing that bothers me,' I ploughed on, trying to head him off.

'What's that then?'

'Why did you come back?'

'I dunno really. I guess -' he sighed.

'You guess what, Floyd?'

'I guess I wanted to say sorry.'

'Oh,' I said, 'now there's the rub. I'd made up my mind to apologize to you.'

For the first time in hours, he grinned. 'Daiz,' he said.

'Floyd,' I said, 'there's something else.'

'Nothing else, it's all behind us.' He squeezed my hand.

'No, hear me out. When you thought I needed help, you didn't hesitate. You came on board in spite of how afraid you are and rescued me. My hero,' I added in a soppy voice. But meaning it.

'I heard you scream,' he said, 'and next thing I was there beside you. I didn't stop to think. Maybe I'm cured now,' he added hopefully.

'Maybe,' I agreed. But I didn't really think so.

At last it was time for me to vacate the trolley for a needier patient. A&E said they didn't have any kind of walking stick to lend me, but thought Physio might be able to help. An intrepid Floyd set off into the hospital's hinterland in search of said department, warning me that like Captain Oates, he might be some time. However, unlike the aforesaid valiant explorer, Floyd returned, eventually, triumphantly bearing the required NHS trophy.

'I'm impressed,' I said, as he hoisted me to my feet and we began the tiresome and protracted expedition towards the exit. 'How did you manage it?'

'It was either my natural charm or the fact that I – well, a lady wouldn't want to know the precise details of my winning strategy,' he said grinning and leaving me wondering how he'd worked it.

As Floyd had come with me in the ambulance, we had to get a cab back. During the ride he did his level best to get me to forsake Louella for the B and B, but I wasn't persuaded. The taxi got us as far as the marina car park from where, with Floyd supporting me whenever the stick got trapped between the planks, we eventually made it onto the pontoon and came alongside Lady Lou.

'Bit of a problem this,' Floyd commented as we gazed at the gap between the deck and us. 'And anyway how are you going to manage if we do get you on board?'

'No worries,' I said grimacing as I tried my weight on the ankle, 'I'll manage perfectly well.'

But it wasn't possible for me to get on board. At least, not with Floyd determined to help. He decided he needed to step on first. He kept looking straight ahead and made one or two stabs at reaching for the shroud, but when he turned back to face me I saw that his eyes were staring and I'd swear his skin was a couple of shades paler. He was shaking. Not cured then. No surprise.

'Sorry, Daiz,' he said, 'one more try.'

And before I could stop him he'd leaned over and grasped Louella's rail with both hands.

Now, this is not a recommended way of getting on board a boat. Even one tightly moored. The weight of Floyd's body pushed Lou away from the side leaving him suspended like a humpback bridge across the water and wailing like a banshee. Having no time to deliberate the finer points of the requisite manoeuvre, I grabbed him round the waist and tugged backwards. We collapsed together in a tangle of arms and legs on the pontoon.

Heroism over and done with I was sharply reminded of my injuries. 'Oh, oh, oh,' I whined, 'my ankle hurts and my ribs. Everywhere hurts.'

'You should worry,' Floyd's voice was muffled, 'I broke your fall.'

It took another huge effort to get back up to the car park giving us plenty of time to argue about, or as Floyd put it, discuss how he'd ended up underneath me when I'd been behind him. We were still talking about it when we were eventually ensconced in the car and were munching our way through a packet of custard creams, which Floyd had found in the glove compartment.

'The B and B methinks, and no arguing,' Floyd said as he crushed the empty packet and flicked the crumbs away, 'you sit tight while I zip over to the pub and get one of your mates to secure Lady Lou so you don't need to worry about her.'

'Could you ask them to bring my jacket and some undies and maybe-'

'I get the picture,' he said. 'Leave it with me.'

'Sorted,' he said a few minutes later as he got in the car and started the engine. 'Breakfast next.'

'More like brunch,' I said checking my watch, 'but I'm not arguing.'

We stopped at the chandler's first where Megan made sympathetic noises and sorted me out a few essentials for a couple of nights ashore in case whoever was boarding Lou for me didn't have the same idea of the rudiments of daily living as I did. From there we went onto the B and B to get me a room, and then adjourned to a café in the old town for a meal.

'I feel better now,' Floyd said as he put down his knife and fork, 'how about you?'

'Mm,' I said.

'Just mm?'

'I guess I was just thinking that all we seem to have done since you got here is eat.'

'I seem to remember that we've put away a few pints as well.'

'One or two,' I conceded, 'but that's hardly the point. I meant we haven't done anything constructive.'

'Did you have something particular in mind?'

And of course I didn't. I suppose that when Floyd had first mooted coming to join me for a few days I'd imagined us, if not exactly sailing off into the sunset together, at least us pottering around on Lady Lou, me showing him the ropes and then perhaps making a couple of day trips. But nothing seemed to have gone to plan. And there'd been a constraint between us that wasn't just Floyd's fear of water, although that certainly didn't help. It was as if-

'Daiz.' Floyd's voice interrupted my train of thought, which disappeared like a white mouse up a conjuror's sleeve. I sighed.

'Big sigh, that,' Floyd said, looking at me intently, 'like someone with something serious on their mind.'

I was alarmed to feel my throat tightening. 'Not really,' I said. 'I suppose I'm just feeling a bit sorry for myself.'

'Well, there are a couple of things I want to talk to you about,' Floyd said, 'but not here.'

We drove a few miles out of town looking for somewhere to stop and eventually parked up on the outskirts of the heath.

'I often come here,' I remarked, 'when I'm on my bike. There are several tracks that are really challenging.'

'Have to leave that for a while,' Floyd said, 'with your ankle and everything.'

'I'll be okay in day or two,' I said moodily. 'Can't afford to let my fitness slip.'

'Thing is, Daiz, I don't think it would be a good idea, even when you're better.'

'Why ever not?' I glanced at him in surprise. He was staring out of the window, but his face had a closed-down look.

'Bit lonely,' he said.

'Floyd, what's the matter with you? You know I spend most of my free time on my own. You've never doubted my ability to take care of myself before. And I have had some training in self-defence.'

'I didn't know that.'

'There you are then.'

'Thing is Daiz,' he said again. 'You may have a black belt in karate or whatever, but that didn't stop someone pushing you down the stairs of your boat.'

Floyd's words hit me over the head like a gybing boom. I was so stunned I couldn't speak, not even to point out he should have said 'companionway'. I felt him slip an arm round my shoulders and pull me towards him.

'Sorry to spring it on you,' he said, his lips close to my ear, 'I've been trying to find a tactful way to tell you for hours, thinking you might mention feeling a thump on your back or something.'

The hairs on the back of my neck were standing to attention by this time but I couldn't decide whether it was Floyd's proximity or his disclosure. I shook my head. 'No, nothing like that, I'd have remembered, surely. You'd better tell me what you think happened.'

'I will,' he said. 'Shall we sit here or d'you want to try walking?'

'Walk, I think,' I said, reluctantly wriggling free of his arm, 'at least to that bench over there.'

With Floyd's hand cupped under my elbow to steady me I made it to the bench, all the while thinking how typical it was of me that I had to be virtually immobile before I noticed my surroundings; a case of being too busy looking at my nose to see what was under it. Like someone trying to cause me an injury and me oblivious. Someone who might have seen me seeing something I wasn't supposed to: the crew of the Tiger Moth for instance. Whom I'd forgotten every word about until that moment.

'What's the matter?' Floyd said as he got me comfortable. 'You've gone quite pale; walk too much for you?'

'Mm,' I said, not meeting his gaze. 'Just a twinge.' And before he could pursue it, I said, 'Tell me.'

'I'd got back,' he said slowly, 'to the B and B. I was pretty wet and pretty fed up. I was telling myself things would be all right in the morning, but that didn't make me feel any better. I'd been pompous and self-opinionated and had sounded off at you. Knowing that I'm liable to get like that if I get onto one of my hobbyhorses only makes it worse. Anyway there was nothing for it except to come back and apologize, then and there.'

'But -' I said.

'How many times have I asked you not to butt in every time I pause for breath?'

I sighed theatrically. 'What was it you were saying about being pompous?' I asked.

We both laughed. He pulled a packet of mints out of his pocket and was fiddling around with the silver paper. I was about to tell him to get on with it when he spoke again. 'Anyway,' he said, 'I'm coming along that walkway thing from the jetty -'

'Pontoon,' I corrected, before I could help myself,

'Towards Lady Lou when I see you moving around on the back of the boat -'

'I suppose you mean the stern,' I said automatically,

'Does it matter, what it's called? I'm trying to tell you what happened.'

'Sorry,' I said, 'I'll try not to do it again.'

'And pigs might fly,' Floyd muttered. 'The point is, I see this figure on your boat and I presume it's you. Why wouldn't I?'

'No reason, except it wasn't me. I was snug as a bug out of sight under the cockpit cover.' I said this in a flippant voice to reassure myself as much as Floyd. Really I was beginning to feel more than a little alarmed, remembering what I'd tried not to see earlier that night.

'I know that now. I'm telling you what I thought at the time. Anyway, next minute the person I think is you is disappearing into the shadows round that hood thing and I think you're going below, so I call out to attract your attention.'

By this time my inclination was to bury my head deeply in the sand so that I couldn't hear what Floyd was saying. Something nasty was crawling up my spine and something else, equally unpleasant was lodged in the pit of my stomach. I absolutely didn't want to know. I was horrified when I heard myself asking, 'What then?'

'And then it all happened at once. I hear a scream and a thump and there's someone making a swift exit from your boat and hammering past me as I'm coming up along side. Had to let him go to get to you. Next thing I know I'm on board and you're unconscious at the foot of the stairs, and I think you've broken your neck.'

I was dismayed to see Floyd's eyes were looking quite watery. 'Not stairs,' I said quickly, 'compan -'

'-nionway,' he finished. 'I know. I know something else as well,' he went on when I didn't reply, 'you're shivering. We'll go back to the car now.'

'Don't mind admitting it, Daiz,' he said as we reached the car and he was helping lever me in, 'I'm worried. Worried about you. These people, whatever they're up to, and you know what I think, aren't in it for love. They're greedy and unscrupulous and I think they've clocked you.'

In the car, he started up the engine.

'Don't let's go yet,' I said, 'I've got something to tell you too.'

'Just running her a while to warm you up. I wish we had some coffee or something,' he said, as he slipped off his jacket and tucked it round me. 'You look done in.'

'Shock, I suppose,' I said. Then I told him about seeing the characters coming off the Tiger Moth not all that long before he'd seen the person exiting Lady Lou.

For a minute or two after I'd finished he didn't say anything. And then he said, 'We'll have to go to the police.'

Floyd's pronouncement about getting the police involved knocked me sideways, or would have done if I hadn't been restrained by the jacket he had tucked round me. As it was, my immediate reaction was that wild horses wouldn't drag me within a mile of the thin blue line, but I couldn't really say why his proposal provoked such a strong reaction. Nevertheless, for the sake of appearances, I gave his suggestion a moment's consideration. Then I said, 'No, I don't think that would be a good idea at all.'

'D'you want to attempt to convince me why we shouldn't?' Floyd sighed in mock weariness as he asked me this and twisted round in his seat so he could look at me eye to eye. I couldn't help noticing how very deep his were, full of understanding and concern. But he needn't think he'd get round me that way.

'You say first why you suggested it.'

'Only that we've run into some sort of people smuggling racket whose operators aren't too keen on witnesses.'

'What proof do we have of that?'

'We've seen them.'

'Not true. You're making assumptions about things from my description of the behaviour of the Tiger Moth's crew and passengers. And probably because of where you work. *You* haven't seen them.'

'That's true. But it's obvious what's going on.'

'To you maybe, from anyone else's viewpoint it's a couple of men with a handful of different women coming and going. There's no proof.'

'We don't have to have proof. That's for others to deal with. Everyone's always telling the public to be observant and to report anything out of the ordinary. The authorities take it from there. And don't forget I kind of am that authority.'

'Now that's not entirely true, is it? You're an administrator in the Home Office. A fairly high-up office person, but not,' I paused, 'a front-line man.'

'Yes, but-'

'But what would happen if you did put your oar in? Suppose you are right and by some fluke someone actually believes you and sets up some sort of observation or whatever it is they do: on the basis of my account, by the way, not yours, as by your own admission you don't know one boat from another. From what I've heard these things can take months. Years even. What happens to me in the meanwhile? Suppose one of the McQueen gang got wind of it and put two and two together? If they're as ruthless as you seem to think, where would that leave me? You won't always be here to look after me.'

'Enough Daiz, enough.' Floyd clapped his hands over his ears and swivelled back into his seat.

There was a minute or two's silence during which I revved up my resistance. Then before Floyd could start again I said, 'And that's not taking into account how you'd feel if you were responsible for some of these presumed 'illegals' being sent back.'

'And you being pushed down the downstairs – don't tell me,' he interrupted himself as he saw my mouth open – 'as I was saying, you being pushed down the companionway, what's your reason for not reporting that?'

'Pushed? Who says I was pushed? I certainly don't. All I know is that I lurched forward. I'd had too much to drink and the water was choppy.'

'You're forgetting I saw him doing a runner from your boat.'

'Saw who?'

'Just a man,' Floyd said in a dejected voice. 'You win, I suppose.'

We drove back to the B and B both avoiding talking about anything to do with the Tiger Moth. I told him about Jeff the barman's complicated love life and he regaled me with a story about a friend of his who'd been discovered in a compromising situation in a used-car showroom.

'Are you sure it wasn't you this happened to?' I queried when I had stopped laughing.

'God's honour, Daiz,' he said. 'There's only one woman in my life and she's not that interested in motor cars.'

It was irrational, I know, but I was quite put out when Floyd admitted having someone special and it was probably just as well that we arrived back at the B and B before I could think of anything to say.

'Guess Megan packed this,' he muttered under his breath as he carried the bulging rucksack, which we'd found waiting for me in the hall, up to my room.

'What now then?' he asked me as he dumped the rucksack on the bed and I bent to unpack it.

'A shower and a couple of hours' shut-eye for me,' I said. 'Don't know about you but my body's telling me that I didn't get any sleep last night.'

'Can't say I'm the least sleepy,' Floyd said, feigning a huge yawn, 'but if that's what you want, I'll go along with it. Think you'll be fit for dinner about eight thirty?'

'Great,' I said, pecking him on the cheek, 'look forward to it.' He turned to go. 'Oh,' I said, 'there's one more thing before you get your head down.'

'What's that?' he asked.

'Your book,' I said. 'If it's as boring as you make out, it'll be just the thing to ensure I get some sleep.'

'Touché,' he said, as he came back from his room a minute later and dropped a slim folder onto my bed.

I felt a mixture of disappointment and relief when I discovered Floyd's literary masterpiece wasn't the entire book. It was a couple of dozen pages, headed 'Introduction and Proposal for An Honest Trade', which to judge by the notes scribbled in the margins, he was still working on.

Introduction to an 'An Honest Trade'

My personal history begins in Sierra Leone. As far back as 1652, Europeans were seizing the people of that country and transporting them to work as slaves on the plantations in the Caribbean and South America, where many thousands died of disease, the terrible hardship of their lives and the punishments inflicted upon them.

Thousands of others never made it to the plantations. They died onboard the vessels which brought them across the oceans, or were drowned when they jumped overboard or were jettisoned by their captors. Increasingly I find myself speculating about their fate and my seemingly irrational fear of water.

I have discovered that my ancestors were slaves on the plantations in British Guyana until the 1830's when they were freed and returned to Freetown in Sierra Leone. Even there, in what might be considered their homeland, they endured much violence from the native population who regarded them as synonymous with British rule.

This hostility may explain my family's migration to Great Britain in 1895, making my great grandfather the first of my forbears to be born here.

***An Honest Trade** is drawn from my own family's story, from our early African origins to my colonial English descent. The story unfolds over the course of a year on a sugar plantation under British control on the mainland of South America. I tell it through the eyes of my forefather, John Wells, the English overseer, who worked on Kings Plantation in Wakenhem in the eighteen thirties. I have devised his narrative from plantation and shipping records held at the William Wilberforce Museum, Hull.*

Floyd Joseph Proivil

Five

Phew! And that was only the introduction. No wonder Floyd was so prickly about my laissez faire attitude. I was surprised I hadn't driven him completely over the top. I simply couldn't imagine how bad he must have felt as he delved into the whole appalling trade and unearthed more and more details about his own origins. The anger and conflict must have been overwhelming when he discovered he was the direct descendant of a slave master.

I put the introduction aside and turned to the outline. I won't say I skimmed through it but I certainly didn't linger over the month by month account of life on the plantation Floyd had sketched out; nevertheless it brought the horrors of slavery home to me in a way that my history lessons at school had never done. That being said, I'm ashamed to admit that Floyd had been right, **An Honest Trade** wasn't my type of book at all. To be truthful, normally I wouldn't have touched it with a bargepole, my personal inclination being to avoid anything much in the way of real emotional content in my reading matter.

Anyway with Floyd's opinion of me in mind, I promised myself I would buckle down and give it some proper attention before getting into any kind of discussion and thought that it would be less likely to put me off if I read a chapter at a time, now and then.

Consequently I was quite happy to say, when Floyd asked me what I thought about it that evening, that it was a very serious subject and I admired him enormously for taking it on and doing all the research and stuff, and that since the subject matter really wasn't my cup of tea I hoped he'd give me a bit of time to get to grips with it. And he'd said to take as long as I liked, as knowing my disposition he'd only given me the outline anyway. I didn't know whether to infer from this that he'd already written the whole thing and thought it prudent not to ask.

It was a beautiful night and I was feeling quite chirpy as Floyd pulled the car to a halt up on the embankment that keeps the sea at bay: it's amazing what an improving book, a short kip, a gourmet dinner and the right company can do for you. Gives you the inclination to study the scenery for one thing. Like the stipples of light from the nearby village, the glow from the distant town shimmering in the cloudless, starry sky and the vast darkness of the sea broken only by the mast lights of the occasional vessel which crossed the horizon.

With the car engine turned off and the window open, the sound of the sea sucking the shingle from the shore was calming, and I thought, romantic, but decidedly chilly. I hurriedly wound up the window again. I could sense Floyd smiling.

'Why are you grinning like a Cheshire Cat?' I asked.

'You got eyes in the back of your head, or what? You're not even looking at me.'

'Don't have to. I can sense it.'

'Pity you're not so perceptive about your own welfare.'

'I suppose you're talking about this blasted smuggling ring again. I thought we'd agreed to draw a line under that.'

'No, nothing of the sort. You've intimidated me into not going to the police, that's all.'

'Yes, but...'

'Thing is, Daiz, he interrupted, 'Even if you're dead set against involving the plod, I can't just leave it. You must see that. I mean if this bunch is prepared to have a go at you because they think you've sussed them, what d'you imagine happens if any of their cargo acts up?'

'Well ...'

'And I'm damn sure you've no idea how illegals are exploited when they do get here: particularly the women. Anyway, I've decided to do some sniffing about myself. See what I can turn up. Maybe get some proof of what you think is a product of my overactive imagination.'

I'd swear the night sky shuddered as Floyd made this pronouncement. But I suppose it might have been me being jolted out of my post-prandial complacency. 'You've what?'

'I just said. I've decided to see what I can find out.'

In spite of my initial shock, I'd have to admit feeling a tremor of something not unlike excitement at the prospect of Floyd as a kind of twenty-first century Batman seeking to right wrongs, and me his Robin. All the same, I couldn't be seen to give in so readily, so I said, 'How do you imagine you're going to do that? You could hardly stake out the Tiger Moth.'

'No,' he said, 'I couldn't do that, but I know a girl who could.' He turned to face me as he said this and I was still trying to decide whether to be flattered or insulted at being called a girl, when his lips brushed my cheek and he added, 'We'll talk about it in the morning.'

'Don't be silly,' I said. 'You can't seriously think I'd get a wink of sleep if you leave everything up in the air like that. We'll have to get one or two things straight right now. First of all you seem to have conveniently forgotten all about my trip. Louella's new sails are due any day. I'll need a couple of test runs to check everything out and maybe a day or two for Phil to make any adjustments. That means I could be away by this time next week.'

'You wouldn't care to postpone your voyage to make a sad old landlubber very happy?'

I felt myself grow rather hot when I considered exactly what I would be prepared to do to make Floyd happy and was relieved that it was too dark for him to see me blush. 'I can't postpone much longer without missing the weather slot,' I said. I wouldn't feel happy making the trip later in the year when I'd be into the hurricane season.'

'I should hope not,' Floyd said, sounding miffed. 'All the same I hadn't realised the time factor was so critical.'

'Anyway,' I said, 'don't put all the blame on me. I seem to remember you only have leave until the end of the week.'

Floyd pulled a face. 'If I decide not to resign I could always apply for a few days more. I've got plenty of holiday entitlement stacked up and it's not as though I'm indispensable to the smooth and efficient running of the Home Office. But there's not much point if you're not going to be around.' He sounded irritable and when I glanced at him out of the corner of my eye I saw that he had his arms folded in a most unfriendly manner.

It struck me that he was on the verge of leaving, there and then. I was casting around for some sort of lame excuse to detain him when I remembered – lame. Me. Exactly. 'My ankle,' I burbled, at the precise moment that he was saying, 'But your ankle; you can't...'

And so it was settled, he'd apply for an extension of his leave, and Lady Lou and I wouldn't go further than out into the bay until I was a hundred percent fit. I didn't know whether to laugh or cry. I'd been so focused on my voyage for so long that I felt as if I was betraying myself. On the other hand - on the other hand there was Floyd.

Next morning found me toying with toast and coffee in the small recess the landlady called the breakfast room, whilst Floyd hovered over me.

'I wish you'd get a move on, Daiz,' he was saying, 'I've told you we've got places to go and things to do.'

'I wish you'd tell me what you've got in mind.'

'It's not that exciting,' he said, 'and we could probably do it all over the phone, or by post or on the net, but what the hell, we've got nothing else to do and it'll be a change of scenery at least.'

'So?'

'So I thought we'd check out the Small Ships Register. See what that turns up, if anything.'

I don't know why I hadn't thought of it myself. There's me, been around boats all my life, and there's Floyd, the absolute last word in landlubberliness. If the Tiger Moth had been registered, the SSR would give her full history, including the listed owners. A brilliant idea in principle, although what we would do with such information wasn't immediately apparent to me.

Anyway, before I could raise any objection, Floyd was hustling me away from breakfast and into the car. He stowed my stick and our bags on the back seat with a breezy, 'Hope you've packed your toothbrush. I've told Mrs M. we won't be back for a couple of days. D'you need to go to the boat for anything first?'

I couldn't really think of anything, but to be on the safe-side, I muttered something about checking the fenders. A few minutes later we pulled into the car park and Floyd began the business of unpacking me. Truth be told, I probably didn't need to hang onto him quite so closely for quite so long, but I wouldn't have liked to think of him feeling surplus to requirements.

The inspection of lines and fenders having been made from the restricted vantage of the pontoon, neither of us being fit or able to go on board, we were back in the car in no time at all.

'Humph,' Floyd said in what I deduced was meant to be a scathing tone of voice, 'that didn't take any time at all, did it?'

'Precisely what I was thinking,' I said, giving him my most disingenuous smile.

We were further delayed by running into a minor traffic jam, caused by a couple of police cars, with sirens wailing and blue lights flashing, forcing their way through the narrow streets towards the marginally faster-flowing ring-road, by which time I'd organized our route. I don't know if

Floyd had forgotten that charts and navigation are second nature to me or whether he really believed that women can't read maps, because I caught him giving me a sideways look as he tossed the Drivers' Atlas onto my lap and announced, 'Cardiff here we come.'

'Somehow,' I said, 'Cardiff doesn't have the same ring to it as California.'

We motored through towns and countryside with the minimum of breaks for nourishment and comfort, but rather more prolonged stops for road works, accidents and those mysterious delays when the traffic comes to a total halt for no apparent reason.

All the same, it was great. Floyd proved to be a laid back driver, not the type to race up behind the car in front in an attempt to save petrol by sitting in its boot, or to cut up other road users, or to hurl insults and rude gestures out of the window when someone did something he didn't approve of. Instead he was calm and authoritative and a pleasure to be with. We chatted about everything and nothing, much more like our old selves when we used to meet in the pub after work, so it seemed hardly any time at all before the new bridge hove into view.

'Chepstow,' I announced, as we drove over and off the other side, 'the gateway to Wales. Only about twenty miles to go now.'

Disappointingly, the motorway snaked past the outskirts of what I'd imagined would have been a quirky medieval Welsh market town. I wondered what Cardiff would have to offer.

My first impression of the city, as we turned off the M4 and picked up the signs for the town centre, was of newish-looking multi-storey buildings without any particular identity. Added to which, with excellent timing, we seemed to have arrived in the rush hour. In a bid to quell the feeling of disappointment, I reminded myself that we weren't there on a sightseeing trip, and as the traffic snarled around us I began to say something to this effect to Floyd. Floyd received my comments with a perfunctory grunt, which I took to be man-speak for 'just a minute I'm concentrating' and I judged it prudent to keep the rest of my thoughts to myself.

It took quite a while to find somewhere to park to get our bearings. We ended up being directed to Cathedral Road, which we were reliably informed, was chock full of hotels and guesthouses and only a fifteen-minute walk from the city centre.

Of course, what we hadn't discussed was what our sleeping arrangements were to be. I can't pretend I hadn't thought about it, off and on, more or less every time there'd been a break in conversation, but to actually broach the subject would have been a whole different ball game. I was really hoping Floyd would make the decision. Women's lib or what?

As it turned out the decision was made for us.

After cruising around for a bit in the leafy environs of Cathedral Road, we'd ended up at reception of an elegant, small hotel, which had been restored in Victorian style with button-leather couches and heavy brocade.

'I can offer you,' the receptionist was saying, 'one of our best rooms, which has,' and here her voice dropped to a stagy whisper, 'a four poster bed.'

Neither of us said anything.

'Or I have a very nice en suite on the top floor that looks out over the river and the park.' She glanced at us appraisingly.

To break the embarrassed silence that ensued, I was muttering something about stairs and my ankle, when she gave us another one of her looks and remarked that they did have a lift. Out of the corner of my eye, I saw that Floyd was giving his undivided attention to a hideous Victorian painting, which was hanging on the adjacent wall. No help there then.

'I didn't know,' I said a touch sharply, after I'd said the en-suite would be fine, thank you, and we'd signed in and were in the lift, 'that you were interested in nineteenth century kitsch.' The picture, of a fire fighter emerging from the flames, bearing the inert body of a curly-haired moppet, was absolutely the last word.

'Just call me sentimental,' he said, grinning.

It was past seven o'clock by the time we emerged into a cool Cardiff evening and a waiting taxi. In the time it had taken us to admire the view from between the fringed and tasselled drapes adorning the window of our room, stow our luggage and freshen up, we had both studiously ignored the large double bed which seemed to be positively pulsating with temptation.

We'd spent ten minutes or so riffling through the assorted tourist maps and brochures in the hotel lobby before deciding to spend the evening in the old dockland area around the bay, which we were informed had been totally transformed by largesse from Europe.

'Pierhead.' The cab driver twitched his head towards the old redbrick building behind us as he drove away.

'The antithesis of taxi drivers,' Floyd remarked. 'Never met one before who wasn't a motor mouth.'

'Never mind him,' I said. 'What shall we do now we're here?'

'Food's definitely high on my agenda,' he said. 'Service station snacks can only sustain a man for so long. How about you?'

'Starving,' I said. 'Let's just walk, or in my case, hobble, shall we, until we find somewhere we fancy? And take in some of the sights at the same time.'

As it turned out, we'd hardly walked any distance and only identified a spaceship-shaped structure as the Millennium Centre, when the cool evening became decidedly nippy. A brisk wind was blowing in from the sea, and finding all those little nooks and crannies normally protected by my oilies. I let go of Floyd's arm to pull the zip of my new fleece up to my chin, thinking much as it was eye-catching colour-wise, and to all appearances cosy, it was certainly no match for my good old Musto's weatherproofing.

'You okay, Daiz?' Floyd asked. 'Here let me.' His hand, warm and strong, closed over mine as I struggled with the zip that I'd managed to catch in the lining. 'You're cold,' he murmured. 'You should have said.'

'A bit,' I admitted. 'Must be due to my ankle slowing me down. I hate not being fit,' I grumbled. 'Makes me feel quite stroppy.'

'"I couldn't possibly comment,"' Floyd said, keeping a very straight face. 'And before you say anything else, is that a mirage or can I see a Chinese restaurant over there?'

As a rule I'm not a great fan of Chinese cooking finding it a bit bland for my taste and that evening's meal put me off for good. I could never look at another bowl of chicken chow mien or a plate of prawn crackers without remembering. Not that there was anything the matter with the service or the food. Nor with the aperitifs, or the wine or the liqueurs, except perhaps for our overindulgence.

It started with a couple of Tiger Beers in the tiny bar while we studied the menu and then a couple more before we ordered. We'd nearly finished our second bottle of wine before I began holding forth on my good fortune on being able to spend my time mucking about in boats. 'I mean,' I heard myself saying, 'who wouldn't swap the daily grind of earning their living in a run of the mill job, for my life?'

I can't remember what Floyd's response was to this observation, maybe I wasn't listening that intently, but whatever it was he'd said, it wasn't until we'd polished off the wine and started on the brandy that I began to notice that he wasn't entirely with me. I was well into the trials and tribulations involved in preparing for my forthcoming voyage by that time and it must have been when I paused for breath that it occurred to me that he wasn't saying anything. Hadn't said anything much for a while actually and nothing at all for the last few minutes. Plus there was a frosty expression in his eyes and a certain set to his mouth that indicated all was not well. This astute observation on my part was further highlighted by the fact that he was sitting bolt upright in his seat and drumming the fingers of the hand that wasn't clenched in a white-knuckle grip round his brandy glass, on the table-top. 'Seething,' was the word that came to mind.

Too late I recalled that Floyd wasn't keen on water. 'I know a life on the ocean wave's not exactly your thing,' I said gaily. At least that's what I meant to say. In truth it may have come out a bit more unsympathetically than that; something about grown men and bottling out. Anyway Floyd bristled.

'Daiz,' he said.

And I didn't like the way he said it.

'Daiz. Sometimes you give the impression of being a selfish airhead.'

It was my turn to take umbrage. 'And who are you to...'

But whoever he was, having decided to resume speech he wasn't to be interrupted. In a few moments he'd gone from repressed fuming to articulated wrath. He was leaning forward in a very intimidating manner, and what's more he was pointing a finger at me. Actually pointing at me, and going on and on about his phobia and me not understanding, or even trying to understand his feelings, although he'd let me read the premise of his book which had set it out clearly enough. And then without noticeably drawing breath he was ranting on about my obsession with my boat and my endless prattle about the difficulty I'd had with the sails.

'Well, I like that,' I spluttered, 'I've hardly said a word about Lou since I had my accident.'

'That's another thing,' he snapped. 'All you've done is sprained your bloody ankle and you're limping around and moaning and groaning as if it's the most important thing in the world. If I weren't being charitable I'd

54

go so far as to say it's symptomatic of your whole attitude. Not caring about anybody but yourself, or having any concept of other people's lives. I bet you've never given a thought to the terrible hardships and deprivations some people endure.'

'That's not fair. You're not being fair. Just because I don't keep on about it like you.'

'Go on then, give me an example. An example of your caring nature.'

'What is this, the Inquisition?' I asked, all the while casting around wildly for some example of my essential humanitarianism.

'Come on then, one example.'

'Charity,' I said desperately, fastening on to his own words. 'I give to charity.'

'Oh,' he said, 'and which charities do you support?'

'Lifeboats,' I said. And even as I said I knew it was just the worst thing to say.

There was a pause, not so much pregnant as ominous, before he pounced.

'That, I think, perfectly proves my case.' He sat back and folded his arms as if there was nothing more to say.

And perhaps there wasn't. I didn't know whether I wanted to round on him for mistakenly seeing me as a shallow, insensitive person, or cry on his shoulder because I was. Maybe if I were better at defending myself or if I'd got it together enough to explain that I've never been good at facing up to things - particularly things I can't do anything about (which is why I hardly ever read a daily paper or watch the news) - or maybe if I'd made it clear that it's a nature and nurture thing, a family trait; maybe if I'd said any of that, it would have helped.

In any case all this was immaterial as before I could say anything at all, a feeling of déjà vu overwhelmed me. We were sitting in The Salty Seadog and Floyd was haranguing me on the iniquity of the global market as if it were my fault.

The upshot of this recollection wasn't the rational explanation that I might have supplied but a furious, 'If this is going to be another of your 'Improving Daisy' lectures, you needn't bother,' rebuttal. The fact that, at that precise moment, I also remembered that we'd had one or two drinks over the top when Floyd had flared up that first time was about as useful as putting lipstick on a pig.

Here followed a short intermission whilst we regrouped. I was chewing over other examples of his short fuse to put to him, when he scowled at me and said, 'I say this more in sorrow than in anger.'

'Really.' I said this in the tone of voice that went with the eyebrow I raised to convey my disdain for the worn out and patronising cliché he'd just used. But being back in full spate he seemed not to notice.

'The trouble is you really don't understand, or more likely don't want to know. If you'd seen what I saw when I was in Africa…' He stopped abruptly.

'What? What did you see?'

'Leave it,' he said savagely. 'Just leave it.'

The cab ride back to the hotel was conducted in stony silence. In the hotel Floyd left me at the lift with a brief word about getting some air, and in our room, I locked myself in the bathroom and spent a long night huddled on the floor in a close embrace with the toilet, the bleak comfort of which was hardly enhanced by bouts of vomiting interspersed with buckets of tears that lasted well into the small hours. I know too much alcohol can have a depressing effect, but honestly, I felt utterly and completely wretched, not helped at all by the fact that each time I closed my eyes the room began spinning in the most alarming manner.

I've often wished I were one of those drinkers who, after a lively night out, claim not to remember anything. Sadly, in my case, every drunken moment is always etched, apparently for evermore, on my mind. Thus, my best efforts under the shower in the morning may slightly have improved my appearance but did absolutely nothing for my mood, so that when I finally plucked up courage to emerge from the bathroom, I was shattered, hung over and mortified. Not to mention a tad bad tempered.

I don't know how he'd managed it, but Floyd was sitting at the window looking as smooth and unflappable as usual. A rush of relief that he hadn't abandoned me was closely followed by the thought that whatever outward appearance Floyd exhibited he wasn't as imperturbable as he liked to portray. However, even in my semi-functioning state, it occurred to me that that particular moment wasn't the best time to pursue the matter.

I think we were both waiting for the other to say something, when mutual face was saved by a rap on the door followed by a voice that announced, 'Room Service.'

'I took the liberty of ordering you breakfast here,' Floyd said. 'Didn't think you'd feel like dealing with the dining room. I've had mine.'

I forced a smile and bit my tongue. The words condescending and patronising passed quickly through my mind while I was trying to think thoughtful and caring.

As I hastily pushed aside scrambled egg and mushrooms and munched my way through a couple of slices of dry toast washed down by a jug of black coffee I felt slightly less piqued and slightly more human. Predictably Floyd had been right; a confrontation with a mass ingestion of the Full English Breakfast would almost certainly have been my undoing.

It was by default rather than agreement that we decided to forgo sightseeing and went straight to the office of the Small Ships Register.

'I expect we're on a fool's errand,' I said gloomily, as we filled out the application form, 'don't suppose she'll be registered. I mean, if they're as dodgy as you seem to think, why would they bother?'

'I don't know, Daiz. You got any better ideas?'

His tone was curt, but an infinitesimal flick of hope pinged inside me as he said my name, that being the first time he had called me anything at all that morning.

But we were in luck. After a short wait and a small fee we found ourselves in possession of the Tiger Moth's registration.

'I'm amazed,' I said, 'I didn't think for one moment they'd have anything on her.'

'Maybe she is straight after all,' Floyd said. 'Or maybe the owner's rented her out or something.'

'Not rented,' I said, before I could help myself. 'You mean chartered.'

Floyd turned his head away and I knew he was really fed up with me. So much for the flutter of hope I'd felt a few minutes earlier.

Anyway, that was effectively the end of our trip to Wales. Floyd carefully folded the form and put it in his jacket pocket. 'I'll check it out when we get back,' he said. 'Can't be sure it's even the right Tiger Moth until then.'

I don't know if it's what he meant, but it seemed to me that he was saying pretty plainly that our combined enterprise was at an end so, somewhat fed up, I decided against mentioning that there was no reason to expect that the Tiger Moth would actually be in harbour when we got back, and that in any case she didn't need 'checking out' as the recorded description supplied by the SSR tallied from bow to stern with the nautical details I'd provided.

The journey home was fraught and interminable. Gone was the placid, considerate driver of the day before. Seated in his place was a post-pubescent Boy Racer, or possibly a thwarted test pilot. Not for him the loosely bent arms with hands resting lightly on the wheel at ten to three as per the Highway Code. Oh no. New Macho Man drove with straight arms from a semi-recumbent position.

Staring straight ahead, Floyd's doppelganger roared recklessly along the fast lane, impervious to the speed limit and to my muttered imprecations about the state my poor old Nissan would be in when we got back, and giving no quarter to any other vehicle on the road. The upshot of this road-hoggish behaviour was that I spent the whole run gripping the door strap with one hand and bracing myself against the dashboard with the other, this tense and uncomfortable position being alleviated only by the movement required for the guzzling of vast quantities of bottled water and the barest words relating to essential stops arising from the former.

In the cheerless respite of one such break I glanced at myself in a mirror in the Ladies and was horrified by the spectre that looked back at me. Dark shadows under sunken eyes in a sallow grey complexion topped by a tangled ginger blanket. Who ever said a thing of beauty is a joy forever obviously hadn't been there the morning after the hen night. 'Never again,' I spluttered to myself as I splashed water on my face, and 'Never, ever again,' as I bent to dry it under the hand drier.

One constructive thing that I did decide during the ride from hell was that I was going to move back onto Lady Lou the next day, whatever Floyd's plans were. Consequently, that night before turning in, I borrowed a kitchen pail and an old washing-up bowl from Mrs M and gave my ankle an intensive 'hot and cold water cure' session, followed by a liberal application of Arnica. That treatment completed I retired to my lonely bed where I spent the best part of the night thrashing over the events of the last two days and only giving way to sleep after tackling the first chapter of the outline for Floyd's novel.

An Honest Trade
July 1833

Homer, the headman, is reported to have died in the Negro yard. Fanny, his wife, two of their children and twelve other slaves are sick with dysentery.

Kitty Mikiel is in isolation in the hospital with lockjaw, having gashed her hand on a machete. The man, Ben, has been sent to the colony jail for neglect of work and insolence.

There is disease amongst the livestock. Heavy rains and cold northerly winds are injurious to the cultivation of the crop, which should be harvested in August.

The sloop, Justina, carrying a new supply of Africans for the estate, is quarantined offshore due to smallpox. Given the conditions prevailing onboard the trading vessels, John Wells, the overseer, knows it is unlikely any of the Africans will survive the outbreak.

This is a bitter blow to Wells as he has suffered a great depletion in his existing labour force since the days when clean-limbed and docile natives from the Gold Coast were readily available.

Weary of the problems that beset him, Wells is inclined to regret his decision to accede to his wife's demands to send his pregnant mistress, Lionoria, away to the neighbouring Beausejour Plantation.

*Guyana was under British control from 1814 and was formerly established as a British colony in 1831.

Six

Floyd didn't put in an appearance at breakfast and it wasn't until I was drinking my coffee that the thought occurred to me that he might have left. The result was somewhat catastrophic. My hand trembled and the cup tipped.

'Don't worry, dear. Have that sorted in a moment.' Mrs M, who was hovering nearby, was there in a flash, whipping off the breakfast paraphernalia, mopping up and replacing it all on a clean cloth. 'There you are.' She paused in her tidying up activity and looked at me closely. 'If you don't mind me saying, you're looking a bit peaky this morning. Ankle playing up? You can't rush these things, you know.'

I was mumbling something about being tired and having recently become very accident prone, when it occurred to me that it hadn't been that long since I'd dumped my cider in my lap and it was entirely probable that I was developing some sort of minor liquid fetish to counter Floyd's aqua phobia. I was going on to say as much to Mrs M who was bustling about not listening and asking me where my nice friend had got to, when the man himself strolled in.

'Any morsels left for me?' he asked as he sat down opposite me. And smiled.

Honestly, it was too much. I was devastated. He'd been awful to me. To say he'd made me feel small would be an understatement. He'd made me feel about as appealing and worthwhile as a slug. And now he was smiling at me. Smiling. As if he liked me. He wasn't being fair.

The best response I could conjure up was a kind of lop-sided grimace that was supposed to be a smile and a shaky gesture to Mrs M. indicating that Floyd would appreciate some breakfast.

'Well, aren't you going to ask me where I've been and what I've been up to?' he asked, reaching for the toast. 'I thought you'd be agog.'

I made a jerky sort of nod, which Floyd didn't notice anyway, having already launched into his story.

'I've been scouring the marina looking for you know who. Been out since the crack of dawn while you've been getting your beauty sleep.

Actually,' here he paused and gazed at me thoughtfully, 'maybe you needed another couple of hours.'

Normally I'd have thrown something at him, or aimed a punch. It wasn't that I didn't know he was joking. But I knew how I looked and it wasn't funny. Luckily Floyd seemed to realise I wasn't in the mood for banter. He reached across the table and gripped my hand.

'Sorry, Daiz,' he said. 'I'm sorry for being thoughtless; sorry for yesterday's behaviour and sorry for flying off the handle in Wales. I get these bees in my bonnet and before I know it I'm taking it out on whomever I'm with at the time. It's not an excuse, but I don't mean to do it. And honestly, it's not personal.'

'It's okay,' I said in a breezy voice. 'I forgive you.' Which was not at all what I wanted to say.

Whilst Floyd was demolishing his breakfast, I went upstairs to throw the last of my belongings into my bag and come back down to settle up with our landlady, by which time Floyd was hanging around in the hall flicking through a magazine as if he'd been there hours.

I glanced at the magazine as he put it back in the 'For Residents' rack and saw that it was a copy of Auto Finder. 'Hope you're not trying to tell me something about my car,' I said.

'It's okay,' he said. 'Don't worry. I was just passing the time after being brought up to speed, no pun intended, by Mrs M. She tells me, that you tell her, that your ankle is much better and you're moving back onto your boat. Today. Are you sure? he asked, looking quite concerned. Then without waiting for an answer said, 'I see you've abandoned your stick. Pushing it a bit, aren't you?'

I managed another of my lopsided grimaces. Couldn't admit I was anything but sure. Couldn't admit I'd had second and third thoughts. Particularly when I remembered that it would mean Floyd wouldn't be with me. 'Time and tide,' I said, 'and as you pointed out so eloquently it's only a bloody sprain.'

It was his turn to grimace. 'Guess I deserved that.'

I shrugged. 'Good job I don't bear grudges. Anyway I've got it well strapped and I can't keep clonking around like Long John Silver.'

He frowned again.

'What?' I asked. 'What are you frowning about now?'

'Was I? Didn't mean to. Must have been your reference to pirates. Put me in mind of the time I failed to win first prize as Captain Hook in a

61

Fancy Dress Competition. Mind, I was eighteen at the time and hoping to take Wendy home.' He laughed.

I squeezed a titter. Was worried for a moment I'd dropped another proverbial brick, although I couldn't see how. Talk about walking on eggshells, I was getting to wonder how we'd ever managed those freewheeling conversations we used to have, without him taking offence. Or, perish the thought; I just hadn't noticed when he was getting huffy then.

I was casting around for some innocuous comment when fortunately Mrs M came out to wish me bon voyage.

'Oh,' I said, 'I shan't be going yet I've got the sails to – '

'Silly. I'm sure you're not fit for sailing your boat yet. It was just my way of saying goodbye. Or should I say au revoir? Expect I'll be seeing you again while Mr Floyd's still here.'

'Mr Floyd?' I queried under my breath, as he picked up my bag, gripped me firmly by the elbow and steered me out of the front door.

'Don't go there,' Floyd warned. 'It's not funny. Sounds like something out of Uncle Tom's Cabin.'

Uh, Uh. Did I mention eggshells?

In the car I was relieved to discover that that day's assigned driver was the proper Floyd, not the one who'd masqueraded as him the day before, consequently our ride to the marina was ordinary and uneventful.

'We'll leave your things in the car until we've checked the Tiger Moth out, shall we?' Floyd said opening the door for me and clearly not expecting an answer.

'Checked her out,' I queried, 'what d'you mean? You can't be expecting to stake her out.'

'No, at least –no, of course not,' he said, as I was thinking that was exactly what he did mean. However he recovered quickly enough and said, 'what I meant was, you can make sure she is the boat whose registration details we've got from the SSR. Then we'll decide what to do next.'

'Hm,' I muttered, trying, and failing, to think of some way of explaining tactfully I already knew she was, so instead I said, 'How are you proposing we get near enough to do that without being spotted?'

'Oh, Daiz,' he said, 'you are being difficult.'

Moi? 'Nonsense,' I said, tact failing me. 'First of all we don't need to physically check her out as her registered description fits to a tee.'

'Oh. And secondly, what?'

'There isn't really a secondly,' I said, 'except that I think it would be a very bad idea to go hanging around the Tiger Moth. If, as you say, someone from her crew was responsible for my accident, the best thing we can do is to keep well out of the way.'

'What do you suggest then?' Floyd asked, looking dejected.

'What I think,' I said slowly, 'is that it's important not to show any signs of anything being wrong. We should give the impression of carrying on as usual. So I'm getting back onboard Lou now my ankle's better and we're meeting up as we were doing before we were so rudely interrupted.'

'But,' he said,

'But me no buts. If they've checked at all they'll know Lou's permanently moored here, so they'll expect me to be around, and the more routine things we do the more likely they are to forget all about us. Plus it'll give us the opportunity to keep an eye on the Tiger Moth without being obvious about it.'

'That's your theory is it?'

I nodded trying not to look smug. 'Better than your plan of keeping the Tiger Moth under surveillance like a pair of amateur private eyes.'

'And what about me?'

I noticed Floyd's voice had a slightly petulant tone as he asked me this, but I pressed on regardless. 'Give me a couple of hours and I'll meet you in The Salty Seadog for a late lunch, we'll talk about it then.'

It was great morning, and I don't mean just the weather, which was warm and sunny. It was great to be getting back onboard and into my natural environment. And it was absolutely wonderful to feel physically independent again, even if my ankle did twinge ominously as I stepped cautiously down the companionway into Lou's unchanging welcome.

A flick of the switch got the turbo heater going to take the chill off the place whilst I stowed my stuff and turned the engine over as I usually do when the boat's been shut up for a few days; after that it was time for a large mug of coffee and another go at Floyd's book, pugged up in my favourite nook in the cockpit.

An Honest Trade
August 1833

Smallpox is in the town. It is believed to have been brought in by seamen fleeing the Justina.

Harry, John Wells' youngest son, succumbs to the disease having been sick for only two days. The boy was eight years of age. Wells fears the extremities of the climate had weakened the child's resistance. His wife, Sarah, entreats him to resign his position so that they can return to England. Such is his grief at the loss of his beloved son, he is minded to comply, and undertakes to write to the London agents by the next mail boat.

The man, Fortune Proivil, is made headman in the Negro yard in place of Homer Searles, who had died the previous month.

Without the consignment of labour Wells expected, the plantation must continue to function with less than half the workers it needs. He reallocates slaves 18, 27 and 29 to shovel and ploughing, number 22 to drilling and sets the rest to cutting canes. He expects the harvest this month to be fair.

The value of the existing slaves in the month of August is estimated as sixteen hundred and fifteen pounds in total, being comprised three head people worth two hundred and ten pounds; fifteen field labourers - eight hundred and twenty five pounds; nine inferior labourers - three hundred and sixty pounds and six children fetching two hundred and twenty pounds.*

The chapter ends with the boy's funeral.

*Need to recheck numbers. Thirty-three seems very few to be working whole plantation. No mention of house slaves.

Seven

Heaving a sigh of relief I dropped the few pages of Floyd's manuscript with which I had been tussling onto my lap and leaned back to let the sun warm my face for a few minutes.

I know it had been in the back of my mind to use this time really constructively - apart from giving some serious attention to Floyd's book I was going to go over everything that had happened regarding the Tiger Moth in the light of Floyd's theory, and subsequently to have oodles of ideas to put to him when we met in The Salty Seadog later.

But something had intervened: whether it was my blanking-off reaction to **An Honest Trade**, or the soothing sounds of harbour life, or the mesmerizing undulation of Lou in the water, or just the sheer pleasure of being there, the few minutes of not thinking about anything at all inexplicably extended to several minutes after I was supposed to be in the pub.

Naturally, although I leapt into immediate action, in so far as someone bravely struggling with a very sore ankle can do, by the time I'd got myself together, Floyd had vacated The Salty Seadog and was calling to me from the pontoon.

'Daiz! Daiz! It's me, Floyd. You all right?'

'Course I'm okay,' I said stumbling up the steps from the cabin – steps for Pete's sake, I found myself mentally calling the companionway 'steps'. Heaven forefend I was succumbing to Floyd's influence.

What kept you?' he asked as, somewhat unsteadily, I joined him on the pontoon.

'I was having another stab at the précis of your book and forgot the time,' I said.

'Oh'. He looked doubtful. 'And might I venture to ask your opinion?'

'Well, it's kind of hard to get a feel for it when you've only got the bare account of what will happen in each chapter, without any dialogue or anything.'

'You don't like it.'

'It's not exactly that I don't like it. I don't like the subject matter, but you knew I wouldn't, so you won't be surprised about that. What I do think is probably unusual is telling the story through the eyes of the villain of the piece – the white overseer. I think his attitude gives the story a different dimension.'

Floyd nodded and I was relieved that my comments seemed to have gone down reasonably well.

'How's the ankle?' he asked, folding the paper he'd been reading and tucking it under his arm, and we started back along the walkway in the direction of the quay.

'All right,' I muttered. 'It's only been a couple of hours, what do you expect, an instant recovery?'

'Tetchy,' he observed. 'Good to know the sea air's put you in a better frame of mind.'

I glared at him but he was laughing and it's very difficult being cross with someone so... so Floydish.

'Come on then, lunch and other serious business lies ahead,' he said, suddenly increasing his pace. 'You won't have seen the paper.'

I don't know if it was a test of the true state of my physical recovery or if it was because he was burning to tell me the news, but whichever it was, disaster followed almost instantly. As I put on a spurt to keep up with him I tripped on a loose duckboard. Inevitably, I caught the plank with my good foot. Having all my weight dumped on it, my benighted ankle gave way. Staggering forwards with arms outstretched in a useless effort to regain my balance, I cannoned against Floyd and before I knew what was happening, he'd gone headfirst into the sea. Right under. Totally submerged.

I'm not thinking as I launch myself over the side and splash the few strokes to where he went down. I'm reaching out and groping for him, but even as I make contact he's rearing up. Ripping through the surface. Hurtling up almost waist high out of the sea. Propelled by terror. Arms threshing. Head thrown back. Mouth wide.

Crashing back beneath the surface.

I'm yelling not to panic, that there's no danger, the tide's out and he's clear of moored boats. But he's not listening. He's drowning. Drowning. And the water wouldn't even come up to his chin.

'You can stand,' I'm shouting at him. 'Put your feet down. You can stand.' But he can't hear me. I doubt he can hear anything, not even his own screams.

He's screaming and floundering, leaping up and plunging back like some berserk butterfly swimmer; churning up the mud, choking on great globs of it thrown up by his own frenzy and he's swallowing water, gallons of it, gagging and retching, gulping and gasping for air. He's pitching and tossing around in the foaming, filthy mayhem, and all I can see of his face are flashes of teeth and the whites of his eyes.

I think I'm still shouting at him, I think I'm repeating over and over, 'Put your feet down and keep still. I'll hold you.' But it may only be in my head. I'm close by him now, half blinded by the deluge and I'm grabbing at him but he's wrenching away and I can't keep hold. I can't keep hold. I'm snatching at water and air and he's totally lost it and his head's under the water and he's not coming up.

I don't know how long all this went on. I do know those wildly thrashing arms had whacked me in the face a couple of times and I definitely wasn't feeling wonderful; I'd been aware I was tiring, my attempts to take hold of him less vigorous than they had been. But what was really awful was the moment when he stopped screaming. A silent capitulation to the sea that was much, much worse.

The rescue, when it came, was fast and effective. No messing about. Three men were in the water beside us. Floyd was unceremoniously hoisted out. I'd like to say I got out under my own steam, but the truth is, I was pretty done in by then and was glad enough to allow myself to be manhandled to safety.

Even before I'd got a foot on dry land, Floyd had been laid face down on the jetty and was being given a serious bout of artificial respiration and by the time I'd been wrapped in enough covers to warm a penguin's backside, he'd been relieved of several pints of seawater, his eyes were open and he was breathing more or less normally. I couldn't say the same about his mental state. Nothing about him suggested the normal Floyd. Everything shouted 'Shock'. Shaking violently, his gaze unfocused, he wasn't responding to his rescuers' prompting. He hardly seemed aware of what was happening as he was lugged to his feet, swiftly swaddled in an assortment of coats and blankets supplied by the small crowd that had gathered around us, packed onto one of the trolleys that are used for moving gear to and from the shore and trundled up to the quay where an ambulance had just arrived.

By this time, a withdrawn and mute Floyd was functioning sufficiently to make it perfectly clear that he rejected the ambulance out of hand, in spite of the advice of everyone around him. Ignoring all protestations, he simply said, 'No, I mean it.' Then lapsed back into silence with a totally uncompromising expression on his face. At which point the ambulance crew gave up and went off to find a more compliant patient.

Talk about misplaced bravado. I must say none of us was convinced about the wisdom of his decision. The few words he'd spoken had been slurred; he was greasy with sweat and his complexion the colour of old putty. I was still worrying about the possible consequences of his pig-headedness when hot sweet tea was administered to both of us and Jeff and Colin from The Salty Seadog were ushering him away to dry him off and warm him up; Jeff, in particular, being expert at that sort of thing with many years of sailing experience behind him.

Sometime later, I was fashionably attired in Megan's winceyette pyjamas and her second-best dressing gown, and Floyd had been kitted out in an equally stylish range of nightwear with the addition of an old grey blanket to wrap round his shoulders, all of which had been loaned by our various well-wishers. We also learned that, not satisfied with attending to our welfare, someone had thoughtfully despatched a bottle of genuine Old Malt to Floyd's rescuers. Anyway, there we were, dressed for bed in mid afternoon, huddled over a fire that had been hastily lit for us in the back bar of The Salty Seadog and I was doing my best to cajole Floyd into conversation. Without much success, I might add.

I'd done the bit about his first attempt to hurl himself into the briny foiled only by my quick-witted action (I think I noticed the flicker of a smile as I said this, but it may have been wishful thinking on my part), and I'd progressed to this latest incident and was flagellating myself for pushing him in, when he'd shaken his head and said, tersely, that it wasn't my fault. Abrupt though his comment was I took it as an indication that he was beginning to feel better and told myself not to spoil it by rushing him. The outcome of which self-admonishment left me holding his hand and smiling in an inane sort of way.

After a while, however, the hand holding and smiling was wearing a bit thin. In fact I was beginning to wonder if my facial muscles would be set for eternity in a live version of rigor mortis. Plus, I had an itch in the middle of my back and my bad foot had gone numb. Don't get me wrong: I was sympathetic. I did know he was in shock and it was more that he couldn't speak, than he wouldn't, but all the same there is a limit and mine was rapidly approaching.

'Floyd,' I was saying tentatively, just as I heard the sound of someone's voice. Someone speaking. Not much above a whisper but definitely speaking.

'How about you, Daiz?' they were asking. 'How's the young woman who saved my life?'

I had a thumping headache, a bloody nose and a split in my lip where he'd put my tooth through it, not to mention an aching ankle. 'Oh Floyd,' I said, 'It was nothing, honestly.'

A brief pause ensued before he laughed. Not much of a laugh, more of a wheezy chuckle, nevertheless another sign he was on the mend.

An hour or so passed before Floyd really got himself together. His improvement came in fits and starts and I kept my chatter as inconsequential and wide ranging as I could. Don't ask me what I talked about, it's not as if I've a vast experience of anything much outside my sailing world, I simply prattled on, knowing that the last thing either of us needed was for him to fly into one of his tirades or relapse back into non-communication due to one of my tactless comments. Tactless. I mulled over the word I'd just applied to myself. It was weird, I thought, that until recently I'd never considered myself a particularly insensitive person, whereas I was fast becoming obsessive about not putting my foot in it. At this rate along with my newly acquired fetish, I'd be developing a phobia as well. Ovi-something phobia perhaps. Fear of eggshells.

Eventually when I judged he was sufficiently recovered, or it might have been when I found I simply couldn't watch my P's and Q's any longer, I gave up skirting around his unwonted immersion and asked him outright. 'So what was it exactly, that suddenly had you all revved up?'

'Sorry, Daiz, not with you.'

'It was something to do with the paper,' I said patiently. 'You said something about my not having seen it.'

He looked at me blankly.

'Newspaper,' I prompted. 'You had a paper you were going to show me. I think it went in the drink with you.'

I could almost see his memory clunking back into place.

'You're right, 'he said. 'I remember now. How could I have forgotten?'

'Your unscheduled dip may have had something to do with it,' I said in my best unsarky voice. 'So now we've cleared that up, would you mind explaining what it was you were going to tell me before we were so rudely interrupted?'

'They've found the body of a young woman. She was washed up a few miles down the coast. It was that morning we were going to Wales.'

'It does happen,' I said. 'Given the currents I expect she came ashore at Wickley Spit.'

'But don't you see the significance?' he asked.

I shook my head.

'Wake up; it's obvious, isn't it?'

'Sorry, you'll have to help me out with this. I'm not with you at all.'

'Ten to one, she's a victim of the Tiger Moth operation.'

I think my mouth dropped open. 'Oh, come on,' I said. 'You can't be serious. How on earth d'you come to that conclusion?'

'Well, of course I do accept it could be anybody, but we know what these people are capable of. And, well, it makes you think, doesn't it?'

'Only if you have a fertile imagination, get real, Floyd. It's all conjecture on your part.'

'They've not been able to identify the woman.'

'Identification can take weeks, months sometimes. You can't base anything on that.'

He glanced at me, registered my sceptical expression. 'If you're going to look like that I won't bother.'

'Like what?'

'You know perfectly well what I'm saying. Probably even think the same. But you'd never admit it.'

'Your point being?'

'No point, 'he said, 'I'm not making a point and there's no point in discussing it further.'

'Don't get huffy with me again,' I said, 'I haven't finished being your life saver yet.'

He had the grace to look sheepish. 'Thing is Daiz, however much you try to convince me I'm wrong, or take the rise out of what you obviously think of as my half-baked ideas, you can't put me off. I've let that happen once too often.'

'I don't know what you're talking about. When have I put you off doing something you're set on?'

'Need you ask? I could mention not reporting illegal immigrants, or, let's see, not reporting someone pushing you – Shall I go on?'

I shook my head.

'Glad that's settled,' he said, 'but actually I didn't mean you. Not you alone anyway. I was thinking about other people; other things.' He gave me a very straight look but didn't say anything else.

His whole demeanour said that he was burning to get whatever it was off his chest but something was preventing him. He was leaning forward, resting his elbows on his knees in an approachable manner, but his hands clasped rigidly together under his chin contradicted this and I'm not sure he wasn't gritting his teeth. I let him struggle with his inner conflict for several seconds before I was forced to chivvy him up. 'Go on then, tell me. Don't clam up on me now.'

No response.

'What, Floyd? What happened?'

His glance held mine for a moment before he looked away; leaving me searching through the backlist of our shared experiences for anything that might prod him into disclosure, anything he'd hinted at in the past or been evasive about. Evasive. The word triggered a memory like a pigeon coming home to roost. 'It's something to do with why you left Africa, isn't it?' I asked making a real effort to keep my voice calm.

He looked startled, really troubled and I knew I'd hit the spot. In normal circumstances, I don't think he'd ever have said anything however much I'd pried, but he was exhausted and vulnerable, and after all who wouldn't be when they'd very nearly drowned themselves? 'Floyd,' I said gently, and this time I didn't have to work at it. 'Please tell me what happened.'

'It's about violence,' he said abruptly. 'Superstitious, barbaric violence which is happening throughout Africa.'

I must admit I was confused by this reply. I mean it's axiomatic to say I don't know the first thing about international affairs, yet even I have gleaned the basic fact that Africa has its problems. And surely that would have been one of the main reasons he'd gone out there, to help people caught up in the conflicts? There must have been something more, I thought, something more than internal unrest that had caused him to walk away or I was seriously off beam somewhere.

I was earnestly engaged in figuring out a way of putting this to him when I realised he wasn't expecting a response.

'There was a lot of stuff leading up to my working in Africa which I won't go into now,' he was saying in an offhand way, so that I guessed that the 'stuff' he'd mentioned hid a whole other story. 'I'll start with when I went out to Sierra Leone to a camp for war-displaced people near the border with Liberia. The charity I was with had been in the area since the end of the war.' He interrupted himself. 'You do know about the war, don't you?'

It was with a mixture of relief and resentment that I recognized the return of the authentic Floyd, the Floyd who was challenging me, knowing I wouldn't have a clue about the fighting.

I rustled up some unconvincing excuse but he was already shaking his head and feigning astonishment at my ignorance and preparing to elaborate. Not that I wanted him to. I've spent my entire life avoiding the horrors of world events and steering well clear of issues that are likely to keep me awake at night, and here was Floyd intent on undoing all my efforts in one short afternoon. I did accept that his dip in the ocean had clearly been a defining moment for him; didn't accept that it had to be for me too. Why is it, I wondered, that those people who take it all on the chin don't understand about those of us who fight shy?

Unsurprisingly, I baulked at saying any of this to him. Inevitably, my backing off meant he supplied a welter of details about the war. He began his account at the time Sierra Leone was colonized by Great Britain and continued with its peaceful transition to independence and the decade or so after that when the country had prospered.

He was well into his stride by the time I noticed the fire needed stoking, and this activity kept me busily occupied through his description of the exploitation of the diamond industry and what he opined was the country's inevitable decline into corruption and poverty. By this stage, the fire was showing signs of being somewhat over-stoked and there was nothing for it but to resume my attentive attitude.

Floyd was holding forth about coups and military rule and I was struggling to prevent my eyes glazing over when I realised he was saying something about the nineteen nineties. Thinking he was nearing the end of the history lesson, I breathed a sigh of relief only to regret it almost instantly when he began to describe the country's eruption into civil war.

With no regard to my obvious distress he went on to enlighten me about rape and abduction of children to fight as rebel soldiers, and the slaughter and mutilation of tens of thousands of innocent people.

I guess it was one of the few times in my life I'd ever been made to face up to anything so dreadful, and I can't say I was the better for it. As I knew would be the case, confronted with the glaring need to do something, I was powerless to do anything. I had the same feeling when I was reading Floyd's manuscript, but at least what he was recounting had happened in the distant past and I was able to put it aside when I'd had enough. This atrocity was in my own lifetime and there was no easy exit.

I felt guilty and weighed down by the intensity of the story. Story. Not the word to describe the brutal inhumanity of it all. Not tragedy either. Tragedy has an element of chance about it. Too much, I thought, as he paused for breath, much too much to know or to bear. Nonetheless, I was painfully aware that he'd still not got to his personal involvement.

'Hardly surprising,' I heard him say, 'that Sierra Leone has been ranked by the UN as the poorest and worst place in the world in which to live. Not that Bendu and Sallay had any option; their village had been destroyed by the rebels. They wouldn't have made it to over the border. Not on their own.'

'Bendu and Sallay?' I queried.

'Girls,' he said, 'very young girls, about nine or ten.' He paused. Spoke again. 'I don't expect you know that, with the exception of one ethnic group, the majority of girls in Sierra Leone are mutilated as part of the puberty rites.' As he said this he turned away from the window and addressed me directly, except that he was looking through me, not at me, and anyway, it was a rhetorical question.

What? I could hardly believe what I was hearing. 'What on earth are you talking about?' I asked.

'Female circumcision,' he said bluntly, 'another way of keeping people in chains. It's estimated that less than twenty percent of girls escape the maiming and those that do are ostracised and never fully accepted into adult society.'

I was stunned. Stunned that what I'd presumed was some long-gone superstitious practice was in reality still widespread: stunned that it had apparently impinged on his own life in some way. It was obvious there was more to come. I didn't say anything. In any case, I don't think Floyd was aware of me then. He was making his report by excising his emotion, as if giving way to the slightest hint of feeling would result in an unstoppable tidal wave of rage. I closed my eyes and shut my mind, but my ears let me down and allowed snatches of the horrific details to penetrate: words about the removal of the female's private parts with basic tools like pen knives, broken glass and razor blades; matchstick size openings for urine and blood, rudimentary healing ointments of herbs, milk, ashes and dung. I felt sick. 'I'm sorry,' I butted in. 'Please, I'm really begging you not to tell me any more.'

The commentary ended abruptly. I opened my eyes warily in case I inadvertently signalled I required more details. I was startled to see that Floyd had got up at some time and was standing by the window still wrapped in his blanket. Seeing him silhouetted by the dusty sunlight beaming through the glass, I was reminded of a picture I'd once seen of a tribal warrior gazing out over the dusty plains of his homeland.

'Had to get out,' my warrior was muttering. 'Had to. Couldn't stand it. Might have done something I'd regret.'

Caught in a dilemma of not wanting to hear any more loathsome details, but needing to know what happened to the little girls, some minutes elapsed before I asked, 'Is that what happened to Bendu and Sallay?'

'It's ironic,' he said, 'a cruel, desperate irony. Their homes were in ruins and the people of the village had been forced to flee into the bush. They'd been hiding there for weeks without food or medicine. Many of the children were sick and dying. Unfortunately, an inadequate word to describe the hideous slaughter that followed, the rebels tracked them down. Many were raped and countless numbers had their limbs hacked off before they were massacred. Few escaped. I've no idea how Bendu and Sallay got away, let alone how they made it to the camp where I was working. Apparently they were in a terrible state when they arrived, exhausted, malnourished and sick.'

'You didn't see them yourself?' I asked, drawn in, in spite of my qualms.

'Not then,' he said. 'You have to understand that almost a quarter of the country's population are now refugees. The camps contain as many as thirty thousand people, all crowded together in mud huts or makeshift shelters of old plastic, bits of wood, anything they can utilise.'

I assume because the figures Floyd had quoted were way beyond my comprehension, I picked up on them and was staring into the fire trying to visualise a camp of thirty thousand people. Me, whose head was usually full of winds and tides, warps and spinnakers, was thinking about refugees hundreds of miles away in another continent.

Floyd had stopped talking. Worried that I might have offended him by not paying sufficient attention, I looked across to him and nodded in what

I trusted was a faintly encouraging manner. Not too encouraging, I hoped; I could do without any more gruesome details. Luckily, in that he didn't seem annoyed, unluckily, in that he pitched back into his account, my body language seemed to have done the trick. I looked back into the fire.

'It was later,' he said, 'when they turned up at one of the camp schools that I came across them. They'd been receiving food and medical aid for a while by then and although they were skinny and undersized, they seemed to be responding fairly well to treatment. They didn't have that blank, haunted look so many of the children had and now and then you might even catch a smile. I knew they were in our programme for trying to locate relatives of the orphans and their particular story was neither worse nor better than many of the others. Yet somehow you couldn't help noticing them. They were always together, usually holding hands; just that bit anxious if they happened to be separated, but not as obviously traumatised as some of the others.'

'Perhaps because they at least had each other,' I murmured.

'It was after – after -'

I continued staring into the fire waiting for him to resume, but all was quiet. After a while I looked up again. He was staring fixedly out of the window. I guessed that all he was seeing was two orphaned girls in a refugee camp in Sierra Leone.

'Floyd,' I said.

He flinched. Drew back from the brink of whatever mental chasm he was staring into. Jerked into speech. 'It was some weeks after I'd first noticed them that they didn't turn up at the school. I'd got used to seeing them, I suppose. Might even have looked out for them; looked for their shy smiles and intertwined hands; two little sparks of hope.'

'Didn't turn up?' I asked.

'Never came back.'

'Go on,' I was saying, as the door of our recuperation room was pushed open.

'How you two doin' then? Jeff asked, glancing at Floyd before ambling over to me bearing a laden tray. 'Thought you might be in need of a peck or two by now. Ship's rations,' he added as he put the tray down on the hearth. 'Come and get it.'

Ship's rations turned out to be hot soup and sandwiches, and coffee laced with rum. Enticing enough to bring Floyd back to join me by the fire. We were mumbling thanks to Jeff as he was closing the door.

We'd demolished the edibles and were making inroads into the drinkables when Floyd suddenly said, 'Fina, one of the field workers, told me what happened. Not voluntarily. I had to really press her; too hard maybe.' He paused, took a sip of coffee.

I gave him one of my semi-encouraging nods, braced myself.

'Fina told me that it's the custom for groups of girls of approximately the same age to be rounded up for initiation into secret societies.' He paused again, glowered at the mug in his hand, resumed. 'The main part of the initiation ritual is the cutting, a euphemistic word to describe genital mutilation.'

With this comment, he banged down his cup, clamped his lips together and glared at me. I recognised the symptoms instantly. It was the seeing red, flying off the handle diatribe syndrome. Not a good idea. Not for either of our sakes. 'Don't go blaming me,' I wanted to shout at him. 'It's not *my* fault.' Instead I said calmly, with the outward appearance of calm anyway, 'Floyd, please finish telling me about Bendu and Sallay.'

Thankfully the furious expression went from his eyes and he said in a flat voice, 'The women who administer the puberty rights are feared and believed to hold supernatural powers. Girls swear never to reveal anything that happens during the ritual and those initiated together form a sisterhood that lasts throughout their lives.'

'What happened to Bendu and Sallay,' I asked again patiently.

'Bendu died,' he said.

I waited.

'Sallay told Fina about it. She must have been desperate to break her oath. Can you imagine her grief after all she and Bendu had been through together?'

I nodded, but I don't think he noticed.

'Sallay said that she was taken to a secret place where she was stripped naked and had a piece of cloth forced into her mouth to stop her screaming. Two women held her legs apart. Another sat on her chest to prevent her from moving. All the women were half-drunk. Then they cut her with a rusty tin lid. After that the raw skin was pulled together and fixed with thorns. A paste that smelled like animal dung was put on and then her legs were bound together. She was ill for a long time, in shock I suppose, and in terrible pain, but she survived. She said that the same things were done to Bendu, only Bendu never got better. She bled and bled and then she died. Her death was attributed to witchcraft.'

He shook his head. 'Sallay just disappeared. I tried to find her. Did my best. Spent all my spare time looking for her, asking questions. Pestered Fina until she complained to my supervisor, who told me to back off. But I couldn't let it rest. Eventually it was put to me, in words of one syllable, that I was becoming disruptive, should take a sabbatical and get my head together.

'That's when you came home?'

'Not immediately; first I made a journey. Against all advice I travelled to what remained of Sallay's village. It was a pitiable place, not more than one or two crumbling walls in a landscape of deforestation and devastation. Utterly deserted. Then I came home.'

'Was Sallay ever found?'

'Who would look for her when I was gone? There are so many there, right under their noses, needing help.'

I didn't say anything for a time. I had the impression that Floyd's coming home had intensified his anguish, not alleviated it. Little wonder he was so uncompromising about injustice; so passionately determined to change things. Little wonder he got so annoyed with me about my sidestepping difficult issues. That being said, it still seemed doubtful to me that after developing my defence mechanism for thirty-odd years I'd be likely to alter my well-honed self-protection strategy any time in the future. I guessed it would be something we'd both have to live with, an incontrovertible fact of life, his ever the weather eye, mine the blind one.

After a while Floyd roused himself and told me briefly about his life between coming home from Africa and joining the Home Office. Apparently he'd applied to the World Health Organisation and spent the time waiting for his application to be processed in doing research for his book. At some stage during this period, he'd become incensed by the iniquities of our Immigration policy and decided he'd be more effective challenging what he saw as 'The Little Englander Mentality'; hence he'd joined the Home Office.

The coffee jug was drained, the soup and sandwiches things of the past and the afternoon dwindling into evening when he returned to the subject of the Tiger Moth. It came right out of the blue. With my head full of images of Africa I'd more or less forgotten the world on my doorstep.

'That's why I'm sure I'm right to pursue this Tiger Moth thing,' he was saying. 'So I'm going back to town to see what I can find out about her owners.'

'But,' I said.

'But me no buts, as someone said to me recently. Face it, Daiz. You mightn't like it, but it makes sense. Water-wise, it's going to take me a time to face anything bigger than a puddle. A couple of days sniffing around on dry land will give me something to do and time to get the phobia back under control.'

So that was it. Really, how could I argue? I'd seen Floyd's fear close-up, too close to ever make light of it again, and as for me I'd done such a good job of downplaying his notion of the Tiger Moth as the mainstay of an illicit immigration gang that I almost believed it myself. Almost.

An Honest Trade
September 1833

The building of five new Negro houses has been completed. Each will contain two families and has a sleeping chamber at the top. The headman, Fortune Proivil, being of good character and respected by the other slaves, will decide how they are allocated.

High winds scorch the canes where the fields are exposed and the windward estates are attacked by crane fly. Second harvest and replanting takes place.

There are arson attacks in the town. The militia are on night guard and there has been an increase in the constabulary force. A reward of £500.00 is offered to anyone, free or slave, who may be the means of bringing the perpetrator to justice.

John Wells comments that such wicked individuals (the arsonists) are more calamitous at this particular time of the year than they would be in any other season because everywhere is bone dry; each blade of grass is parched and the Negroes' houses of wattle and daub with palm-thatched roofs are exceptionally combustible.

He is seriously alarmed at the extent of the damage that could result from a fire and writes to the London agents requesting a portable fire-engine of sufficient power to quench a fire of, say a small English cottage. The engine would be worked by 4 – 6 men and the cost would not exceed £20-£30 since he would not require leather buckets or a great length of hose.

After he has despatched his letter he realises he has not notified the Agents of his intention to resign. On hearing of this omission, Sarah, his wife, is distressed and retires to her bed. His conjugal rights having been withdrawn, Wells considers selecting another woman to replace Lionoria.

Eight

Our goodbye on the windy wastes of the marina car park next morning was prolonged. One thing I knew for certain was that I didn't want Floyd to go. If he'd asked me I'd have been buckled up in the front seat of the Nissan without a by your leave. But he didn't. And I couldn't ask him to stay. Not with all he'd been through.

'Promise to ring me tonight,' he was saying, as he pecked me on the forehead, 'and get yourself a mobile today. You must be the only person in the UK who hasn't got one.'

'Never felt the need before now,' I said. 'Always had the ship's radio for emergencies.'

'Life's about more than emergencies,' he said, pulling me close and wrapping me in a hug. 'I'd have thought you'd have realised that by now. It's about what's important and what's not. And if there's a few miles between you and the one you want to talk to about those things, the telephone's a wonderful thing.'

I was mumbling that I'd miss him, when he loosened his hold on me, wiped the tears from my eyes with the back of his hand and kissed me full on the lips.

I felt desolate as he drove away.

I had it in mind to restart my cycling regime that had been so rudely interrupted by the ankle incident, and had brought my bike with me to the car park. I stood and watched the car disappear into the distance and gave Floyd plenty of time to come back for me. When he didn't, there was nothing for it but to mount up. A couple of miles at the most, I decided.

Pedalling along the old harbour lane, I was doing a pretty good job of convincing myself it was good to be back in the saddle; ankle not too bad, no visible signs of loss of fitness, weather brightening up and the prospect of getting away on my trip in the not very distant future. Hunky dory, all things considered: so why did I feel so fed up?

Too fed up for this futile cycling, going nowhere, for no good reason. Without thinking, I pulled hard on the handlebars and performed a perfect u-turn. Almost perfect, I should say. In the instant I found myself skidding broadside along the unmade carriageway spouting gravel and mud in all directions, until, hitting a particularly spiteful rut, the bike slewed over and I executed a couple of acrobatic manoeuvres I hadn't realised I had in my repertoire.

Disengaging myself from the brambles which lined the banks of the lane, and recovering the cycle from its equally prickly landing place took a while. The bicycle was more or less unharmed, a couple of scratches but nothing buckled or bent. The rider hadn't fared so well. I'd scraped the skin off both palms, grazed my chin and ripped the knee out my jeans. I won't even mention the pain in the already afflicted joint.

Not much of a morning so far, I moaned, as, cross and snivelling, I pedalled back to Lady Louella. There I restowed the bike in the aft locker with the promise of another day, dabbed TCP on my assorted abrasions and changed my jeans. Next I had coffee and half a pack of chocolate digestives, and after that I proceeded to the town centre in search of a mobile phone.

That evening I rang Floyd from the pay phone in The Salty Seadog. Having been so overwhelmed by the amazing features of my new mobile, which included such mysteries as PINS and ring-tones, text messaging and imaging, I'd failed to work out how to put money on the damn thing to allow me to use it.

Floyd didn't sound all that sympathetic when I told him about my day.

'Daiz,' he kept saying, in between what sounded like someone in paroxysms of mirth, 'tell me you're making it up; especially the bit about the brambles. Oh, and the ring-tones. I particularly like your description of mastering the ring tones.'

'Glad to have made you laugh,' I sniffed. 'Can't say it seemed all that amusing to me.'

'Daiz? Daiz? You crying?'

'No,' I lied.

'Didn't mean to upset you,' he said, sounding contrite. 'It's just that I've been missing you and it's so good to hear your voice and you tell your stories in such a deadpan way, laughing is like a safety valve if you see what I mean.'

'Not really,' I said, 'but it doesn't matter. I've been missing you too. Tell me what you've been up to since you got back.'

'Nothing much; unpacked my stuff; chucked some washing in the machine; had something to eat. You know the kind of thing.'

'Oh,' I said.

'Listen,' he said. 'I was thinking things over all the way home, going over and over everything. About you and me and this Tiger Moth matter. Seems to me there's only one solution. One obvious solution.'

'Don't keep me in suspense, then.'

'Thought maybe you could come here for a few days. Stay with me. I've got a spare room. You could come any time. There's plenty needs checking out. More than enough to keep both of us occupied. Don't say no. I'm going to put in for the rest of my leave allowance, which will give me nearly a month - might even tuck my resignation in with it, haven't decided yet.'

Me, say no? The only problem I had was not saying yes too fervently. Have some dignity woman, I told myself. Don't bite his hand off. I managed a 'hm,' as if I was considering his suggestion, whilst I was casting about for a couple of weak excuses as to why it wouldn't be feasible, which in turn could be dismissed with the verbal equivalent of a flap of the hand.

'Don't say no,' he repeated. 'Please. Just come for a day or two. No pressure.'

'Well,' I said, 'I suppose I could squeeze a short break into my hectic schedule.'

'Brilliant,' he said. 'To be frank I wasn't about to take no for an answer, which is why I put my spare keys in the post to you. I sent them by special delivery to your mailbox as soon as I got home. They should be there by tomorrow.'

'You what?'

'Sent you my key so you can come whenever you like. I'd hate to slip out for an hour and come back to find you waiting on my doorstep. So just come, Daiz. Whenever you like. But make it soon.'

After I said goodbye to Floyd, I hovered by the phone for a few minutes while I mulled over what he'd said. He'd said he was sending me his house keys. He'd definitely said that. His keys. So I could come when I liked. No big deal.

Not to him, maybe.

I stayed in The Salty Seadog an hour or so after that while a team of regulars sorted out my phone for me, and I was somewhat gratified to hear a note or two of dissension amongst the techies as they wrestled with the instructions. I sank a couple of pints of cider during this interval and finally left the pub armed with a PIN based on Lady Lou's registration number, a debit of £50 on my credit card and a phone that played 'What shall we do with the Drunken Sailor' instead of ringing. Who says I'm not up to speed?

First thing next morning, I was in town picking up my mail from my P.O. Box. I normally only pop in two or three times a month, so there was quite a pile waiting for me, Floyd's parcel included. He'd stuck a silly card in with the keys, with a message about Hercule Poirot, although I was thinking more on the lines of Travis McGee, him being my favourite knight errant cum private eye, and his houseboat the Busted Flush coming a close second to Lady Lou in my choices for living accommodation. But I liked the card anyway. I guess the mood I was in I'd have liked anything that meant the two of us being together.

Next job was to coast round to Sealine Rigging to see what state my new sails were in. Phil was a tad short tempered.

'About time,' he snapped. 'Thought this job of yours was urgent. I dropped other stuff to get your rig sorted out and pushed the order for your new canvas to the front of the queue.' He glared at me while he caught his breath and I took the opportunity to explain about my near fatal fall down the companionway, and to grovel.

The upshot of this encounter was that Phil forgave me and arranged to bring the sails round to Lady Lou later that afternoon. Limping out of the workshop I chided myself for exaggeration and for taking advantage of a friend, at the same time reminding myself that it wasn't all eye-wash. The incident with the bicycle having taken its toll, I'd had to resort to strapping the dratted ankle up in several feet of stretch bandage and even gone so far as to swallow a couple of pain killers.

Getting the new rig sorted took the best part of the afternoon and I was delighted with the result. I think Phil was too, but more especially with the handsome tip I gave him. Having skipped lunch, by the time we'd got everything ship shape I was tired and hungry and I decided to leave the sea trials until the next day and to go to Floyd's the day after that, providing there were no hitches on the test run. After a swift shower I set off in search of calories and company and luckily found both in The Salty Seadog.

Next day I whizzed Louella round the bay a couple of times. There wasn't much wind, so, although everything seemed okay, I couldn't be entirely satisfied. Obviously she handled differently, I'd expected that, but I couldn't decide whether it was her or me who was feeling so sluggish. One thing I did know was that we'd both have to perk up if we were going to undertake our much-vaunted voyage in the next week or two.

To be truthful, by mid afternoon when I was moored up again in my customary berth, it wasn't the trip to the Azores that was taking my attention. Rather it was a forthcoming visit to a two bedroom flat in South London. So much so that, after a bite to eat and an excited attempt to 'phone Floyd, only to be disappointed to find that there wasn't a signal, I'd thrown my prescribed reading matter and a couple of more essential items into my rucksack and had my bicycle ready to go on the pontoon.

I stopped off at the chandler's to instigate the usual arrangements I made with Megan if I wasn't going to be around for a while, and spent fifteen minutes or so parrying the questions and innuendo arising from a single woman staying for an unspecified time in the home of an eligible bachelor. My difficulty was, of course, that I couldn't explain about Floyd's suspicions regarding the Tiger Moth. Consequently, the more I equivocated, the more unconvincing I sounded, giving Megan plenty of scope for gossip in The Salty Seadog that evening.

'We're just good friends,' I was saying for the umpteenth time. 'You're barking up the wrong tree. Honestly.'

Judging by Megan's reaction, 'honestly' was the wrong word to use. 'I think that's called over-egging the pudding,' she said, smirking.

It wasn't until I was cycling over the downs that I remembered I'd intended to 'phone Floyd from the chandler's to let him know I was on my way. And, living up to my recently acquired description as an airhead, I entirely forgot about my new mobile packed carefully in the pocket of my rucksack, so I never did make the call.

I can't say I enjoyed the ride once I was on the main road. Being overtaken; cut up and cut in; having names hurled at me and obscene gestures waved in my direction did not make for a pleasant experience. The puncture was the icing on the cake. It happened on the outskirts of the city. No drama, just a bloody puncture. Not difficult to fix, but a nuisance, and, I discovered, a hazardous operation when stranded on the kerb with London traffic snapping at my ankles, one of which wasn't up to scratch anyway.

The final phase in my journey related to locating Floyd's address. Arriving in the right neighbourhood armed with an A to Z and the rough diagram Floyd had enclosed with his keys should have made things easy. Not so. After a frustrating tour of blind alleys and dead ends, of backtracking and going round in circles, it struck me, as I dismounted to squint at his scrawled instructions once again, that maybe diagrams weren't his forte.

The result was that it was well after ten p.m. when I arrived in a mansion-house block, three floors up on the landing outside Floyd's front door. Sweaty and nervous I ran a hand through my hair, shuffled around for a bit, did the hair thing again, wished I had a mirror, fixed a big smile on my face and finally screwed up my courage and rang the bell.

Then I rang again.

A little while after that I rang again.

My big smile slipped a smidgen as it dawned on me that he wasn't in. It occurred to me that I should have telephoned.

Letting myself in wasn't physically difficult. Mentally it was hard. Disappointment and apprehension held me tremulous on the doorstep. I had to have several stern words with my Yin before my Yang propelled me into the hall.

I'm no kind of connoisseur of interior decoration, unless it relates to Lady Lou's brass fittings, pale oak wood finish and the size of her sail locker, but Floyd's hall looked pretty plain to me. Swish, but plain. Linen-look walls, glossy woodblock floor, long mirror, chromium up-lights and four doors leading off.

A sheet of paper was taped to one of them. I took a couple of steps, read, 'See note in kitchen.'

I pushed through into what was obviously the lounge. Minimalist didn't come into it. Acres of woodblock hosted a pair of sofas upholstered in ivory cord and set either side of the hearth, a glass topped table and chrome chairs in the window bay and little else. Floyd didn't seem to have got round to finishing touches like cushions or pictures or curtains. Maybe at three floors up he didn't think he'd be overlooked or, more likely, he didn't have the money.

I headed for what I presumed was the door to the kitchen.

There are kitchens and there are lifestyle statements and Floyd's black marble tops and sleek honey coloured units definitely came in the latter category. I was thinking that I'd have to take him to task about this conspicuous expenditure, when I remembered him telling me that it was the fixtures and fittings which came with the flat that had bumped up the price, but that he thought he'd be quids in, in the long run.

The note, or rather the tome, was waiting for me, next to a plate piled high with sandwiches.

Daiz,

I know you said you'd probably come tomorrow, but I'm leaving you a sandwich on the off chance that you make it tonight. Hope you like Brie and grape. Help yourself to tea and coffee, or there's beer in the fridge if you fancy it. Make yourself comfortable. The bed's made up in the spare-room if you want to turn in before I get back.

No doubt all you say about my overactive imagination is true, because having done some running around, I applied some lateral thinking and some cross checking, and now I've put two and two together and made five. All of which adds up to why I'm not here.

It's nearly nine forty five and I'm unable to contain myself any longer. Consequently I'm shooting out to do a proper reccy of one of the addresses we got from the Small Ships Register, apropos the owners of the Tiger Moth. I'm pretty sure you'll agree that there's no reason for us both to go chasing wild geese.

One other thing, Daiz, I guess there's a fifty-fifty chance that I'll be reading this to myself while I'm washing down the sarnie with a Budweiser. But if you are reading it, it means you're in and I'm out, and I just want to say I'm sorry I'm not there and I'm glad you came and I'll see you soon.

Love Floyd.

Oh! 'Pretty sure' indeed. What planet was the man on? I'd come all this way to be with him and he hadn't waited. I checked my watch. Couldn't have missed him by much more than half an hour. If I hadn't had that damned puncture …

I'd cycled miles and miles to be with him and my ankle was sore and I'd been really looking forward to seeing him and now he was out and I was totally hacked off. And he thought he'd appease me with a sandwich, when I wasn't even hungry. I'd take one bite just to show him. Then I'd be on my bike. No note or anything. That would definitely show him.

I took a bite. The cheese was creamy, the grapes sweet and the bread crusty; olive and rosemary, I thought. Not that a tasty sandwich would appease me. I wasn't in the mood for coffee just then, but thought I might have a cup before I left, for the caffeine. I opened a few unit doors until I located the fridge, and the beer. Opened a few more to discover the glasses.

Sandwich and beer in hand I came out of the kitchen into the lounge where I glanced at the labelled boxes stacked against the long wall, still unpacked from the move by the looks of it, noted his T.V. and sound system languishing amongst them.

I wandered back out into the hall.

There I peeked through the other three doors. With the front door behind me, to my immediate left was the bathroom, a bit of an eye opener. The lavender tiles and stainless steel taps and fittings had probably been inherited from the previous occupiers. But even so, putting the matching purple towels aside, what exactly was going on with the myriad bottles of crystals, oils and lotions which were set along the tiered glass shelves, as shiny as a Christmas window display at Boots?

Directly opposite the bathroom was the box room, neat and tidy and nothing exciting. In front of me, on the left-hand side, was the door to the lounge, and to the right the main bedroom.

I hovered on the threshold of Floyd's bedroom, took in the fitted cupboards, futon with midnight blue bedding, pale window blinds and plain rug by the side of the bed. Save for a single native shield standing on a low bank of drawers in a recess between the wardrobes, the room was totally unornamented, almost puritan. Was its lack of embellishment something to do with Floyd's ethics or more prosaically about his pecuniary position, I wondered? As I tiptoed through the room to where I could see another door, I had the feeling that whatever the underlying reason, Floyd would never be comfortable with drinking wine or eating chocolate biscuits in bed. What a loss!

The room off the bedroom was Floyd's study. Now I could see the man I'd known when we worked together. Well, not exactly together, not with his status and my lack of it, but in the same place. And I suppose I should also say, 'thought I knew'. I'd thought of him then as warm and serious and meticulous; come to think of him more recently as intense and ultra scrupulous. So I was probably kidding myself in seeing anything significant at all in the neat piles of papers and folders spread along the desktop; the shelves of books, the filing cabinet, the laptop computer he'd brought with him when he came to visit, something I presumed was a printer, and other equipment that was a complete mystery to me.

I won't pretend it was an idle whim that drove me to start riffling through the papers on Floyd's desk. More like a grim determination to find out where he'd gone. I was hoping, as I flipped over the top few pages, that he would have entered the details of the SSR form on his computer and printed a copy to take with him, leaving the original behind.

I didn't find the form among the papers on the desk. Hope springing eternal, I tried the filing cabinet. The top drawer was labelled 'Miscellaneous', the one below 'Research'. Sure enough, the form was filed under 'Tiger Moth' amidst the general filing.

Scribbling down the details, three names and addresses, I returned the form to the drawer and myself to the hall to get the A to Z from my rucksack. Back in the kitchen, I managed another sandwich and made myself a coffee, while I studied the map. Best leave the beer if I was off on another marathon. Need a clear head to deal with London's little idiosyncrasies.

All the addresses turned out to be within the M25 ring, and it seemed logical to me that Floyd would have headed for the nearest one first, which, as far as I could make out, was about eight miles from his flat. A thirty minute ride at the most, I thought, plus a maximum of fifteen minutes to get lost in.

After rinsing my cup and glass and putting the single remaining sandwich in the fridge, I availed myself of Floyd's facilities, unbuckled my Musto from the rucksack and then dumped the bag on the bed in the spare room. With the map and our quarries' addresses stowed in separate pockets and carrying my jacket rolled under my arm, I locked the front door carefully behind me.

Threading my way through the labyrinth that is the nation's capital wasn't much fun. Being dark didn't help, nor did the drizzle, but not for nothing do my friends call me obstinate and trenchant. And that's to my face. I think pig-headed and bloody-minded have also been mentioned.

Personally I prefer to think of myself as resolute and tenacious and maybe a little impatient; all of which might explain why some thirty-five minutes later I was in the right road and looking for somewhere safe to park my bike. The drizzle having given way to rain I unfastened my jacket from the saddle clips and pulled it on before making the bike as secure as I could. One couldn't go investigating without thinking about the return journey.

Obviously the first thing to do was to locate the precise address, where, with any luck, I would find Floyd loitering, presumably with moustaches waxed and little grey cells running riot, ready to clue me in, in a pronounced Belgian accent.

The address turned out to be a barber's at one end of a parade of shops. I don't know why this was a surprise. As far as I know there's no law about barbers owning boats. Of course the shop was in darkness, why wouldn't it be? It was late. I squinted at my watch: eleven fifty: I hadn't realised how late. Of course there was no sign of Floyd. I just knew that whilst I'd been cycling towards him, he'd been driving back in the opposite direction.

It was raining hard and I moved into the doorway of the shop next door to the barber's. I was glancing up and down the street, still hoping I might spot Floyd, when a car drew into the kerb, the passenger window slid down and a man's head bobbed into sight. It wasn't until I'd been propositioned and we'd had a somewhat heated exchange about my availability that I realised I was sheltering in the entrance of a sex shop. Mortified isn't the word. I fled. Scuttling past the barber's and into the side street, I ducked into the first opening that presented itself and found myself in the area behind the shops.

Hiding in the shadows I listened fearfully for the sound of footsteps, but fortunately none came. Waiting a moment or two to be on the safe side, and to recover my equilibrium, I began to see the funny side of the incident, although how any one could mistake someone togged up in oilskins for a working girl was a bit of a mystery. Unless he had some kind of fetish …

Anyway, no harm done and no time for aimless speculation, I was here to find Floyd and, chance having intervened, I'd landed up in a gloomy hinterland, which was much more likely where Floyd would be, if he weren't already sitting on his sofa supping Budweiser.

I moved closer towards the buildings, checked I had the right door.

Would Floyd have gone in? Broken and entered?   No, no, of course not. Yes, yes, definitely, the mood he was in.

To the best of my knowledge, I'd never done anything downright illegal before, but there's always a first time and I did just want to be certain he wasn't there, before I went back with my tail between my legs.

Tentatively I pushed the door, my hand on the handle. Of course it would be locked.

The door moved. I pushed harder; stepped inside.

Nine

I'm crouched in the dark in the barber's shop on the corner of the parade. I've been here, not knowing what to do, since the slim beam of the LED torch on my key ring located Floyd and I'd forced myself to bend down to check his pulse even though it was obvious he was dead.

He's still there, only a couple of yards away from me. I can make out his shape, slumped on the floor between the row of stainless steel basins and the fixed swivel chairs, and I know his head is lying in a sticky pool of his own blood.

In as far as my brain is working at all, I'm wondering if there's a chance anyone saw or heard anything suspicious; one of the late-night motorists brought to a temporary halt by the traffic lights a yard or two away on the opposite side of the plate glass window perhaps, someone who'll come forward when the police put up their notices.

Then I notice the slatted window blinds closed against witnesses.

The sound of a vehicle approaching the junction jolts me back into action. I lurch forward, hunched over my torch, keeping the beam low. I grope in my pocket for a tissue, then I'm creeping around wiping at things I think I might have touched because I don't want anyone to know I've been here - and I'm trying not to bang into other things and I'm looking for clues. Clues to what, I don't know. I do know it's pointless, futile. But I can't seem to stop. Compulsively wiping and lurching and wiping, all the time swearing and cursing under my breath and promising retribution on the people that did this terrible thing.

Until the noise. Not from outside this time.

From upstairs.

I'm listening now. Not lurching or wiping. Not even breathing. Just listening.

I can't tell how long I'm crouched there listening. Straining my ears. It seems ages. I don't hear anything else.

Imagination, I say.

Time to go.

Past time to go.

91

I don't know how to say goodbye to Floyd.
Not saying it takes a long time.
Going takes longer.

Ten

When I finally dragged myself out of my berth on Lady Lou, I was feeling like hell. Crippled and exhausted from the long cycle ride home I'd drunk much too much whiskey and crawled into my bunk only a few hours earlier. Huddled up in my sleeping bag, freezing one minute, sweating the next, I'd tried to make the world go away.

All I could think about was that Floyd was dead and I didn't think I'd ever care about anything ever again. What was there to care about? Floyd was dead and nothing could change that. I could try to emulate his example, take up his causes, devote myself to good works, but that could never change the fact that he was dead. Dead, like mum and Louise, the only two other people in the whole world I'd ever cared about. Caring didn't stop them dying either.

I thrashed all this around until I couldn't bear it any longer. Thinking was driving me into the buffers. Physical action was the only solution. I needed to be physically nearer to Floyd, nearer to where he'd lived. And died. And maybe if I were there, there'd be something I could do to avenge his death. Something I couldn't do hiding out on Lady Lou.

My mind made up, I hobbled into the heads for a lick and promise and was poking around wondering where the devil I'd put my toothbrush, when I remembered my rucksack casually abandoned on Floyd's spare bed.

And then I remembered my car. How could I have forgotten my car? My battered but trustworthy Nissan, last seen being driven away by Floyd – how many years ago? Two days. Just two days. Forty-eight hours when my comfortable, selfish world had been dashed away. Destroyed by murder.

I swabbed my eyes, sniffed and blew my nose. Couldn't afford to let misery get the upper hand. I glanced in the mirror. A pasty-faced individual, with bloodshot eyes and matted hair, stared back. Not a pretty sight. I shrugged, turned away. What did it matter?

Washed and dressed, I drank two glasses of water and swallowed a couple of aspirins. Next I scrambled up a few more items of kit and threw into my sailing bag together with a full size torch and my multi-function gizmo, slung the bag across my back, grabbed my jacket and went up on deck.

Two minutes later, I was below again, scrabbling around for my spare car keys, trying not to think about the other set …

Spares located and the sigh of relief hardly expelled, when I was panicking again. Only this time about Floyd's door keys. After a frantic search, I discovered them safely zipped into a pocket of my Musto and some sanity returned, although I couldn't honestly say I was on top of things.

On deck, I collected my bike from where I'd dumped it only a few hours before, and hoisted it over the rail.

'Sorry Lou,' I whispered as I climbed down to join it on the pontoon. 'I have to go. I know you understand. Wait for me.'

And then I slipped away from Mullion Quay.

I hated the ride. Hated the scenery, the weather, the traffic, the world. Hated arriving in the hustle and mayhem of the urban sprawl, but most of all hated seeing the barber's open for business, as if everything was perfectly normal. There was no yellow tape; no police guarding the premises; nothing out of the ordinary. As I lent my bicycle against the side of a bus shelter on the other side of the junction I asked myself how they could possibly have managed it, I mean, surely it's not that easy to dispose of a dead body?

Fiddling around for the painkillers in my pocket, I surveyed the premises. They must have been practically dogging my footsteps to have been able to spirit Floyd away in the time between my escape and the town waking up. Had they seen me? Been watching me as I crept away? Perhaps I'd actually interrupted them – there'd been that thud I'd heard – but if so, why had they let me go? They? He? Too many questions and no answers, I was in danger of questioning myself to a standstill. Time to find my car. It wouldn't be that far away, surely. Out of sight of the shop, certainly, but not hidden, just a parked car.

I eventually found it on a residential road outside the no parking zone.

Good. First hurdle jumped.

Bike folded and stowed in the boot, I hovered indecisively on the kerb, not wanting to open the driver's door. Not wanting to dispel the last picture I had of Floyd alive.

An elderly couple walked by. I caught the man giving me a suspicious look out of the corner of his eye. It occurred to me that I probably looked as if I were about to break into the car. I dredged up the ghost of my practical self and got in.

Floyd's flat was as stark and bleak as a lighthouse whose lamp has been suddenly extinguished. The fact that he hadn't even finished unpacking made it more awful.

The mauve bathroom horrified me: too full of his personal foibles. I took his purple towels down, folded them carefully and put them in the airing cupboard. Next I dug out a couple of plain white versions from my rucksack and hung them in their place. I filched a box of paper from the study, emptied it and packed the glittery toiletries away. When I'd finished the bathroom was still lavender but only sported such essentials as toothpaste and soap.

Creeping from room to room I began to be thankful for Floyd's minimalist approach - there were less personal bits and pieces to jump out at me, to remind me I was treading on his life.

I was in the kitchen drinking coffee and eating the sandwich I'd left in the fridge when the next phase of anxiety assailed me. What about Floyd's family? Would they be expecting frequent contact with him, or did weeks go past before he remembered to phone? What about his work —had he resigned? What were his financial arrangements? How about his neighbours? Did they know him well, know his movements, or did he keep himself to himself? Dozens of questions, if not hundreds sprang to mind. Every one remained unanswered. Anyway all these unsolvable problems merely confirmed my belief that my stay in the flat had to be brief, a couple of days at the most, which meant I had no time to waste on worrying about things I was powerless to do anything about. I washed up under the tap, left the crocks to drain and went back to the study.

I needed to know precisely what Floyd had discovered. Whether he had anything more than the registered owners of the Tiger Moth. Obviously he'd been right all along about her nefarious activities. The odds would have to be pretty long for him to have stumbled on some other criminal activity, some other crime lucrative enough to have necessitated his murder.

I tried the desk first but found nothing. Next I flicked through the filing cabinet, skimming the first few docs at the front of each category. I'd got as far as Tiger Moth's registration and was glancing over the details making sure there wasn't anything I'd overlooked, when something clicked. There was something I'd missed, not on this form, but relating to it. Something I'd skipped over without realising its significance. I stared at the names listed on the form and this time it was more of a clunk than a click, like something important falling into place.

I had it in a trice, neatly filed under C for Companies House. A print out from the computer, which provided, to my uncomprehending inspection, a lot of bumf on a chain of shops trading as 'Cutting it Fine'. A rather less perfunctory study elicited the information that the main man in charge of said shops was one Martin Boyle.

Well, Floyd had been busy in the hours before I arrived. Apart from investigating the addresses on the SSR form, I presumed he'd found other stuff on the internet. A closed book to me.

I folded up the printout and tucked it in my wallet with the registration form, then completed my speed-reading of the rest of the filing. Nothing else turned up. Hadn't I got enough to be going on with? Another unanswered question.

On my way out of the study, I glared at Floyd's computer and it glared back without giving anything away. I'd have to come up with a total zilch before I was prepared to dice with that.

I'd been mulling over the possibility of breezing into the barber's on the pretence of looking for a casual job, but the minuses outweighed the pluses. What would that achieve? There would hardly be a chalk-marked outline on the floor where Floyd's body had lain, nor was it likely that the McQueen look-a-like would be in there busily cutting hair. So my plan, in so far as I had one, was to repeat my movements of the night before, gain entry to the shop somehow, and make a search. Cloak and dagger stuff, I know, but what were my options? Right then I couldn't think of anything better.

Time dragged while I was waiting for it to be late enough for my raid on the barber's. It wasn't as if there was nothing wrong. Everything was wrong. Floyd was dead and I hadn't reported it and I was there in his flat and I doubted anything would ever be right again.

I did know, as I took Floyd's manuscript from my rucksack, that it wouldn't make me feel any better. But I doubted it could make me feel any worse.

An Honest Trade
October 1833

Wells is out of sorts. His wife still languishes in her bed and his cargo is still in quarantine. He remembers an earlier age when, unencumbered by marital restraints, he'd sailed on the Elvera, a freebooting brig, which worked the lucrative Gulf of Guinea for several years and successfully evaded the ships of the British navy that patrolled the coast.

He describes a vessel subject to attacks of shipworm, rot, barnacles and leaking, and a crew subject to fever, scurvy and weals, a disease that caused languor and pain in the limbs that was generally treated with mercury.

Drunkenness was common. He illustrates this with a snippet of information about a seaman by name of McPherson who jumped overboard in a state of intoxication. After a perfunctory search, he was presumed 'drowned'. Wells concludes this account with a shrug of the shoulders and quotes the old saying 'they lie on deck, they die on deck.' Or he adds, as in McPherson's case, in the sea.

Still wallowing in nostalgia, Wells recalls one particular voyage when, running up the largely surf bound coast of West Africa, the Elvira was caught in a ferocious storm that carried away the jib boom and damaged both whiskers and the light rigging. With a semi-crippled vessel, they'd come to the estuary of the River Sierra Leone, which afforded a harbour, despite the treacherous rocks at the mouth.

Having successfully navigated the rocks, Wells goes onto explain that they needed an extraordinary 130 fathoms of chain to hold fast on their mooring.*

Finding the land about them swampy and too dense with forest to traverse on foot, those of the crew not left onboard to make the repairs made their way inland along the creeks and rivers in the extra long canoes made especially for the purpose.* Coming ashore at night, the men hid amongst the bushes when they neared a village.

At daylight, they sprang out of their hiding places, seizing everyone within their reach and leaving behind only those too old or sick to be of any use. The natives were then handcuffed and brought to the canoes. In this way they proceeded up the river until the boats were full and they returned to the Elvera.

Once the hold was packed and the repairs completed, the Elvera set course for the West Indies but was intercepted by a naval cutter a few miles out. After a chase lasting 14 hours in which the Elvera was forced to ditch more than a third of her cargo to lighten the load, they managed to get a shot off, which carried away the mainmast of the cutter and allowed them to escape.

Coming back to the present, Wells concludes by saying that as a good Christian he believes that the trade in slaves is a way of redeeming an unhappy people from inconceivable misery.

*Pirate ships were able to operate fairly freely as it was impossible for the naval vessels to watch 3000 miles of coastline. The patrols could stop no more than one in four of the slaving vessels. As late as 1840 the number of slaves taken from West Africa was as high as it had ever been.

*Recheck this. 130 fathoms would mean nearly 240 meters of chain.

*Need to find out how canoes were obtained or whether they were brought over on the main vessel.

Eleven

The afternoon faded into evening. I spent an hour or so going over the instructions for the more baffling features of my mobile phone. Not that I had anyone to text. Nor was there anyone I could think of who might ring me. Not now Floyd was dead. I don't think I'd ever felt lonely before Floyd was killed; now the isolation was absolute.

It goes without saying that I was togged up and ready to go far too early. I'd gone for the inconspicuous look and come up with a sweater and my navy tracksuit with the hooded top; then, given the vagaries of an English spring, I'd stripped off again and pulled my long johns on underneath, to keep my nether regions warm. I'd stashed the torch and my gizmo in my bum bag and confined my luminescent Musto to the wardrobe, banking on the weather staying dry.

With a supreme effort, I delayed my departure until eleven. The postponement reminded me of how edgy Floyd must have felt when he'd been shilly-shallying around, wondering if I was going to put in an appearance. I was busy winding myself up about how things might have turned out if I hadn't had the bloody puncture, when I suddenly remembered Aunt Louise's advice about not trying to put the genie back in the bottle. It was such a relief to hear another voice - even if it was only in my head - that I was distracted enough to make my way downstairs to the car.

I parked in more or less the same spot as Floyd had. Before getting out of the car I topped up with painkillers and pulled up my hood to hide my hair. Then, as if I hadn't a care in the world, did my best to pass myself off as a jogger, until I reached the parade.

There wasn't much activity along the way: a few cars, a desultory fox scavenging in the gutter, the wail of a siren in the distance, not much else. It wasn't the sort of area to attract evening revellers - no pub on the corner, no Eight to Late convenience store, just a parade of slightly run-down shops. Even the sex shop closed at six according to the notice on its door.

Be grateful for small mercies, I thought, as I hurried down the side of the barber's and slipped into the backyard. The last thing you need is a hoard of witnesses.

Safely shrouded in the shadows, I sussed out the lie of the land. There wasn't a light to be seen and, as far as I could tell, no guard dogs or muscle men lurking in the shadows, which I supposed meant they didn't expect anyone to come looking for Floyd. I wondered briefly about CCTV cameras, but thought them unlikely, considering a dead body had apparently been removed unobserved.

Dodging between a couple of commercial sized wheelie bins and an old car, I crept towards my target.

I'll try the easy way first, I thought, as, reaching the door, I cautiously grasped the handle. Not that easy. Locked. As if I hadn't expected it to be. I mean, who leaves their doors unlocked nowadays? Especially if they have something to hide: something like murder.

I stepped back to get a proper view of the building- a standard block of ground and upper floor, which, I recalled from the frontage, housed a dozen or so shops, some of which were vacant. Obviously I couldn't tell for sure, but none of the top floor looked occupied. No light chinked from behind closed curtains, no muffled sounds of T.V. broke the silence and no prowling cat rubbed round my legs hoping to be let in. Storage then, I decided, not residential, clinched by the fact there wasn't a communal fire escape. A firm enough decision to outweigh not much proof, I know, but I wasn't looking for obstacles. I was looking for a way in.

Ground level access to the barber's was the door and a boarded up window. The first floor offered a couple more windows, not boarded up, but not conveniently ajar either, and there was a sky light in the roof. Open or not I just didn't see myself as Spider Woman. How had Floyd got in, I wondered? Was the boarded up window the result of his forced entry? If so why hadn't I noticed a broken window the first time I'd come? More crucially, could it be my way in now?

Under the probing beam of my torch the timber panel proved to be screwed into the window frame. A hasty job, I thought, probably to secure the window after Floyd had been taken away. I hadn't gone there like a thief in the night with a jemmy in my back pocket, but I did have my Hi Tech gizmo (a kind of Swiss Army Knife with knobs on) in my bum bag, and it was an even hastier job to remove a few screws, insert the tip of a blade behind the boarding and begin prising it away.

Inside, I took a moment to get my bearings. The window had let me into a narrow storage room lined with a couple of shelves of towels, boxes of shampoo, a washing machine and drier, and a toilet and basin installed behind a flimsy partition. I didn't loiter.

Coming out of the storeroom, I found myself in the passage, which I knew led through another door directly into the salon. No point going that way, I thought; whatever had been there would be gone by now. Every last trace of Floyd, swabbed away, disinfected, wiped out. I was looking for something else, something, somewhere on the premises, vital enough to be protected by murder. Which meant broaching the staircase.

I don't know why going upstairs should have been extra scary, but it was. I crept up with my back to the wall.

The area that awaited me was one large non-partitioned floor, which stretched from the front to the rear of the building. It was a place full of shadows, dimly lit by the moonlight filtering past tattered blinds masking the windows set in both end walls. The whole space had a derelict air; a few bits of broken furniture, a couple of rolls of carpet, a door still on its hinges propped against a wall and a jumble of boxes and packing cases, none of which looked as if they'd been disturbed for years.

Disappointment threatened to overwhelm me. There was nothing here. Nothing. So why had Floyd had to die? It didn't make sense. If there wasn't anything to hide, why kill Floyd? Why not let him creep away empty-handed? There had to be something. Had to be. Something someone was hiding, but where?

I started again. Flicking the beam of my torch systematically round the room, I took in the naked light bulb hanging from its flex, the cobwebs, the layer of dust over everything and everywhere, except, that is, where it had been scuffed away. Like, for instance, from where I was standing at the top of the stairs to a point a few feet away, where, partially covered by an old tarpaulin casually thrown over it, I discovered a step-ladder; modern and lightweight, and eminently suitable for gaining access to a loft. Looking up I saw a trap door in the ceiling directly above me. Belatedly I recalled the skylight.

Carefully, quietly, I stood the stepladder upright and set it in place. Then, having slipped the torch into my pocket, I went up the first few steps, pushed open the hatch and poked my head into the gloom.

In contrast with the floor below the loft was in darkness, with only a faint glimmer percolating from the skylight. A couple more rungs took me up to waist level and there, blowing caution to the wind, I fished the torch out of my pocket and switched it on.

Twelve

The shock, when the light of the torch flickered on the figure huddled under the eaves, was as tangible as a slap in the face. Instinctively I jerked backwards. The steps tilted with me. Off balance, with one foot flaying in the air, I half threw, half dragged myself forwards through the opening of the trap door. I heard the racket of the stepladder landing on the floor below and the crack of the torch hitting something hard as my chest thumped down against a beam and the breath went out of me. The darkness was instant and the silence that followed, absolute.

I was seriously frightened. Lying on my stomach, with my legs still dangling through the hatch, I was winded and vulnerable and trying not to imagine the figure moving towards me.

My impulse was to slither backwards through the hatch and get the hell out of there, but my stubborn streak wasn't having any. Probably what I'd glimpsed in the torchlight had been nothing more sinister than the product of an overactive imagination, after all it had been a couple of minutes at least since my precipitate entry and nothing had happened. I decided to make a move.

Still partially winded, I took a couple of deep breaths and wriggled forwards; stopped, snatched a couple more breaths, wriggled again, breathed again. It was about then that I became aware of the most disgusting smell – a nauseating mixture of mouldy food and public lavatories. Don't think about, I told myself, breathe through your mouth and get on with it. Another wriggle and I had one knee on the lip of the hatchway, then the other; then I was up in a crawling position. I went swiftly from all fours to standing; upright, I remembered the Mag Light on my key ring.

She, for I saw immediately it was a woman, was still there, under the eaves. Further under if anything. She was wrapped in a blanket and cowering down on an old mattress. She didn't look like a killer; she looked totally wretched and scared out of her wits, but just to be sure there wasn't someone a damn sight more threatening lurking in the dark I swept the beam of my miniature torch round the whole space. Not much to see except for the bags overflowing with rubbish crammed into one corner and the plastic bucket in another, which kind of explained the smell.

I've heard it said that women are like teabags – they don't know their own strength until they're in hot water. I guess mine must have been at boiling point because balancing precariously on the rafters; I began picking my way towards her, keeping the torch slanted to one side so that she could see me coming and wouldn't be blinded by the light. I'd swear she didn't move an eyelash as I approached her. I stopped a few feet away from where she was crouched, dropped down on my haunches. Still she didn't move. I put a hand out towards her.

'Come out,' I said. She cringed, drew further back. I stayed quite still, my hand extended.

'Come out,' I said again. Still no movement, even her expression was frozen. Leaning forward, I touched the blanket where I judged her arm would be. I felt her flinch under my hand. 'Don't be afraid,' I said. 'I won't hurt you. I want to help you.'

'Help me,' she said bleakly, her eyes filling with tears. 'Everyone saying that.'

'Look,' I said, 'I don't know what the hell's going on, but I do know that whatever it is, there's no way you should be hiding in a foul smelling, filthy attic. And there's one thing for sure, we've got to get you out of here before we can discuss it. You're going to have to trust me on this.'

'No. I not,' she started to protest as I grasped her arm through the blanket and tried to haul her to her feet.

'You can,' I said. 'Honestly. What have you got to lose?' Still she hadn't started to get up. 'Let's go,' I said giving her another tug, but she must have got her feet tangled in the blanket or something because she just kind of toppled forwards.

She wasn't wearing a stitch of clothing beneath the blanket.

'Get this on,' I said, as I stripped off my tracksuit and tossed it over to her. 'Good job I wore my long-johns, and luckily the car's not far away.'

A second or two passed and I was ready to go and still she was just standing there, clutching my clothes to her body and staring at me. 'Look,' I said again, 'get dressed and don't argue. Whatever way you look at it clothes are preferable to a blanket in anyone's book.'

In the end I had to help her. I can't say I've ever dressed a naked woman before and it wasn't a great experience. Her flesh felt cold and clammy and she flinched each time I touched her, plus she was kind of limp and rigid at the same time, so it was a bit of a tussle to get her limbs in the right holes what with balancing on the beams so that a stray foot didn't go crashing through the ceiling. But the whole time she never said a word.

'Right,' I said, as I took her hand and led her across to the trapdoor. 'I'll go first. You hold the torch, such as it is, so I can see where the ladder landed. My name's Daisy, by the way.'

I eased myself carefully through the loft opening until I was resting on my elbows, then shifted my weight and lowered myself right through until I was hanging by my hands. All of which was simple compared to the effort it took to swing myself clear of the steps, which were lying directly beneath me, illuminated by the puny light being directed on them from above.

Feeling somewhat stretched, I could have done without the image of Jane swinging effortlessly through the jungle in one of the old black and white Tarzan films, which chose that moment to come into my head. About the only consolation I had, as I let go of my hand-hold and landed, stifling a scream of pain, was that I doubted I could have done it at all if it hadn't been for the hours I'd spent shinning up and down Louella's rigging.

In spite of the urgency of the situation I had to wait a minute or two for the pain in my ankle to subside before getting gingerly to my feet. 'You can come down now,' I hissed as I righted the stepladder, 'and close the trap door behind you.'

No response. 'Hurry,' I urged, jiggling the steps a bit. 'Come now. Hurry.' Still nothing. Leading with my good foot I went back up the steps to coax her down. Found her at the top, the torch clenched in her hand. 'Come on,' I said grasping her wrist. 'Hurry.'

'Why you taking me?' she asked abruptly. 'Why you coming here?'

Relief and worry jockeyed for pole position. I was relieved she wasn't so traumatised she couldn't think for herself; worried about her timing. She'd picked a pretty bad moment to start asking questions.

'It's a long story,' I said. 'I came looking for something and I found you and it's pretty obvious you need help. So that's what I'm trying to do. My aim now is to get us safely away from here. Then we'll talk. O.K.?'

I didn't wait for an answer. Somehow I got her down the ladder. Then I hid it back under the tarpaulin. I was pulling her down the stairs before I remembered the torch I'd dropped. I had my teeth so tightly gritted that I had a pain in my jaw as well as my ankle as I went back up the stairs to retrieve it.

I was drenched in sweat, my ankle was complaining about my exertions and I was functioning on straight adrenalin when I came back down to where the girl was huddled against the wall. I took her arm again, edged her down the remaining stairs, whispering to her that nothing was going to prevent us getting away, all the while looking over my shoulder for the character who'd already gunned Floyd down.

Out in the yard, me still holding her by the wrist, we were creeping towards the side road when she stumbled and let out a smothered yelp. Too late I remembered her bare feet. God knows what she'd trodden on. 'How bad is it?' I asked, trying to sound calm. 'Is it bleeding? Can you walk?'

'It not so bad,' she said in a shaky voice.

'Look,' I said, 'you stay here. Hide. I'll fetch the car.'

'No,' she said and clutched my arm. 'Daysee, please not leaving me.'

'I don't know,' I muttered, 'one minute you're frightened to death of me, next you're holding me so tightly you're cutting off the blood supply.'

She loosened her grip a fraction. 'I walking now,' she said. 'Foot not hurting.'

'What we have to do pronto is get away from here. The quicker the better. Which is difficult without shoes.'

'We going now,' she said. 'I walking okay.'

'Wait,' I said, bending over and pulling off my trainers and one sock. 'It's your left foot, isn't it?'

'Please?' she said.

'Never mind.' I passed her my left shoe. 'Put this on your sore foot and the sock on the other, and I'll wear the other pair. That way we'll both have some protection. And it'll be easier on the road when we can see where we're going.'

'Why you helping me, Daysee?' she asked suddenly. 'You not knowing me.'

Why was I helping her? I hadn't stopped to think from the moment I'd poked my head through that trapdoor and seen a pale face with staring eyes gawping at me. 'Good question,' I said. 'All I can say it's pretty clear someone has to help you. Plus, I firmly believe that what goes round comes round. I help you today; tomorrow someone helps me.' It wasn't much of an answer but she didn't say anything else and I was pleased to see that she finished tying the shoe without further prompting from me.

It took a few cautious minutes more to negotiate our escape from the yard, but once we hit the pavement, I linked my arm through hers so our socked feet came together and edged her into an easy jog, which was no mean achievement considering the state of her foot and my ankle. Loping along, side by side, our pace, by necessity, unsteady, it struck me that we must look for all the world like a couple of parents in the three-legged race at the school sports day. Any other time it would have been comic.

I'm fond of my old car, battered though it is, and when its familiar shape parked by the kerb hove into view, I could have hugged it. As it was, the joy drained away when I couldn't find the keys in my bum bag, only to come to life again when I remembered they were zipped into my track suit pocket, now being worn by my companion.

I herded her into the car and we were out of there.

The drive back to Floyd's seemed to take forever. I kept checking the rear view mirror all the time expecting to see headlights following us - never mind the fact that that's what they do in films, it was one hundred percent real to me, and no one could convince me that finding themselves in the same circumstances they wouldn't be looking over their shoulder too.

She didn't speak a word during the journey, not even to ask where we were going. She just sat there with her arms wrapped round herself, staring straight ahead, and shaking. Really shaking. Shock, not cold, I thought, like Floyd when we hauled him out of the sea.

Floyd.

I turned the heater up full blast and pushed the accelerator nearer the floor. Whatever it is that's going on, Floyd, I promised, I'll get to the bottom of it, if it's the last thing I ever do.

It was tricky knowing how to make the third floor of Floyd's apartment building without drawing attention to ourselves. I'd parked near the flat, having decided not to risk the residents' car park and was contemplating waiting it out until early morning, when hopefully a couple of joggers wouldn't look so conspicuous. Set against that was the fact there'd be more people about then and my companion didn't look that great. Or smell that wonderful either. With hindsight, I decided the heater hadn't been a brilliant idea.

A couple of minutes' further deliberation and the smell convinced me. I swapped my remaining shoe for her sock, less noticeable I thought than the temporised arrangement and we took off for the lift.

The relief when I closed Floyd's front door behind us was overwhelming.

I don't know how long I stood in the hall, my companion beside me weeping copiously but never releasing her grip on my arm or uttering a single word. I do know my feet were cold and sore, my ankle was throbbing, my arms felt as if they'd been wrenched out of their sockets and I was veering between great surges of exhilaration and equally enormous waves of fear. What the hell had I got myself into?

After a while, the charms of Floyd's hall began to pall. 'We'll go in here,' I murmured, steering the woman into the lounge, only to change my mind immediately and propel her out again and into the bathroom. 'A nice bath, I think,' I said as I turned on the taps and went to find one of Floyd's exotic oils to gee it up for her. She was still standing where I'd left her when I came back with briefs and socks and my spare jeans and shirt. I turned off the taps, splashed in the oil, rooted around in the cabinet for TCP and plasters and left her to it.

In the kitchen, I shed my sweater and long johns and balancing on one leg, gingerly plunged my cranky ankle into a bowl of cold water; that torture over I had a head to toe swab down at the sink, emerging, if not a new woman, certainly a completely revitalised old one, which I guess is a lot to do with the fact that, prior to owning Lady Lou, I'd never sailed on a boat with the luxury of a shower onboard and was always grateful for a supply of hot water wherever it cropped up.

It didn't take me long to freshen up, so I gave her another ten minutes before I went to investigate.

Getting no answer to my rapping on the bathroom door, I let myself in. She was sitting hunched up at one end of the bath, knees drawn tightly under her chin, wet hair clinging closely to her scalp. She didn't even look round as I came over to her.

'What's the matter?' I asked as I knelt down by the side of the bath. 'Are you ill?'

She turned her head slowly towards me. 'I not ill,' she said.

Not ill, but judging by the welter of bruises I could see on her arms and upper body, not unharmed. 'That's O.K then,' I said. 'You've finished washing?' She nodded. 'Wait a tic,' I said, 'and then we'll get you out and dry.'

I came back with one of Floyd's vast purple towels to wrap her in.

During the drying and dressing process I couldn't help noticing the other bruises. I didn't know what she'd been going through but it wasn't hard to guess. I was dabbing antiseptic cream on some of the less intimate places when she suddenly said, 'You very kind me, Daysee.'

Feeling the prickle of tears and finding myself suddenly tongue-tied, I resorted to the hand-patting tactic I'd adopted after Floyd's near drowning. 'It's okay,' I managed, 'honestly.' I don't how long I'd have gone on with the patting thing if I hadn't spotted my tracksuit discarded on the floor. I bent to scoop it up saying as I did so, 'I'll shove this in the wash with my other stuff if I can figure out how to work Floyd's washing-machine.'

She drew away from me. 'Floyd. Who Floyd?'

'He's my friend. This is his flat.'

'He coming here?' she asked in a low voice.

'No,' I said. 'He's not coming. He's ... away.'

'Away?'

'Yes,' I said firmly. 'Away. Now let's go and find something to eat and a hot drink, and then we'll talk.'

Thirteen

Floyd, being a fresh food fanatic, didn't keep much in on the fast food front. I consigned the end of a loaf of stale bread, a mildewing aubergine and three very brown bananas to the bin. The milk in the fridge was off and went down the drain, but luckily I discovered half a dozen packs of long life stored in a cupboard with his supply of bottled water and spare toilet rolls.

I rummaged around in the kitchen units and came up with a can of lentil soup, and a search of the fridge produced enough to knock up a couple of cheese omelettes. It wasn't a feast and not what I'd normally serve up for breakfast but she ate everything I gave her and followed me out to the kitchen to help with the washing up as soon as we'd finished.

I doubt we'd exchanged a dozen words since entering the flat, what with me having to concentrate on not thinking about Floyd and her being so plainly traumatised, so it wasn't until I'd flicked on one of the bars of the swish electric fire set in the wall and got us both settled in front of it with mugs of coffee laced with rum from my hip flask that I got round to asking her about herself.

'Will you tell me your name now?' I asked gently.

'No,' she whispered. 'Please not asking.'

'But I must call you something,' I said, 'and I've told you my name.'

'Daysee,' she whispered. 'Your name Daysee.'

I nodded encouragingly. 'So what may I call you?'

She shook her head.

'Look,' I said, 'I know you don't know me and you might believe right now that you've no reason to trust me, but think about it. I got you out of that awful place by lending you my own clothes and now I've brought you here and fed you and lent you more of my things and maybe, if you think about it, you'll see you can tell me your name.'

She looked down at her hands wrapped round the coffee mug.

There was a very long pause. 'My name Ileana,' she said at last.

I gave her a big smile. 'You're Ileana and I'm Daisy,' I said. 'It's a start.'

Whilst we returned to sipping our coffee I looked at her properly. Behind the haunted expression I was startled to see the face of a very young woman - well, in reality hardly more than a girl; about eighteen or nineteen, I thought, at the most. She had olive skin, dark eyebrows and very long, very dark hair pushed back from her face. She had a high forehead and deep-set, almost black eyes. From the way my clothes hung on her I guessed she was thinner than I am but about an inch taller, and from what I'd seen in the bathroom she didn't have any muscle tone at all. It occurred to me that whilst we could probably get by sharing my not very vast wardrobe, given the height difference we were unlikely to take the same size shoes. And one thing's for sure, you can't go for any length of time with your size sixes crammed into someone else's size fours.

I'd made more coffee and added more rum and was brooding about making myself at home in Floyd's flat when he hadn't even finished unpacking and wouldn't ever now, when a small voice interrupted my morose thoughts.

'Daysee,' it was saying, 'when I must going?'

'Go?' I was bewildered. 'We just got here.'

'Your friend: this his place.'

'Yes. The flat belongs to Floyd. But don't worry, I'm looking after it for him for a while,' which was true, 'and he wouldn't mind my having a friend stay with me.'

'I your friend, Daysee?'

'Well,' I said, 'we've been kind of thrown together, and you know that I'm Daisy and I know you're Ileana and friendship is usually based on a bit more than that. But I'm prepared to work on it if you are.'

'I liking very much be your friend,' she said. 'I having no friend and you helping me.'

A backhanded compliment, but something of a breakthrough. 'Good,' I said. 'We'll take it as read then.'

She frowned. 'I not understanding. What I read?'

'My fault,' I said. 'It's an expression that kind of means we'll accept the position and go on from there.'

'O.K,' she said, nodding. 'I think I understanding now.'

'Good,' I said again. 'So maybe we should start by talking about how we both came to be in that place.' Uh, uh. The wrong thing to say: that frozen expression again. 'Tell you what,' I said as if I hadn't noticed. 'I'll start. The thing is I wouldn't ask you to talk about it if it wasn't for the fact that I'm pretty sure that what's been happening to you is only part of the picture. Actually I know it is.' All the time I was saying this she was just sitting there, white-faced and stiff with fear. 'You remember,' I said ploughing on, 'that when I found you, you asked me what I was doing there and I said I was looking for something. You remember that?'

'I remembering, Daysee,' she said, her rigid expression relaxing a fraction as she waited to hear what I had to say.

'Well, it might sound silly, but I didn't know what I was looking for.'

'I not understanding,' she said.

'I don't understand myself, entirely. All I can say is that someone had done a terrible thing to my friend – to Floyd,' I paused, breathed, pressed on, 'to Floyd, whose flat we're staying in at the moment, and I was trying to find out who was responsible for it.'

'What happening Floyd?' she asked me quietly, and I noticed that her eyes were quite alert.

'Floyd was killed,' I said, brushing tears away with the back of my hand, 'two nights ago. He was shot in the head. I found his body on the ground floor of that place where they were keeping you.'

'I maybe knowing this,' she said.

'You know,' I repeated, half incredulous, half unsurprised. 'How could you know?'

'I not knowing any person dead. Men coming always in night to empty room below roof. Making ladder ready. Sometime they allowing me coming down for lavatory. Most time they coming up ladder...' her voice dropped to a whisper, trailed away.

I braced myself. 'What happened that night,' I asked her, needing but not wanting to hear the answer, 'while you were waiting to see what they were going to do?'

'I hearing noise like glass break. All going quiet. Then I hearing

113

shot of gun. I very afraid. Men going quickly and not putting ladder for me. I waiting long time and thinking I hearing them again but they not coming to me. Soon I needing lavatory so bad I must using bucket.'

'I did hear a noise,' I said.

Once I'd got her talking, or perhaps I should say once I'd regained my self control sufficiently to recap what she'd told me and add my own conjectures to her account, I thought I could risk asking her directly about herself. But not until I'd got us both more coffee. I needed a couple of minutes' space.

She was leaning back against the sofa with her eyes closed when I came back into the lounge. Setting the cups down, I touched her lightly on the shoulder. 'Ileana, are you awake?' I asked.

Instantly her eyes snapped open and she jerked away from me, hunching over and clamping her arms tightly around herself in the same movement.

'It's okay,' I said. 'It's me, Daisy, your friend. I'm sorry. I didn't mean to frighten you.'

'Daysee,' she said, her eyes brimming with tears, 'I thinking... thinking....'

'I think I know what you thought,' I said, 'and that's what I need to talk to you about. About why you were being kept in that horrible place.' I could see her shrinking into herself as I said this and her eyes were filling with tears.

I got up to find some tissues.

'Perhaps,' I said when I came back, 'it would help if I told you what I think.'

She sniffed and made a slight movement of her head, which I took to be a nod.

'Well,' I said, 'it's my guess that you've entered the country illegally. For some reason you've upset the people that brought you in, and either as a punishment or to get you to do as they say, they've kept you a prisoner by taking your clothes away and doing awful things to you.'

She mopped her eyes and nodded. Passing her the box of tissues, I pressed on.

The day had run into afternoon by the time I'd confirmed that Floyd's assumption about the Tiger Moth being used to smuggle people was accurate enough. The fact that I'd pooh-poohed Floyd's ideas didn't bear thinking about.

Ileana told me that, in the hope of finding a better life in the West, she'd paid a local fixer to get her out of Romania. She said she'd been brought by truck overland to the French coast, where she'd been put onto a small sailing boat with another single woman, a mother and her twelve-year old daughter, plus a two-man crew.

At some point during the crossing there had been an altercation between the women and the crew.

'Man coming,' she said, 'to girl. He doing very bad things. She hurting very much. I taking off my scarf, making it tightly like this.' Here she interrupted herself coiling her hands so I could see what she meant, 'Putting round man's neck. Pulling very hard. I wishing him dying.'

I gathered from the way Ileana went on to describe it, that while she was attacking that one man, the other two women had rushed up on deck in the hope of disabling the helmsman. But the man Ileana was trying to throttle had thrown her off without much trouble and gone roaring up on the deck.

Ileana was scrambling up the companionway after him when the boat had gybed. She was in time to see her two companions struggling with the men before the boom came round hitting one of the women and knocking her into the sea.

'Much happening,' Ileana said. 'Screaming. Shouting. I grabbing wheel of boat, wishing save Marta.'

'Marta was the women who'd fallen in the sea?'

She nodded.

'What happened then?'

'I turning wheel all my strength. Man's arm is trap in wheel. He hollering like dog but I not letting go.'

But she'd had to let go when the uninjured man had wrenched her away from the wheel by her hair.

'What about Marta, the woman who went overboard?' I asked her when she'd drawn her harrowing story to a close by telling me how she and the other woman had then been forced below deck and locked in the forepeak for the rest of the voyage. 'Did they go back for her?'

She shook her head. 'No, not go back,' she said. 'She must drowning, I think.'

It came back to me then, Floyd's theory about the body washed up on Wickling Spit. It didn't seem so far fetched anymore.

'What about Marta's daughter?' I asked.

'Girl falling down, all shaking and howling like mad person. Maybe she soon dying.'

A few more questions ascertained that, once ashore, the women had been taken by car to a lay-by, where other men were waiting for them. Ileana had been separated from her companions and taken on to the premises where I'd found her. They'd stripped and raped her before leaving her there. Her continuing obedience had been ensured by a regime of beatings, rape and humiliation.

'Did they ever say why they were doing those things to you?' I asked her gently.

'They saying I trying kill man. I saying I wish he dying.'

'How long had you been kept there before I found you?'

'Not knowing. Maybe one week. Men coming often to that bad place, saying I must learning lesson,' she said. 'They hurting me very much. They laughing and asking why I crying. They saying I making sex in Romania, I making sex with them. I saying I coming to this country to making proper job in factory. No more sex job. They saying they owning me. I must doing always as they saying.'

Bloody Hell! 'Do you know what happened to the other women?' I asked.

'Not knowing,' she said shaking her head.

Already exhausted by her ordeal, relating all this to me, a virtual stranger, had clearly been a huge effort for Ileana and when I reached out and took her hand she kind of sighed and subsided back against the cushions of the sofa.

So, for a while, we just sat there, staring into the distance, each thinking our own thoughts, which, in my case, were about as bleak as thoughts can get and which I wouldn't think were any better for Ileana. I guess we'd have sunk without trace into the trough of despondency if I hadn't got my act together sufficiently to make more coffee. As it was, the caffeine gave me enough lift to struggle to the surface again and remind me that it wouldn't be doing Floyd any favours if I simply gave up.

'Right,' I said as I drained my cup and stood up, 'I've got a couple of things to do. You still need to rest and I need to whip out for some supplies. We've eaten practically all Floyd had in. Plus,' I was looking at her feet as I spoke, 'I'll see if I can pick up a pair of shoes for you. Can't have you wearing mine, we don't even know if they're the right size for you.'

'No, Daysee,' she said jumping up. 'Please not leaving me. I afraid staying alone. I not hungry and not needing shoes.'

After a brief verbal struggle, it transpired that apart from not wanting me to leave her, she was worried about having no money. I assured her that friends help each other out in times of crisis and said I was sure she'd help me if I were in difficulties.

In the end we both went out.

We weren't out long, a few groceries, a large bottle of rum, some basics for Ileana and of course shoes —she was a size and a half bigger than me so how she'd coped in mine was anybody's guess. Then back in the safety of Floyd's flat, I settled Ileana on the sofa, unpacked the shopping and rustled up a couple of helpings of scrambled eggs on toast. An hour or so passed after that, while we dozed in front of the fire.

The noise on the landing shocked us out of our lethargy. We went from sofa to standing in a split second. I saw Ileana's eyes gaping wide with shock, her mouth opening to scream. I caught her wrist, cupped my hand over her mouth, my expression warning her into silence. We stopped breathing. Listened as the sounds of human life moved off: heard a door slam in the distance: gasped breath in.

'False alarm,' I said when we were breathing normally again. 'But we shouldn't get complacent. They'll be looking for you, for sure. Will they think you got away on your own? Unlikely, I'd say, with no clothes and nowhere to go. If someone helped you, who was it and what was he or she doing there? Conclusion; someone connected somehow to Floyd.'

'Soon they coming here,' she whispered.

'It depends, I suppose, on whether Floyd had anything on him that would identify him and-' I cut myself off in mid sentence remembering a conversation Floyd and I had had about young black men habitually carrying their driving licences because of the police's stop and search policy, '- which they could get his address from.'

'They finding you also? she asked.

'I don't think so,' I said, mustering up the shreds of my optimism to make it sound convincing. 'They'd have to link me with Floyd first and as far as I can see the only way they'd do that was if the people here were to contact the men who brought you over from France. And I can't see why they would. Why they'd make that link.'

I don't think either of us believed this theory but it was the best I could do and anyway I just didn't want to talk about it anymore. Being a great believer in comfort food I made hot chocolate laced with plenty of rum for both of us before putting her to bed in the spare room, hoiking Floyd's duvet from his futon and huddling up on the sofa.

My ability to sleep almost anywhere, almost instantly is the result of being a regular sailor. It's a discipline you learn the hard way; if you don't get your head down when you're off watch, the time will be past and you'll be on duty again. So it was somewhat aggravating to find that as my head hit the pillow I was wide-awake. After a few minutes I wriggled free of the duvet and went to find my bedtime reading matter.

An Honest Trade
November 1833

There are 24 square-riggers moored in Demerary River. The brig Rople Helm has unloaded her cargo and reports a high number dead – 165 out of the 400 it carried. Given the need for labour on all the estates, Wells thinks it unlikely he will be able to secure the 50 Africans he requires for Kings Plantation.*

The Rople Helm is carrying 89 passengers for the homeward journey, of whom 75 are from 3 local estates. Sarah, Wells' wife and his surviving children, Susan and Oliver, are amongst them. Wells' family are returning to England to live with his wife's sister. There was anger and grief at the parting.

Wells reports that he hopes to ship 30 keels of sugar and 300 hogshead of good Muscovado from the next crop, as the canes are currently presenting a favourable appearance. This estimate is dependent on the canes ripening early. If the profit from the harvest does not meet expectations, he will instruct Fortune Proivil to reduce the rations allocated to the slaves to make good any shortfall.

Wells goes on to explain that the rum is generally disposed of locally to defray expenses but the price of the last crop was so low that it had to be shipped and the net proceeds set against the debts.

He concludes this month's account by stating he has word from Beausejour plantation that Lionoria has given birth to a boy, whom she has named John.

*Of the slaves that survived the journey one third died within a few months of arrival and infant mortality was around 500 per 1000 live births.

Fourteen

I suppose it's awful to admit that even then, so soon after Floyd's death, I was quite unable to manage more than one chapter of his book at a time. In fact, if anything, it was harder than before. I put the manuscript aside and got up again. Wandering into the kitchen, I made another cup of hot chocolate and stared out at the night sky for a while, before bracing myself sufficiently to slip through Floyd's bedroom and into the study. What I needed was, as Monty Python would have it, something entirely different; something to take my mind off things; something like, my gaze flicked round the room, alighted on the filing cabinet, Floyd's research.

I got slightly more than I bargained for when I opened the drawer. It contained a whole bundle of files. Having spent a good many of my formative years working in various guises in offices, files do not excite my interest. In fact they bore the pants off me. I carried them back to my makeshift bed knowing I had found my sleeping pill.

I was right. My eyelids were drooping as I noticed that Floyd had been to museums in Liverpool, Bristol and Hull to further his enquiries and by the time I'd skimmed over his reading list for the project, which was probably more than I'd read in all my thirty, soon to be thirty one, years, I was drifting into sleep.

I got up reasonably early next morning, to give myself plenty of time to think things through before Ileana and I vacated the premises, because the one conclusion I had come to the day before was that Floyd's flat was definitely not the place to be.

However, before we could leave, there was the matter of contacting what I vaguely thought of as refugee organisations – the sort of institutions whose acronyms Floyd had frequently bandied about, but whose names were eluding me now when I needed them.

Leaving tracking down the appropriate body aside for the moment, the real problem was how to approach such an organisation without revealing the whole story. It didn't seem exactly feasible that I'd strayed into that loft on a whim.

The unpalatable fact was, that whatever way I looked at it, it was obvious that everything would have to be disclosed, and I couldn't see any institution with a public profile being party to keeping a murder under wraps. So the whole matter would be passed over to the police, with the inevitable repercussions arising from my not reporting it, which, it was plain to see, had given the killers plenty of time to remove any incriminating evidence. Not, on reflection, one of my best decisions, not that this changed anything. I had to get Ileana in contact with the people who could help her, and if I got a bloody nose in the process, I had no one to blame but myself.

Having found the phonebook, I was making more coffee and a couple of slices of toast before settling down to my task, when Ileana came banging out of the bedroom. She was pulling on Floyd's bathrobe and half falling over the trailing belt as she hurried over to stand beside me.

'What's the matter,' I asked looking at her anxious expression. 'Did you think I'd left without you?'

'I sleeping long time,' she said. 'I waking. Hearing nothing. I thinking maybe you going. I not knowing what I do.'

'I'm still here though, aren't I?' I said, 'so you needn't have worried, need you?'

She sighed but didn't look any less nervous.

'What's the matter?' I asked, taking her hand in what I realised was becoming my habitual gesture when I was trying to reassure her.

'I not knowing what happening me now,' she said.

'Get washed and dressed and I'll rustle up some breakfast,' I said, 'and then we'll talk.'

By the time she was ready, I'd put cereal, coffee and more toast on the table and had unearthed a couple of telephone numbers that looked relevant.

I waited until we'd got breakfast out of the way before I broached the subject.

'You told me earlier that you didn't know what was going to happen now,' I said, 'and I can understand that, as I'm out of my depth myself.'

She looked puzzled. 'What depth meaning?'

'I'm sorry,' I said. 'I shouldn't take it for granted that you understand everything I say.'

'What granted meaning?'

We both laughed.

'How long did you study English at school?' I asked her when I'd finished trying to explain both turns of phrase. 'It's very good.'

'Not going school,' she said.

'But you can read and write,' I said.

'My brother, Florin, teaching me some. He very clever, maybe one day being doctor.'

I didn't say anything for a moment or two expecting her to elaborate, but when she didn't I changed the subject. 'I've been thinking about what we should do now,' I said. 'It seems to me that our priority is to get you to a place of safety.'

'I safe with you,' she said.

'No,' I said, 'I don't think you can stay with me.'

She was on her feet in a trice, knocking her chair over backwards in her haste. 'You saying you my friend. Why I not staying with you?'

I stood up and took her arm, guided her over to the sofa. How many hours, I wondered, had we sat talking there already?

'I am your friend,' I said as we settled down. 'Please believe me. Let me try to explain things to you.' I went on without giving her chance to reply. 'We were talking last night about the chances of the people who were imprisoning you, tracking you down. We've every reason to believe Floyd was killed by the same people. People, who may, or may not, come looking for you here.'

'They killing Floyd before I running away. Why they thinking he helping me?'

I sighed. 'I don't know. All I can say is, as far as I can see, he's their only lead. They might not make the connection, but I've been thinking about it for hours and I don't think we can take the chance.'

She was asking how they'd find out where Floyd lived and I was explaining that we just didn't know what identification he might have been carrying when he was killed, when another alarming thought struck me. 'There's another thing to worry about as well,' I said, 'I'm not sure about Floyd's employer. I know Floyd was thinking about giving up his job, but if he hasn't got round to it, his boss will start to wonder why he doesn't go back to work after his holiday. He might make enquiries. Discover Floyd has disappeared. I don't know what might happen then. He might or might not notify the police. I've no idea.'

'Police coming this place?'

'They might. I don't know. But you can see why we can't stay here?'

'We staying different place.'

'It's not that easy, though. You need professional help. The kind of organisations that know the law; that are used to helping people who've come into the country without the proper papers. I wouldn't know where to start. I think they'd be able to find you somewhere to stay - a hostel or something - whilst they were sorting things out with the authorities.'

As I was saying this, I was aware that Ileana's breathing was getting faster and she was moving forwards until she was perched on the edge of the sofa as if poised for flight. She'd also crossed her arms in that protective gesture I'd seen her use before, gripping her upper arms so tightly that her knuckles had turned white. When I bent forward to reassure her she slid from the sofa to her knees at the same pressing her head into my lap. I was mortified.

'Ileana, get up. There's no need -'

She interrupted. 'Not authorities, Daysee, please. Please not making authorities knowing I here. They sending me away. Back Romania. Please not. Please.'

What could I say? All I could see was a girl on her knees begging me not to betray her. 'One thing's for sure, we can't discuss it with you down there,' I said abruptly. 'If you don't get up this minute I'll -.' I'll what? I'd no idea what I was going to threaten but, fortunately, she was scrambling to her feet and I didn't need to elaborate. 'That's better,' I said, 'and if you'll let go of my hand as well so that I can get the circulation back, we can have a proper conversation.'

'Would it be so bad,' I asked her when we were sitting more comfortably again, 'if you were sent back to the place where you were born?'

'All being poor in village,' she said. 'Factory not working many years. Old people only now. Nothing for me. I must going Bucharest. Bad men catching me again. Making me same as before. Also beating me much for run away. Very bad. Please not making authorities knowing I here. Please not, Daysee. Please not.'

All this came out in a rush and left me speechless. Hadn't I talked myself out of not reporting Floyd's murder to another set of authorities on a lot more spurious grounds than Ileana had just put forward? How could I be instrumental in sending her back to a life of prostitution and who knew what else?

Fifteen

The result of not making a decision about Ileana's future found us clearing up the obvious signs of having stayed in Floyd's flat, collecting his laptop to take with us, and packing the bundle of research files into my sailing bag for reading later. The least I could do was to take the time to read everything properly.

Relief and sadness were vying for level pegging as I locked the flat door behind us. I was thankful to be going back to my home territory, upset about leaving Floyd behind. I didn't know how Ileana was feeling; she hadn't said anything since she'd thrown her arms round me when I'd agreed not to contact anyone about her. At least for the time being. To be truthful I was feeling exactly like that woman in the poem - far too far out and not waving but drowning. And, offhand, I couldn't think of anyone who was about to throw me a life belt.

We'd been driving about ten minutes before Ileana broke the silence.

'Why you crying, Daysee?' she asked. 'I sorry I making you much trouble.'

'It's not you,' I sniffed, wiping my face with the back of my hand. 'It's everything. I don't know what to do for the best. Floyd's been murdered and I miss him dreadfully and I never told him how much I cared about him and I haven't told the police and I know I should and I've never felt so awful.'

'Police bad people,' she said in a flat voice.

'What? Oh, I see what you mean. No, not in this country, not all of them anyway. Or maybe I mean not most of them. Oh,' I said again. 'I don't know what I think.'

'So why you not telling about Floyd?'

'I suppose I was frightened. Frightened of getting involved. I made a lot of excuses to myself that seemed good enough at the time.'

125

'I thinking you brave person. Not frighten at all. You helping me escaping that bad place.'

'Finding you's part of it, I suppose,' I said, steering with one hand while I rummaged around for the tissue I'd stuffed up my sleeve, 'like the moment of truth. It seemed clear that I had to get you proper help, which, even though it was bound to have repercussions, was a kind of relief. But that isn't what you want. And I can see why. Not that that makes anything any better. I'm worried about you. I'm worried about what will happen if I give you up, what will happen if I don't. All of which in answer to your question is why I'm crying.'

'Daysee,' she said, tears running down her own cheeks, 'I your friend. You helping me. I thinking repercussions meaning much trouble. I not wanting you getting trouble. We going police. Saying all. Maybe I knowing things helping catch men killing Floyd. Maybe I helping they not sending me back Romania.'

Too much. I checked my mirror and pulled into the kerb.

It wasn't a great place to stop: on a double yellow line on a busy road on a weekday morning, but hey, who can pick where they have their defining moments? We sat for a couple of minutes, the car juddering in the whoosh of air from the passing vehicles, until we'd got the tears under control. I was starting to say something about her not worrying and I wouldn't do anything to hurt her, when I spotted an approaching traffic warden. 'Time to go,' I said. 'Trouble's looming and suddenly I know for certain that this is as near as I want to get to authority.'

For all that I'd got over that particular hump, at least for the time being, I still couldn't have been thinking clearly, because I was fully intending to drive straight back to the marina. In fact, it wasn't until we were only twenty miles or so away and we'd made a stop for petrol that I said something about Lady Lou to Ileana.

'Is Ladeeloo friend?' she asked.

'Yes,' I said. 'My friend and my home.'

'I not understanding.'

'Lady Lou's my boat. You remember I mentioned her when we were talking about the boat that had brought you over from France.'

She grabbed my arm. 'Not boat, Daysee,' she said urgently.

'Bad men seeing me.'

Which is why we ended up at the house.

Halnaker House is an old stone house at the head of a muddy inlet from the sea. The lane that leads to the house is bordered on both sides by deep drainage ditches, but they don't stop it flooding when the land's waterlogged and the weather's bad. The house is raised up on a man-made bank between the marsh and the shore and is protected by a small copse planted by an earlier tenant, which may be why, as far as I can remember, the house itself has never flooded. There's a path from the house to the sea, which is not too far away to make humping the outboard motor for the dinghy a problem, and not too near to make high tides a worry; not at present levels anyway. I've lived in the house all my life.

I guess Ileana was feeling apprehensive as I pulled up in the yard. I let her have minute or two to take it in before I chivvied her out of the car and passed her a couple of the bags.

'You'll have to make allowances for the state of the place,' I said as I unlocked the front door and ushered her in. 'I'm not much of a one for housework and it's been closed up since I've been living on Lady Lou.'

Her gaze was darting around the low-ceilinged, stone-flagged hall. 'Why you living on boat when you having house?' she asked me in a bewildered voice.

'Well,' I said, 'I don't usually. But the opportunity came up for me to make a long sea voyage, something I've always wanted to do, so I'd moved onto Louella in readiness and if Floyd hadn't -'

'What readiness meaning?'

'Readiness,' I said, 'means being ready.'

She shook her head. 'I not understanding.'

'Ready means being fit and able to do something.'

She looked doubtful.

'I know,' I said, 'I'll see if I can find a dictionary which will help me explain words to you properly. There ought to be one in the house somewhere. I'll look later when we're sorted out.'

'Sorted?' she asked.

'Now you're taking the mickey,' I said, putting my fingers to her lips before she could ask.

It was great to see the wide grin that creased her face.

We spent a couple of constructive hours shaking out the curtains and flicking away the dust before we made the beds up. I put Ileana in what had been Mum's room. Luckily Aunt Louise and I had cleared it out in a flurry of emotional activity a few months after she'd died. Needless to say, left to my own devices, I hadn't got round to doing anything about Louise's room, and the other bedrooms hadn't been used for years.

'I liking this place very much,' Ileana said, as we finished smoothing out the eiderdown and she turned towards the window, which overlooks the rocks and sandy earth that passes for the garden. 'Other people living here also?'

'No,' I said, 'just us. My relatives have all passed away.'

'Is 'passed away' meaning dying?'

'Yes,' I said.

By this time she'd crossed the room and was staring out of the window that faces across the reed beds. 'My family also are dying,' she said.

My own bedroom is on the other side of the house and looks down the inlet to the sea. The room's been converted from the barn that was once an integral part of the house. In addition to its ordinary door off the landing, it still has the original entrance at the top of a flight of deep stone steps that climb up the outside of the building, and the winch they used to use to hoist up their stores still hangs over the door. I think it's a wonderful room. For as long as I can remember I've slipped in and out of the house by my very own private staircase and I never thought of locking the door until Aunt Louise had to go away.

By the time I'd finished showing Ileana my quarters in what I suppose may have been over proud detail and had whizzed her round the rest of the house, it was time to eat again. I wonder why it is that when you live on your own, food just kind of happens, but when someone else is with you, eating has to turn into meals? Anyway, after a scratch affair of frozen chicken and oven chips, which I'd discovered loitering in the bottom of the freezer, I stuck a couple of logs in the grate and we settled down in the wing armchairs on either side of the fire. Since I've been living on my own in the house I've got in the habit of lighting a fire in the evenings, unless it's the height of summer, and that night it was especially gratifying to see Ileana gradually relaxing in its friendly warmth. I think perhaps I was unwinding a little too: staying in an environment away from all that had gone on in the last few days had been a good idea and I was glad Ileana had baulked at going back to Lady Lou.

I'd drawn the curtains, switched the lamps on, put another log on the fire and poured us both a drink before I took Ileana up on the remark she'd made in the bedroom. 'When we were upstairs you said that your family had died. Is that why you left Romania?'

The question startled her. She jerked out of the comfortable slump she'd slipped into and glanced towards me.

Realising I'd put it too abruptly, I hurried on. 'I thought maybe you'd like to talk about it,' I said, 'now we've got some time to ourselves.'

She shook her head.

'Tell you what,' I said. 'I'll start by telling you a bit about me. O.K?'

A nod.

'First off, you know my name's Daisy. I'm thirty years old, and an only child. My mother passed away quite a few years ago and I lived with my Aunt Louise until she died last year. That's when I inherited the house. I've never lived anywhere else. Now my only family is my boat named Lady Louella.' I paused. 'I never knew my father.'

'Why you not knowing your papa?' she asked.

'He left just after I was born; I suppose he didn't want the responsibility of a family. I never knew him so I never missed him,' I said. 'Anyway that's enough about me. Now it's your turn.'

Maybe I was imagining things, but I thought I saw the wary expression that usually clouded her eyes clear as she turned to answer me.

'Daysee,' she said, 'I telling you some about my life.'

I nodded, and mentally braced myself.

'I coming from village by Timisoara,' she began. 'I having three brothers and one sister; two brothers dead, other brother and sister going away. Mamma and Papa both dead also.'

I was taken aback. 'But what happened,' I asked, 'that caused so many of your family to die?'

'Papa being arrest before revolution. He dying in the prison.'

I interrupted. 'Why was he arrested?'

'They saying he plotting against State.'

'You mean he was a terrorist?' I asked, trying to keep my voice level.

'No! Papa good man. He making complain about waste from factory. Is polluting water.'

'But surely he couldn't be imprisoned for that?' I asked.

She looked surprised. 'It always dangerous criticising Party. This day, Papa very angry. He saying factory committee filling own pockets. Not caring animals die and people sick.'

It seemed incredible to me that someone could be imprisoned for protesting about a legitimate issue, but what did I know? Anyway it hardly seemed likely she'd be making it up. 'What happened to the other members of your family?' I asked her. 'Did they fall foul of the authorities too?'

She didn't reply and I realised she was mulling over the idiom I'd used. 'I meant,' I said, 'did they also suffer because they disobeyed the rules?'

She nodded. 'Securitate shooting two my brothers during uprising. They running to cathedral to find the safety but priests locking doors. Many people dying there.'

I needed a minute to deal with this statement. I could see the dead and dying clearly and my mind's eye had put Floyd there with them. He was sprawled on his back amongst the bodies at the entrance to the Cathedral. He had a gunshot wound in his forehead.

Ileana began speaking again before the images had faded from my imagination. It struck me that it must have been a very long while since she'd told anyone about her family. It was like taking the plug out of a bath so that all the water came flowing out at once and didn't stop until the bath was empty.

'Every day and night after Papa dying, Mamma praying. The time Nuta being born, Mamma getting sick but she still praying all the day. When she hearing what happening to Florin and Aurel she going crazy. She saying God punishing her. She begging him forgiving her. Praying all the time. Soon she dying. I never believing in God from that day.'

What can you say to that? 'How old were you when your mother died,' I asked her.

'Oh,' she murmured, staring fixedly at the flames flickering up the chimney. 'I five years old.'

'But how did you manage?'

'Brother finding food and I looking after Nuta. She crying all the whole time and there is no milk.'

'Nuta was just a baby?'

'Yes, she being born after Papa dying.' She paused. 'She gone now.'

I couldn't ask. 'How old was your brother?' I asked instead.

'I thinking Janos ten or eleven. Is very hard for him and one day he not coming home. I not knowing what happening him.'

It was awful going on asking the questions, but I had to know. 'What happened when Janos disappeared?'

'We going in orphanage. After Revolution people coming, taking Nuta to America. They not wanting me also. Soon I running away orphanage. Staying with other kids in pipes under railway. Then I going city.' She stopped as abruptly as she'd started; turned her head away; picked up her drink; put it down again.

I was feeling the same – not knowing where to look or what to do with my hands. My first instinct was that it was so unfair when she'd been through so much. But then of course, I realised it was the other way around. She'd suffered all that before she fell into the hands of the people smugglers. And from there, it wasn't a great leap to come to the conclusion that none of it would have happened if her father hadn't been arrested.

Whilst Ileana had been talking, I'd become acutely aware of my total lack of knowledge about Romania. Lately there'd been more and more times when I regretted the head in the sand stance I'd adopted about current affairs over the years.

Because of this, it was some time before I found a way of asking about her decision to leave Romania. From the sketchy details she provided, I concluded that in many of the countries of the former Eastern Bloc, living conditions were grim and it wasn't uncommon for people desperate to get out to be promised well-paid jobs in the West. The snag was, of course, that the would-be workers invariably found themselves in hock to the traffickers, women in particular being vulnerable to the iniquities of the sex trade.

I hadn't realised how long we'd been sitting there in front of the fire, sipping whiskey and chewing over events, until I noticed Ileana's eyelids drooping.

'Time you were in bed,' I said.

'I not tired, Daysee,' she said. 'I liking sit here with you.'

'Plenty of time for sitting here, right now we both need our beauty sleep.'

'What beauty meaning?' she asked sleepily as I switched off her bedroom light and pulled the door to, her question reminding me of my promise to look out a dictionary for her.

I had a quick search through the bookshelves in the sitting room with no luck and couldn't find my pocket version anywhere, only remembering belatedly that it was amongst my stuff on Lady Lou, so I turned my attention to Auntie's room.

As far as I can remember, the house has always been furnished the same way: whitewashed walls, rough rugs on the floors and old-fashioned farmhouse style furniture. During the years, a few modern innovations like oil-fired central heating, an electric cooker and microwave to back up the range in the kitchen and a downstairs cloakroom in the old scullery have squeezed themselves in, but the feel of the house stays the same. I guess Louise's taste in soft furnishing would be described as traditional. I can remember what seems like forever when she'd sat by the window in the study, stitching together a patchwork bedspread to blend with her curtains and rugs. Not that she ever criticized me for wanting a bolder colour scheme.

It wasn't as if I hadn't been in her room since she'd died. I'd run the hoover round from time to time and I'd slipped her handbag that had come back from the nursing home and hadn't gone to the charity shop with her other things, into the bottom of the wardrobe, but I had successfully avoided anything more emotionally taxing. Consequently, the feeling of sadness that overtook me as I started my search was entirely unexpected.

I made straight for the bookcase which stored most of the volumes she'd accumulated since her schooldays. No dictionary. I swapped my search to the bedside cabinet, where she'd always kept her night-time reading; her own books and those exchanged in the mobile library that arrived once every three weeks for half an hour at the junction at the end of the lane.

I think it was the lack of the library books that upset me so much; the loss of the volumes that had been returned for the last time when it had become obvious she couldn't cope anymore. Books had always been such a big part of her life that it had felt like a betrayal not getting any more out for her, and coming across the space where they should have been brought it all back and added to my pool of misery.

Another part of the space was where a dictionary might have been kept. I glanced wearily round the room wondering if there was anywhere I might have missed. The only place that seemed remotely likely were the drawers in the dressing table.

Sixteen

I didn't find the dictionary in the drawer but I did find a letter – a letter addressed to me in the tiny, shaky hand-writing that had been Louise's in her later years.

'My dearest Daisy,

Sensible of the encroaching ravages of physical weakness and mental decline, I'm writing to you now whilst I'm still able to do so. Knowing your strengths and weaknesses only too well I think it's unlikely you'll discover this note until some time after my death, which is how I want it to be.

The plain facts are, my dear, there are certain things you need to know: things that, rightly or wrongly, have been kept from you over the years. Far better if Ellen and I had grasped the bull by the horns when you were old enough to understand, but somehow the time never seemed exactly right and I'm sorry to say we let matters slide.

Another opportunity to set the record straight came and went when Ellen died, and now, on my own with you, I haven't the courage. I have therefore deposited a package at our bank, which will be released to you on production of this letter. There are also other papers relating to the family business, which may be of interest to you, stored in box in a large leather trunk in the attic.

I hope, my dear, you'll forgive us for keeping these things from you and will find it in yourself to overcome any anger you may feel. Please believe me when I tell you that all we ever wanted was to protect you and ensure your happiness.

Fondest love,
Aunt Louise.

For a moment I stared at the letter in my hand and then I started to read it again. But I wasn't taking it in. I'll readily admit I wasn't wholly in charge of myself. I mean, who wouldn't be knocked sideways, if all the people they'd ever loved had died, but in spite of that they were bravely trying to carry on and were going about their lawful business doing nobody any harm - except perhaps for concealing a murder and hiding an illegal immigrant - and then being told, suddenly, out of the blue, that they might have some terrible skeleton in the family cupboard? I think anyone might have felt weak-kneed in those circumstances.

So it took me a little while to get myself together. Then I did read the letter again. Then I told Aunt Louise to tell Mum that whatever it was, I'd forgive them, though it might not be immediately. Then I drank a couple of glasses of water from the bathroom tap and prepared to tackle the attic.

Apprehension about what I was going to find, even without the twinge in my ankle to remind me, as if I needed any reminding, of what I'd found in that other place only a couple of nights before, made climbing the loft ladder a huge effort, and without the reassurance of electric light, which lit the whole shebang at the flick of a switch, might well have proved one rung too far.

The space under the eaves of Halnaker House is a rambling kind of arrangement. It steps down into the cavity above the barn, picks its way into dusty corners, skirts round the chimney flues and comes out onto a biggish boarded area under the main part of the slate roof. I couldn't remember the last time I'd ventured up there and I noticed, with one of those sinking feelings that one gets when they're confronted with a job that needs doing fairly urgently, that countless generations appeared to have been dumping their not quite unwanted possessions there for years.

I was dusty, nervous and resentful by the time I'd located the trunk. 'If this is a test,' I muttered to myself, 'there'd better be a bloody good prize for passing.'

Inside the trunk was a cardboard-box, as Aunt Louise had described. I carried it carefully down the ladder. I retired to bed with the box and the bottle of whiskey.

I was asleep in a trice. I put it down, not to a drop too much whiskey, but to the cumulative effects of the last few days combined with the wad of papers in faded spidery writing on yellowing paper, which confronted me when I tackled the family's archives, and which, I decided, would need me to be feeling a good deal more alert than I was at that particular moment to decipher them. Anyway, I remember thinking, as I clonked the box onto the floor by the side of the bed, the papers had obviously been mouldering in the box for years, so another day or two wasn't going to hurt.

Ileana was busying around in the kitchen when I found her. She'd washed up the dishes from the night before, raked out the ashes and set the table for breakfast. She was bright-eyed and bushy-tailed in complete contrast to me, who was red-eyed and bushed.

'Daysee,' she said, 'I making breakfast today.'

'Haven't you had something already?' I asked.

She shook her head. 'I waiting we eating together.'

Ileana's breakfast turned out to be cooked potatoes and onions in a kind of omelette come pancake. 'I can tell you're a much better cook than I am,' I said between mouthfuls. 'This is delicious. Is it your national dish?'

She flushed and giggled. 'No, I making,' she paused while she trawled her memory for the word she wanted, didn't come up with it. 'How you saying putting many things in pot to making good taste?'

'Do you mean inventing a recipe?' I asked.

'Maybe,' she said. 'I not being sure.'

Another of those pauses.

'Daysee?'

'Yes?'

'Maybe you finding dictionary. You saying you looking in house.'

'Oh, I'm sorry. I got side-tracked.'

'What ...'

'Side tracked meaning?' I finished for her.

After we'd finished laughing, I told her about the letter from Aunt Louise and the papers I'd found in the attic.

'What papers telling?' Ileana asked.

'They're just stuffy papers from the old days' I said, 'I've only glanced at them. There's no rush. And as I can't do anything about this other blasted package until the bank opens tomorrow I think we should get out in the fresh air now, while the sun's shining.'

I dug out some old jeans and a pair of ancient deck shoes with the toes cut out, for Ileana to wear, and then we went down to the beach. Carrying the outboard between us, we had to make numerous stops for Ileana to point at the birds and ask their names and that of the plant life we encountered on the way. I'd have to admit most of the flowers were as much of a mystery to me as they were to her, although I made a reasonable stab at identifying the gulls.

Down on the shore we wandered along the waterline picking up the bits of plastic and tin cans discarded by the tide and checked out the crabs and their associates left behind in the sandy eddies. When we tired of that I connected the outboard up to the dinghy, pushed it out and called to Ileana to jump in. The water was cold but she came splashing through the sea to join me without a second thought. Squealing and giggling like a couple of kids we scrambled in and took off, phutting out of the inlet and heading along the coast. It didn't occur to me until we'd been underway for several minutes that she might have been uneasy about being in a boat, and I was trying to think of a tactful way of saying so, when she said, 'Is good, Daysee, in little boat. I not used to making nice time.'

Well! It was ages since I'd had someone to share the sheer pleasure of being afloat with, and now, here was Ileana, traumatised, abused as she'd been, trailing her hand over the side, tipping her head back to feel the sun on her face, laughing and chattering and a positive pleasure to be with – as I'd anticipated things being with Floyd and me onboard Lady Lou before my plans were thwarted; but then Ileana was evidently not afraid of water.

We were trudging along the path back to the house, taking it in turns to carry the outboard motor and the bag of litter we'd collected from the beach, and I was wondering why I never got round to buying one of those sack trucks or at least remembered to use the wheelbarrow, when I realised Ileana had stopped her excited chattering.

'Let's have a rest,' I said easing the outboard to the ground, 'I'm out of breath and I don't want to overtax my ankle.'

'Daysee,' she said, after we'd stood there a while. 'How I paying all the things you giving me?'

'So that's what you've been worrying about,' I said. 'I thought you'd gone quiet.'

'I needing working,' she said, 'but not having papers. Maybe you knowing working place not asking papers?'

'Daft goose,' I said, bending to pick up the outboard, 'we'll discuss it when we get back.'

'What meaning 'daft goose?' she asked me later when we were washed and fed and were finishing off the chores.

'Well,' I said, 'daft means foolish and a goose is a big long-necked fluffy duck. Somehow the two words come out as an affectionate way of saying don't be silly.'

She looked at me blankly.

'Tell you what,' I said. 'I need to go into town tomorrow to collect this mysterious package Auntie's left for me at the bank, and to stock up at the supermarket. How would you feel about seeing if we could pick up a dictionary, and maybe a book of everyday English sayings while we're there? We might even find a Romanian / English phrase book that I guess would come in useful.' I glanced at her as I said this expecting to see a pleased expression. Instead of which she looked glum. 'What's the matter? I asked. 'Don't you want to go shopping?'

She shook her head, didn't reply.

'What's up?' I asked again.

'I not having money,' she said.

It took a while. I had to explain what a difference it made to me to have someone to share things with and how it made me feel less self indulgent about having inherited the windfall from my family: but for all that it wasn't until we agreed that if she weren't happy being my guest, she would do the cooking for us until we could think of something else. I don't know who was more thrilled, she at the prospect of earning her keep, or me in anticipation of not worrying about getting meals anymore.

The evening was slipping away uneventfully until the clang of metal against the cobbles shattered the peace.

Ileana leapt out of the chair like a deer with the hunt on its heels and launched herself at me across the hearth; the drink she'd been nursing, forgotten in her panic, fell from her hand and exploded on the flagstones splattering whiskey and glass in all directions, closely followed by my own as it was jolted out of my hand.

'They coming, Daysee,' she gabbled. 'Bad men finding me. They coming, making me going back that place. Daysee -'

'Shush,' I whispered, wriggling my hand free from where she had it pinned between her body and the chair, and holding her to me. 'Listen.'

We must have stayed like that, her trembling against me, me trying to be calm, for some minutes; might perhaps be sitting there still if I hadn't got cramp and had to eject her from my lap.

I couldn't describe it as a relief when it became apparent that masked men weren't about to burst open the door - relief is such an inadequate word - it was a mixture of exhilaration, reprieve and the realisation, that in spite of the short time we'd known each other, Ileana was my friend and I'd be devastated if anything happened to her.

When we were functioning again and had cleaned up the mess of glass and booze, I suggested I make a quick reccy outside. She wouldn't have it of course; didn't want me to leave her, tried her best to persuade me not to go; insisted on coming with me when she realised I wasn't to be dissuaded.

As it turned out it was nothing; less than nothing, yet the alarm it had engendered was real enough.

You have to use your imagination when you're looking for an intangible thing like a noise. For instance, has your bike toppled over from the wall where you thought you'd propped it, or do you find it still in the boot of the car? Has a slate come off the roof? Or maybe, given the rubbish scattered around the yard, has a fox after the chicken bones from last night's dinner, upset the dustbin?

Mundane though the explanation was, the incident did give me pause for thought. Although I couldn't see any way that the scum who'd kidnapped Ileana and murdered Floyd could track us down to Halnaker House, it wouldn't do to let my guard down.

An Honest Trade
December 1833

John Wells has received notice from the London agents advising him that a bill ordering the final abolition of slavery was passed in Parliament in July. Children, under the age of six, are to be freed immediately, while slaves over that age are to be given a period of apprenticeship that will be phased out by 1837.

Wells notes that the abolitionist, William Wilberforce, died a day or two before the date the bill became effective. To Wells' mind this is some comfort, considering the harm Wilberforce and his cronies have done to an honest trade over the many years they'd campaigned for abolition.

Wells also receives a letter from an acquaintance from England who has recently been appointed overseer for an estate on Grenada, the owner having returned to England on the back of the compensation he will receive from the government for the loss of his slaves. The London agents have been deputed to receive all future consignments of produce from the estate and will require news and regular journals from the manager.

Wells bemoans the character of the absentee landlord who expects the overseer to hand over quick profits in spite of the shortage of labour and the vagaries of the weather. He (Wells) highlights the difficulties he has maintaining the fine mansion on the estate. The house is deteriorating in the absence of the owner, who makes inadequate provision for its upkeep.

Fortune Proivil reports much ill feeling in the yard. The 26 new Africans Wells has indentured are proving to be fractious, stirring up trouble and making many demands for shorter working hours, increased rations and better living quarters.

Without the company of his wife and children or the diversions he was accustomed to in the arms of Lionoria, Christmas for John Wells is a lonely occasion.

From as early as 1773 the Human Rights and Social Justice Movement had some impact on slaving in Britain. Trading in slaves was abolished throughout the British colonies in 1807 and slavery itself in 1833/34. The last slaves were freed in British Guyana in 1838.

Seventeen

Next morning, Ileana concocted a meagre breakfast from the bits and pieces which had been hiding out at the back of a cupboard and whose history was lost in the mists of time. As we were down to the dregs of the milk, it meant a single cup of almost-black coffee each, and I promised Ileana a large cappuccino as soon as we got into town to make up for it.

It was busyish in town; not the teeming throng it can be at the height of the season when the schools have broken up, but the couple of coaches in the car park near the bridge were as sure a sign of the onset of visitors as that first cuckoo that heralds spring.

We had frothy coffee in Starbucks before tackling the shopping, which turned out to be a real marathon. It took ages: ages and ages. An aisle or two in and Ileana was hooked; fascinated by the range of products she would have checked out the whole store shelf by shelf if I hadn't put my foot down. As it was she wanted to know about everything she didn't recognise and chattered on about the different packaging of those items she did. Needless to say it cost a fortune at the checkout.

'That's a relief. Shouldn't think we'd need to shop again for a month,' I said to Ileana as we packed it all in the car.

She gave me an old-fashioned look.

'What?' I asked.

'I making you spending much money. You so good to me, Daysee,' she said. 'I not knowing how making thank you.'

'We discussed all this last night,' I said, 'and I thought it was settled. We're friends. We'll do things for each other because that's what friends do. We'll have a look for those books we talked about now, shall we?'

We tried Smiths first, where we purchased a huge Oxford English Reference Dictionary, then Waterstones, then the second-hand bookshop, where we found a copy of Brewer's Twentieth Century Phrase and Fable and whose helpful proprietor suggested we try the

142

library for our other requirements. The library's sole reading matter on Romania was a travel guide, which, after a protracted search to find my library ticket, we took away with us along with their advice to order the other volumes we wanted from one of the chain stores.

Back in Waterstones, I whiled away the odd half an hour leaning over the counter whilst the assistant trawled through the stock list on the computer. My order completed, I went to find Ileana. She was exploring the Cookery Section.

'Daysee,' she said excitedly, 'they having many books showing how cooking things. Maybe,' she paused, couldn't ask.

We finally left the shop with a brightly illustrated cookery book, a receipt for the long list of books we'd ordered and a wishy-washy promise that everything should be in within a couple of weeks. Personally, I had my doubts.

'I'll take you to see the cathedral now we've finished the essential stuff, if you like,' I said. 'It's very old, and –'

'Not liking seeing cathedral,' she said in a flat voice.

I was about to ask what her objection was, when I noticed her expression. The word stony-faced came to mind. And then I remembered the other time I'd seen that expression and heard the same deadpan intonation. When she was describing the shooting of her brothers. When I'd seen Floyd so clearly lying amongst the slaughtered bodies.

How could I have been so tactless; so crass? How could I have forgotten such a terrible incident? Red-faced and speechless I took Ileana's arm, steered us back to the car.

We didn't talk much as we drove home. I tried pointing out one or two local landmarks but my heart wasn't in it and I could tell from the stiff way Ileana was sitting that she'd taken a step back into herself as a result of my insensitivity.

I guess the atmosphere had lifted a smidgen in the evening. Ileana had curled up in the armchair with her books and looked more relaxed, although she still didn't have much to say. Unused to being at a loose end, I wandered up to my room in search of diversion, which I soon found when I began looking through the files I'd filched from Floyd's flat.

The first thing I discovered was Floyd's journal, a loose-leafed affair in an ordinary folder, which was probably why I'd overlooked it when I'd first poked my nose into Floyd's filing cabinet.

I was telling myself that it would be a total no-no to read it, even as I was busily thumbing through to see if he'd written anything about me. Rewarded with a glimpse of my name towards the end I was happy enough to go back and start at the beginning.

I could imagine well enough his mixed feelings as he stepped off the plane into what he noted was Sierra Leone's rainy season.

"More humid than I'd imagined," he remarked, "and desperate for a long cool drink by the time we finally cleared Customs. Had to make do with a mouthful from my ration of tepid bottled water, which is supposed to last me until we get to the camp."

He went on to describe a sweaty, juddering journey incarcerated in the back of a truck, through mangrove swamps and vast tracks of deforestation, until eventually arriving in the Eastern Province of the country.

"In spite of all the induction training," he wrote that first night, "nothing really prepares you for the reality: thousands of people in a sprawl of mud huts and plastic shelters, in an area reduced to rubble by Civil War. What makes it all the more sickening is that one in three children will die before they're five years old because although the country is rich in diamonds, it's riddled by corruption and rebellion. I just hope I'm up to this."

How typical of Floyd, I thought, to doubt himself, when it was perfectly obvious to me he had all the courage and skills that anyone could possibly need to work in his chosen field. Quite apart from the fact I thought it unlikely his employer would have invested what I imagined would have been considerable time and expense in training him if they hadn't thought he was up to the job.

Whether it was due to something as prosaic as lack of time, or whether that hint of doubt grew rapidly into something more specific, it transpired that after the first few days Floyd had only kept his diary spasmodically. So it wasn't until I came to his first mention of the two little girls, Bendu and Sallay, with their sunny smiles, that I realised it had been quite a few weeks since he'd described anything so positively. Not surprising really: surrounded by so much misery it must be awfully difficult to keep your sunny side up.

I'd have to admit that knowing what had happened to Bendu and Sallay, I skipped over that part of his account until I reached the record of his expedition to their village.

It had been well into the dry season when, after a tortuous journey through an arid, depleted countryside, he'd reached the village – "a place of ruin and destruction swept by dust-storms and dry sand-laden winds blowing in from the Sahara." Like your anger, I thought, which as I'm reading this, is billowing up from the page in great choking clouds.

There were very few entries when he got back to the camp. He spoke briefly about rehabilitation initiatives, water and sanitation programmes and the small farming enterprises set up on the outskirts of the camp, but I could tell his heart wasn't in it. The last entry he made before he returned to England said baldly, 'It hasn't turned out as I expected. I hoped to do so much but have achieved so little. I am thankful for the fortitude of those of my colleagues who battle on.'

I don't know whether Floyd had always kept a diary or if his deployment to Africa had prompted him to begin, at any rate he'd more or less given it up when he returned to England. He was still making entries, but they were more along the lines of recording dentist's appointments and birthdays than life experiences. I flicked over several months until I saw a note he'd made about coming down to Mullion Quay to meet me, followed a day or so later by, 'a disastrous excursion to Cardiff.' His near drowning had a cursory 'fell in the sea' and his very last entry said, 'Daiz arriving today or tomorrow. Can't wait.'

'Why didn't you tell me, Floyd?' I asked him as I gulped down the lump in my throat and wiped my nose.

'He did try, Daisy, but you wouldn't listen,' someone answered for him.

I pushed the journal aside and picked up one of the other folders. It turned out to be crammed with facts about his own family's background and a mass of material on Africa.

Glancing at the family tree in pride of place on the top page, I saw that he'd traced his family back to when they arrived in Britain at the end of the nineteenth century. As far as I could see, he was still working on his ancestry before that date. He'd apparently gleaned some information about his earlier forebears from his grandfather, who had been told the story by one of his own aged uncles. Floyd's family had come to Britain from Sierra Leone where they'd been settled since the mid 1800's. There was evidence that Floyd was still researching his even earlier ancestors through museum records he'd unearthed, which recorded people with his surname in servitude on a sugar plantation in South America, which was obviously the material he'd used as the basis for his book.

Sated by what, for me, was proving to be a literary marathon, I was relieved when I heard a tap on my door.

'Daysee,' Ileana said quietly as she took a couple of steps into my room and waited for me to sit up before handing me a mug of coffee, 'why you staying in bedroom?'

'I'm sorry,' I said, 'I didn't mean to neglect you. I've been reading.'

'I thinking you angry I not wanting see cathedral.'

'Daft goose,' I said, patting the bed. 'Get your coffee and come and sit by me and I'll tell you about Floyd's writing.'

'What Floyd writing about?' she asked, when she'd settled herself beside me.

'This stuff is mostly about Africa and his experiences there,' I said, pointing to Floyd's journal, 'but he's done masses of research since he came home and has traced his roots back nearly two hundred years. In fact he was using the material he'd collected to write a novel about life on a sugar plantation before slavery was finally abolished'

'You looking very sad,' Ileana said.

'Thinking about Floyd,' I said. 'He had such plans. It's all wasted now.'

Ileana was looking thoughtful. 'I having idea,' she said. 'Maybe you writing Floyd's book.'

'I wish,' I said. 'I'm a sailor not a writer. I wouldn't know where to start.'

'You learning quickly,' she said. 'Later you making book for Floyd.'

She said this with such calm assurance that she almost had me convinced, so that for a moment I was turning over the pages of the recently published ' An Honest Trade', ghost written on behalf of Floyd Joseph Proivil, by Daisy Davenport.

'What 'plantation' meaning?' Ileana's question came out of the blue. She'd obviously been mulling our conversation over as well.

'It means,' I started, pausing to think what I thought it did mean, and said instead, 'While I'm thinking about that, I'll explain about something else. When you want to ask the meaning of a word, it would be better English to say, 'What does so and so mean?'

'What does 'so and so' mean?'

I laughed. 'Okay. I suppose 'so and so' can be used instead of the proper name for anything. Do you understand?'

'Maybe,' she said, looking unconvinced. And then asked carefully, 'What does 'plantation' mean?'

I took a deep breath and plunged into a rambling and I'm sure inaccurate explanation.

Ileana looked bewildered.

I laboured on. 'Of course that's my impression of what a plantation was like a hundred and fifty years ago. I'm sure things are different now. Perhaps you could check it out in your new dictionary. Or maybe you'll need something like an encyclopaedia.'

'What does 'encyclopaedia' mean?'

'It's a reference book that tells you a lot of facts about a lot of different things. We'll get you one when we next go shopping. I can see you need something a good deal more precise than my woolly explanations.'

'You helping me very much,' she said, 'and making me very happy, so why you looking sad again, Daysee?'

'I'm still thinking about Floyd. I don't know what to do about what's happened to him. I keep thinking about his family. What should I do about his family?'

'You knowing Floyd's family?'

'No,' I said. 'We've never met.'

'You knowing where Floyd's family living?'

'It would be better to ask me, 'Do you know where Floyd's family lives?' I said. 'It's got something to do with the verbs only I can't explain what, I'm afraid.'

'I sorry, Daysee,' she said. 'English is very difficult.'

'No need to apologize,' I said, 'your English is excellent. I wish I could speak Romanian half as well.'

She looked astonished. 'You speaking … No.' She tried again. 'Do you do speaking… speak Romanian?'

'No,' I said, 'not at all. That's the point.' By this time Ileana was looking totally baffled. 'Let's not worry with any more English lessons today,' I said. 'What were we talking about before we interrupted ourselves?'

'We talking about Floyd,' she said.

'Yes,' I agreed, 'we were. But there's something else at the back of my mind. Something to do with his book that I can't put my finger on.'

'You forgetting. When you reading Floyd's book?'

'The first time was a week or two ago when Floyd came to visit me.'

'When you living on boat?'

'Yes,' I agreed. 'Thing is, I've got quite a good memory and I know it's to do with the book, but that that's only part of it.'

'What is other part?'

'I wish I knew.'

'You thinking what book tells about. You remembering other thing.'

'Yes, you're probably right.'

'Where slaves living in book?'

'You could ask, 'Where do the slaves live in Floyd's book? The answer is that I can't remember exactly, except they were near a river estuary in Guyana in South America. I remember that because he mentions many different ships being moored there.'

'You still having Floyd's writing?'

'I have.' I jumped up. 'I've got it here. I reread it now and then.' I flicked through, until I came to what I was looking for. 'Here it is. There's a vessel called the Rople Helm moored in the River Demerary. Mean anything to you?'

Ileana shook her head.

'Me neither - except … except… the name of the ship, the Rople Helm. The Rople Helm,' I repeated. 'It's that name that I've heard before. But where, where on earth could I have come across it?

It's hardly a modern name.' I stared vacantly at the ceiling willing the boat to heave into view: nothing, not a sail in sight, but still that irritating, evasive feeling of nearly having my finger on it. My gaze left the ceiling and travelled round the room, alighted on Auntie's box of papers. The recognition was instant.

I took a couple of steps over to the chest of drawers to grab the box.

It didn't take long to put two and two together. 'I must have noticed the name before I fell asleep,' I said, 'without even realising.'

I flicked out the top sheet.

'Here it is,' I announced, and immediately began reading it aloud to Ileana, which, given the uncomfortable feeling I was doing my best to ignore, had the merit of providing several minutes' diversion.

Dear Sirs,

It is with pleasure and thanks to God for a safe voyage that I make this report to you.

The Agent's vessel being in dock, I proceeded immediately to take command of the brig Rople Helm in accordance with your instructions. Finding her to be sound and all her rigging in good order I gave the order for departure.

I am able to report that the helm of the vessel is quick and with a squally wind blowing through the gulls she stands well enough under her canvas, being neither too stiff nor too crank. Close-hauled and under double-reefed topsails and jib she steers with little weather-helm. However when becalmed she pitches heavy causing much seasickness amongst passengers and crew.

After one hundred and two days we arrived in Demarary in heavy rains, thunder and lightning. With high surf running in the bay, we had to let out 25 tons of chain to secure safe anchorage. The voyage was completed without serious incident, a petty disturbance amongst the crew about rotten rations being put down easily enough.

It is my intention to lie up here for two to three weeks to make repairs, load the sugar and put on stores and fresh water before proceeding to Madeira.

With God's blessing we may be home for Christmas.

Captain J.A.Williamson.

In spite of my interest in the description of the ship's seaworthiness, the bell that had begun as a tinkle was ringing at full peal by the time I came to the name of the vessel and I certainly wasn't happy about what the rest of the stuff in the box would reveal.

Wading through plantation records, agents' documents, letters from captains and passengers, supply sheets, trading accounts, ships' logs and numerous other papers all relating in one way or another to the slave trade, foreboding changed rapidly into reality and it wasn't easy to go on with the task to the very last sheet.

Floyd's choice of the name Rople Helm for use in his manuscript wasn't lost on me. The vessel, probably owned by my own flesh and blood, had obviously been a prominent slave ship working the Caribbean and South American colonies.

It was very late, or very early, depending which way you look at it, when I closed the box and pushed it away from me.

What it boiled down to, was that my forebears were directly involved in the slave trade. Belatedly, I recalled that when Auntie died, the solicitor had said something about merchant shipping: a pretty euphemistic description of the truth.

It was like waking up from a nightmare only to find it still going on in reality.

The arm that curled itself round my shoulders, followed by the hand wiping my face with a tissue, reminded me that Ileana was still sitting beside me. She'd been reading the papers as I finished them. What she'd made of them I didn't know. I vaguely remembered her asking a few questions at the beginning, but I'd shaken my head and hadn't answered. I think she'd left the room once or twice, perhaps to fetch her dictionary as I could see it on the bed beside her, or maybe to make more coffee. Whatever way she'd coped, now she was hugging me and whispering something about not crying about old papers.

'I sorry, Daysee,' she was saying. 'Papers very difficult for me to reading. I not understanding all words and too,' she broke off and made a complicated gesture with her hand, 'and hard to see.'

I had to smile. 'By', I repeated the gesture she'd just made, 'I expect you mean, with lots of curls and flourishes, and I guess it's hard to see because the ink has faded over the years.'

She nodded. 'I thinking papers telling about slaves,' she said. 'Like Floyd's book.'

It was my turn to nod. 'Yes,' I said. 'Exactly like Floyd's book.'

'Is very sad,' she said, 'but all finished now, so not to crying.'

'It's not as easy as that,' I said. 'I only wish it was. The horrible thing is, I gather from these documents that my own family was directly involved in the trade.'

Ileana shrugged. 'Maybe family doing bad things in old times. You doing good things. You saving me, Daysee. Saving me from that place and the bad men. Bringing me here in your house. Giving me food and books and being my friend. You very good person, Daysee.'

'Don't be daft,' I said, 'and anyway it's hardly in the same league. Can't you see everything I have, have ever had, this house, my boat, everything, it all comes from tainted inherited wealth.'

Of course it was my own fault for spouting off. 'What meaning "tainted inherited wealth"?'

Oh lor! 'Well, 'tainted' kind of means poisoned, like something that's been corrupted or spoiled by something bad, 'wealth' mainly means money, but it includes other valuables like jewels or fast cars or fur coats, and 'inherited' means things that are passed down to you when someone dies.'

'I understand some,' she said. 'Who passing things down to you?'

'I got everything from my Aunt Louise, who was the last of the three daughters to die. I suppose they'd inherited from my grandparents. I don't know how things were willed to them.'

'I thinking many people born and die in your family since old times when making wealth from slaves. I thinking some people farmers, maybe some working in factory, maybe some being soldiers. Not all money from slaves.'

I hugged her. 'Ileana, you're a star. Everyone should have a friend like you.'

'Daysee?'

'Mm?'

'Maybe we going to bed now?'

An Honest Trade
January 1834

There has been an uprising amongst the Negroes, the women being the most outrageous and disobedient. The mothers are refusing to apprentice their children and are demanding the compensation money. As with the unrest on neighbouring estates, the men in the field gang are turning out late and performing only half a day's labour. Special Magistrates have been appointed to check the spirit of insubordination throughout the area.

In the presence of the field gangs, 5 ringleaders are selected, examined and found guilty. The punishment for each is 30 lashes on the back with the cat-o'-nine-tails. Others are sentenced to hard labour on the treadmill. There are public floggings in the town and the jail is full of rebellious slaves. Wells comments that the punishments eventually have the desired effect and order is restored. Meanwhile he has applied to London for fifty indentured Portuguese workers to be sent from Madeira to add to his workforce.

The overseer's problems are intensified when he receives a letter from the Agents blaming him for not managing the Negroes with sufficient rigour. He writes back stating the recent imported Africans are too liberated - their crimes include behaving indecently, insolence and neglect of duty, and riding one of the horses. He requests they are transferred to Jamaica.

Alice, the girl Wells has selected to replace Lionoria, rejects his advances as she already has a man. Wells is furious. He punishes Alice by relegating her from the cosseted life she enjoys as a housemaid, to labouring in the fields, and sentences the unfortunate man to castration.

Fortune reports that life will be difficult for Alice in the Negro yard as the labourers are resentful of those that have had an easier life.

Eighteen

Morning had slithered into midday before we woke up, consequently it wasn't until we were washing up after lunch that I fell to brooding about Floyd and the chains that linked my family to his.

I'd got to the stage of wondering whether Mum and Louise had ever worried about the source of the family fortune or if they'd been able to shrug it off as ancient history, much as Ileana had on my behalf, when I fell to thinking about Floyd's book. Could some recompense be achieved if, as Ileana had kind of suggested, I could get **An Honest Trade** published for him? The snag was, of course, that apart from not knowing what stage the work was at, Floyd was dead; his death was unreported; and his body was missing. Some snag.

'You looking very sad again, Daysee. You not liking making plates dry?'

Absorbed in my grim thoughts and not really paying attention I only half took hold of the wet plate Ileana was holding out to me, definitely not firmly enough to prevent it slipping through my fingers and shattering on the flagstones.

'We're certainly getting used to clearing up broken crockery,' I said as we scurried into action with dustpan and brush. 'I wish I could sort out all the other stuff so easily.'

'What you wanting – no –what do you want to sort out? Ileana asked.

'Oh, nothing to speak of,' I said, and it came out much more sharply than I intended. 'Not unless you count Floyd's murder, your incarceration in that bloody attic, and my family's record on Human Rights. Apart from those things, there's not that much worrying me.'

'What is "Human Rights"?'

'And having to explain every word I bloody say, doesn't help,' I snapped before I could help myself.

Ileana froze. Then, her hand flying to her mouth, she rushed from the room.

I found her, face down on her bed, sobbing. I don't think I've ever seen anyone so distraught. Dropping onto the bed beside her, I pulled her up to me and held her as close as I could. She was stiff and unyielding and gasping for breath through her tears.

'Shush,' I whispered. 'Shush. It's all right. Honestly. It's all right. Really it is. Come on now. It's me, your friend Daysee. I'm sorry if I sounded angry. I'm angry with myself not with you.'

She pulled away from and muttered something I couldn't make out. I thought afterwards that she must have spoken in Romanian. Whatever it was, her tone of voice was laden with reproach and betrayal.

I didn't know what to say. How could I describe the guilt I felt about covering up Floyd's murder? How could I explain about living with it day after day only by blanking it out or say how I dealt with the days when that strategy failed? And what was there to say in justification of my family's gory antecedents? So I didn't say anything.

After a while Ileana raised her head and glanced listlessly at me. 'I being big trouble to you; making you angry. I go away,' she said.

'No. No, please. Don't say that. Don't even think about it. I like you being here with me, being my friend. Think about the good things we've done together already. The fun we've had.' I cast around for an example. 'Remember being out in the dinghy; you liked that, didn't you? And you like your books. And cooking.' I could hear my voice cracking. 'Don't go, Ileana. Please. This is your home now.'

'My home?' she asked.

'Our home,' I said.

After a great deal of hugging and mutual reassurance, and tea laced with brandy, I chanced asking her what it was she'd said in Romanian.

'Is old saying,' she said, blushing.

'What saying?' I asked.

'I not knowing all English words,' she said. 'Needing to find many in dictionary.'

'Oh,' I said. 'Perhaps you'll be able to explain when we've got that English / Romanian phrase book for you.'

'Maybe,' she said, looking sheepish. Then added abruptly 'We going out after drinking tea? Sun shining. We going in little boat?'

'Good idea,' I said. 'We've been cooped up too long.'

She beamed. 'Do you having bag? I making things to eat by sea.'

'A picnic; what a good idea.'

'Is – does picnic meaning eat food outside?' she asked.

'Exactly,' I said.

We had a great afternoon. We paddled and swam and punted around in the dinghy and then sat on the sand and ate our picnic washed down with lemonade and a bottle of Pimms, which had tucked itself into our shopping trolley with a couple of its friends during our expedition to the supermarket.

It wasn't until later, when we were pottering around indoors and Ileana remarked how much she'd enjoyed being out in the dinghy, and I'd said I'd liked it too, that I realised just how much I was missing Lady Lou.

'It was fun,' I said, 'and I'm sure you'd enjoy proper sailing even more.'

'What is 'proper sailing'?'

'You know, like the boat you came over on.' Even as I was saying it I couldn't believe I was. Talk about putting your foot in your mouth. I didn't know where to look and I could feel my face burning up. Please, please, please, don't let me have hurt her again.

I was still begging the ground to swallow me up, when I realised Ileana was asking something about Lady Lou.

'Sorry,' I said. 'I didn't hear what you were saying.'

'I asking if you going on your boat often.'

'Oh yes. Most weekends, and I'd been living onboard until Floyd … until Floyd died.'

'Is Floyd staying on boat?'

'No. I wanted him to, but he couldn't. He was afraid of water; really frightened. Once, when he came to see me, he fell in and nearly drowned. It was awful. Terrible.'

156

'Why Floyd afraid?'

'I don't know. Come to that, he didn't really know himself. I gathered, when I read his ideas for his book, that he thought it might be an inborn trait – something dating back to when his people had been enslaved and transported across the high seas. I don't know whether that's likely, or whether it's one of those things that people have phobias about, like flying or spiders.'

She shuddered. 'I not liking spiders.' She paused. 'But I thinking I like little boat very much.'

'We'll take her out again soon,' I said. 'Perhaps tomorrow, if it's fine.'

The evening passed quietly enough with Ileana mesmerised by the TV and me, in an effort to put recent revelations out of my mind for a while, engaging myself in maps and charts and tide-tables.

I got us up early next morning.

'How would it be,' I asked Ileana over breakfast, 'if I moved Lady Lou from Mullion Quay so that you wouldn't be worried about being seen if we went sailing together?'

Her spoon, laden with milk and cereal en route to her mouth, dropped messily onto the floor. She gaped at me in astonishment.

'Close your mouth,' I said, 'it's not a pretty sight.'

She clamped her mouth tightly shut and continued to stare at me.

I laboured on. 'It would be nice to have someone to sail with, but it's not entirely for your benefit. Obviously I've been thinking about things since Floyd was murdered and it seems to me to be a pretty good idea to tuck Lady Lou out of sight for a while. What d'you think?'

She bent down to pick up the spoon. When she bobbed up again she had a soppy expression on her face.

'I thinking you the goodest friend in all the world,' she said.

'It's best, not goodest,' I said, 'which leads me nicely to the other thing I've been thinking about – trying to fix up some English lessons for you.'

Her face was a picture. 'I learning English like school?'

'Something like that, I'm not sure what's available locally. We'll look into it as soon as we've moved Lou.'

Having made the decision, I couldn't wait to get started. Louella had been berthed in the same place for the best part of ten years and the first thing to decide was where to move her to, which was, of course, why I'd been poring over my charts the night before. You do get used to mooring in a marina; even a smallish one like Mullion Quay has a shower block and water and diesel readily available, and there's no doubt that I'd miss those facilities if I moved onto a floating anchorage as I planned; but not as much as I was already missing Lou, and not nearly so much as I'd miss her in the future if I didn't take decisive action now.

'It's a bit convoluted,' I said as we were loading things in the car, 'but it's the best I can do. I've picked out a spot a few miles east on the other side of the peninsular, where I'm pretty sure I'll be able to get an anchorage on the mud up one of the inlets. What I'm intending to do is drive over there now and secure a mooring. Once that's sorted, I'll park you up in the car somewhere nearby, then cycle back to the quay, collect Louella and bring her round to her new berth. As long as there are no hitches, I'll catch the tide in plenty of time to come and fetch you in the dinghy.'

She caught hold of my arm as I said this. 'No, Daysee. Plan not working. Dinghy being here near house. Little boat too big going in car.'

I grinned. 'I'm sorry, I should have explained. I keep an inflatable onboard Lady Lou.'

'What meaning – what does 'inflatable' mean?'

'It means you can blow it up.'

'Blow up like bomb?' She looked dumbfounded.

'No,' I said, trying, but not succeeding, to smother a laugh, 'I'm afraid I'm not explaining very well. 'Blow up' can also mean to fill up with air. Do you understand?'

She shook her head.

'The little boat we keep here on the beach is made of wood. The dinghy on Lou is made of rubber, so you can pump it up like a tyre on a bicycle. Do you understand now?'

We struck lucky in one of the numerous boat clubs that pepper this part of the coast. Leaving Ileana in the car, I'd gone in to make enquiries. Almost the first thing I spotted was a card on the notice board advertising a temporary mooring whilst the resident-occupier was away for the summer. Judging by the date, the ad had only been up for a couple of days.

I unpinned the card and went to find the steward.

'You're in luck,' he said. 'It's only been free a week. The bloke who was supposed to take it had his mind changed for him at the last minute. Ran into a little marital difficulty apparently. Had a new cabin cruiser, 'had' being the operative word, as before he could get it in the water, he found it was to constitute part of his divorce settlement. Poor sod. You want a drink while I get the stuff out of the safe?'

Conscious of Ileana waiting in the car, I shook my head and muttered something about it being a little early. He was back with the ubiquitous brown envelope and emptying the contents onto the bar while I was still thinking of changing my mind about a drink.

The formalities were completed in minutes. With the contract signed and three months paid up front, I had immediate possession.

Lady Lou's new home had to be approached by a rough track from the road. The mooring was located in an arm, or perhaps I should say finger, of a fairly quiet inlet about three quarters of a mile out of the village. Half a dozen small craft lay in the mud on our side of the sliver of water flowing along the channel. There was a tiny pier from which you could launch a dinghy to get to and from your boat when the tide was in, otherwise you'd be pretty much stranded, as the shoreline in the area is treacherously muddy.

Apart from the pier, and the mud, and the seagulls, we seemed to have the place to ourselves, although there'd been a couple of cars parked along the track so it was quite likely there were people out of sight onboard their boats. Anyway, as far as I could see, it was the ideal location for Louella.

'You're sure you're going to be all right waiting here for me?' I asked Ileana when we got back to the car and I was lifting my bike out of the boot and unfolding it.

'Not needing to worry. I having my books and coffee, also water and many sandwich. If I needing toilet I must going in bushes.'

'You could walk back to the village if you get bored, look at the boats, and have a drink in the pub if you felt brave enough. Just remember to lock the car.'

'I not leaving car. I waiting here for you, Daysee.'

'I'm going to give you my phone,' I said. 'It's switched on. To answer it all you have to do is press this green button. You understand?'

'Is fine,' she said, nodding.

'I'll try to ring you from a call box if I'm delayed at the marina for any reason. The tide's still going out now so I've got at least six hours until high tide, and a bit more because of Lou's lifting keel.'

'What is 'lifting keel?' she asked.

'It's part of the bottom of the boat that can be raised up so you don't need so much water to float in.'

She was about to ask something else, but I pecked her lightly on the cheek and climbed onto my bike. 'I'm sorry to dash off, but if this is going to work I have to get going. Once I'm onboard Lou I've no way of getting in touch with you if I miss the tide, which means you're going to be hanging around hours without knowing what's going on. You've got to promise me you won't panic; you'll wait it out until I can get in on the next tide early tomorrow morning.'

'I waiting, Daysee,' she said. 'Not to worrying.'

Even so, as I reached a bend in the road and turned to wave goodbye, I was very conscious of how vulnerable she looked, standing there, alone in the road.

Nineteen

Cycling back to the marina gave me the opportunity to work through the finer points of my strategy. Obviously the hardest part was the Floyd factor. I really hated the idea of lying about Floyd, but what else could I do? It would be common knowledge that I'd gone to stay with him in London, and yet here I was on my own, and taking Lou away to boot.

With only the twinge in my ankle to divert my attention as I started to pedal, by the time I reached Mullion Quay I'd worked myself up into quite a state, and was pretty hot and flustered when I propped my bike against the wall of the chandlers and went in to see Megan.

'Daisy,' she said, vaulting over the counter to hug me, 'where've you been? What've you been doing? Where's the delectable Floyd? Tell me all. Instantly.'

I guess in some perverse way my guilty conscience saved me.

'Megan, I...I can't talk about it. I'm sorry,' I managed to stammer before I found myself bawling my eyes out. Real blubbing, not a wishy-washy pretence at it, a deluge of sobbing, more akin, I thought afterwards, to Ileana's recent breakdown than to anything I thought myself capable of.

'Didn't work out then,' I could hear Megan murmuring as she steered me surreptitiously towards her office. 'You poor thing. We'll have a cup of tea and you can tell me all about it.'

'I can't,' I blurted out. 'I just can't. I'm sorry. Please don't ask me.'

'Oh,' she said, and I could tell she was miffed. 'Are you sure? Only we've all been wondering about you.'

The thought of the gossip sloshing round the marina provoked another spasm of snivelling and it was as much as I could do to hang on to my plan.

'Thing is,' I mumbled, 'I can't face anyone. Need time by myself.' I could sense she was about to say something consoling and went on quickly before she could get a word in. 'I've decided I need to get right away, but I'm not up to a long voyage on my own, so I'm going to have a stab at the British Isles. Take my time. Stop off wherever I fancy and see how far round the coast I can get.'

'Yes,' she said, 'I can see the merit in that, but wouldn't you -'

I had to interrupt. 'So I'm going today. Now, as soon as I leave here.'

She let go of my arm and turned to face me. I could see I'd taken her by surprise by the way her mouth was opening and closing although she wasn't saying anything. The word 'goldfish' swam into my mind. 'And you'd be doing me the most enormous favour if you'd tell the others after I've gone.'

And that was that really, apart from a couple of hugs and a promise to send a postcard or two.

I was half out of the door when she caught up with me again.

'Two minutes,' she said. 'Hang on two minutes while I get your Musto pants you left for repair.'

I know I snatched them from her. I know it was rude and thoughtless and she must have thought I'd gone completely bonkers. I knew all that even as I was waving away the bill and thrusting fifty pounds into her hand. 'I have to go.'

I fairly flew down to Lou, praying I wouldn't bump into anyone else, heaved my bike over the side onto the deck, did the barest minimum in the way of essential checks, and cast off, motoring up the channel and out into the bay.

I can't begin to describe the mixture of emotions that swept over me as we left Mullion Quay behind, other than to say I was feeling distinctly wobbly, so much so that, out of the blue, I found myself doubting my ability to manage Louella's new rig; a doubly alarming sensation, I suppose, in that I can't remember ever doubting my sailing competence before.

Whilst I was still mentally quagmired, habit and experience were fortunately reasserting themselves, so that I'd eased off the throttle and got the engine driving gently forward whilst I put the main up, hardly realising I was doing it. I guess it's like driving a car; if you think about how to do it, your mind goes blank, but once you're behind the wheel you do it automatically.

With the bit of a blow that was coming in from the west, we were soon heeled over and breezing along the coast with the headsails set and a reef in the main. There was definitely more weather helm than there would have been with the old sail layout, but I was easy enough with it. Gradually the wind picked up, and, judging by the clouds, I thought we were in for a squall so I took the opportunity to put another reef in before it got too gusty.

Sure enough, as we approached the point the wind changed and I felt the first few spots of rain. I shot below for my jacket and was hardly back on deck before it began bucketing down. Then the wind veered again and I decided to leave gybing until I was well clear of the headland. I'd say being under sail in squally weather is much the same as powering an off-road vehicle round an assault course. But sailing's infinitely more exciting; bucking up on the crests of the waves, plunging into the troughs, fighting the sea for control of the wheel, the wind howling round your ears and the sting of saltwater against your face. Exhilarating stuff and exactly what I needed to take my mind off my troubles, at least for a while.

As I came round onto the other tack and into the lee of the peninsular, the rain petered out and the wind dropped. I let out the second reef and checked to see how I was doing for time. Although it was only about four and half miles to Louella's new berth by road, it was more than double that distance to sail round the coast. It had taken me the best part of an hour and a half to cycle back to Mullion Quay, speak to Megan and make my get-away with Lou. We'd been at sea another couple of hours and I reckoned we had the best part of three miles still to go. With a good wind we'd make it in plenty of time to fetch Ileana.

Half an hour later, the wind had vanished and it was raining. I switched on the engine and lowered the headsails, leaving the main to catch any wind there might be. After that I uncovered the dinghy and pumped it up, ready for swift disembarking.

The tide was on the turn as we came chugging up the inlet. I dropped the main into the stack-pack bag and made ready to come alongside the mooring. Once Lou was made fast I lowered the dinghy over the side and scrambled in.

I'm not saying I'm an expert rower, but I reckon if there'd been an Olympic scout in the vicinity he'd have signed me up then and there. I went like the wind. Or as fast as you can in a small rubber boat with a couple of paddles. Oh, oh, oh, for the outboard safely stored in the garage at home.

When I got to the car Ileana wasn't there. I suppose I should say, 'when I got to where I'd left the car', because that wasn't there either.

I couldn't believe it. There was absolutely no sign of Ileana or the Nissan.

I told myself firmly, very firmly, that I'd left it further on, round the next bend; knowing I hadn't. And, needless to say, it wasn't round the next bend. Nor was Ileana.

There had to be a perfectly reasonable explanation; for instance - but what instance? I couldn't think of anything; not a single sensible explanation as to how or why car and refugee might have vanished.

What I could think of were a hundred and one permutations of disaster, top of the list being that the bastards who killed Floyd had caught up with us and taken Ileana. Taken her away to do God knows what to her, leaving me there, kicking my heels in the rain, looking at the space where the car ought to be and trying to think what the hell to do next.

Time's a funny old thing: one minute it's ticking along, regular as clockwork, the next it's sped unaccountably forwards so that you've missed that important matter you shouldn't miss on any account and then, just as mysteriously, it slows right down and takes an hour to pass five minutes. Which was approximately when Ileana, driving my car, came back.

She tumbled out of the car and threw her arms round me. 'Daysee, you not waiting long time? I hoping you not waiting. I thinking maybe you coming soon. I thinking you being hungry. Riding your bike and sailing the boat. I buying fish and chips.' She was beaming.

What could I say? That's all very well, but you gave me the shock of my life, or, that was a very kind thought, but you scared me out of my wits. I thought you-know-who had found you. Instead I said weakly, 'I didn't know you could drive.'

'I can drive, but not having permit. Shall we eating chips here or on boat?'

'I don't know if they'll be enough water to get back to Lou now. We can go and see and may be able to park the car nearer as well.'

Louella was still afloat, but separated from us by several yards of mud. We ate our chips in the car.

'It seems to me we have two options now,' I said, as I screwed up the paper and wiped my mouth. 'We can sit here for the best part of twelve hours or we can go home again and come back tomorrow.'

Pausing only long enough to deflate the dinghy and stow it in the car, we went back to Halnaker House, unlocked everything we'd locked up, switched on everything we'd switched off, had a couple of drinks and a conversation about driving lessons as well as English ones, and retired to bed relatively early.

We had coffee in the house, and breakfast onboard. Ileana was like a cat with two tails, not knowing where to turn next. And the questions. Talk about thick and fast, it was like being grilled by that Anne Thingy person on TV. In the galley she asked, 'How stove working?' 'How to cooking when sea very rough?' 'Why things not falling out of cupboards?' 'Is refrigerator like in house?' 'Where is water being kept for washing up?' Then she was in the saloon inspecting the gimble table, the sofa / bunk arrangements, my pilot berth, the chart table; then the heads and the sail locker; I'd swear, there wasn't a cupboard, hatch, porthole or locker, she didn't open and peer into or out of, or a handle or switch she didn't want to pull, press or push. By the time we'd got to the forepeak cabin, which was to be her domain, my brain was hurting. And that was before she wanted to know about the technical stuff. I was going cross-eyed with the strain and the voice in my head. 'Daisy. You are the Weakest Link. Goodbye.'

I could only describe the session that followed on deck as the equivalent of a Competent Crew Course done in a couple of hours and without the benefit of coffee breaks. Or sailing.

She'd just discovered the life raft when I cracked. 'That's it. No more questions,' I said, clapping my hands over my ears. 'If we don't go now, we'll miss the blasted tide again.'

165

Weather wise it wasn't a brilliant day, overcast and not much wind about, but we were happy. Putting sails up; taking them down; motoring; putting sails up again, and so on. And so on. Ileana was keen to try everything and by golly, as we used to say at school, she was a quick learner. Although I'd joked about it earlier, I could see she'd really blossom on a proper sailing course. Another thing to add to my list?

Ileana made supper. We ate under the cover in the cockpit, looking up at the stars and out across the mud. There was nobody around; no lights on the other boats, nothing to disturb our thoughts.

Apart from my commenting on how much meals had improved since Ileana had been in charge, we didn't talk much. I was getting acclimatised to being berthed with no water under me, feeling the different stresses and hearing different noises as Lady Lou settled down into the mud. I thought Ileana was contented enough; she seemed to be anyway, propped up in the corner, sipping Bicardi and coke, her legs stretched out along the bench; but how could I know for sure? After what she'd been through on the Tiger Moth, was I asking too much of her?

People have contrary views about the sea. There's that heartfelt yearning for the 'lonely sea and the sky' hard up against the 'snotgreen' 'scrotumtightening sea', but what does it for me is the notion that 'it's always ourselves we find in the sea'. Which, I guess is why, when I woke up the following day, I was feeling as if I'd lost a pound and found a penny. It's not as if I hadn't realised, when I decided to move Louella, how much it would affect me. But I was thinking about the practical difficulties, like having to go much further for water and diesel, no hot showers, and no comforting pub to while away the shore-based hours in the company of reliable like-minded friends. What I hadn't really considered was how I'd feel about leaving ten years of my sailing life behind. I'd swapped a huge part of myself for a mud berth with no facilities, where I couldn't even get onboard Lady Lou if I cocked up the tide. The fact that Ileana was safe, Lou was away from prying eyes and I wouldn't have to tell any more lies about

Floyd failed to lift my spirits.

I was lying in my bunk, staring at the ceiling and feeling about as bouncy as a deflated balloon, when Ileana drifted into view. She was holding a mug out towards me.

'You maybe getting up soon?' she asked. 'I making breakfast.'

'Sure,' I said, sitting up and taking the mug from her.

'Daysee,' she said, 'you drinking coffee now, eat soon, before all getting cold.'

'Of course,' I said, taking a couple of swigs of coffee and wriggling out of my sleeping bag.

Breakfast was weird. I could hear my voice and see myself over my own shoulder. I wasn't hungry, wasn't not hungry. I just ate until it was gone, and then I stopped.

'Is all o.k?' Ileana asked.

'Fine. Why d'you ask?'

'I thinking you not happy.' She screwed up her face. 'I not knowing how to say exactly. You like,' she fluttered her hand, 'not standing on ground. Like you flying about. And your face very red.'

'That'll be the wind from yesterday. I expect my skin has softened up because I haven't been sailing for a couple of weeks. And, yes, I am a bit down this morning; a dose of anticlimax, most likely, although there is something else niggling at the back of my mind. Something else I know I should be doing.'

'What is anti...? She checked herself. 'No, I looking in dictionary later. What else needing doing?'

I sighed. 'Can't remember, that's the problem. Perhaps it'll come to me when we get home.'

'We not sailing today?'

'No,' I said. 'I think I need to get my head into gear before we go out again. Anyway we've got plenty of time for sailing in the future, now Lou's out of the lime-light.'

We were standing by the car and I was rooting around in my bag looking for my keys when I came across Auntie's letter. Auntie's letter, alluding to more family secrets, which I was supposed to present to our bank and which had been my main reason for going into town last time, had completely slipped my mind.

I brandished the letter. 'Obviously it's this that's been fidgeting me. I can't think why I didn't notice it. It's been in my bag all the time.'

'You thinking about moving boat to hide from bad men. Now boat safe, you see in bag. Seeing letter.'

'If it's not one thing, it's another,' I said. 'And that's the understatement of all time. By any normal standards, having your boyfriend murdered, discovering a naked girl held prisoner in an attic, and finding out about your own family's unspeakable background, would be considered sufficient unto the day. But it doesn't stop there. Oh no. Now I've got something else to deal with. Something so secret and unpleasant I can't be told about it until after all my relatives are dead.'

Ileana took my hand. 'Many bad things in my life also. You helping me. I trying help you. Is maybe good thing, we being together, Daysee.'

'Is good definitely. All the same I can't help feeling someone's trying to tell me something; something about chickens coming home to roost. I just wish someone had told me to build a bloody coop.'

We drove straight into town. I can't pretend I wasn't nervous when the clerk handed me the package. In spite of Ileana's efforts to reassure me, I couldn't just shrug off the knowledge that my ancestors were active in something as barbaric as slavery. And if that particular skeleton had only been stored in the attic, how grisly was the corpse that was locked up in the vaults of the bank?

Deciding where to open the package was the next problem. My first impulse was to find a quiet pub where a spot of Dutch courage could be imbibed. We found quite a decent place near the bridge, but second thoughts imposed themselves before I reached the bar and I decided to drive straight home, only stopping off long enough to top up with groceries, to whiz into Waterstones for an encyclopaedia, and to pick up a couple of local newspapers, a copy of Loot and a prospectus for the adult education college. Not that all of this didn't take at least an hour and a half, with Auntie's packet burning a hole in my pocket all the way through, so it was an enormous relief to get back to Halnaker House.

The package contained my birth certificate.

Big deal.

Bigger perhaps if you notice your mother isn't your mother. Your real mother is apparently your Aunt Victoria and the person you thought was your mum is, ipso facto, your aunt. Your father's name is not recorded, which presumably means you're illegitimate, born out of wedlock to use the old phrase.

Before you give yourself chance to take this in, you look at the other documents, the death certificates for your grandparents, which confirm their deaths by drowning. No surprises there.

But it occurs to you, even in your shell-shocked state, that there's no death certificate for Victoria, your real mother, who you've always understood died in the boating accident with your grandparents.

What conclusion do you draw from that?

Did I mention corpses in vaults? It's all completely unbelievable, like the plot of some tacky soap opera, which stretches credibility to its limits and then gives it another tweak just to be sure you're not getting complacent.

And the explanatory letter from Louise was anything but.

Dearest Daisy,

My hands are shaking as I slip your birth certificate into this envelope for you, so monstrously unforgivable is the deception we have perpetrated against you. But still I do beg you to forgive us. Circumstances at the time were so terrible - even now I can't bear to think about them - that it seemed the only way to protect you.

I hope, Daisy, that you've enjoyed your life so far: you've blossomed from an intrepid toddler into a competent, self-reliant young woman and I trust your strength of character will sustain you through this period.

I'm so sorry, my dear, that much as I intended to set things straight now, the deception sustained over the years is now so ingrained, so deep-rooted, I find I cannot say as much as I intended.

I justify myself by postulating that it might be enough for you to know that Victoria was unmarried and in poor health at the time of your birth, and not in any position to care for you, and that after much soul-searching it was decided to bring you up as Ellen's daughter.

It may be some relief to you to see that, although we withheld the truth from you, you were properly registered as Victoria's daughter, so you are in no way compromised with the authorities. Your passport was properly obtained – you might recall signing the form before passing it over to Ellen to fill in for you - fortunately a sixteen year old girl has more exciting things to do than to complete bureaucratic forms and hang around in boring government offices, waiting to have her birth certificate verified against her application.

On the other hand, you may well feel that conforming to rules and regulations is trivial compared to the enormity of being lied to about your true mother. And, my dear, I can't pretend I don't feel that too. You were entitled to the truth, but were misled by those closest to you, those from whom you rightly expected honesty and integrity.

No amount of regret or guilt can change the past. What's done is done. I am asking you to find it in your heart to forgive us: asking, but not wholly confident of your response. So needful am I for your forgiveness, my dearest Daisy, I find I must, in spite of my misgivings, say a little more.

A search of the newspapers in the year you were born would be enlightening; enlightening, but I must emphasize, far from easy reading. I would caution you only to adopt this course of action in the knowledge that whilst I believe you would come to understand why we acted as we did, you might wish you had let matters lie.
Your ever-loving aunt
Louise.

I'm fairly sure I was on the point of making some quip to Ileana about it being a wise child who knows its own mother, when someone hit me over the head with a metaphorical sandbag. Next thing I knew, I was propped up against the sofa, with Florence Nightingale, minus her lamp, wittering over me.

'I'm fine,' I snapped, after I'd drunk the tea she'd insisted I have and was still going on, 'bit of a shock to the system is all.'

'I knowing you having very bad shock. I not minding you

sounding angry.'

'Daysee?'

'Yes?'

'I needing say something.'

'Spit it out then,' I said, 'but could you top me up with tea and you know what first? In fact you can dispense with the tea and just bring the brandy.'

'Where's yours?' I asked her when she came back with my drink.

'Daysee, I not having drink. I must telling something. Something bad.'

'I can't imagine what you've done that's so bad you can't have a drink,' I said, 'apart from dropping the bottle. That would be bad.'

'Not to joking, Daysee. I must telling bad thing.'

'Get it over with then. I'm all ears.'

'I reading your letter,' she burbled, 'while you passing out.'

Talk about after the Lord Mayor's Show. All that build up and then nothing. 'Daft goose,' I said, 'I'd have told you all about it anyway. Who else have I got to share things with? You think I could find out about something so earth-shaking and not tell you?'

We passed the rest of the evening with a lot of alcohol, food to mop it up, and me getting trying to get to grips with Louise's revelations. And poor Ileana was on the other end of it all. Did she get bored with my worrying about clues I might have missed when I was growing up, like birthdays and Christmas when I imagined cards coming in the post but never reaching me? Was she worn out by my endless speculation about what cataclysm had overtaken the family, which had led to my aunts perpetuating such a terrible fraud, not to mention my monotonous theorising about why Victoria had agreed to give me up? If she did, she didn't show it. She didn't offer advice, or suggestions, she was just there, listening and supporting me while I fought my way through to a sort of resolution: that however grim the outcome, I had to know.

An Honest Trade
February 1834

There is a measles epidemic on the plantation. The hospital is completely filled. Wells needs 6 young and healthy workers immediately and makes application for an additional 50 Africans. He also requires a ploughman and a blacksmith, who, in addition to their pay would be provided with a small garden where they could keep a cow, and whose wives could teach reading 2-3 hours a day.

The disorder amongst the insubordinate Negroes rumbles on. Wells cites numerous cases of people refusing to work and using improper language. Ten have been lashed in the yard to little effect. He has heard from Beausejour Plantation that Lionoria is being disruptive and uncooperative. She is resentful about being sent away from Kings, is neglecting her child and refusing to work.

A Man-of War moored in Mangrove Bay reports an alarming state of affairs in Jamaica with slaves in outright rebellion and crops unharvested in the fields.

Wells seduces Nelly, the thirteen-year old daughter of Fortune Proivil.

Twenty

We went to the library first. Of course if I'd known how to use Floyd's computer, I expect I could have found most of what I was looking for on the web. As it was I thought briefly about the dormant laptop in my bedroom, before handing Ileana paper and pen and asking her to keep a few notes.

'I reading slowly,' she said, 'and not writing English.'

'It doesn't matter,' I said. 'Just copy the words, we'll remember most of it anyway.'

In response to my enquiry the librarian in the Local Studies Section presented me with a microfilm, rather than the actual newspapers, which, in my old-fashioned little way, I'd expected to be poring over. I can't say I was very impressed. With hindsight, though, it may have been for the best, as scrolling through the spool on the reader/printer, with Ileana sitting beside me scratching away, was, to begin with at any rate, a lot more impersonal than it would have been splashed all over the front page. I found the first reference on page 3 of the local paper in February.

"Local Girl Has Miraculous Escape."

"Nineteen year old Victoria Davenport was thrown clear following an explosion onboard the yacht, The Maiden. Her parents, keen sailors Jack and Reva Davenport are missing, presumed dead. Initial enquiries indicate the blast was probably caused by a gas leak. The Davenports are survived by Victoria and her two elder sisters."

The next edition contained more details. A reporter, one Josie Pimm to judge by the by-line, had apparently been despatched to interview the family.

"Two Die In Sail Boat Drama."

"After an extensive search the bodies of Jack and Reva Davenport have been recovered from the sea following the serious explosion which destroyed the family yacht in Bellchester Bay last week. The accident is believed to have been caused by a spark igniting leaking gas. Nineteen year old, Victoria Davenport, who had been onboard with her parents, survived the disaster and suffered only minor injuries.

"A friend of the family said, 'Victoria has had a terrifying experience. She attributes her survival to the fact that she was at the wheel when the blast occurred, whilst Jack and Reva were below deck. Victoria is thankful to have survived although her happiness is naturally tempered by the tragic loss of her parents.'

"A spokesman from the RYA gave the following brief statement. 'The use of gas on board sailing boats has to be a matter of constant vigilance. Gas can all too readily collect in the bilges without the crew being aware of it. Simple safety precautions like having a drain through the hull in the locker in which the gas cylinder is stored, and fitting a detector below, would prevent very many of these accidents.'"

I must admit I heaved a small sigh of relief at this stage and Ileana must have been feeling the same because she squeezed my hand and whispered, 'There, not so bad as you thinking. Victoria being very brave escaping from burning boat. Why auntie making big fuss about newspaper?'

'I don't know,' I muttered. 'Have a feeling this is only the tip of the iceberg.'

Ileana looked baffled. 'What ice-?'

'Before you ask,' I interrupted, 'it means that, like an iceberg, you can only see the bit that sticks out of the water, and there's a lot more out of sight below the surface.'

'You thinking more in paper?'

'Yes,' I said, 'I'm afraid so.'

I guess it sounds like a simple procedure to scroll through a microfilm and it is – simple, but time consuming. You've more-or-less got to check every page, with the exception of the ads at the back, and you've got to view it sideways or spend the time rotating the pages so it reads the right way up. Consequently I had quite a crick in my neck by the time I found the next clue. It came in an edition two or three weeks later and was hidden away in a couple of lines on an inside page. The gist of it was that marine insurance investigators were looking into the sinking of The Maiden.

It was an innocuous statement; I'd guess that ninety-nine times out of a hundred an accident as serious as that which had overtaken The Maiden, would be thoroughly investigated - so why did I have this crawling sensation round the back of my ears? I ran my hands through my hair to brush it away, but the feeling persisted.

The kick in the teeth came in a report a month later.

"Local Girl Arrested."
"A Police Spokesman confirmed today that Victoria Davenport, who escaped the explosion and fire which destroyed the family's yacht last month, has been arrested in connection with the death of her parents, Jack and Reva."

I had to take a series of very deep breaths before I could bring myself to read through the short report that followed, which stated that the arrest had been made following an initial report by insurance investigators. No wonder I'd been feeling spooked.

I like to think I'm fairly tough, but there is a limit. Putting everything else aside, even the revelation that your aunt is in fact your mother - that mother was apparently suspected of being responsible for the death of her parents. I doubt anyone could take that in their stride without a break in their step.

I could feel myself breathing too quickly; I know I was getting increasingly hot and sweaty; I was shaking and my heart was thumping fit to burst as I worked through several more pages of newsprint looking for the follow-up. I was anticipating some heading about accidental death caused by negligence – what else could a gas leak be? – not the banner headline that announced; "Girl Remanded On Double Murder Charge."

Then I lost it. Before I knew it I was on my feet and throwing a tantrum – completely out of control. With hindsight I'd say it was understandable; I'd had to deal with too much over too short a time and something was bound to give sooner or later. I would have preferred it, however, if I hadn't made such a spectacle of myself. Raging about liars and mothers, kicking and shouting, knocking the furniture aside and beating the screen with my fists and yelling that it must be a mistake may have been a little over the top. The librarian and Ileana who were trying to restrain me almost certainly thought so. But I couldn't help it. Just couldn't, because I knew. I knew in my heart it was true. My mother was a murderer.

At last, when my anger had given way to inertia, and Ileana was driving me home, even though I knew she shouldn't be driving, I could see it all quite clearly and I tried to tell her. I explained that, coming from a long line of slavers and murderers, it was hardly surprising I'd let Floyd die, rather than have the inconvenience of reporting his suspicions to the proper authorities. And she'd said that I shouldn't say such things, that Floyd's death hadn't been my fault, and had I forgotten that she'd still be in that terrible place if I hadn't rescued her? All this was delivered to me, wallowing in self-pity and not inclined to hear words of reassurance, in her fractured English so that by the time we got home, I was still feeling pretty bleak. In search of a quick-fix to put me out of my misery for a while, I spurned the food Ileana offered me, drank the best part of a bottle of Night Nurse I found in the medicine cabinet, followed it with several glasses of brandy and thought about going to bed.

I had no idea how long I'd been out for the count when I eventually woke up. I was lying in bed, wondering if I should get up, when Ileana tiptoed into the room. Her face, solemn and full of concern, lit up as she saw I was awake.
    'You sleeping long time, Daysee. I worrying a little.'
    There's not a lot you can say to that. I crinkled up my mouth in what I hoped was a cheery smile before turning my attention to the tea she was offering me. I wasn't so dopey I'd lost the power of reasoning and I was going to say something obvious about it being the shock I'd had, when she said she thought maybe I'd drunk a drop too much brandy, and she'd drunk some too after she'd got me into bed and there wasn't much left and she hoped I didn't mind. I assured her that given the way things had gone recently, being a tad short of brandy wasn't of any great significance, which was enough of an opening for her to ask me if I remembered what had happened in the library.

'Unfortunately,' I said, 'it's all crystal clear. From the moment of reading the headline right through my fit of hysterics to you steering me up the stairs to bed. I know exactly what it said in the newspaper and don't doubt that Victoria was subsequently convicted of murder. What other reason could there be for the cover-up?'

'Is all accident,' Ileana said.

'No way. If it all got ironed out eventually, there'd be no reason to hide the truth.'

'You still angry?'

'Strangely,' I said, 'I'm not. Bewildered and hurt, but not angry. I don't know if my subconscious was working overtime while I was zonked out, but in actual fact I'm relieved that somehow Ellen and Louise contrived to deceive not only me, but the outside world as well. There was never a hint of scandal in all my thirty years. Imagine it at school if anything had leaked out. "There's that Davenport girl – the one whose mother murdered her grandparents." How would any child deal with that? Or people whispering about you; turning to watch you walk along the road; friends shying away. My life would have been a misery. Instead it was wonderful. I guess I've got a whole lot to thank Mum and Louise for. God knows what they went through.'

'They loving you. Making best for you. Not minding hard for them.'

'Mm,' I said.

'The thing is,' I said, once I was up and about, 'I don't exactly fancy another trip to the library for a while, but I can't think what to do next.'

'You thinking more in papers?'

'Well, as I said, it seems clear Victoria was subsequently convicted otherwise there'd have been no need for the cover-up.'

Ileana nodded. 'Maybe newspaper office keeping old papers, like library.'

'Of course. What was the name of the paper?'

'I not remembering, but I making note. Where I putting?' She jumped up and vanished into the hall. 'In pocket,' she said, as she came back, waving a notepad at me.

'Are you sure this is English?' I asked her as I squinted at the squiggles. 'Looks more like ancient hieroglyphics.'

'I saying I not writing good,' she said and I thought her voice wavered a little.

'Just joking,' I said quickly. 'It's great. 'Look, here's the name, 'The Gazette'. Thank goodness you wrote it down.'

She nodded and looked pleased.

'And here,' I went on, 'you've written the reporter's name - Rosie, no, Josie Pimm. That's plenty to be going on with.'

'What we doing now?'

'We need to find out whether the paper's still being published. Not being a newspaper reader I haven't a clue.'

Merged, but not thankfully out of print, the paper had transmogrified into The Gazette and Advertiser. We came out of the shop with our copy, scrambled into the car, flicked through the pages looking for the phone number, flicked back again until we found it. 'Here it is,' I said stabbing the page with my finger. I checked my watch. 'If we get a move on, I reckon we can get home in time to catch them before they pack up for the night.'

Ileana laid a restraining hand on my arm. 'Maybe telephoning now on small phone, Daysee.'

'Do you realise I haven't used this yet,' I said, as I ferreted around for my mobile in my bag, 'and how many weeks have I had it?'

I was put through to the Personnel Section. 'I wonder if you could help me?' I began politely. 'I'm trying to get in touch with a reporter who was working on The Gazette in the nineteen seventies.'

'Names and addresses of employees are confidential,' an impersonal voice replied.

'Her name is Josie Pimm,' I said.

'As I said, we can't supply any personal details, I'm afraid.'

'Thing is,' I said, 'I know she was working on the paper about thirty years ago; she might even be retired by now. If I sent her a letter, care of the paper, could you at least forward it to her? It's important. Honestly. Really important.' I could hear my voice cracking. 'I don't know where else to turn.'

'Hold on a moment.'

Was it my imagination or was the voice on the other end less frosty? I held my breath.

'You may send a sealed letter, under cover of a letter to the Head of Personnel, for onward transmission to the third party. You must understand that the newspaper cannot accept any further correspondence from you after that, nor any responsibility for soliciting a response.' The voice hung up.

I turned to Ileana. 'They'll do it. They'll forward a letter to the reporter who covered the case.'

We had the letter written and had been out to post it by the time we went to bed that night. Reasoning that even if Josie Pimm had retired or changed her job, her journalistic instinct would prevail, I explained who I was - not precisely I should say, only giving my name, deciding that if Ellen had been my mother for thirty years, there wasn't any cause for the world to know otherwise in year thirty one - and saying that I'd recently uncovered the allegations relating to Victoria's part in the death of my grandparents. I said that I'd found Josie's by-line on a brief report of the incident and that I was trying to obtain more details, in particular to ascertain what had happened to Victoria. I concluded by hoping she'd feel able to contact me and generally throwing myself on her mercy.

It occurred to me, as I dropped the letter in the box, that there'd been a positive glut of letters over the last few weeks - real letters, not bills or mail-shots - Floyd's letter enclosing his house keys; the note he'd left me in his flat; (Where had I put that?); the first letter from Aunt Louise that had led me to those documents; the second devastating missive from Louise; and now this, mine to Josie Pimm. I could hardly imagine the content of any letter she might write back to me, if she contacted me at all.

The next few days went quickly enough. We decided a priority was to get Ileana a provisional driving licence. Of course we immediately came up against a brick wall. The form required identification to be submitted with the application.

'I'm positive I didn't have to send anything when I applied for mine,' I said. 'Although, on second thoughts, given my track record with forms, and mum and Louise's vested interest, it's perfectly possible I just signed and left it for them to post off. Not that any of that helps with our current problem.'

Ileana shrugged. 'Soon maybe Romania becoming in Europe community and I not needing papers.'

'Fancy you knowing about that. I don't keep up with politics at all,' I said, desperately trying to ignore the echo of Floyd's voice belabouring me for my lack of interest in current affairs.

'I knowing many old communist countries hoping to joining. People thinking life better all being together.'

'We'll see what we can find out when I can face the library again,' I said. 'But I can't help thinking it's not going to happen overnight, and meanwhile we're back to square one when it comes to legitimising your driving.'

'Not important,' Ileana said. 'I thinking I not needing permit to sailing Lady Louella.'

And thankfully she was right about that. The weather was mixed - sunny, showery, windy, calm -ideal for a novice sailor to start to learn the ropes. Ileana blossomed: from port to starboard, bow to stern, she was on her toes and scampering around the deck to haul this up or make that off when the words were hardly out of my mouth.

I decided, in a quiet moment when Ileana was at the wheel and I was lounging beside her, that her need to know, coupled with her startling ability to process information, must be the result of having to look after herself from such a young age. In spite of, or perhaps because of, the dreadful life she'd had, she had a resilience and strength of mind that would put Ellen MacArthur to shame.

Josie Pimm didn't write back. She rang to ask when we could meet.

Ileana and I were watching from the window when her car, a sporty-looking job with a customised number plate, NEWS 1, came down the lane. I hurried across the yard to meet her, Ileana on my heels.

It was probably the result of the hypersensitive state I was in, that I thought her smile slipped a smidgeon as I approached her, because she was positively beaming as she clasped my hand and said how glad she was that I'd got in touch.

My impression was of a woman in her late sixties with short blonde hair streaked with grey, or it may have been short grey hair enlivened with blonde highlights; I decided the latter in view of the ostentatious number plate. She was wearing glasses with those special lenses that adjust to the sunlight and used a stick to help her across the yard to the house.

'Hip playing up,' she explained as she chose one of the upright chairs at the table in the window. 'I'm waiting for the op. Can't get into a decent pair of shoes.'

'Aren't Hush Puppies decent?' I asked her, glancing at her suede brogues.

'Oh, they're all right for clumping around in. I like something more elegant myself.'

I glanced down at my own well-worn trainers. I couldn't remember the last time I'd lashed out on anything more stylish than a pair of sea boots or a good pair of deck mates: shoes weren't really my thing. Would I be able to speak freely to a person who obviously put some store in her footwear?

My expression must have conveyed a hint of my anxiety because she said, 'I knew I wanted to meet you the minute I opened your letter.'

I let the breath I hadn't realised I was holding, out. 'I, Ms Pimm, I...'

'Let's agree to first names, shall we,' she said briskly. 'You know I'm Josie. I know you're Daisy, which only leaves this young lady.' She smiled at Ileana.

'My name is Ileana,' Ileana said carefully. 'I am Daysee's friend.'

'I'm very pleased to meet you. I expect you're a great support to each other. Now,' she paused, 'I'm wondering where to start. You said in your letter that you'd only recently learned about the unfortunate circumstances which lead to the death of your grandparents.'

'That's true,' I said. 'I always understood they'd died in the sailing accident with my aunt before I was born. It's only in the last week or so I've discovered that Victoria survived the incident and in fact,' I faltered, had to force the words out, 'was subsequently

181

charged with causing their death.'

Josie nodded. 'May I ask how you came by that information?'

'Louise, my other aunt, who died this year, had left a letter for me that has only just come to light. She said that the family had covered up the real story to protect me.'

'And how do you feel about that?'

'Well,' I said, 'mostly I'm relieved now I can think about it rationally. I know that sounds terribly selfish, but imagine what growing up would have like knowing that your grandparents were killed by their own daughter. I can't think how I would have dealt with that knowledge as a child, it's hard enough now.'

'I'm sure the family acted in your best interests. So what did you actually glean from the newspaper accounts?'

'Ileana and I went to the library to look through the old records,' I said, thinking as I answered her, that so far instead of me asking the questions, Josie was definitely making the running - the result of a career as a journalist I supposed - not that I wasn't more relieved than put out.

'We found reports of a gas explosion onboard The Maiden,' I went on. 'Victoria survived. My grandparents were killed. Following investigations into the accident Victoria was arrested on a double murder charge. You'll understand it all came as a terrible shock to me. I'm afraid I didn't take the news very well, and we didn't get any further.'

'It must have been devastating for you.'

I nodded.

Ileana reached out and touched my hand. 'Daysee very brave,' she said.

'Yes,' Josie said, looking thoughtful, 'I'd say brave and resourceful.'

I felt my face flush. 'So I'm hoping you'll be able to fill in the details,' I said quickly, to cover my embarrassment.

Twenty-one

'The first thing I did after reading your letter,' Josie said, 'was to dig out my cuttings and refresh my memory. I always kept a file for the big stories I covered on the Gazette as I had aspirations of moving on to the Nationals. At least, I fostered those hopes in the early days; I'd have to admit there came a time when I decided it was better to be a big fish in a small pond than the other way round, but keeping my records was routine by then.'

'So you have a note of the whole case, even after it came to court?'

'Oh yes,' Josie agreed. 'I've got the file in the car if you want to look at it. Not that I ever forgot the nub of it, being one of the biggest stories I ever worked on.'

'I must admit I don't relish banner headlines,' I said. 'I'd prefer to talk about it if you don't mind. Unless you think you won't remember everything. Thirty years is a long time.'

'My colleagues used to say I had the hide of a rhinoceros and the memory of an elephant, not very flattering but I couldn't really argue with the description. Anyway, as I mentioned, I did go through the case again before I came to meet you. I could start by recapping the details you already know about if that would make things easier for you?'

I nodded.

'Well,' she began, 'The Maiden was a few miles out of harbour when the explosion occurred. There were three people onboard, Victoria and her parents, Jack and Reva. The lifeboat put out from Holworth and subsequently picked Victoria up from the water -'

'Victoria very lucky being saved.' Ileana interrupted. 'With burning and many wounds from explosion even excellent swimmer may drowning.'

'As a matter of fact that was one of the salient points of the investigation, the question of how she'd come through it sustaining only minor injuries - concussion, a couple of cracked ribs and

183

superficial burns and contusions - as I recall. Experts were of the opinion that being caught in a blast of such intensity that the boat was virtually reduced to splinters, would have resulted in much more serious injuries. They would have expected to see signs of lung, ear and eye damage, abdominal ruptures, and penetration wounds from flying debris. Victoria was pretty well unscathed in those terms.'

'My grandparents...?'

'I'm afraid only body parts were recovered. I'm pleased to say The Gazette was fairly tactful about that: we didn't wallow in the gory details then.'

'It must have been a terrible explosion.'

'It was. You could still see the plume of smoke coming up from oil and wreckage out at sea hours afterwards, and vessels that had been in the vicinity when the explosion occurred, reported burning debris dropping out of the sky like ash from a volcano.'

'Newspaper saying gas leaking making explosion. Why they thinking Victoria doing bad thing?'

'You do have a way of asking the pertinent question,' Josie said, looking at Ileana. 'That came out at the trial. Victoria had opened the gas tap before they left port. It was stated the bilges would have been flooded with it by the time the smell reached them on deck.'

'I can hardly take this in,' I said feebly.

'It must be difficult for you. Are you sure you want to go on with it?'

'Not at all sure, but what option do I have?'

'Perhaps it will help you to know that when the case came to court Victoria's legal representatives submitted she was unfit to plead.' Josie glanced from one to other of us. 'I should explain that. It means the person acting on Victoria's behalf said that she was unable to understand the charges against her because of her mental illness.'

'Victoria was mad,' I said. It was a statement not a question.

'I suppose it depends on the definition of 'mad'. Victoria was certainly seriously deranged: words like psycho and schizo were being bandied about pretty freely in the newspapers, but I don't think those in charge ever came up with a precise diagnosis, at least not during the trial. It did come to light that Victoria had been

184

exhibiting chronic symptoms for some time without them being recognised or treated, which I gather could often happen in those days. Anyway ...'

'Sorry,' I said interrupting, 'but I don't understand. If her symptoms were so severe, why wasn't anything done about them?'

'I can only tell you what I learned at the time. Apparently people could suffer for years without diagnosis or treatment then. We must hope things have improved now; it was a long time ago.

'How illness making Victoria into bad person?' Ileana asked. 'I knowing how being hot angry making people do bad things, but making plan for gas leak to blow up boat and killing parents is,' she paused and looked at me. 'How you saying, thinking a long time before doing?'

'Do you mean plan ahead?'

'Yes,' she nodded. 'Make plan before.'

'We'd call that premeditate,' I said.

Ileana nodded again. 'Why illness making Victoria premeditating kill Jack and Reva?'

'I see what you're asking,' Josie said. 'You mean it wasn't done in the heat of the moment. But you know, to some extent it was. It came out that Victoria was bearing a huge grudge against her parents. Think how it might be if you combine an overwhelming feeling of resentment with mood and thoughts distorted by illness; it's easy enough to see how it could happen.'

'She didn't care that she was likely to be killed herself?' I asked.

'They said it was very unlikely she ever considered the danger to her own life.'

'I still not understanding about illness making Victoria having grudge to mamma and papa,' Ileana murmured.

'Well,' Josie said, 'I gathered it was a chicken and egg situation. Victoria's resentment had been festering over the years with their opposition to her affair with a local boy and the illness may have been the catalyst that pushed her over the top. Or it may have been the other way round. Frankly, the medical evidence was couched in so many ifs, buts and maybes it was hard to tell.'

My mind was in turmoil as Josie said this. Dozens of questions were in need of immediate answers: I didn't know where to start. Questions about the grudge and the man Josie had mentioned were forming on my lips, when I realised Josie was staring at me and Ileana was looking decidedly worried. 'I'm sorry,' I said, pushing back my chair and scrambling to my feet, 'you'll have to excuse me while I fetch a glass of water.'

It was quite a while before I rejoined Ileana and Josie. I really felt as though my brain was in danger of imploding with the pressure of it all. I remember standing at the sink running cold water over my wrists: when that didn't help, I filled the bowl with more cold water and plunged my face in: after that, I tipped ice cubes from the freezer into a towel and applied them to my forehead. Dripping, but calmer, I finally went back for the rest of the grisly details.

Ileana and Josie were drinking tea and chatting. Well, Josie was talking and Ileana was listening politely. I managed a smile, thinking how much I'd learned to rely on Ileana's good judgment – it hadn't occurred to me she'd let a stray word slip or would confide in a stranger. It wasn't that I didn't trust Josie – I hadn't known her long enough to form an opinion – I just wasn't taking any chances, she was a journalist after all, albeit a retired one. And as I've said, I wasn't ready for the world to know I was the child of a murderess: the niece maybe, but not the daughter.

'I know I asked you earlier, but are you certain you want to go on with this?' Josie asked as I rejoined them at the table. 'You're looking very pale.'

'I'm fine,' I said. 'Anyway, how can I back off now?'

'Mm.' Josie didn't look or sound convinced.

'Daysee must knowing what happening to Victoria,' Ileana said, breaking into the exchange. 'If you going and not telling Daysee, she worrying more and we having find other way of knowing what happened.'

'If you really are sure …' Josie hesitated, and then easing herself into a more comfortable position, said, 'I'll explain first about the plea procedure. It's long-winded rather than complicated. The burden of proof rests with the defendant who submits that he or she is unfit to plead. The court is allowed to defer consideration of the plea until the close of the case for the prosecution, which means that a defendant can be convicted, even if the jury is not satisfied beyond reasonable doubt that he or she is fit to be tried. This is what happened to Victoria. The jury decided the evidence presented by the prosecution established that she committed what is termed legally the 'actus reus' of the offence, that's to say she did the actual deed. I don't see how they could have done otherwise, given her statement.'

I mopped at the drips running down my forehead from my improvised icepack and asked, 'Are you saying she admitted killing her parents?'

'She denied it when they first brought her in. Of course this was before anyone realised how ill she was. She stuck to her story of Jack and Reva going below to investigate the smell of gas and that being more or less all she knew of it before she found herself in the sea.'

'Why she changing mind, saying she did bad thing?' Ileana asked. 'Is police torturing her?'

Josie looked surprised. 'I'd be the first to agree our police force is far from perfect, but in general I'd say we breed bullies rather than tyrants.'

'You were telling us about Victoria changing her statement,' I said.

'Ah yes. I'm of the opinion that interrogation techniques in those days might be regarded as robust,' she glanced at Ileana, 'and there was certainly no doctor present at the initial interviews - the way the Prosecution presented it, the breakthrough came when it was put to her that she was lucky to have escaped with her life. "Luck, she was alleged to have said indignantly, hadn't come into it. It had been due to her exemplary planning and exceptional physical prowess."'

In the wake of this pronouncement, I could feel my chest tightening and my temperature rising again. 'I don't know about you two,' I said, jumping up, 'but I'm in desperate need of fresh air. Shall we go down to the sea?'

Naturally, I'd forgotten every word about Josie's dodgy hip until she reached for her stick, but she insisted she could manage.

While I was rooting around for something to sit on, Josie went to the bathroom, and Ileana made a flask of coffee. Thus prepared we set out for the beach.

Other than Josie admiring the scenery on the walk down, we

didn't talk much until we were settled, like three old biddies on a Sunday outing, on the assortment of foldaway chairs I'd unearthed in the shed.

'I suppose,' I said, as I stared into my coffee, 'that it was then they realised how ill she was?'

'They may have, but you know, it wasn't in their interests to acknowledge it: not until she'd made a revised statement. And my goodness, once they'd found the trigger, she went off like a machine gun.'

'Wasn't anyone with her? Where were Ellen and Louise? Didn't she have a solicitor?'

'She wouldn't speak to her sisters. She said they were plotting with Jack and Reva against her. The solicitor didn't have a ghost's chance, as I understand it. Advised her of her rights and not to say any more, and that was about it before she showed him the door. They got the works down on paper while he was still huffing and puffing about a doctor. I don't imagine they'd get away with it today - although one does still hear about falsified statements.' She paused. 'Not that I'm saying her statement was false, but I'd say it was come by dubiously. She was seriously disturbed and didn't have any protection.'

'So what was her explanation,' I asked. 'What had driven her to do such a terrible thing?'

'I don't know how much you know about your grandparents. At the trial they were presented as a wealthy, middle class couple; their money had come down from Reva's side of the family, Jack was a Magistrate and Commodore of the local yacht club. They were respectable and respected amongst their set in the community.'

'What is 'set'?' Ileana asked.

'I think Josie means a group of people who have similar interests,' I said. 'But it implies a kind of narrowness, as if people outside that particular 'set' wouldn't have the same views.'

Josie nodded. 'Thirty years ago this area was far less developed than it is now; even with the new council estate that had been built in the teeth of the opposition led by your grandfather, it was still very much a backwater, with, in some quarters anyway, startlingly reactionary ideas.'

Ileana gave me an enquiring glance.

'Reactionary means backward-looking,' I said, interpreting her question, 'like someone who doesn't have a modern outlook.'

'You two do know each other well,' Josie remarked. 'You must have been friends a long while. How -?'

'Ages,' I said before she could ask. 'So you're saying my grandfather was a prominent local bigot.' I said, and it came more angrily than I intended.

'No. Not at all,' Josie said calmly. 'I'm trying to explain that he was a popular, respected man within his own social class, and that Victoria's association with the son of a convicted felon – a felon moreover convicted on more than one occasion, by the bench over which Jack presided, was simply not acceptable.'

'Oh God,' I said. 'I can see it coming.'

'And so could everybody else – after it had come.'

'Jack and Reva forbade Victoria's affair with someone they believed would sully their good name. What was his name?'

'Marlon Boyce.'

'OH MY GOD!' I said slowly. 'Marlon Boyce. What a name. I can just imagine how that went down. "She, 'I'm going to marry Marlon. I don't care what you say.' He, 'I forbid it. You're under age and you can't marry without my consent.'"'

'You've got it in a nut shell,' Josie said. 'And actually there was plenty more said about him being the dregs of society; his father in and out of prison; his youngest brother AWOL from the Army; the other two totally beyond the pale. And there were a string of sisters that no one had a good word to say for, as well. The irony was that Marlon had got a job as soon as he'd left school and was working as a tool-maker for a small engineering firm.'

'And after the row,' I asked, 'what happened then?'

'Victoria stormed out and went to find Marlon. She turned up at his work and caused a scene demanding to see him immediately. She was in such a state his boss had to let him leave, then and there.'

'I thinking Marlon not dregs,' Ileana said. 'I thinking he love Victoria.'

'Yes,' Josie agreed. 'I thought so too. And he stood by her, right through the trial.'

'You still haven't told us what she did,' I said.

Josie sighed. 'I have been putting it off,' she said, 'but there seems to be so much to tell.'

'One thing I don't understand is how Victoria came to be out sailing with her parents after the bust-up they'd had.'

'Marlon had calmed her down by saying they'd run away together and marry in Scotland. I'm sure he was sincere about it. He'd told her he needed a week or two to set up a job and find somewhere for them to live. In the meantime she was to persuade her parents she'd given him up. The trip was to cement that idea. He knew it had been quite a while since Victoria had shown any inclination to go sailing with them, although she was an extremely competent sailor, and he surmised correctly that a reawakening of interest would do the trick. What Marlon didn't know was how ill Victoria was.'

'Is Marlon not seeing Victoria's bad thoughts?'

'Yes and no. He,' Josie hesitated. 'He-'

'What? What else is crawling out from under this bloody stone?' I shrieked. I couldn't help it. Honestly. Luckily we'd finished the coffee or it could have been a messy business. 'It's too long-drawn out,' I protested. 'For God's sake cut to the chase.'

'The thing is,' Josie said, 'Victoria had been using acid – you might remember it as LSD, a drug popular with hippies in the swinging sixties - so Marlon was used to her mood swings.'

I swore then. I don't usually swear and by the time I'd finished I guess I'd used up my life's worth of imprecations. Ileana and Josie just sat there with their mouths hanging open – two old biddies having their outing ruined by a ranting, foul-mouthed fish-wife.

I was exhausted by the time I'd run out of steam and neither Ileana nor Josie said a word about my outburst. After a while Ileana collected up the chairs and we went wearily back to the house.

Changing venues again didn't really help. After the shortest of respites I was at it again like a dog with a bone, frantically gnawing to get to the marrow.

'Please just tell me,' I said, 'as bluntly as you like. Don't try to protect me. I have to get to the end of this. We'll try not to interrupt.'

'I'm inclined to agree with you. We do need to finalise this. I told you on the beach that Victoria was taking LSD. Again you should understand that the abuse of drugs was probably a side effect of her disorder. As, most likely, was her utter obsession with the Boyce boy; so obsessed she thought killing her parents was the only way to get what she wanted. Incidentally the court was satisfied that Marlon Boyce was not a drug user. Or her supplier.'

'That's it, is it?' I asked abruptly. 'All the factors that led to her doing what she did?'

'I believe so,' Josie said.

'Telling what happening next please,' Ileana said.

'The thrust of Victoria's statement was that her parents were overjoyed when she suggested they took The Maiden out together. Just the three of them to show there were no hard feelings on either side. It was all there in her confession – how stupid they were – how easily taken in - their docile little girl who'd given up that bad-lot she'd fallen in with: and the bragging about getting one over on Ellen and Louise – who were apparently 'wetting their knickers' at the prospect.

A day or two later they set off. As soon as they were underway, Victoria went below, ostensibly to use the heads, and opened the gas tap. Obviously it was tremendously risky; Jack or Reva could have gone below at any time, smelt the gas and averted the whole plan. But luck, if you could call it that, was with Victoria. They were a fair way out before the smell reached them. Jack went below. When he called out, Reva bent down to answer him. Victoria gave her a hefty shove from behind, pitching her mother down the stairs to the cabin.'

I couldn't suppress a gasp as Josie said this.

'Oh nothing,' I said as they both glanced at me, 'only I fell down the companionway myself recently. Please go on.'

Josie began speaking again. 'With chaos below, Victoria jumped out of the cockpit and climbed over the safety rail to balance on the stern. Holding on with one hand, with the other she pulled a mini flare out of her pocket, broke off the cap and tossed it forwards through the companionway hatch, letting go of her hand-hold and thrusting herself backwards at the same time. It was a miracle she wasn't killed too.' Josie stopped, took a deep breath, ran her palm across her forehead and leaned back in her seat.

When it came down to it, I suppose the 'how' didn't make much impression on me. I already knew the outcome and the prolonged explanation of the 'why' had in some way taken the edge off that final act, which may be what Josie had intended, like the splutter of a damp squib against the blaze of a rocket.

I thought it was over – at least I'd got round to wondering, as obliquely as I could, if Josie had had an ulterior motive, like a follow-up article or worse, in coming to see me and she'd reassured me that it had been a matter of principle for her to set the record straight for me, and I was inclined to take her at her word - when I realised I still didn't know what had happened to Victoria.

'You said at the beginning that although the court accepted that Victoria was unfit to plead, she was still convicted. I presume you meant convicted of murder. What ...? She wasn't-?' I couldn't say it.

Josie reached across the table and took my hand. 'Victoria was sent to a special hospital.'

'A special hospital,' I repeated. 'What sort of special hospital?' And then the penny dropped. 'You mean Broadmoor, don't you?' I said.

'You wanting eat now?' Ileana asked, as Josie's car vanished up the lane. 'Or maybe phoning hospital first?'

'You're reading my mind,' I said.

'I must knowing quickly if it being my mamma,' she said. 'You knowing number?'

'Haven't a clue. Don't even know where it is. We'll have to see if Directory Enquiries can help.'

Of course that wasn't as easy as it sounds. The demise of the old 192 number had passed me by and I hadn't the least idea what the new one was. When we did get hold of an operator from BT, he couldn't help without knowing the location. And so it went on. I don't suppose it took more than half a dozen calls to end up with the Communications Office for the West London Health Authority, which, I learned, administers Broadmoor.

Obviously they couldn't tell me anything on the phone. The

procedure, I ascertained, was to apply in writing under the provisions of The Data Protection Act of 1998, to the Medical Records Office of the Hospital, which they said was located in Crowthorne, Berkshire. I was also advised to enclose a form of identification, either a copy of my birth certificate, or my passport or marriage certificate.

I guess it was when I put the phone down, the worst of the thoughts crowded in. Broadmoor - the name alone strikes fear into your heart. Everyone has heard of it: the hospital for the criminally insane. An institution I imagine as being a cross between Bedlam and Newgate.

Images from Hogarth and Dickens were filling my head when I heard a distant voice saying I was looking very pale again and please to drinking water she'd brought for me.

Water didn't help. Broadmoor. That was where they held people like The Yorkshire Ripper and The Moors Murderer.

And my mother.

I can't think how I would have dealt with this latest trauma without Ileana. Imagine trying to get to grips with this sort of ordeal on your own. As it was I could feel myself losing control. I know I was ranting about evil bitches getting their just desserts, when Ileana said calmly, 'Victoria having very bad illness, making her not knowing what being right or wrong; nobody helping her get better, not even seeing she sick, except maybe Marlon, but he not being doctor. You not to swearing and saying Victoria like the devil. Is okay you being sad about bad things, but must understanding what happening and not being so angry.'

I guess I snivelled some more about my hard lot, but Ileana's words had taken the heat out of my whining and after a while I buckled down and wrote the letter. 'Another letter for the Davenport annals,' I exclaimed, as I put down my pen and went to find my recently acquired birth certificate.

Which was when I suffered the next shock.

'What was the address we got for Broadmoor?' I asked Ileana as I came back into the room.

She picked it out from the papers on the table and read carefully, 'Crowt horney.'

193

'Look at this,' I commanded, thrusting the certificate under her nose.

She studied the form for some seconds.

'Well?' I asked.

'Place of hospital is same name as being on birth certificate,' she said.

I collapsed onto the chair next to her. 'You realise what this means?' I said.

She shook her head.

'It means I was born in Broadmoor,' I said.

Poor Ileana, I thought, as I lolled on the chair, after all she's been through, now she finds herself shacked up with someone in their own living hell. Instead of me helping her, she's supporting me.

This time it was a glass of brandy she put in my hand. 'I see you see I'm too far gone for water,' I muttered, as I took a hefty slurp.

'Is good for shock,' she said and giggled.

I was mystified. 'Why are you looking so pleased with yourself?' I asked.

'I not having shock, but having brandy also,' she said. 'Now, you sitting thinking what mattering where you born; who is real mamma; why is all stuff coming bing-bong on head, you still being Daysee. Daysee, who coming alone to bad place to find who killing Floyd. And finding me and saving me. And bringing me to home and being my true friend.' She pecked me lightly on the cheek. 'We knowing how bad things being for each. Also we knowing how good and strong being together. So, I making dinner, then we thinking what we doing tomorrow.'

And that was the way it was. After dinner and a couple more brandies we meandered up the lane and posted the letter. Then, having decided against the longish walk to the pub, meandered down the lane again, had a few more brandies and fell into bed.

An Honest Trade
March 1834

Wells awaits word that his family have arrived safely in Madeira.

Matters deteriorate on the plantation. Life is miserable. The curing house, the sick house and the dwelling houses are in bad order. Two children die in one day. The Negroes are sullen and resentful. Punishments of lashings, solitary confinement and days in the stocks make little difference.

Wells knows that it will be many months before he has word of the indentured workers he has requested and in the meanwhile there is insufficient labour to plant the new sets.

Wells receives a report that 'o-be-ah', a superstitious belief, which involves sorcery is being practiced amongst some of the Negroes who have refused to abandon their African paganism.

He sends for Fortune Proivil, who is a good Christian man, and tells him great efforts must be made to stamp out the practice; he must seek out the perpetrators and bring them to him (Wells) for punishment. But Wells notices a change in the headman. Fortune is sullen and ill at ease. When pressed by Wells Fortune states that he has heard that a noxious charm has been put into the ground to cause the crop to fail and to bring sickness and death to the plantation.

On reflection Wells puts the change in Fortune's attitude down to his primitive credulity.

In addition to the worry and aggravation arising from the management of the estate, Wells is mired in complications arising from the three young women he has chosen for his pleasure.

Alice, demoted due to her insolence in rebutting Wells, and her man, Jimmy, have committed suicide by taking poison. Nelly Proivil has been taken away from the plantation and is believed to be hiding somewhere in the town. Lionoria has been sentenced to three days in the stocks for her continuing insubordination on Beausejour Plantation.

Twenty-two

I don't know what sort of time-scale one would normally expect when setting out to resolve a query with an official body, but the word 'prompt' doesn't immediately spring to mind. Which was why I was surprised to receive a formal acknowledgement of my letter by return post, and even more taken aback to receive the full reply by the end of the week, during which brief interlude we'd hardly had time to set Ileana up with her first English lessons.

Obviously there were certain pitfalls to be considered when selecting a tutor for Ileana. Presuming tuition would be on a one to one basis, how inquisitive was the instructor likely to be and what cover story could we devise for Ileana? We were mired in developing a complex tale about her being in the country to learn English whilst working as an au pair for a professional couple with one child, who, we decided, were to reside several miles away from wherever the tutor happened to live. But the more we tried to tie up the loose ends, the more problems arose. How would she deal with questions about her own background? What were the details of her working day? How would she remember all the gumph she'd have to invent on the spur of the moment?

'No,' I was saying as I ran my finger down the Business Column, 'I can't help thinking it's too risky. Maybe you should wait until the autumn term starts at the College. You could do 'English as a Foreign Language' there and you'd be in a class with lots of others so wouldn't stick out, unless,' my finger slid to a halt, 'unless we could tackle it differently. There's this ad here. See.' She peered over my shoulder as I read, 'English Graduate requires temporary employment whilst waiting permanent position. Anything reasonable considered.'

We telephoned. It transpired that the English Graduate was called Greg. He'd qualified a year ago and had immediately left England to seek his fortune in the USA, where he'd been able to secure enough cash-in-hand employment to tide him over. However, without a green card he'd not been able to obtain a proper job and had returned to GB to secure the necessary documentation. As soon as it came through he'd be back to the States, where, he'd added, using a rather more colloquial expression, a stunning American beauty eagerly awaited his return. He sounded perfect. We agreed to meet tout de suite.

Greg was renting a bed-sit on the top floor of a crumbling, multi-occupancy Victorian villa on the outskirts of town. Numerous stairs and any number of anonymous doors, through which a startlingly disparate range of musical taste became apparent, divided up the house. Greg seemed pleasant enough and on first impression too self-engrossed to want to get involved with Ileana's personal circumstances, which couldn't have suited us better. We agreed that it would be a pay as you go arrangement since Greg hoped to be back to the States armed with required papers at the drop of a hat.

'Hell,' he said, when I asked him about his prospects there, 'anyone can make a buck in the black economy particularly if you're not too bothered about staying on the right side of the law. Which is okay in the short term but I didn't relish spending the rest of my life looking over my shoulder.'

We agreed Ileana would start by having three lessons a week whenever we could fit them in. The initial lesson would be the next afternoon, by which time Greg would have obtained whatever teaching aids he required and have an idea of what books Ileana would need.

On the way home Ileana and I talked logistics. I said that until we knew Greg better, I'd drive her and wait outside. She said no, too much trouble, she going on bus, and I said no, not too much trouble, she going with me.

Ileana was immersed in her new textbooks and I was planning a weekend sail to the Isle of Wight when the reply came from Broadmoor. It thanked me for my enquiry, returned my birth certificate, quoted the Data Protection Act and advised me that my mother had been transferred from Broadmoor to a Medium Secure Unit in 1993, and that a copy of my letter had been forwarded to that facility, to which I should address any further correspondence.

I skimmed over the sheet of general information they'd enclosed with the letter. Apparently Broadmoor was one of three high security units for patients with mental illness who require treatment in a secure environment. I read that three hundred and twenty six patients were currently in confinement, of whom forty-nine were women. The average stay was apparently nine years. What was I supposed to deduct from the fact that Victoria had been held there for eighteen years? Was she twice as ill as most patients? Two times more dangerous? Double the risk to the outside world? Crossly I tossed the paper aside. I couldn't think why they'd included it. Victoria hadn't been there for years and surely they hadn't imagined I was about to take up philanthropic prison visiting. I was having enough trouble steeling myself for my forthcoming appointment with my mother, wherever she was currently incarcerated.

Instead of sailing to the Isle of Wight in Lady Louella, we went to Humberside by train - but not until we had got over a couple more hurdles. The first was relatively easy to deal with. I was on the telephone to the unit to which Victoria had been moved, and was waiting to be transferred to the Patients' Welfare Officer, when Ileana whispered she had a small pain and was going to rest for a while.

When I'd ascertained that Victoria had been moved on to yet another institution and my letter had been forwarded to that establishment, I hung up and went to find Ileana.

She was curled up on her bed and crying into her pillow.

'Where does it hurt?' I asked as I knelt down by the side of the bed. 'When did it come on? Have you had it before?'

'Pain is not so bad,' she mumbled, 'but bleeding and having nothing to put is not good. I sorry I...' Her voice trailed off.

The problem is that I've lived on my own for such a long time, other people's needs tend to pass me by, although there's really no excuse for having become quite so insular. One thing that did come out of this episode, once we sorted out where supplies were kept in the bathroom, was that it brought home to me that Ileana didn't have a single penny to call her own.

'You have to have some cash for your personal needs,' I said, when we were settled downstairs again. 'I simply don't want you having to ask me for everything.'

'No, Daysee, I not wanting money. I liking you buying what we needing.'

'Well,' I said, 'that's fine as far as it goes. But supposing something untoward happened to me –'

She interrupted. 'Is 'untoward' meaning bad?'

'More or less. Inconvenient anyway. Where was I? Oh yes. Suppose something happened –'

She interrupted again. 'Not to thinking about untoward happenings.'

I laboured on. 'We can't take account of everything. Look what I've discovered about my family in the last few days; who knows what else is about to crawl out of the woodwork?' She opened her mouth to butt in for the umpteenth time but I held up a restraining hand. 'Before you manage to side-track me again, that was a rhetorical question.'

'What –?'

'A rhetorical question is one that doesn't need an answer. I'm trying to say that you'd be in difficulty if anything cropped up and I wasn't around. We have to make some sort of financial arrangement for you.'

'No. I not staying if you not being here.'

'Illy,' I said, 'please try to understand. In addition to Lady Lou, I have this house and a sizeable sum in the bank. You might even call me an heiress. An heiress to a fortune made from slaving. Try to imagine what that feels like. My own flesh and blood traded in people: took them from their native lands, subjugated them and kept them in servitude, all to line their own pockets. And I'm still living, very comfortably, on the proceeds. So until I decide what I should do about it, you might help me salve my conscience by letting me make you an allowance. It's not as though I've got anyone else to share anything with.'

She listened to all this without comment only saying, 'Why you calling me different name?' as I drew to a close.

'Pardon?'

'You calling me "Illy".'

'So I did. Not that I imagine you'd dream of trying to distract me from what I was talking about, I suppose I'll have to try to explain about nicknames before we go any further.'

She grinned. 'What does nickname mean?'

By the time I'd finished that explanation, I had, of course, lost the thread of my original argument and could only summon up a wishy-washy proposal about her at least having pocket money. Seeing her take a deep breath, no doubt to embark on some new diversionary ploy, I had a flash of inspiration. 'What was it you said in Romanian the other day?' I asked, apropos of nothing we'd been talking about and putting the boot neatly on the other foot.

She looked at me blankly.

'When I was grumpy and you were upset?'

She flushed and looked away. 'I not remembering.'

'Don't give me that. You remember perfectly well. Come on. Out with it.'

'I saying only old Romanian words.'

'Which were?'

She muttered something under her breath, not looking at me.

'Which means?'

'I cannot saying. I not knowing all English words.'

'I'm sure you know enough.'

'No.'

'Try,' I said. 'I'll bear with you.'

'Is about saying good things but ...'

'Spit it out,' I said.

'I not meaning. I very upset.'

'I know,' I said.

'Is like, with tongue he giving you sweetness and with tail he plucking out your eyes.'

'Oh,' I said. 'I see.'

'Daysee ...'

'No. I deserved it. That's another thing you've got to let me make amends for. Not just for you, for Floyd as well. I was unkind to you and downright pigheaded with him. He'd be alive today if I hadn't been so obstinate.'

'Daysee...?'

'Yes?'

'If you really wanting, you giving me little money sometimes, and maybe one day I making special place in garden for Floyd.'

So that at least was one hurdle over. The second turned out to be higher. My initial thought was to set up a bank account for Ileana. But new bank accounts, I discovered, require identification documents. I was mulling over the possibility of opening a second account in my name and making Illy an independent signatory to it, when I decided to cut my losses and give it to her in cash. 'It's not as if it's a fortune,' I said as I handed the envelope over. 'You'll have to keep it under the mattress until we can think of a better arrangement.'

'I telling you I not needing money,' she said.

'Don't start that again. Remember Floyd's memorial fund. All the same,' I added, 'I can't help noticing the number of dead-ends we've already run into because you don't have any papers.'

The next step was to organise the trip to Hull. My first call was to Bewdeth House, where I'd been advised Victoria was currently being held. After a couple of false starts I was put through to the Charge Nurse on duty. She seemed surprised when I asked if I could arrange a visit.

'Of course we're delighted for our residents to have visitors. So many never see anyone from one year to the next.'

I heard the reproach in her voice and said I'd anticipated some restrictions, to which she replied, sounding even more reproving, 'I can't imagine why you might think that. Bewdeth House is no different to any other nursing home for residents with mental health problems.'

After mumbling that I didn't know what to expect, I said I hoped to be there within the next few days, to which comments she imparted a few basic directions and advised me I could visit anytime between 10am and 7pm, seven days a week.

'She didn't even ask me who I was,' I remarked to Ileana when I came off the phone.

'Much time has passing since Victoria doing bad thing, maybe this place not knowing what happening then.'

'Who knows? Anyway now I've got to tackle our travel arrangements.'

'We not sailing in Lady Lou?'

I smiled. 'Nice idea, but it would take too long. I need to get this over and done with.'

Half an hour later when my blood pressure must have gone up by several degrees, I decided that one day in the not too distant future, I simply had to master the computer. Life is just too short to waste any more of it in a frustrating telephonic queue for National Rail Enquiries.

We went by train from Waterloo to Hull and asked at the taxi rank outside the station to be taken to a decent hotel. The cab duly dropped us off at a Travel Lodge on the Beverley Road.

I'm not much of a shopper, tending to wear my clothes into the ground before I think of replacing them, so having a couple of hours on our hands before the shops closed was a good opportunity to have a look round the town centre and add a few items to Ileana's scant wardrobe.

Sometime later we toted our goodies back to the hotel, freshened up and went out to find somewhere to eat.

We rounded off the night in our hotel room, lying on our beds watching cable television, with a bottle of red wine and assorted packets of savouries to keep our strength up.

First impressions of Bewdeth House were uninspiring - a low-level, municipal-type building, with a ramp leading up to the door. It was fronted by a parking area and a few blades of grass and was on the outskirts of a sprawling estate dominated by a sixties style tower block. And the weather didn't make it any better, grey skies and drizzle. I couldn't help wrinkling up my nose as we climbed out of the taxi.

'Why you making face?' Ileana asked.

'It's not a very nice area, is it?' I said.

'Is okay. Many people living in tall building and all around. I thinking not all having much money. I knowing many like places in Romania.'

'I suppose it's possible,' I said as we walked up the ramp and rang the bell, 'that people with mental health problems aren't aware of their surroundings, but I can't believe such a drab setting does anyone any good.'

Once inside my opinion was confirmed - grubbyish, smellyish and depressing. An elderly gentleman shuffled past on a zimmer frame; another stood motionless staring into space. I felt my spirits flag, and that was before I met the person who purported to be my mother. I'd hardly finished explaining who we were there to see to the harassed-looking assistant who'd let us in, before we were speeding along the corridor after her. We followed her into the patients' lounge, and before I had time to take it in, she'd stridden over to one of the occupied armchairs set round the walls.

'You should realise,' she said, making no attempt to lower her voice, 'Victoria has serious mental health problems and is inclined to bouts of violent temper. Try not to upset her.' She turned to her patient. 'Wake up, Victoria, there's some nice young ladies come to see you.'

Not that there was any need for introductions on either side. The woman she'd called Victoria was clearly well past the need for formalities. She was slumped sideways in her chair, a thin drool of saliva slithering from the corner of her open mouth, traces of her last meal dribbled down her front, one trouser leg pushed up above her painfully thin knee. Her hair, though lank and greying at the temples, was still the family red, and the eyes that glanced emptily up were unmistakably blue - faded and unfocused - but blue all the same.

So much for any false hopes I was harbouring about Ellen being my mother after all. No birth certificate could have proved so effective. The blue eyes were conclusive. I was Victoria's daughter. Which was why, I realised, as I continued to stare at the betraying characteristics, Josie Pimm had looked so startled when she first saw me – she'd seen the relationship as clearly as I could now.

It was a blessing, I thought, that the care attendant, who was wiping Victoria's mouth with a scrap of mucky tissue she'd dug out of her overall pocket and telling her to sit up nicely and talk to her visitors was far too preoccupied to make the connection.

'That's better,' she commented, as she levered Victoria upright and wedged her in place with a couple of cushions. 'I'll leave you to chat now.'

I had no idea where to begin. Suddenly struck dumb, I was shuffling from foot to foot and glancing round the room at the other residents, when Ileana whispered something about me not being able to talk properly standing up. In a moment she'd fetched a couple of chairs from a stack she'd spotted in the corner and was chivvying me onto the one she'd put down in front of Victoria.

'Speaking to Victoria now,' she commanded.

'Victoria,' I said. As I spoke her name the faded blue eyes opened and she looked at me. I kept very still. Were her eyes clearing? Was the focus sharpening? Slowly I put my hand up to my hair. My red hair. Her gaze followed my hand. Gently I patted my hair. Just the once. There was the briefest instant when I thought her eyes flickered, and then they drifted away. Relief or some other emotion flooded through me. I took a deep breath, blinked and lowered my hand.

When I glanced at Ileana I discovered she was watching me intently.

'You staring at Victoria,' she whispered. 'You think she knowing you?'

'No chance,' I said shrugging. 'The lights are on, but there's no-one in.'

Ileana took a moment to digest this. Her eyes rounded when she worked out what I'd meant. 'Not to saying such bad thing,' she whispered, sounding shocked.

'I'm sorry,' I whispered back, 'but I simply don't feel anything for this woman other than slight revulsion. It doesn't help that I've been expecting a monster and I'm confronted with this pathetic shell of a person.'

'Must remembering she having big problem in head for long, long time. Maybe not many talking kindly to her.'

'I know all that but I still can't help it.'

At Ileana's insistence we stayed about half an hour. It seemed like years.

'We'll go now,' I whispered to Ileana after I'd muttered a few words about the weather and the food and the people looking after her, and received no reaction from Victoria at all.

Ileana shook her head. 'Should trying more,' she said. 'Victoria very sick. You talking about her sisters, seeing if she remembering.'

'I don't know what to say.' Which was an understatement. Anyway, the longer I stayed, the more doubts I had about mentioning the past at all - what good would it do to remind her? It seemed to me, albeit from a totally non-professional viewpoint, that it was a godsend if her mind had blotted everything out. From what I could see she was in her own world, which hopefully was untroubled by her past sins. Would it help her to discover I was her long-lost daughter: the daughter who had presumably been wrenched from her bosom within hours of the birth as a result of the terrible crime she'd committed? What good would it do this shrunken old – old: that stopped me in my tracks. How old was she? I did a rapid calculation and was horrified when I came up with the answer – fifty-one or two at the most. My mind went into overdrive. How old had Mum been when she died? When had her illness set in? I couldn't remember. And what about Louise? More calculations. Answer, she'd only been in her mid sixties. I could feel my throat tightening. Were all three sisters victims of the same illness? Was it a genetic thing - something I was likely to inherit? Did I want to know?

By this time I was desperate to get away. It's not easy looking at what derangement might mean for you, full in the face. 'Time to go,' I said abruptly, checking my watch. 'The taxi will be waiting.'

'You wanting asking doctor about Victoria?' Ileana asked as we made for the exit.

'No,' I said. 'Definitely not.'

In the taxi Ileana asked when I'd be visiting Victoria again. Her question startled me. 'I wasn't thinking of going again,' I replied. 'As far as I can see there's only one thing to be thankful for – although Victoria undoubtedly gave birth to me, Ellen was and always will be my mother.'

Ileana didn't reply. Didn't need to, I could see it written all over her face. She'd sown the seed and would leave it up to my conscience to reap it. I could only hope my conscience wouldn't come up to scratch.

By this time I'd worked myself up into a real sweat. Worrying about future dementia and agonizing about the past I was in serious danger of complete melt down, consequently it was a massive relief when it suddenly occurred to me that Hull had been one of the towns Floyd had visited in the course of his research.

'I've just remembered,' I said, 'Floyd came here to work on his book. I don't think I should miss the opportunity to see where he studied.'

The cabbie dropped us off outside William Wilberforce House, which he advised us had been the actual home of the abolitionist.

It turned out to be an incredibly short-sighted move on my part. Out of the frying pan into the fire. In trying to distance myself from Victoria and her crimes, I put myself hard up against the rest of my despicable history. Traversing galleries illustrating the horrors of slavery in minute detail, knowing that my kith and kin were up to their necks in the whole ghastly business, was not going to help me sleep at night.

I was standing in a darkened corner of one room, mesmerised by a sickening tableau of slaves crammed into the hold of a ship, their cries echoing around me from a hidden sound system, when Ileana tugged at my sleeve.

'We going now,' she whispered. 'Not good you being here.'

I was so, so glad to be out of that place.

'What we doing now?' Ileana asked, taking my arm. 'Shall we having drink or two while thinking?'

We idled the rest of the day away, drinking, eating and shopping, and then reversed the process before making our way back to the hotel.

'We seem to have a lot more bags than when we came,' I said later, as I surveyed our purchases spread around the room. 'I don't know how we're going to carry them all home on the train. It's a good job my ankle's practically better.'

Twenty-three

'**I** don't know about you,' I said to Ileana when we got home, 'but I've had enough excitement to last me a life-time.'

She looked very serious. 'We each making long journey. I thinking not ending soon.'

'Blimey,' I said, 'you been reading Satre, or what?'

She screwed up her face. 'I not understanding 'Sart'.

'Me neither. I don't think many people do. Not that I've met, anyway.'

She looked thoroughly perplexed.

'I'm teasing you,' I said. 'I think Satre was a famous philosopher or something like that. I haven't a clue really.'

'What meaning, no, what is a filosofer?'

'A person who thinks very deeply about things. When are you are going to Greg next?'

'I saying I telephoning. He will fitting me in.'

'Why don't you arrange something for tomorrow morning fairly early? If you went then we could get out on Lou for the rest of the day.'

I dropped Illy at Greg's at nine thirty next morning, which, by all accounts, was the crack of dawn for him. I fully intended to idle the hour away doing nothing more productive than listening to the car radio. I was tuned into a local station that was hosting a phone-in on custody battles, and was half listening to a succession of horror stories, when some chap from 'Families Need Fathers' came on the line.

I suppose it was inevitable.

Who was my father?

No, you do not want to go there. Absolutely not. Look what finding Victoria has done for you; not only do you have to come to terms with her knocking off a couple of inconvenient relatives, you've also got to face the likelihood of early dementia. It isn't as if Louise didn't warn you. Do not open another can of worms.

No, I wouldn't be so stupid. I've been perfectly happy all these years without giving him a thought. Why upset the applecart now?

That's settled then.

Yes. Only...

Only what?

I guess I need to know the whole story.

You've made up your mind?

Seems so.

What now?

I don't know. No one's named on my birth certificate, but there is someone firmly in the frame. Marlon Boyce, the boy Josie had spoken about – Victoria's childhood sweetheart.

I was racking my brains wondering where to start, when Ileana rapped on the passenger window. Greg was standing behind her.

'Greg liking speaking with you,' Ileana said, as I scrambled out of the car to join them on the pavement, 'about computer. I saying we not knowing how to making Internet work.'

It was too good an opportunity to miss.

'A friend's lent us his laptop,' I explained, 'but it's a closed book to me.'

'Bring it along next time, and I'll show you how to set yourself up with a provider,' he said.

I must have looked utterly stupid, because he said, 'Don't worry, you'll soon get used to it. Tell you what, give it a whirl in the library first, or you could try the Internet café in the High Street.'

Oh, oh, some choice - the library, where I'd made that awful scene or some trendy place with a lot of geeks, who'd pretend not to notice when the extent of my ignorance became apparent.

Thankfully word of my hysterical outburst didn't seem to have extended outside the Local Studies Centre in the library since no one stared open-mouthed at us as we made our way to the computer suite. For a minimal sum we were hooked up to the web, assured we wouldn't bring the whole of the western world to a standstill if we pressed the wrong button, and left to our own devices. Half an hour later we were none the wiser. Roll on Greg's crash course.

After that we adjourned for coffee. I told Ileana about the decision I'd made whilst she was having her English lesson, and added that I didn't know where to start looking for my father.

'I thinking Marlon not living far away. Josie saying your grandpapa knowing Marlon's family. Saying they bad lot.'

We went back into the library and asked to see the electoral register.

Thankfully it hadn't been computerised. 'We'll need something to write on,' I said to Illy, flicking through the wad of papers in front of me.

'I having notebook in car,' she said. 'I getting.'

She was gone in a trice, but was quite a while coming back.

'I forgetting car keys,' she said, 'so finding shop to buying.'

'Looks like you bought half of Smiths,' I said, eyeing her packages.

'I looking at books about computers.' She rummaged in one of the bags. 'I buying this, "Windows in Easy Steps".'

'You're a braver man than I am, Gunga Din.'

She looked at me blankly.

'It was a joke,' I said.

'I not...'

'We'd better get on with this list,' I said hastily. 'We'll take half each, shall we? It'll mean going through every ward in the borough and listing all the Boyces.'

It turned out that there were quite a few and none was called Marlon.

I sighed. 'I suppose it was a long-shot,' I said, 'expecting him still to be in the area after all this time.'

'But maybe some these people belonging to Marlon. Josie saying he having many brothers and sisters.'

'It's a good job one of us was paying attention.' I scanned the list. 'I suppose the easiest option is to phone any of the names we can find in the directory, and ask to speak to Marlon.'

Ileana nodded. 'We go to Lou now, while sun shining and making phoning later?'

We were bobbing aimlessly about in the bay getting a suntan and trying to catch the odd puff of wind, when Illy disappeared below. When she reappeared she was grinning like a Cheshire cat.

'I knowing secret,' she said.

'What secret?'

She produced a small parcel from behind her back. 'I knowing today being your birthday,' she said. 'I hoping you liking.'

'But how did you know?' I asked, noticing a sudden prickling in my eyes and rummaging in my pockets for a tissue. 'How could you possibly know?'

'Is simple. You showing me birth certificate.'

'I ...'

'I taking wheel while you opening gift.'

I can't begin to say how much it meant to me. The field of daisies on the card had me sniffing and dabbing incipient tears, but there was no holding them back when I unwrapped the tiny anchor on a slender silver chain. I blinked and turned away.

'You not liking,' I heard a small voice saying, 'I not having much time for finding.'

I turned back and threw my arms round her. 'I liking so much you've rendered me speechless.'

Her face lit up. 'You liking truly?'

'Really and truly,' I said.

'Please holding wheel, I having more surprise.'

She vanished below again. There was a short interval before she called, 'Please to taking from me.'

I wrested a tray bearing chocolate gateaux and a bottle of champagne from her; didn't trust myself to speak.

'I buying cake and nice wine while you waiting in library,' she said, as she scrambled up to join me on deck, 'and card and necklace when we shopping in Hull. Is very hard to buying with you not to seeing.'

We were like a couple of loopy schoolgirls when we popped the cork of the champagne. 'To absent friends,' I said as we clinked our glasses together.

'I saying big thank you to Floyd for making you my friend.'

We looked solemnly at each other as we clinked glasses again.

'Thinking of birthdays,' I said thoughtfully, as I drained my glass and forked up a mouthful of chocolate and cream, 'has kind of brought things home to me. To all intents and purposes we're both in the same boat.'

'In Louella,' Illy said, giggling and refilling our glasses.

'I was endeavouring to make an important point,' I said, hiccupping, 'something profound about us both being orphans.'

'Bubbles making nose tickling,' Ileana said, obviously enthralled by my insightfulness.

I hiccupped again. 'You have a missing brother and I have a missing father.'

She nodded and looked as if she was on the brink of making a momentously perceptive observation. 'I thinking I liking more cake. You wanting more also?' she asked.

Next morning we set about phoning all the local Boyces for whom we'd found numbers; Ileana assigned to the home phone and me on the mobile. We'd spent ages deciding what to say before we started.

'You liking me phoning also?' Ileana had asked when I handed her the script we'd come up with.

'Why not?'

'I not having English voice.'

'That's true. Perhaps we should amend your script a bit.'

We ended up just adding a sentence about her helping a friend out.

'You start,' I said, 'so I can hear how it sounds.'

She rang the first number. 'May I speak to Marlon Boyce,' she asked very precisely.

I couldn't hear the reply but gathered from her expression that whoever had answered had given her short shrift. 'She saying "Wrong number" and hanging up,' she said.

'I expect there'll be a lot of those,' I said.

'I know is quicker if I phoning also, but I thinking not to taking chances any person putting phone down because I sounding foreign.'

'Oh, I don't think so.'

'I thinking so. Begin phoning now. I helping later if you really being tired or having sore neck.'

'You mean throat,' I said. 'Your neck is on the outside. Perhaps I'd better make the calls.'

'I doing homework from Greg and soon no one knowing I am

being from Romania.'

Some were curt, some were abusive, some were out, some were curious, some suspicious, some indifferent, but eventually one was taken sufficiently by surprise to blurt out, 'Our Marlon hasn't lived 'ere for years.' Before adding warily, 'And who wants to know?'

Not that the surprise wasn't entirely mutual. My prepared script went out of the window. 'I...' I said. 'I have information for Mr Boyce that may be to his advantage.'

'You a solicitor or what?'

'Not exactly,' I said.

'What's your game then?' the voice asked, sounding even more cagey.

'It's personal,' I said. 'And I prefer not to talk about it on the phone. May I intrude on your generosity and call round to discuss it in person?' I wondered where the hell that pompous phrase had come from, as I waited anxiously for the reply.

The sound of wheezy breathing filled the earpiece, as my quarry appeared to be considering my request. Thinking that the lengthening silence was boding a negative response, I said, in the silkiest tone I could drum up, 'I thought it only polite to phone before I came round. Not everyone likes unexpected visitors turning up on the doorstep.'

'And you reckon it's to our Marlon's advantage?'

'I think he'd like to know,' I said, sounding a great deal more positive than I felt.

'Maybe I should phone 'im first. See what 'e thinks.'

'Yes,' I said. 'That's a good idea,' hoping she wouldn't do any such thing. 'Or I could come round, talk it through with you, and see what you think. I feel I could talk to you.' Funnily enough as I said it, I knew that was true. It would be a damn sight easier to see how the land lay with another member of the family before contacting a man who might, or might not, be my father.

'You got our address?'

'Yes,' I said. 'Number thirty - four The Meadway.'

'When you thinkin' of coming?'

'Would today be okay?'

'Yeah, but don't come before two o'clock, I gotta give ma 'er

213

dinner.'

It wasn't until I'd hung up I realised I had no idea who I'd been talking to. I checked our list again. There were two women listed at the address, Mrs Alma Boyce and Miss Marilyn Boyce. Since the person on the phone had mentioned getting her mother's lunch, I presumed I'd been speaking to Marilyn. Either way would this 'phone call prove to be my first contact with the missing side of my family?

Over lunch, Illy and I inevitably fell to talking about families. Well, to be truthful, for the most part I did the talking and she listened. Predictably, I started going over the ramifications arising from the days when my people were slavers. This was in itself bad enough, until it occurred to me that I was perpetuating the evil by conspiring with modern-day traffickers to conceal Floyd's death. Uh. That was a real downer.

'You looking unsmiley,' I heard Illy saying. 'Many people keeping slaves in old days. Is silly to thinking your family being only one. One day maybe you seeing this.'

That's all very well, I thought, but the fact is Floyd's dead, and, in spite of the promise I made myself, I haven't done a damn thing about finding his killers, and what's more, it's highly likely I'm using your safety as an excuse for doing nothing.

And then of course the same unanswerable questions about Floyd's nearest and dearest were piling in. Were they in regular frequent contact with him or was the odd phone-call, out of the blue, the norm? If they had missed him, had they been to the flat, contacted his employer, phoned the police? The more I strived for answers, the more uncertain I became. I was going round in the same old frantic circles, not getting any nearer breaking out of the loop.

'Is waste of time worrying about these things,' Illy's voice broke into my thoughts. 'You having to think about finding own father.'

'That's your philosophy, is it?'

'Yes,' she nodded and grinned. 'I like Satre maybe?'

There was no doubt about it, I thought, as we were washing up, Ileana had an old head on young shoulders. Again my thoughts brought me up short. When had I last asked Ileana about herself?

For instance how old was she? She'd been perceptive enough to suss out my birthday and buy me a present. I hadn't even asked her the most basic questions. How on earth had I got to be so shallow and self-centred?

'Illy,' I said taking the tea towel from her, 'let's leave this a minute.'

'You making long face again. I doing something bad?'

'Of course not, it's not you, it's me. I'm so self-obsessed. I never ask you about yourself. It's as if getting you out of that bloody attic was the end of all your troubles. But honestly -'

She interrupted. 'Is end. I never so happy in my whole life.'

'That's not saying much considering the awful things that have happened to you.'

She looked surprised. 'I not thinking about sad life all the whole time. But sometimes I having bad,' she paused, wrinkled her forehead. 'What you calling thoughts when you sleeping?'

'I think you mean "dreams",' I said.

'Bad dreams,' she said. 'But when I waking, shivering and shaking, I saying to myself, "You living with Daysee now. Daysee, who saving life and making you like sister. Not to worrying about old times, being glad for now, for new times with Daysee."'

Sometimes she knocked me for six.

When I'd recovered my equilibrium, I did ask her a couple of things about herself, like her age, and when her birthday was, and if there were any other relations still living in Romania. She said she was nineteen or twenty, she wasn't quite sure, and she thought her birthday was early in the year. She had no idea of the whereabouts of her birth certificate, other than to suggest that if it existed it might have been handed over to the orphanage authorities, although she couldn't think who might have done so. I also discovered she didn't remember any other relatives outside her immediate family, I suppose because she'd been so young when she was taken into the orphanage.

'Well,' I said, 'we can't do anything about your birth certificate but you could be like the Queen and have an official birthday, irrespective of when the real day is. When d'you fancy celebrating?'

She blushed and didn't say anything.

'Cat got your tongue?' I asked.

She shook her head, looking mystified.

'It's a saying,' I said, 'like the Romanian one we were talking about the other day.'

She flushed again. 'I not liking remembering that.'

My turn to blush, 'Me and my big mouth. How did we get onto this? We were talking about birthdays.'

'I not wanting official birthday like Queen,' she said.

'I'm not suggesting a red carpet and a banquet,' I said, 'just a special day like everyone has for their birthday.'

She took the tea towel from me and began wiping up again. 'When is Floyd's birthday?' she asked quietly.

'Oh,' I said, 'the beginning of December as I remember. Why?'

'I share Floyd's special day, maybe?'

'Don't you think you merit a day of your own?'

She shook her head.

'Tell you what, if you really don't want to have a birthday, we'll nominate the day we got you out of that place. We'll call it "Ileana's Escape Day". That's got to be worth celebrating.'

She beamed and I could see I'd won the day.

'Is like the day I born again,' she said. Then she looked thoughtful. 'I finishing putting things away while you getting ready. We talking so long is nearly time to see lady about Marlon.'

Number thirty-four The Meadway was one of the old cottages on what had been the edge of the village before the council estate was built. It had new windows and a modern porch. The front garden had been partially paved to accommodate a newish car with a disabled sticker on the windscreen.

'I'm quite nervous,' I said to Ileana.

Illy took my hand. 'I not knowing what will happening, maybe good, maybe not. But you needing finding out about Marlon. I staying in car and reading book and when you coming back, we seeing what we must doing.'

The front door was opening as I walked up a ramp from the path. The woman met me on the step. Standing there, staring stiffly at each other, I became aware of her expression. To say she was astonished would be like describing a tidal wave as a ripple. For a second neither of us spoke. Then she said, 'I don't believe it.'

I held out my hand. I noticed it was shaking. 'My name's Daisy,' I said.

Her hand came slowly forward to take mine. 'You'll be a Boyce or I'm a monkey's uncle.'

Still holding my hand, she drew me inside, carefully guiding me past the wheelchair in the hall. Only when we were standing in the living room, did she say, 'It's the 'air. There's no mistakin' the 'air. All us Boyces 'as red 'air.'

She must have seen me glance at her own hair. 'Bottle blonde,' she said, 'since I were fourteen. Had to do somethin' to make me stand out, there bein' so many of us. Not that it made no difference in the long run.'

When she'd settled me on the sofa, her scrutiny never seeming to leave my face, she said, 'And you've got the blue eyes too, like Ginger.' Her voice was husky.

'Who's Ginger?' I asked.

'Our Ma,' she said. 'Real name's Alma.' She stopped abruptly.

'Why are you looking at me like that?'

'You asked for Marlon when you phoned.'

'Well, yes. Perhaps I could explain.'

'No need. I can see it, clear as day. Out of all of us, only our Marlon got Ma's blue eyes as well.' At last she drew her gaze away from my face and said, 'I'll get you a cuppa.'

I looked around the room whilst she chinked cups in the kitchen. Dark green and cream swirly-patterned carpet, light walls, pale green curtains; a table and chairs in the front window, a sofa, with an ashtray and a half-smoked cigarette on one arm and a newspaper folded to the crossword next to it, a large flat screen T.V in the corner, a clock, an air freshener and a few ornaments on the mantelpiece above the coal-effect gas fire and French windows opening on to a modern conservatory. All very spic and span.

I stood up as the woman came back in, carrying a tray. 'You never said what your second name were,' she said, as she put it down on the table.

'Davenport,' I said.

She nodded. 'Davenport,' she repeated. 'Might've guessed.'

'You know the name?'

217

'Oh yeah, I know the name all right. There'd be no forgettin' it after what happened.'

'You mean that my mother caused the death of my grandparents.'

'You know, then.'

'I've just found out. It's hard to take in.'

'True enough all the same.'

'Seems like my aunts conspired to keep it from me.'

She nodded, busied herself pouring tea, then she said, 'Gotta confess I'm all shook up inside. You turnin' up after all this time. I won't say it's not a shock.'

'I don't want to upset you or cause any trouble, really, I don't. But now I've got half the story, I need to know the rest.'

'Don't get me wrong; I always knew there were somethin' on our Marlon's mind. But 'e never let on; never said a word.' She gestured to me to sit down and handed me a mug.

'I haven't got any proof of anything. In fact this visit is a stab in the dark. I'm hoping to get some information from you.'

'You saying they never told you who your dad were?' She took a couple of paces over to the sofa and picked up the ashtray. 'Trying to give up,' she remarked, 'gotta cough.'

I'd been wondering about her croaky voice. 'I had to get those patches,' I said, 'and it was still a struggle.'

'Gotta try, seein' the way our Sabrina suffered at the end,' she said. 'She weren't all that much older 'n me.'

I waited whilst she went into the kitchen to dispose of the cigarette.

'I was told my father left after I was born and there are no details, other than my mother's name, on my birth certificate,' I said when she came back.

'Victoria Davenport, nothin' but trouble. Don't know 'ow they had the nerve.'

I looked away.

'Sorry luv. Don't take offence. Only it makes my blood boil. Our Marlon, 'e stood by her, and she were off 'er trolley. Raving nutcase. The things they said about 'im. Tried to make out he'd put 'er up to it. Well, it weren't fair, he never knew nothin' about it. 'He loved her, 'e did. Tried to protect 'er. Never knew how ill she were. Thought it were the drugs makin' her peculiar. "Them

218

bloody trips" he called 'em.' Her voice crackled and she took a deep wheezy breath.

'It must have been a terrible shock when he found out what she'd done.'

'Shock, that's not the 'alf of it. He went beserk. The worse thing were, they wouldn't let 'im see 'er. Said he were in it up to his neck. Questioned 'im for days. Give 'im a terrible time.' She paused long enough to turn her head away and cough. 'It were all over the papers, ' she said when she'd got her breath back. 'A lotta damage were done by the time she confessed it were all down to her and they saw reason. He were a decent lad and his employer stood up for 'im, but that never stopped the whispering.'

'Poor Marlon.'

'Yeah. Well.' She wheezed, looked round in what I recognised as the desire for nicotine, shook her head, and glanced back at me. 'In the end she were found guilty and were put in that place where they send criminals who aren't right in the 'ead. Broadmoor they call it. We always said she were trouble. And our Marlon, 'e never really settled in the village after that.'

I swallowed hard before I asked, 'So you don't doubt I'm his daughter?'

'I wouldn't say you was the spittin' image, but you got the hair and the eyes and his look about you, and I never 'eard no rumours about her goin' with no-one else.'

'Do you remember how long they'd been going out together before it happened?'

'Well, they'd kind of grown up together. Ginge and Charlie was always goin' on about them Davenports bein' so 'oity toity and reckoning our Marlon weren't good enough for their swanky daughter.' She paused and reached out in a habitual gesture for cigarettes, closed on space, withdrew her hand.

I thought it was high time Marilyn gave up smoking; hoped it wasn't too late.

She looked at me vaguely, her train of thought interrupted by her habit. 'Where were I?'

'You were telling me how Marlon and Victoria met.'

She nodded. 'It were a small village in them days and the kids was bound to run into one another, bein' at the school and all and only a year or so between 'em. Them Davenports sent 'er off private when they saw the way the wind were blowin'.

'So my mother's parents tried to keep them apart?'

'You could say. And for a while it seemed to be workin'. But they was still seeing each other. 'Had us all fooled. 'Course her sisters was older and 'er parents – what was their names?'

'Jack and Reva,' I supplied.

'Oh, yeah.' She chuckled to herself and I noticed how throaty she sounded. 'What kind of name's Reva when it's at 'ome?' This didn't seem to need an answer as she went on, 'Anyway 'e were a local big shot and by all accounts she had money and they thought that made 'em better 'n the rest of us. Didn't do no good though.' She sighed and added bleakly, 'No point cryin' over spilt milk.'

'Could you tell me some more about Marlon?' I asked timidly.

'There was seven of us kids, three girls and four boys. There's me, Marilyn, I'm the youngest. That's why I'm still stuck 'ere. All the rest got away, one way or anover. Next up were Marlon, then Dirk, then it would've bin Sabrina, then Zsa Zsa. Or was it Spence? No I'm right Zsa Zsa, then Spence, that's short for Spencer after Spencer Tracy as I 'spect you guessed, and the oldest, that were our Orson.'

She must have read my expression, as before I could ask, she said, 'Not much to do in them days 'cept go to the flicks; big fans, Ginger and Charlie. That's the pity of it now, Ma losin' her sight on top of everythin' else.'

I was lost for words. From having no living relatives I now apparently had a father, grandparents, six uncles and aunts and presumably a whole host of cousins. Another thought struck me with some force – stepmother, half brothers and sisters? I reached out for my tea but my hand was trembling so much I couldn't pick it up.

'You're looking right peaky,' I heard Marilyn saying. 'Put your 'ead between your knees.' A firm hand pushed my head down. 'Don't come up 'til I say.'

Feeling decidedly groggy, it didn't cross my mind to argue. Presently something pungent was wafted under my nose. I twisted my head away.

'Up now. Easy does it.'

I did as I was told. Leant back against the sofa and closed my eyes. My head began to clear. I opened my eyes. Marilyn was standing in front of me. She handed me a glass of water. 'Steady,' she admonished. 'Don't go gulpin' it down.'

'Sorry,' I burbled, when I was feeling better. 'Don't know what came over me.'

'Thought of being related to a couple of dozen Boyces, I imagin'.' She said tartly.

I blinked. There didn't seem to be anything to say.

'Tell you what,' she said. 'I'll get them old photo albums out. It'll be easier for you puttin' names to faces. Won't be a tick.' Half out of the door she stepped back and twitched the front curtains.

'My friend's waiting in the car,' I said.

She didn't say anything. Let the curtain drop back. She went out into the hall and I heard the sound of the front door being opened. A minute or two later I heard the slam of a car door and then Ileana was ushered into the room.

'No point 'er sittin' out there,' Marilyn said. 'Why don't you make us a fresh pot of tea while I check on Ma and find the photos.' She vanished.

'I hoping you not minding I coming in,' Illy whispered. 'Lady telling me come. She saying she your papa's sister. I saying I your friend.'

'I'm glad you're here,' I said, and started making the tea whilst telling her what I'd learned so far. Marilyn was back before the kettle had boiled.

'Ma's sleepin',' she said, dumping a shoebox and three or four albums on the table.

Once the three of us were settled round the table with a plentiful supply of tea and biscuits, Marilyn reached for the box and took off the lid. 'These 'll be the oldest. Mostly black and white.' She began rummaging around in the box. 'They're all mixed up but most'll have dates on the back. I'll see if I can find one of our Marlon first. 'Him bein' the reason you're 'ere.' She hunted through for a minute or two before declaring, 'Can't find none. Mostly Charlie and Ginger and our Orson. Marlon 'll be in the albums.'

The first picture I was to see of my father was a black and white photo taken outside the village school in 1963. There were about twenty children in the photograph arranged in three rows; the youngest sitting cross-legged at the front, the second row on chairs either side of the headmaster and the older children standing along the back.

'That's our Marlon,' Marilyn said, stabbing a finger at a boy seated at the end of the second row. 'And that's me, and that's the Davenport girl, if I'm not mistaken,' she pointed at a couple of the tots in the first row. 'Our Dirk and Sabrina should be 'ere somewhere as well.' She squinted at the back row. 'Can't see neither of 'em. Playin' hookey I shouldn't wonder,' she added, breathless.

I took the print from her while she recovered herself. Studied the image of a serious-faced schoolboy; tried to imagine him with red hair; tried to imagine him as my father; failed dismally. Looked at the child called Victoria. Wondered how she'd grown into the woman I'd met in the Nursing Home. Wasn't surprised that I couldn't make the connection; if meeting her in person had left me cold, why should a forty-odd year old photograph make any difference?

But now, sitting next to Marilyn, I could see this new aunt in the dimpled, curly-haired child in the photo. It made me smile. I wasn't surprised she'd stayed at home to look after her ailing mother. 'Have you always lived here?' I asked her.

She shrugged. 'Never had no option. By the time I left school, Ma'd had the accident, Charlie were doin' a longish stretch and our Orson's whereabouts was unknown. Spence were doin' his best to carry on the family business, but were 'aving a little local difficulty.'

Marilyn stopped and picked up her tea, whether to collect her thoughts, or save her voice, I couldn't tell.

When she'd set the cup down again she said, as if there'd been no interruption, 'And Zsa Zsa, livin' up to 'er name-sake, had married her first husband. Sabrina, far as I recall, 'ad gone to London to seek her fortune. Dirk were doin' 'is best to avoid the Military Police and our Marlon were obsessed by your ma. Marvel he kept goin' to work everyday, considerin'.'

Ileana must have been thinking about Marilyn's plight because she said quietly. 'Is hard looking after family when mama sick and papa not there.'

Marilyn didn't say anything to this but I could see her sizing Ileana up. I thought that not much got past Marilyn.

Picking our way through the family's pictorial records took ages. As each photograph was turned up I learned a little more about my father and his family. I discovered the Boyces were from a seafaring tradition. Marilyn didn't say so in so many words, but I gathered that, by and large, they sailed pretty close to the wind. She did say that Marlon had taken a lot of flack when he'd opted to work in a nine to five job in an engineering firm.

Marlon, she'd said, when she saw me framing the question, had made good, in spite of everything that had happened. He had a number of business interests, one of those posh apartments in London overlooking the Thames, and a string of glamorous girlfriends.

As to the others - three of the immediate family were dead. Charlie, my grandfather, had died in prison. Orson had been shot dead in an incident involving a luxury yacht in the South China Seas, and, as already indicated, Sabrina had smoked herself to death.

Of the surviving siblings, my uncle Spencer had retired to his villa on the Costa del Sol, and Dirk was working on the cross channel ferries. Marilyn didn't say anymore about these two. Zsa Zsa, recently widowed by husband number four, was sheltering from the demands of the taxman in the Channel Islands. Overall there didn't seem to be as many cousins as I'd been anticipating.

I think we were all drooping as we closed the last album and the feeling of anticlimax was palpable.

Ileana broke the silence that descended on us. 'You telling Daysee so much about Marlon and all the family, I thinking she needing time for thinking. You maybe knowing if Marlon liking to know about Daysee?'

'Well now, that I can't say. All I know is, he loved that Davenport girl, and he stuck by 'er til she drove 'im away. I know it broke 'is 'eart.'

'Then why, why d'you think he gave me up?' I asked.

'Maybe 'e didn't know she were pregnant. Or perhaps 'e thought it were best for you. I dunno.'

'He might not have known. My aunts covered a lot of things up.'

'You'd need to ask him.' Suddenly she smiled. 'Tell you what, I'll give 'im a bell if you like. I phone 'im now and then, let 'im know how Ma's doin', thank 'im for the money he sends. I'll tell 'im you've bin in touch. Break it to him gently. 'He can decide what 'e wants to do. What d'you think?'

'That would be great,' I said. 'And I promise I won't make a fuss if he decides against meeting me.'

On that understanding we agreed she'd ring me as soon as she'd spoken to him.

She walked down the front path with us to the car. 'There's somethin' I'd like to ask before you go,' she said.

'Ask away.'

'I were goin' to ask if you would come and see me and Ma sometimes, whatever our Marlon decides.'

'I'd love to.'

'There then. Make a lovely surprise for Ma havin' a granddaughter come to visit. She don't 'ave many visitors.'

An Honest Trade
April 1834

There is still no letter regarding Wells' family.

The man Fortune Proivil is angry about the debauching of his daughter. He has seen Lionoria sent away and Alice so degraded that she took her own life. He will not allow Nelly to suffer a similar fate when Wells tires of her. He is demanding Wells makes restitution by providing a passage to Freetown for the whole family together with a sum of money to allow them to build a house and buy a plot of land to farm.

To make matters worse, Wells hears that as soon as she was sufficiently recovered from her punishment in the stocks, Lionoria ran away from Beausejour Plantation, leaving the child behind.

The labour shortages escalate when the Proivil family (numbering six in all) refuse to work.

Fortune refuses to name the slave responsible for burying the fetish. Without specific information about the 'o-be-ah', Wells takes matters into his own hands. He summarily accuses two men and a woman of practicing sorcery and sentences them to twenty lashes each and two weeks in the stocks.

Twenty-four

I was more than a little on edge by the time Marilyn rang. I was chopping wood in the yard when Ileana came charging out of the house calling to please hurry as Marilyn was on the phone.

'Sorry luv,' she said, 'for not ringin' before. You probably bin climbing the walls.'

'Oh,' I said, trying to sound casual, 'don't worry about it. It's only been a few days. I'm sure you have your hands full looking after Ginger.'

'Yeah, well, like that's true, but that's not the reason. Turns out our Marlon's away on business. Got 'is answer phone a couple times, then struck lucky and Beryl, his cleaner, picked up the phone. She says 'e's away 'til the end of the month.'

I mumbled something about one or two more days not counting for much after thirty years, but I can't say I didn't feel deflated. I suppose it was a coincidence that Marilyn said, 'I were that excited after you left, I 'phoned our Marlon straightaway. Went down like a burst balloon when I couldn't get an answer.'

'I must admit my friend and I were up half the night talking about it.'

'So I'm sittin' here, and I'm dyin' for a fag and I need to talk to someone about you, and it don't seem fair to get Ma all worked up in case you change your mind about comin' to visit her, so I give our Zsa Zsa a bell. I know it's a liberty an' all.'

'I don't mind,' I said. 'But how d'you think Marlon will feel about it?'

I heard the sound of breath being sucked between teeth.

'His own sister, well it's not like blabbin' to all an' sundry, is it?'

Taking that to be a rhetorical question, I asked, 'What was Zsa Zsa's reaction?'

'She were over the moon. Talkin' about flyin' over to meet you.'

'Blimey!' I said.

A raspy chuckle, followed by a fit of coughing, sounded in my

226

ear. ''Scuse me,' she said when she'd recovered. 'You remember I told you our Zsa Zsa's not short of a bob or two. She don't say so in so many words but I 'ave a feeling she's bin a bit bored since Den died. Not used to bein' on her own. 'Spect she'll be looking out for husband number five, soon enough.'

I felt a flush of indignation warming my cheeks. What did Zsa Zsa think I was, a novelty to fill the gap between husbands?

I think Marilyn must have sensed she hadn't expressed herself very well because she said hurriedly, 'Don't get me wrong, I'm only sayin' she and Den was always jettin' off one place or anover. She'd get on a plane like I'd get a bus. She's really keen on meeting you.'

I had mixed feelings about meeting another member of the family before I knew what Marlon's reaction would be, but it was nearly two weeks until he'd be back and I didn't relish the wait. 'When was she thinking of coming?' I asked Marilyn.

'More'n likely got 'er bags packed as we speak.'

'Well,' I said, 'I'll leave it up to you.'

'There's a hitch,' Marilyn said when she phoned back. 'Baggage-'andlers strike or some such at the airport. Zsa Zsa says she'll get the boat over.'

I suppose it was the use of the word 'boat' in conjunction with the time lapse which was going to ensue before I had an inkling of Marlon's feelings about the possibility of being the father of a thirty-one year-old daughter, that gave me the idea. 'Thing is,' I said, gathering my thoughts, 'I've got a boat. How d'you suppose Zsa Zsa would feel if I went to her instead of her coming here?'

After a few more phone calls it was all arranged. Ileana and I would take Lady Lou across to Alderney to meet the second one of my father's sisters.

'Is interesting,' Illy said when I finally put the phone down, 'you not even meeting Marlon, but you thinking he your papa. And Marilyn not mention Ellen, only Victoria.'

'I know,' I said. 'I seem to have jumped to an enormous conclusion without any real evidence.'

'When you meeting Marlon, if you wanting truth, maybe doctor making test, to seeing if he your papa.' She wrinkled her forehead.

'Is wrong English. Is Marlon, not doctor, who maybe papa. How I should say this?'

'Oh lor! I don't know. I understood what you meant, anyway.'

'I asking Greg at next lesson. Is wasting money if you not telling when English wrong.'

'I like the way you speak,' I said, 'and correcting you would spoil our conversations.'

'Is true we always talking. I never having friend to talk to before.'

'There you go then. It'll come in time. There's no rush. Now let's get on with planning our trip to Alderney.'

'We needing many plans to going there?'

'Not really. I just need to set a course and check the tide times. I've sailed into Alderney plenty of times. It's not complicated. It's when you're leaving Alderney to go, say to Guernsey, you want to get The Race right.'

She looked puzzled. 'I thinking race meaning running full speed.'

'Yes, it does. It's also the name of the very strong current that flows past Alderney. If you time it wrongly, you can find that the island seems to be overtaking you. That's because although the wind might be filling your sails, or you have the engine on full throttle and think you're driving forwards, you are actually being pushed backwards by the force of the tide.'

'Is very dangerous?'

'Not very, unless the weather is particularly bad. Usually it's just a matter of waiting for the tide to turn and starting again.'

'We trying getting tide right first time.'

'We certainly will. Actually I did once get it wrong and that was when I mixed up 1700 hours with 7 o'clock, instead of 5 o'clock. I don't think I'll make that mistake again. But as I said, it won't affect us on this trip anyway.'

'Daysee?'

'Yes?'

'I not knowing where is Alderney.'

'It's an island off the coast of France in the group we call the Channel Islands.'

Her face changed.

'What's the matter?'

'Daysee, I cannot going to France. I not having papers.'

'Oh,' I said, 'don't worry about that. The islands are British not French. You won't need a passport.'

'You knowing this?'

'Well, I've never been asked for mine.'

'But you not having foreign voice. Authorities speaking to me, will asking what country I coming from.'

'Well,' I said, 'I suppose it's a possibility, but it's very unlikely.'

She shook her head, 'I thinking not good idea. I staying in house.'

'No. I wouldn't want to go without you.'

'I afraid to go. I meeting Zsa Zsa, maybe she asking many questions about me.'

'From what Marilyn's said, I don't think the Boyces have much truck with the forces of law and order, but I take your point. How about we agree you stay on Louella while I go to see Zsa Zsa; keep your head down. Would you be bored on your own?'

'Not bored. Afraid someone coming.'

We kicked it around for another ten minutes or so before I capitulated. I can't say I wasn't disappointed, but the plain fact was I didn't want to go without her, and she, for perfectly valid reasons, didn't want to risk it. So we were effectively back to square one.

'Thing is,' I said, 'a trip to the Channel Islands is neither here nor there. I'm sure I can fix something else up with Zsa Zsa. But we're still left with the same problem - how to get on with all the things we want to do in the future, with you having to look over your shoulder the whole time.'

'I needing papers.'

'Yes, and I've no idea how to go about legitimising your presence in this country.'

'I thinking very difficult. Is why I paying bad men much money to make false papers. And they never giving to me.'

'You're not saying you paid the people that did those terrible things to you?'

'Oh, yes. All money I have saving and must also promising to paying when I having job.'

I gave her a hug.

'Why you squeezing me up?' she asked, her voice muffled.

'It's my way of showing I want to keep you safe,' I said.

The upshot of all this was that I called Marilyn yet again and explained that I had a problem with Lady Lou's engine and consequently wouldn't be able to make the trip to see Zsa Zsa for the time being.

'Pity,' she said. 'She's bin like a cat on an hot tin roof since I told 'er the news.'

I hadn't been off the phone fifteen minutes when she called back.

'She'll be here by the end of the week. She suggests meetin' up at the Holiday Inn in town. She usually stays there when she comes over to see Ma.'

Having a few days free, Illy and I decided to take Lady Lou to the Isle of Wight. There wasn't much wind about on the outward journey and we motored most of the way, giving me rather more time for introspection than I would have chosen. It wasn't that I didn't think about Floyd, but I tried not to let what had happened to him obliterate the person I'd known, as if his death meant more than his life. And keeping busy seemed to help me do that; consequently I was extremely pleased when this enforced period of inactivity was brought to end by our arrival at Cowes.

I'd given Illy a book on knots to keep her occupied on the way over and was confident enough to throw her a line as I brought Lou up to the mooring.

'Step off when I say and take a turn or two round that bollard,' I told her. 'Then make her off with a couple of those half-hitches you've been practicing.'

She didn't need any prompting. We had Lou made fast in a couple of shakes.

Fortunately, it was still nearly two weeks until Cowes Regatta or we'd never have got a berth, not withstanding the exorbitant fee. All the same the town was packed. We edged through the throng, which was sprawling off the pavements and clogging up the roads, until we found a pub. With the tenacity for which I'm famous, I fought my way to the bar and secured our drinks. But, crammed cheek by jowl into a corner, there wasn't much pleasure in it, and finishing our cider, we decided to forgo a second and escaped back into the crush outside.

Later, armed with a great bundle of purchases including a safety-line, thermals, sea-boots and a full set of oilies for Ileana, and fish and chips for both of us, we climbed back onboard Lady Lou, expecting to spend a quiet evening watching the world go by.

Things didn't work out that way. We'd demolished our supper and were well into the wine when we were hailed from the pontoon. A rather dashing young man was addressing us.

Suffice it to say the young man was called Harry and was from a sea-training vessel moored at the end of the pontoon. He was inviting us onboard to share an impromptu barbeque along with several other crews he'd rounded up. I'd like to say I don't remember anything much of the evening that followed. That of course wouldn't be true. And anyway, even if it were, Ileana insisted on reminding me of every little detail next morning, even going so far as to regale me with my own story.

'You making all listen,' she said. 'Is very exciting. I feeling proud I being friend of such a brave person.'

Oh no! Not the Channel Island story. But yes. In explicit detail.

'You saying you sailing with four others. You going to Alderney. I remember this, because is where Zsa Zsa living and you telling me about The Race and time you making mistake about tides.'

'I did, didn't I?'

She beamed. 'I telling again now.'

'No, honestly. There's no need.'

She looked offended. 'You thinking I not telling properly.'

I shook my head. A mistake, considering the headache.

'Good.' She settled herself more comfortably. 'I begin. You and friends having many drinks in pub on Alderney. You knowing you must leaving by seventeen hours but you thinking this being seven o'clock, when really is five o'clock. So when you all going at last to boat is really two hours late. And outside harbour, very, very dark and you not seeing lights on the island and thinking maybe power cut. But big storm is coming, is why so dark and none ready on boat.' She looked at me for confirmation.

I tried to smile.

'Soon sea and wind being very strong. Crashing and splashing all about boat. Boat is tipped over on side, like this,' she lent over to one side, came up again, 'and wind roaring and main sail is down in water. When wave is pushing boat up, sail is scooping water and throwing into boat. And cockpit flooding. All crew afraid, thinking boat sinking and all drowning.'

I cringed.

'You knowing must taking big sail down, and making little sail for storms. But thing for making sail come down is broken and you must pull down with ropes. You going to front of boat in fierce wind and sea splashing all about, and you making sail come down, and hoisting jib sail, but alas wind is so strong and sail having small rip, and whoosh, suddenly is all tearing and tattered and no good. And then engine breaking. All is lost.' She stopped dramatically.

'I see you were listening very intently,' I said. 'And where did you learn words like 'alas' and 'hoist'?'

'You saying both when you telling story. I thinking I remembering all you telling.'

'I might have exaggerated a little,' I muttered.

She wrinkled her forehead. 'I not remember you saying exajerr – word you just saying – I remember, you alone putting up storm sail when all the whole time wind and sea crashing around and then must mending engine. Then crew seeing not drowning and you saving all and being most brave.'

'That's it, is it?' I asked.

'I think so. I thinking after that you having a few more drinks, also others telling stories. But none so brave as Daysee. Then we coming back to Lady Lou, and now waking up and we going sailing together.'

'Hangovers and tides permitting,' I said, 'we'll move round to Yarmouth to sample the hospitality on offer there.'

Albeit boats were rafted up three deep on the town quay at Yarmouth, it was quieter. Not what you'd call peaceful, being where the ferry comes in, but at least you could find standing room in the pubs. We idled the rest of the day away swimming and sunbathing. Fortunately I was sufficiently on the ball to get a post card off to Megan saying I was well but that as she could see I had only got as far as the Isle of Wight. We left the following morning.

'We'll go westward first,' I said as we were preparing to cast off, 'so you can see The Needles. Then back along the Hampshire coast.'

'What are needles?'

'They're a line of jagged chalk rocks that stick up out of the sea, like the backbone of a sea monster,' I said. 'Quite spectacular. And there's a lighthouse at the tip of the tail.'

'I liking seeing sea monster,' she said.

'It won't all be sight-seeing,' I warned her as we got underway. 'The Solent can be quite tricky to navigate in this area.'

She glanced at me enquiringly.

'What I'm trying to say is, Fiddlers' Race, the rip tide off Yarmouth heading towards Sconce Point, the way we need to go, is the fastest in The Solent. That's because it's where the water is deepest. Luckily it's easy to see because the water is always choppy there.'

'What is choppy meaning?'

I made an up and down flappy movement with my hand.

She nodded.

'And before you ask, as far as I know it's called Fiddlers' Race after a band of musicians who were returning from Yarmouth when their boat got caught in the current and they were all drowned. I don't know whether there's any truth in the story. The point is, we don't get near enough to find out.'

'I thinking you knowing where we must sailing. I not worrying.'

'Thank you for that vote of confidence; all the same it doesn't do to get complacent,' I said. 'We'll hug the shore as much as we can without venturing into shallow water.'

'We not wanting Lady Lou going bump-bump on ground.

'We certainly don't,' I agreed.

As it happens, it was just as well we'd got Illy her waterproofs. It rained more or less solidly the whole trip. That's not to say we didn't have a great time because we did. Safely navigating the many hazards that mark this passage, by the time we'd anchored up in the Beaulieu River we were wet, windswept, tired and happy.

'No doubt about it,' I said to Illy after we'd showered and were eating supper, 'you should feel proud of yourself, especially when you remember the terrible time you had on that other boat.'

'I not thinking about that time. I loving being on Lady Lou.'

'Not like Floyd,' I said.

'Is big pity, he missing very nice time.'

'Yes,' I said. 'I think so. I couldn't really understand anyone being so afraid of water and on the other hand, he couldn't understand my obsession with sailing. I don't know if we'd ever have worked it out …'

'Daysee?'

'Yes?'

'Maybe I getting chart and showing where I remember we have sailing today?'

'Not bad for a beginner,' I said, when she'd successfully identified The Needles, Hurst Castle and Lepe Bank. 'You're getting a real feel for it. We need to think about a proper course for you when we get back. I'm sure you'd love it.'

'I not sure. How is course?'

'Well, to be truthful I've never done one. But they're run by the RYA and are for people at different stages of experience.'

'What is RYA?'

'Royal Yachting Association.'

'You coming also?'

'No, it would be for you. And it would be nice for you to meet some new people.'

'I not liking meeting new people. They asking where I coming from.'

Not again. Not another blind alley because of her illegal status. I was getting heartily sick of it. 'There has to be away round this,' I said grumpily.

'I must waiting Romania joining European Union,' she said.

'And who knows when that might be?'

'I sorry, I making you cross.'

'Illy, you do not make me cross. Not knowing how to get round your situation makes me cross.'

Twenty-five

We got home in plenty of time for the appointment with Zsa Zsa. Well, we would have if we hadn't been stranded on Lou waiting for enough water to get ashore. As it was we had time to rush indoors, dump our stuff in the hall, powder our noses, and jump back in the car. Then I dropped Illy at the library, her favourite place in town, told her to make sure she got something to eat, and shot through the traffic to the Holiday Inn.

Zsa Zsa met me in the foyer. She was waiting just inside the revolving doors and virtually swept me off my feet as I emerged. Mutual recognition not being an issue given the striking superfluity of curly red hair, introductions were swiftly dispensed with and I was whisked upstairs to her suite, where a cold buffet had been laid out.

'Well I never! Who'd've thought it? I can't get over it!' I had to remind myself not to stare at the extremely elegant woman, in, I judged, her early sixties, who was showering me with platitudes. She was so different from Marilyn. Everything about her breathed affluence and the confidence that goes with it. From her artfully organised casual hairstyle, through the perfect makeup ornamenting her unlined face, past the pearls and the décolletage to the neatly crossed ankles and undoubtedly hand-made court shoes, she was certainly a credit to what money could buy and, I thought, liberal doses of HRT, if not Botox. She reminded me of Deborah Kerr in The King and I, but without the crinoline, obviously.

'Well, then,' she exclaimed, as she poured me a drink. 'Our Marlon's girl. Who'd have thought it?'

I said I hoped she didn't think I was being presumptuous, considering I hadn't even met Marlon and reiterated that the whole thing was only guesswork on my part.

'Not much doubt in my mind,' she retorted. 'It explains a lot of things. We all knew something was afoot soon after the Davenport girl was put away. Marlon was that loyal at first, visiting her

235

whenever he could, still wouldn't have a word said against her.'

'Did he dispute the verdict?' I asked.

'He did in a way. Not that she hadn't done it, but that she was so ill she couldn't see it was wrong and that she should be getting treatment, not punishment. Since everybody accepted she was unfit to plead, I suppose he had a point.'

'Didn't she get any help in Broadmoor?'

'I couldn't really say. I didn't live at home then. All I know is, he used to visit her regularly and then one day when he got back, he told Ginger he wasn't going anymore.'

'Didn't he give any explanation?' I asked.

'No. Wouldn't discuss it at all apparently.'

'What do you think happened?'

'Well, of course we all had our own ideas. Maybe she'd turned against him. Or maybe they were keeping her so drugged up she didn't know him anymore. Or more likely the Davenports had bought him off.'

'But why would they?'

'Well, at the time, we thought it was because those aunts of yours blamed him for everything. They hated him, you know; said he'd got her into drugs and they were what had sent her loopy.'

'That wasn't true though, was it? I've found out about the trial. Victoria had been mentally ill for years. The LSD may have pushed her over the edge but Marlon had nothing to do with it. He was totally exonerated.'

'I know. Still, you've got to understand how it was in those days. There was a good deal of prejudice about then. The Boyces were working-class scum; the Davenports stood for middle-class respectability. No contest.'

'But it's so unfair,' I said.

'To be perfectly truthful, we weren't exactly pillars of the community. Our bad reputation wasn't wholly undeserved. Charlie was a right swine, Orson was a thug and Spence looked after Charlie's business whenever the old man was being detained at Her Majesty's Pleasure.'

'Didn't anyone speak up for you, apart from Marlon's employer?'

'Why should they? We were all tarred with the same brush. Spence didn't have the same violent reputation as Charlie and

Orson and he was clever enough not to get caught. Doesn't mean he wasn't a crook all the same. Dirk's more shiftless than shifty, not that that kept him out of trouble. No-one would believe Marlon was straight, coming from a family like that, whatever his boss said.'

I'd finished my lunch whilst Zsa Zsa was speaking and she stood up to take my plate from me. 'Rum lot, the Boyces,' she remarked, walking over to put it on the table. 'How do you feel about being related to us?'

'Well,' I said, 'as yet there's no proof I am.' I thought I noticed a stiffening in her stance as I said this so went on hurriedly. 'It seems impertinent to assume anything before I've even spoken to Marlon. But if it turns out he is my father,' I paused, didn't know how to go on, felt the tears welling up in my eyes, 'If he is my father -' My voice broke.

Zsa Zsa came over and sat down beside. 'Don't take on,' she said. 'I wasn't getting at you. Must have come as a bolt out of the blue, all this. Marilyn tells me you've only recently found out what happened.'

'I'm glad I didn't know before,' I muttered as I wiped my eyes. 'Who wants to grow up knowing their mother murdered their grandparents?'

'You've got a point there,' she said. 'Mind you, I don't know how they managed to cover up a scandal like that. I'd have thought someone would have said something over the years.'

'It is odd, isn't it? Yet it's true. I didn't have an inkling.'

'You were brought up round here?'

'Yes. Well, yes and no. I can't remember much about when I was really little. I know I went to boarding school until I was eleven and I seem to remember spending every spare moment of the holidays on one boat or another with,' I was going to say Mum and Louise, checked myself just in time, 'Ellen and Louise. After that I went to Radnor Hall, which is about twenty-five miles from here, and again I spent most of my free time sailing. I suppose, now I come to think about it, I haven't spent that much time just knocking about locally.'

'No doubt why your aunts arranged it that way. The other thing to remember is that the place changed completely when the estate was built and the newcomers moved in.   Nasty backbiting, incestuous rats' nest before that.'

I shuddered as she said this, thought about how it must have been for Ellen, posing as an abandoned mother in that environment. How on earth had she managed?'

We chatted on about the two families as I worked my way through the cheese and biscuits and coffee. I realised, as I reached for the liqueur Zsa Zsa poured me, I was finding her extremely easy to talk to. All the same, I didn't say a single word about Ellen bringing me up as her own daughter. I don't know why.

I'd made a comment about feeling guilty about swanning through my life without a care in the world whilst Ellen and Louise must have been going through hell, when Zsa Zsa said, 'Now there's a thing. I feel guilty about leaving Marilyn to cope with Ginger.'

'I saw the wheelchair in the hall and Marilyn mentioned that your mum had lost the use of her legs a long time ago.'

'She's blind as well, you know. And it's all down to Charlie.'

'No!'

'He was a nasty bit of work, especially when he'd had a drink. Ginger got the worst of it. When I look back now, I can see it was only a matter of time. She was just a walking punch bag for him.'

Did I want to know about this? On top of everything else, did I have to discover that the man, who was likely to be my paternal grandfather, was a wife-beater? Absolutely, definitely not. So what perverse quirk drove me to ask, 'What happened?'

'Nothing more than the usual, only she was at the top of the stairs when he got her. By the time she'd bounced down to the bottom, she was unconscious and had suffered a serious spinal injury. She was in hospital for months. Never walked again. They put Charlie away for it, but he was out in eighteen months and as bad as ever. About the only thing we can be thankful for was that he wasn't out that long before he was in trouble again. And that time, when he went down he didn't come out.'

'He died in prison?'

'He was in a fight apparently. Stabbed with a screwdriver by another inmate. We all breathed a sigh of relief, believe me.'

Bloody Hell, I thought, I wouldn't have been breathing sighs of relief; I would have been dancing on his grave. 'It's a lot to take in,' I said.

'Yes, I know, I'm sorry. It's worse than East Enders.'

I must admit I was flagging by this time. Surely there's only so much family drama a person can be reasonably expected to deal with; a history of murderers, wife-beaters, thugs, crooks and slavers would be over the top by anyone's standards. My family made the skeleton in the cupboard look like a fairy story. Unfortunately there was any number of things I still wanted to know. 'D'you think I could have another drink?' I asked boldly. 'Something bracing.'

Zsa Zsa grinned. 'A drop of Dutch courage. I'm not surprised.'

'What else is on your mind?' she asked when she'd got us both a brandy.

I asked her about Marilyn staying at home and Ginger losing her sight. She said Marilyn had got the short straw. Being the youngest, her sisters had already left home by the time she was old enough to leave school, and no one would have expected the boys to do it. So it was a fait accompli. Zsa Zsa, Spencer and Marlon sent money, and Marilyn and Ginger didn't want for anything, but Zsa Zsa knew it wasn't the same. The fact was Marilyn had never had a life of her own, and now she had that awful cough and you couldn't help thinking about Sabrina. She added that Ginger's blindness was also to do with nerve damage from the accident.

We'd been talking for ages when I remembered Ileana. 'Oh!' I started to my feet.

'What's the matter?'

'I've completely forgotten my friend. She's waiting in the library. At least she should be if it hasn't closed by now.'

'This would be the girl with the foreign name you took to Ma's with you?'

'How did you?' I interrupted myself. 'Of course Marilyn mentioned her to you. Actually I didn't intend to take Ileana in. I'd left her waiting in the car and when Marilyn saw her there, she went and got her.'

Zsa Zsa raised one elegant eyebrow. 'Marilyn's got no side to her but she did wonder …?'

I left the question hanging in the air.

I needn't have worried; the library was still open. I found Illy at a

239

table on the first floor, a heap of books piled up in front of her.

She jumped to her feet when she saw me. 'Daysee, I hoping all is good when you seeing Zsa Zsa?'

'I'll tell you about it when we get home. How have you been? I hope you had some lunch.'

'I loving this place,' she said. 'You can finding book about everything you wanting to know in the whole world.'

'I don't know about that,' I said. 'I'm sure it's quite limited compared to the ones in the big cities.'

'Even if I coming every day of my life, I not reading all.'

'But would you want to?'

She looked baffled. 'Yes, I do wanting. You not wanting also?'

'Not really,' I said. 'I wouldn't say I was an avid reader.'

The next chapter in the unravelling of my family saga was supposed to be meeting Ginger. Marilyn and Zsa Zsa had more or less got it arranged when I panicked. 'I can't,' I said, 'honestly. Not until I know what Marlon's reaction will be when he discovers there's some redhead claiming to be his daughter. Just suppose you're wrong and he's not my father. I will come to see Ginger, I promise, but I've got to know where I stand first. I mean, I'd be pretty miffed if I were Marlon and all this was going on behind my back.'

'Oh,' Marilyn sighed. 'Are you sure? Only me and Zsa Zsa thought it'd perk Ma up no end. We was lookin' forward to seeing you again too.'

I managed to stick to my guns about delaying my visit to Ginger; failed to put them off their next idea – that Ileana and I meet them for a pub lunch when Ginger was next at the Day Hospital.

I'd describe this period as similar to being out at sea with a weather system coming in; the wind is picking up and there are some ominous clouds on the horizon. You're aware of the heavy weather markers and should be going about, but for some insane reason you're forging on, into the eye of the storm.

Illy and I eventually devised an account of our friendship which we hoped would stave off the inevitable questions from Marilyn and Zsa Zsa. We'd met, we decided, when I was on a sailing holiday on the Black Sea and she was working in one of the hotels in Constanta, which, she thought, was a big enough town to have some sort of tourist industry, although she'd never been there and didn't really know anything about it. We could both see it was a very flimsy story.

'I not wanting to coming. They will asking many questions. Is better to saying I being ill and not coming,' she wailed. 'Please Daysee.'

Which was how I came to be sitting in the garden of The Bell with Marilyn and Zsa Zsa, studying the menu and sipping a gin and tonic, whilst Illy waited at home with her books and daytime TV.

'Such a pity your friend couldn't come,' Zsa Zsa said. 'I was looking forward to meeting her. I hope it's nothing serious.'

'Oh, no, just a sore throat and headache. Probably a cold coming on,' I said.

'Shame though, innit?' Marilyn said. 'Would 'ave bin nice, the four of us havin' a chat.'

I nodded, studying the menu even more intently.

'Marilyn says she thinks your friend comes from Eastern Europe,' Zsa Zsa said, when we'd ordered lunch.

'Yes, that's right. The view's great from here, isn't it?' I said, looking down the garden to the bank and the river beyond. Out of the corner of my eye I saw Marilyn give Zsa Zsa a nudge. 'Have you heard anything from Marlon yet?' I asked.

'Not yet, Beryl said she'd leave 'im a message. I bet 'e'll be on the blower the minit he reads it.'

'You didn't tell her what it was about did you?'

'Course not. Be more'n my life's worth, discussin' his business with the cleaner.'

I breathed a sigh of relief, 'Are you nervous about telling him?' I asked.

'Well, not as you'd notice. 'He's gotta know after all.'

'I think he'd be pretty hacked off if he thought we'd been making his decisions for him, whatever we imagined his reaction might be,' Zsa Zsa said.

'I agree with you there. Even if 'e thought it were all a lot of tosh, 'e'd 'ave to say it. I mean, you can't leave that sort of thing to other people to decide.'

'I'm worried that he'll be angry about me speaking to you two

241

first.'

'Well, 'ow was you supposed to find him otherwise?'

'Perhaps I should have advertised or something. Or gone to an agency that specialises in this kind of thing.'

'And what was the first thing they'd have done? Asked you what you knew about where he'd lived, what family he had; whether any were still living in the neighbourhood, and who would they have found? Ma and Marilyn of course.'

'You make it sound quite reasonable. I hope Marlon takes it that way.'

'Don't you go worryin' yourself. It'll all come out in the wash. Me and Zsa Zsa just wants a chat, so we can get to know each other.'

Ileana was agog for news by the time I got home and I was buzzing, partly with apprehension and partly excitement. It took enormous willpower, and a couple of hastily swallowed drinks, until I was steady enough to be sure I wouldn't blurt it all out at once. My strategy, such as it was, was to save the surprise until last. I began recounting the meeting from the moment I'd sat down in the pub.

'And that was how it was all the way through the meal,' I said as I drew towards the climax. 'They were off, like a dog after a rabbit. Honestly, there was no stopping them.'

'They trying to tricking you?' she asked.

'Oh no, nothing like that. I really like both of them. They're just extremely inquisitive and being two of them, each time one stopped for breath, the other jumped in. They seemed to want to know about my whole life.'

'Is good finding new family, only I hoping,' she faltered, 'I hoping you not liking so much you ...' she came to a complete standstill.

'What? What is it? Spit it out.'

She shook her head. 'I cannot saying.'

'Tell me what's going on in that head of yours,' I said, putting my arm round her shoulders.

There was a moment's silence and then it all came bubbling out. 'You finding Zsa Zsa and Marilyn, and if Marlon is papa, maybe you not wanting I living with you, or maybe I being big trouble because of not having papers, and many, many questions about me from all these new people, and so I must going away from Daysee and Lady Lou, and I not wanting to leaving and not being anymore with my true friend Daysee, and, '

'That was an awfully long sentence,' I interrupted, 'and I think it had any number of grammatical mistakes. I can see you'll be going to Greg's for years yet.'

She looked at me, her eyes wide, and wrinkled her forehead in the way she always did when she was puzzled. 'I not understanding. I explaining all these things and still you saying about Greg.' She stopped abruptly.

'Well?'

She grinned. 'I cannot going to Greg for years if I not living with my true friend, Daysee.'

'So all this moody is about what, exactly?'

'What is this 'moody'?

'I meant unnecessary worrying, but I don't think that's exactly what it means; perhaps I should have lessons with Greg as well.'

This time she laughed. Thank heavens. 'Illy,' I said, 'I'm going to say this once and then the subject's closed. We've not known each other very long but I can honestly say I can't imagine you not being here. The only thing that bothers me is your illegal entry into the country.'

'I sorry I doing bad thing against law.'

'No, it's not that. From what Floyd told me, I don't think it's a very fair system anyway – it's because it's stopping you doing lots of things and because of always having to be looking over our shoulders. There are so many instances already. For example, you can't apply for a driving licence, or go to college. We daren't venture far in Lady Lou and it's difficult for you to meet people. Like today.'

'I being big trouble.'

'No, you - are - not - any - trouble. Don't keep saying that. I want to get it sorted out that's all. It's gone on long enough.'

'I not minding not doing these things. I having plenty good things to doing now. In future maybe something changing. I waiting. No hurry.'

'Of course there's a hurry. We've got our lives to get on with.

You should know how impatient I am. Anyway it's immaterial now.'

'I not knowing what immaterial meaning.'

'It means it's of no consequence,' I saw her mouth opening, 'or, it doesn't matter. And do you know why it doesn't matter anymore?'

She shook her head.

I could hardly contain myself. 'Because we're getting you some papers!'

I don't think I explained in any kind of logical way. I know I started by going on about the Marilyn and Zsa Zsa double act; the way they seemed to be totally in tune with each other so that one would take up the other's theme with no noticeable break in the conversation, and the way, when they'd got round to asking about Ileana, they'd kept the questions coming, bouncing corollaries between themselves without giving me time to think. The result being, that in spite of my feeble efforts to prevaricate, they had her position laid bare by the time we were on to dessert.

'Marilyn just came out with it,' I said. 'She said, "She's not legit, is she?" I didn't know what to say. I must have got it together enough to mutter that I had no idea what they were talking about, but they weren't having any. "Don't be silly, dear," Zsa Zsa said. "We're not daft. It sticks out a mile."

'They wanted to know how we'd really met, but had to make do with me insisting I couldn't add anything to what I'd already said. After that it just seemed to be accepted – I didn't admit anything. Marilyn said you looked like a nice girl and were obviously devoted to me.'

I paused to catch my breath and organise my thoughts. I noticed, belatedly, that Ileana, who hadn't said a single word since I'd made the announcement about her papers, was looking petrified.

'It's okay,' I said. 'Honestly. They want to help.' Even as I said it, I heard my own words that other time - that time when I'd found a poor naked creature being held prisoner in an attic. And whilst I was remembering that, she was saying, in an eerie echo of her reply then, 'Why they helping me? They not knowing me.' It was spooky.

Spooky or not, what was clear as daylight to me was that Marilyn and Zsa Zsa wanted to help. Wouldn't, in fact, be diverted from helping. Why, wasn't so clear. Whether it was an over-reaction to having their brother's child sprung upon them, when both of them were childless, or whether it was an innate Boyce reaction to thwarting authority, or some other reason I couldn't even guess at, they'd already got the process underway.

'Illy,' I said, when I'd poured us both a brandy and managed to persuade her to stop pacing round the room and sit down beside me, 'I know it's hard but we have to trust them. What else can we do?'

'We going on Lou to different place and I not speaking to people and being like shadow only and no-one will noticing me. Please Daysee, I so frightened to staying here.'

I didn't know how to comfort her. She was sitting bolt upright, her arms wrapped tightly around herself, her face pinched – the girl on Floyd's sofa all over again.

'We could go away,' I said. 'We could do exactly what I told Megan I was going to do. We could sail round the British Isles. Take as long as we like.' I noticed a slight easing in her position. 'But I have to get this stuff with Marlon out of the way first. You understand that, don't you?'

She stiffened again, and then said slowly, 'Yes, I knowing you must doing this but I not knowing what to do.' She started to cry. 'I sorry, Daysee, I so afraid Marilyn and Zsa Zsa knowing about me and telling authorities and police coming and locking me in prison and then making me going back to Romania. I so afraid.'

'That's not going to happen. You're going to have to trust me on this.' For the second time in as many minutes I heard myself repeating the assurances I'd made to her when we were escaping from the barber's. Not that they were any less valid. 'Let me try and convince you. You remember Marilyn telling us about Charlie and Orson and Spencer?'

She nodded and dabbed her eyes.

'What was your impression of them?'

'Is impression meaning how I thinking about them?'

'Yes, that's right.'

She nodded again. 'I thinking Charlie and Orson are very bad lot. Very bad. I thinking Spencer also is scoundrel,' (I smothered a smile) 'but Police not catching him and now he is living in big house in Spain with swimming pool.'

'So if I tell you that Spencer could get you some papers, what would you think about that?'

To say Illy sagged, would be something of an understatement. She simply collapsed.

'Good job you were sitting down' I said, when we'd reassembled her, 'or you'd have done yourself a mischief. You're still looking rather wobbly.'

'I suddenly feeling all hot and shivery and shaky and like I having no bones in my whole body.'

'I noticed that,' I said. 'You looked like a rag doll. Do you want a glass of water?'

'I thinking maybe brandy, to steady nerves,' she said with a small smile.

'I'd better have another one as well in case of emergencies.'

This time it was a proper smile. 'We always thinking of good reason for having drink.'

'Absolutely,' I said.

She was more settled by the time we'd had supper and had progressed to asking for details before we went to bed. I explained that Zsa Zsa had indicated that one of her husbands had had a little trouble of his own and that Spencer, or people he knew, had fixed it for him.

Having been persuaded to put our toes into what could only be described as very murky water, in no time at all we were in it up to our necks.

Several sets of photographs of Illy taken in the booth in the Leisure Centre on different occasions, in different clothes, some with her hair up, some with it tied back after swimming, some with it loose on her shoulders before she went in, were delivered to Zsa Zsa as per instructions. And in spite of her protestations that it was a family thing and Spencer wouldn't want payment, I'd insisted on enclosing fifteen hundred pounds for onward transmission to Spain. In fact, to be truthful, paying for the phoney ID for Illy had been my way of distancing myself from the family connection, so that I could think of it merely as a financial transaction between me and someone I'd never met.

Once the practicalities had been concluded Illy and I didn't talk about it anymore, but, for obvious reasons, we were both a bit edgy. To take our minds off her illegal documents and my forthcoming contact with Marlon, we kept ourselves busy.

Instead of my normal haphazard method of explaining things to Ileana when we were onboard Lady Lou, I did my best to instruct her properly in what I imagined would be the basics of a Competent Crew course.

Ashore we embarked on computer training under Greg's expert eye, which, combined with Illy's English lessons, must have significantly improved his bank-balance.

I was hoping, somewhat unrealistically given that I hadn't noticed any particular improvement in Illy's English, my investment in Greg's prosperity would, in time, reveal the contents of Floyd's laptop to me.

An Honest Trade
May 1834

Wells finally receives a letter from Sarah and the children who arrived in Madeira in February after a passage of more than three months in heavy seas and torrential rain. Crossing the tropics took five days in contrary winds. In spite of this, Sarah reports that passengers are in good health and there have been no losses amongst the seamen except for one, Richard Moffat, an old-hand, who apparently absconded when they docked. There is a feeling that something untoward has happened to him, as he has left his traps onboard.

The main crop should be harvested this month, but the weather is poor and the scarcity of labour has reached crisis point. In general, it is Wells' belief that the attitude and behaviour of the Negroes is as bad now as it was at the time of the major uprising in Demerara a dozen years previously, when scores of slaves had to be hung to quell the revolt.

Fortune Proivil advises Wells that Nelly is with child. Wells finally agrees to write to the London Agents requesting permission to release the family and asking for sufficient money to cover their passage and set them up in Freetown.

Twenty-six

We'd been out on Louella all day, practicing, with much hilarity, the drill for man-overboard and launching the dinghy, and were in the best of spirits when we got home. The message from Marilyn, asking me to ring her as soon as possible, was on the answer phone.

'Our Marlon 'ud like to meet you,' she said.

I did try to reply but all that came out was a series of strangled grunts.

Marilyn chuckled. 'I knew you'd be chuffed. He suggests meetin' for lunch one day soon. He's give me a few dates 'e could make it.'

'Does he want me to ring him?' I asked, finding my voice.

'No, 'e says best I'm in the middle, case things don't work out. I didn't give him your number neither.'

'That was very considerate.'

'Like I said, 'owever it goes with our Marlon, I feel you're one of us and that's good enough for me.'

'I don't know what to say.'

'For starters you could say when you could meet 'im.'

I can hardly begin to describe the planning required for a meeting with someone who might, or might not, be your father. Firstly there are the relatively easy preparations like your travel arrangements. Will you drive or take the train? What's the nearest station? Should you travel up the night before? Then there's the venue itself. Is it modern and trendy, or chic and sophisticated? Either way, it seems unlikely the dress code is jeans and trainers. So what the hell do you wear? This is the real blinder. You turn out the entire contents of your wardrobe. Realise it must be quite a time since you wore anything formal. You have a fairly smart knee-length jacket and two pairs of black trousers you used to wear to work; a third pair you bought for Louise's funeral, half a dozen tidy shirts, one pair of flat-heeled slip-ons and a couple of reasonable sweaters: everything else, including a hardly-worn blue fleece, is so casual it's practically sloppy. You do have an extensive range of thermal underwear, hats, gloves, scarves, Henry Lloyd and Musto deck wear, heavy-weather clothing, jeans, shorts and tops, sea boots and sailing shoes, but nevertheless, you do know, in your heart of hearts, that none of these items is entirely suitable for the forthcoming occasion.

So it was off to the shops.

I decided that I wasn't a frock person. Unfortunately, I didn't come to this conclusion before I'd tried on dozens, with humiliatingly depressing results.

'You standing in funny way when you trying on nice dress,' Illy giggled. 'All flippy-floppy. And making grumpy face.'

'It's all very well for you,' I said, 'standing there, making facetious comments.'

'What is faseeshous?'

'Never mind. Help me out of this, would you, before I explode. I feel like a bunch of gardenias.'

'I not understanding what you meaning.'

'Trussed up with all these bloody flowers. Surely they've got something plainer.'

'I think you putting all on. Maybe you trying skirt instead. I looking for you.'

About half the High Street later, I had the skirt – a slim brown affair that flared slightly at the ankle. We had the creamy top to go with it just before lunch and snapped up a rather handsome linen jacket shortly after. Footwear, however, nearly defeated us.

'I can't,' I moaned, from the dizzying height of some strappy affair I'd squashed my feet into. 'Honestly. I can't walk a single step. They're far too high and this bit here cuts in, plus I'd only have to put a foot out of place and I'd do my ankle in again.'

The assistant gave me a frosty look as I discarded the shoes. 'I thought madam said she was looking for something stylish.'

'I said stylish, not stilts with a couple of laces,' I said, as she went away to see what else she could find. 'And did you see how much they were?'

Illy didn't answer. I think she may have sensed I was getting a tad bad tempered. I'd more or less decided to give up the whole enterprise when the assistant reappeared carrying a pair of boots. I'd never have thought of boots, especially not boots in pale leather with square toes and Cuban heels. I lusted after them the minute I saw them.

'They're perfect,' I said as I hitched up my jeans and eased them on before standing to admire myself in the mirror. 'Beautiful.'

It wasn't until later when I realised they'd cost twice as much as the stilettos, that I found myself wondering if the sudden desire for the boots was the top of the slippery slope that that dictator's wife, whose name eluded me, had slithered down. I really hoped not.

Anyway, that was the clothes sorted out.

Illy and I went up to London before my appointment with Marlon. Greg had booked us a hotel on the Internet and had lined up some very touristy things for us to do during our short break.

The hotel was modern and comfortable. We unpacked, freshened up and hit the town in time to pick up an open-top tour bus at Piccadilly Circus. We were lucky to get two seats together on the top deck.

Illy was tremendously excited and there was the added bonus of finding herself surrounded by tourists of every nationality. 'So many foreign people on bus I not sticking out like wounded finger,' she whispered before turning her attention to the itinerary we'd been given.

'Or a sore thumb,' I murmured, but she wasn't listening. She was intent on the voice of our guide coming over the microphone.

And then we were off.

Ohing and ahing with our fellow passengers, she craned over the side of the bus to marvel at Eros conducting the traffic, and to see if she could glimpse the Queen at Buckingham Palace. Then there were the Houses of Parliament, Downing Street and Westminster Abbey to gawp at. We could have got off at any of these stops, taken our time to look around and picked up a later bus, but she was much too happy to break the spell. So we stayed in our seats at the National Gallery and St Paul's Cathedral, and London Bridge too, and even at the Tower of London, secure in being part of the cosmopolitan crowd on the bus.

She was walking on air when we finally alighted and linked her arm through mine as we threaded our way through the crowds. 'I having wonderful time,' she said, 'seeing all these fine places.'

'Remember we've got more lined up over the next couple of days,' I said. 'I hope you won't get bored.'

'I never being bored,' she said.

Which was true. She was like a bee collecting nectar, drawing up and processing the stuff of life wherever she found it.

That evening we went to see 'The Woman in White'; Andrew Lloyd Webber's version of the old Wilkie Collins story. I can number the times I've been to the theatre on one hand, so thought we were extremely lucky to get tickets for a popular show at short notice. I don't know if it was because it was a weekday, or because word had got around that apart from the scenic effects it was a fairly mediocre musical, but the theatre was half empty. Not that that mattered to Illy. As with everything she did, she gave it her full attention and was busy unpicking the production when we came out.

'What did you make of it overall?' I asked, when she'd finished explaining that she hadn't quite grasped the plot.

'Maybe I reading book. You thinking we can borrowing from library?'

'Positive. We'll get it next time we go in.'

We'd decided that Illy would be safe and happy in one of the museums whilst I was meeting my putative father, so next morning I got up early, took ages in the bathroom and eventually fitted myself into my new finery.

'You looking like film star,' Illy said, when I'd asked her for the umpteenth time if I looked all right. 'When Marlon seeing you, he is wondering who is beautiful woman. And when you saying you Daysee, he fainting dead away.'

'Daft goose,' I said, giving her a peck on the cheek. 'I think you're biased.'

'What is biased meaning?'

We took a taxi to the British Museum. Inside we got Illy a ticket, ascertained where the ladies, restaurant and shop were located, and agreed that I'd meet her in the entrance hall at four o'clock. I gave her my mobile and said I'd ring her if there were any change of plan.

Another taxi dropped me off at the assigned rendezvous on Park Lane. I was literally quaking with nerves. I walked up to the door of the hotel to pass the flunkey in the gold braid and forced the semblance of a smile through gritted teeth. As I came into the reception area, the polite description of my physical state would be 'glowing'; it was hard enough wondering if I was about to meet the person who'd been missing from my life for thirty years, I was also having to do it on alien territory - I'd never been in any of the really swish London hotels before.

Given the preponderance of curly red hair that existed between us, Marilyn had decided there'd be no problem with mutual recognition. Fortunately her assumption was accurate. I'd hardly paused to glance around when I saw Marlon striding towards me. I didn't doubt it was he for a moment. Quite apart from the dark auburn hair, thick and close-cut, he fitted his sister's description to a tee. Mid fifties; not over tall - well under six feet, I thought - and stocky; not strikingly handsome but having a presence about him, so that you immediately noticed him. Slightly flashily dressed in a light grey suit and navy shirt and tie, I was immediately reminded of old films I'd seen on T.V featuring his name-sake and almost in the same thought dismissed the resemblance; the hair colour was all wrong and I think Brando had a swarthy complexion, whereas Marlon had pale skin, like me.

I suppose all this was a case of the subconscious working overtime in the vacuum caused by the conscious not working at all. I hope I wasn't standing in the lobby of that pretty fancy real estate with my mouth gaping like a Koi Carp. I suspect I was.

'You must be Daisy,' he said, extending his hand to clasp mine.

I couldn't help noticing his eyes. The colours I could see in my own eyes when I looked in a mirror, reflected back at me; the blue shaded by violet, the tiny specks of orange. No trick of the light, then.

I wanted to smile. I think all I managed was a stiff sort of twitch. Marlon seemed undeterred. Murmuring pleasantries he took me gently by the elbow and steered me smoothly into the bar. (Or maybe *a* bar. Who knows how many a really swanky hotel has?) In between the small talk, he settled me into a plush armchair and summoned the waiter. I don't think I said anything until I'd drunk at least half of my vodka martini.

'Mr Boyce,' I began.

'Marlon,' he said.

'The thing is, well, I know Marilyn's told you, but, well, the thing is, my mother was, I suppose I should say 'is', is Victoria Davenport and I think, I don't know, but I think you might be my father.' It wasn't the calm and collected speech I'd rehearsed, more a semi-coherent babble, but at least it was out.

I realised after a moment or two's silence, that I was staring intently at Marlon, and he was gazing at me, equally fixedly. At last he nodded. 'Can't say I wasn't gobsmacked when Marlilyn said you'd turned up. Didn't know what to think. After all these years,' his voice faded away.

I took a hasty slurp of my drink. Far too hasty. When I'd recovered my breath, I said, 'You knew Victoria had had a child?'

'Yeah, they told me that much.'

'Could you tell me about that time? What it was like?'

'You sure you want to know?'

I nodded, not sure I wanted to know; positive I needed to.

He finished his drink and signalled the waiter to replenish our glasses before he said, 'When they first put Vicky away I used to visit 'er whenever I could. But over the weeks I could tell she was slippin' away from me, kind of sinking into herself. At first I put it down to them keeping her drugged up, then I realised she probably weren't on that much, being pregnant and all, and I see how ill she was, and I knew she'd never be able to bring you up. Not that she could 'ave anyway, not in that place.'

'She couldn't have been the first woman, who was pregnant, to be committed. What did they usually do about the babies?'

'Haven't a clue. All I know is what were decided for you. Not that I had any say in the matter. They cooked it up between 'em.'

'Was I going to be legally adopted?'

He shook his head. 'I think the idea was they'd look after you until she was released; nothing official.'

'But surely you had some right …?'

He shook his head again. 'They said it 'ad to be a clean break. I never saw her again after the decision was made. Not that I didn't want to. It was like cuttin' off my right arm.'

'But surely,' I said again, 'surely if you felt so strongly you couldn't just turn your back on her.'

"Just", his face tightened with anger. 'You've no idea. We'd been together since we were kids and you think I 'just' walked away. You tell me what I was supposed to do, when they're tellin' me I've gotta take the blame for what Vicky did; that I'd turned her against her own flesh and blood. And that if I gave a toss for her and the kid she was expectin' I'd get out of their lives and stay out.' He sighed and fell silent; his face pinched and white.

'I'm sorry,' I muttered, when the enormity of what had been done to him had sunk in. 'I'd no idea.'

He shrugged and tried a smile. 'I dunno. Maybe they had a point. I never liked her family, never made no secret of it. Could be she took her cue from me. Who knows?'

I shook my head. 'Certainly not me. I'm struggling with an account of what was apparently done on my behalf that doesn't exactly fill me with delight.'

'Thing is, kiddo, in the end I had to try to do what was best for you. No point you growin' up with that kind of stigma when it could be avoided. And I've never regretted makin' that decision. As to me and Vicky, well she was out of it and I got out soon after.'

'A fait accompli.'

'Yeah, in those first weeks when I was visitin' her in Broadmoor she was pretty far gone and I couldn't get through to the Vicky I'd known at all. So I can't pretend it were all bad news havin' a reason to stop going, and it got easier still as time went on. Not that I ever forgot my Vicky.'

'It is hard when you feel yourself losing contact with someone you love. I felt like that when I was visiting my aunt before she died last year.'

I saw him register the news of Louise's death before he asked, 'And Ellen, the one that brought you up, is she dead too?'

'Yes, she died a long while ago. Both she and Louise were suffering from dementia when they died. And now I've found out about Victoria, I can't help wondering ...'

He covered the shadow that crossed his face when he realised what I'd meant, by asking quickly, 'But Vicky, she can't be dead, have you seen her?'

'Yes, she's in a Nursing Home.'

He nodded. 'I see.' Waited for me to go on.

'I only met her recently. Louise left me a letter.'

'Yeah.'

I ploughed on, 'Now I've found out what happened, I need to- um, I thought maybe ...'

After a pause he said, 'I've never talked about it, you know. Not to no one. And now you've turned up out of the blue and I don't know what to say to you.'

'You say you think you are my father, yet you've never contacted me, in all these years.'

'Like I said, that was the deal. It was grim what Vicky did, doin' away with her ma and pa. Not somethin' you'd want your kid to grow up knowin'. I thought it were for the best, particularly since everybody made out she did it for me.'

'You thought I'd turn against you too?'

'Yeah. Scandalmongers, tabloids, all having a field day, what chance did I have against them? How could I prove it weren't the whole story?'

'But if you'd explained, when I was old enough to understand, I'd have been on your side.'

'Would you? Would you have believed she hated them, even when she was a kid?'

'What happened to make her feel that way?' I asked, wondering, as I spoke, whether I would have taken his word for it.

'I never got to the bottom of it. The quacks said it were an early symptom of her illness. I dunno. Seems to me it's easy to spout that kind of medical claptrap after the event. If that was the reason you'd 'ave thought someone might have noticed the way things were shapin' up. Would have saved us all a lot of grief.'

'But you were close to her. Couldn't you see something was wrong?'

He shook his head. 'We were kids and in love. She did have a temper - I'll say that. Now and then she'd let fly at me but I could always calm her down. All I know is, she got much worse when they sent her away to that bloody private school.'

'Didn't the teachers notice the warning signs?'

'Noticed the school fees they'd lose if she were chucked out.'

'What about her sisters?'

'She didn't care for them two. They were too prim and proper. I remember the younger one,' he broke off in mid sentence.

'Ellen,' I said, when he didn't go on, 'the one who brought me up.'

'Yeah,' he said, 'her. Ironic, when you come to think about it. I never liked her, a right prissy little madam, always telling tales. The last person I'd have chosen to mother my child.'

Tears welled up in my eyes. I wanted to defend her, my proper mum; to explain how brilliant she'd been to me, how happy we'd been, but I couldn't find the words.

Marlon seemed to realise he'd been pretty tactless. 'Don't get me wrong,' he said hastily, 'I don't mean to say she didn't do a great job, bringin' you up. I'm just saying she weren't my type.'

I made some comment about the responsibility of looking after a younger sibling.

'I don't know about that,' he said. 'She was too stuck up for me. Not like my Vicky.' (My heart plummeted when he said this, and I thought I understood what people meant when they talked about being on an emotional roller-coaster.) 'She was wild; didn't care what she did. Always looking for thrills. That's why she started taking acid. I told her she didn't need it. She said it was a real mind-bender and she could handle it. Could have been that pushed her over the edge.'

'You didn't take it?'

'No, I like to be in possession of all my faculties.'

'You were telling me about the school,' I said, when it became obvious he wasn't going to elaborate.

'Yeah, the school.' He drew a deep breath. 'We met most nights. She'd climb out of the window. For a posh school it was pretty free and easy. This went on until we were caught in the act; then they didn't have no option. Had to chuck her out.'

'I didn't know that.'

He shrugged. 'Her old man went mad. He said I was leading her astray - blackening the family name - him being a local bigwig and her so hoity toity. The upshot was they forbid Vicky to see me. But short of locking her in, or trumpin' up some charge against me, what could they do?'

'Surely my grandfather wouldn't have done that.'

'He would've if he'd had the balls.'

His strong language grated though I tried not to show it.

'They blamed me for everything,' he went on. 'I went to the house one night, determined to have it out. He wouldn't let me across the doorstep. Threatened to have me horsewhipped if I didn't get off his land. Like he was the lord of the manor, and I were some bloody serf.' He paused as the waiter approached.

'Your table is ready, Sir,' he said.

We ate on the balcony overlooking Hyde Park. No doubt it was a fabulous meal; I was too keyed up to notice, only thinking, as Marlon dotted the i's and crossed the t's of the horrifying family saga, that however unreasonable my grandparents had been, that hardly warranted being blown to bits by their youngest daughter.

At last we got to the nub of it.

The remnants of the food had been cleared away and we were sipping brandy when he set down his glass and reached across the table to take my hand. 'We could have blood tests to be certain, but I never doubted it were my child that Vicky was carrying,' he said.

I didn't know how I was feeling. I was elated and dubious at the same time. Apparently I'd found my father. Which should be wonderful. Which was wonderful. But what if it didn't go well? I could think of a thousand reasons why it might not. Wouldn't that be worse than not having found him at all? It had certainly been worse seeing Victoria in the flesh. Why on earth hadn't I heeded Louise's advice and let sleeping dogs lie?

Trying not to show the doubts, I slid my hand from his and picked up my bag.

'This is my birth certificate,' I said, as I pulled it out and passed it over for him to look at.

He gazed at it for a minute or two before he said anything. Then he said, 'It's a shock seein' it in black and white, her name and that place shown on it. Tells me I was right to try and protect you.'

I nodded. 'The plan worked perfectly. I didn't know anything about it until a few weeks ago.'

I was pleased to see the look of relief that crossed his face. He muttered something under his breath I didn't quite catch, before he said, 'You've no idea what it was like givin' you up. Seein' that sister Vicky despised plodding round the village with cushions stuck up her jumper, makin' out she were pregnant and knowing Vicky was carrying you and I was never goin' to see you, was bloody murder.'

Both of us flinched as he said that word.

'It must have been very hard for Ellen too,' I said quickly. 'Being an unmarried mother in those days wasn't easy.'

I could see he was reluctant to admit it. Eventually he said, 'She did take a lot of flack; I'll give her that. They put it around she'd bin married to some flash Italian git she'd met on holiday, and he'd got cold feet when the scandal erupted. No one believed it but they stuck to the story and by the time she come back it were old news.'

'Came back from where?'

'I've no idea. She disappeared when she was supposed to be about six months gone, and come back when you was about two years old. I think the story were she'd gone out to Italy to be reconciled with the baby's father.'

Another shock to be digested. Two years when Ellen had disappeared with a new baby and no one I could think of to tell me where she'd spent them. 'There's so much I still don't know,' I said, thinking as I spoke, that that was an understatement by anyone's standards. 'Marilyn remembers a bit about the village then,' I said, clutching at straws. 'Do you mind if I ask her more about it when I see her? Maybe she'll know something.' Or maybe I'd never know. Might it not be better to settle for knowing Ellen put up with the slur of being an unmarried mother for me: to protect me from the consequences of Victoria's doings, and after all, what more could any child ask for?

Marlon was speaking. 'The cat's out of the bag now. Odds-on they guessed years ago anyhow, but Boyces ain't blabber-mouths; not like the rest of the population.'

'Zsa Zsa called the village an "incestuous rats-nest".' I said.

His laugh was strained 'True enough. Don't know how Marilyn stuck it out. I do know all of us that got away send conscience money.'

Twenty-seven

After lunch we walked in the park.

'Why do Zsa Zsa and Marilyn describe the village as incestuous?' I asked. We were sitting on a bench watching the ducks on the Serpentine.

'Are you sure you want to know?' he answered, not looking at me.

My heart missed a beat. Was something else slimy and unpleasant about to come crawling out of the woodwork? 'Of course I do,' I said stoutly.

He lent forward to cup his chin in his hands, resting his elbows on his knees so that I couldn't see his face. 'You'll 'ave noticed the red hair: all us Boyce's have it and Reva Davenport were a redhead too. There's those that say there's a reason for that.'

His shoulders rose and fell before he spoke again. 'There's those that hold,' he repeated, 'that the Davenports and the Boyces are pretty much indistinguishable. That's why old man Davenport was so set against me.'

Light didn't so much dawn, as explode. 'You're saying the two families are related.'

He looked round at me. 'Yeah.' Looked away.

After a little while I said, 'Would you tell me about it?'

'If you like. There's nothin' you couldn't find out for yourself anyway.'

I studied the vast variety of ducks on parade while I waited for him to speak, wondered about the effects of crossbreeding on their plumage.

'It was common gossip when Charlie and Ma was growin' up,' he said at last. 'Ma's maiden name is Allen. Her folks had bin in the village for generations; Charlie's come from further up the coast. His grandfather Samuel, who wed Susan Allen, was the first Boyce to live in the village. The Allens were known for their red hair. One's even got somethin' about it on his tombstone.'

'In the parish churchyard?'

'Yeah, along with all the other Allens and Boyces, who've bin buried there over the years. More'n likely paved over by now.'

'Oh, I don't think so, that's where,' I nearly said 'mum's buried', said 'my aunts are buried' instead.

'Yeah,' he said moodily. 'Allens and Boyces, Jauberts and Johnny-come-lately Davenports, might as well chuck 'em all in one big pit.'

I bridled; bit my tongue; told myself to remember what he'd been through. Wanted, anyway, to hear the rest of the story.

'You were telling me about Susan and Samuel,' I said, when I thought he'd simmered down.

'Same old story,' he said. 'Susan were the scullery-maid at the big house; James was squire Jaubert's second son. Result – one bundle of trouble. Lucky Susan were walkin' out with Samuel Boyce and he stuck by her. Brought the kid up and added a dozen more of his own over the years. The only fact that stands out is that the Jauberts had red hair. Red haired Jauberts and red haired Allens – who knows 'ow long it had been goin' on? They say the Jauberts could trace their ancestors back to William the Conqueror.'

I mulled this over before I spoke. 'Reva was a 'Jaubert'?'

He sat up, and swivelled round to look at me, said, 'Yeah. The name died out when she married Jack Davenport.' Adding as an afterthought, 'He landed on his feet when he married her.'

He went on to explain that the Jauberts were loaded. I asked if he knew how they'd made their money. He shook his head. 'Old money,' he said, 'Who knows?'

I thought I did.

We were rather quiet as we walked back to Park Lane. I guess we both had enough to think about. I was wondering how to draw the meeting to an end when Marlon said abruptly, 'One thing's clear, I want to get to know you. If it's not too late.'

'We won't know unless we try.'

'Fair enough. Say we meet next week. No pressure. I'll give Marilyn a bell when I've fixed somethin' up.'

I was still muttering clichés about the super lunch he'd treated me to, when he'd hailed me a taxi, helped me in, thrust money into the driver's hand and instructed him to take me wherever I wanted to go. He lent in and kissed me on the forehead. 'Take care, kiddo,' he said. 'I don't want to lose my daughter when I've only just found her.'

'Honestly,' I said to Ileana, after I'd finished recounting everything to her and she'd asked how I was feeling, 'I don't know. I wouldn't describe it as relaxing. There's so much to think about, apart from the small matter of finding my long-lost father, there's all the other interrelated stuff about the alleged inbreeding proved by the dreaded red hair, and whether that's got anything to do with Victoria being off her trolley, and if it has, whether I'm going to lose my marbles too.'

Illy was looking at me open-mouthed. 'I liking to ask what is trolley and marbles but you maybe not wanting to explain just this very minute. Your face all red and hot looking. You telling instead if you liking Marlon to be your papa.'

'I'm not sure. I suppose that's the problem. You don't usually have to think about whether you like your relatives or not.'

She looked puzzled.

'Having grown up with them, you just know. It's different when you meet a stranger.'

'I liking you straight away we meeting.'

'I think that's rose-coloured glasses,' I said. 'As I remember it took quite a time for you to come round.'

'You having froffy stuff on nose,' she said.

We were drinking cappuccinos in the museum café, having repaired there from the front steps where I'd found her, sitting in the sun, her nose in a book on the Ancient Egyptians. 'I think you mean 'frothy',' I said, 'and don't think I don't notice when you try to change the subject.'

'Maybe I being very afraid in that horrid place, but quickly I am knowing you being good person who I liking very much. And then, whoosh, you are my true friend, Daysee.'

'Mm.'

'What you thinking?'

'I'm thinking there's a grain of truth in what you say. Perhaps we do make snap judgements.'

262

'So you liking Marlon?'

'I couldn't say that. He was pleasant and generous. I guess we were both trying to find out about the other one without giving too much of ourselves away. D'you understand?'

She nodded. 'I thinking you both worrying what other is thinking. You each saying to yourself, I have making my life so good, the other will being full of pride. But also thinking, maybe other's life is not so good, so must not be having big head.'

'You're a gem,' I said, laughing. 'Have you thought about taking up counselling?'

'What is 'counselling'?'

'Will I never learn? A counsellor is someone you could turn to if you run into trouble.'

'Is running into trouble, having many problems?'

'Yes,' I said. 'I'm glad we've settled that. Unfortunately, I've entirely forgotten what we were talking about.'

She giggled. 'I asking about Marlon. If you liking him to be your papa. '

'I don't know. Maybe thirty-one's a bit old to be adopting a father. Especially if you've been used to doing your own thing.'

Her expression became serious. 'I thinking maybe you making good point. You used to sailing about on Lady Lou. We not knowing how Marlon making his life. Very bad if he not liking boats.' She looked at me solemnly. Then beamed. 'I making joke,' she said.

As it happened Ileana needn't have worried about Marlon not liking boats. He had one of his own. Fair to say, she wasn't my kind of boat, not having any sails, but as gin palaces go, she certainly went.

Her name was Firefly. She was a deluxe motor cruiser with sleek lines, an impressive superstructure and twin cruiser engines. Below was sumptuously appointed, glossy teak veneer, pristine fitted carpets and swanky upholstery. She had air-conditioning, two refrigerators and an icemaker, and was moored within sight of Tower Bridge at St Katherine's dock in the Port of London. She must have cost a fortune.

I'd left Illy sightseeing amongst the crowds at the Tower of London, only a stone's throw away, while I went to my second meeting with Marlon. I knew Illy would be fine; armed with a guide and her insatiable curiosity, she couldn't help but be as happy as Larry. I wasn't so sanguine about my own arrangements for the day.

Marlon was waiting for me near the pier. The hair being something of a give-away, I spotted him easily amongst the sightseers who were leaning on the parapet looking out over the river, and angled my approach to come up alongside him.

For some reason I couldn't account for, since I'd had some reservations about our first meeting, I was suddenly overcome with so strong a notion that he might have changed his mind about getting to know me I had to keep reminding myself to breathe. Marlon, however, was looking relaxed and confident as he turned to greet me, and as quickly as my anxiety had surged, it subsided when he smiled at me. I thought afterwards that my relief must have had something to do with the eyes, as if I saw myself in them and was reassured.

'Kiddo,' he said, catching both my hands and pecking me on the cheek, apparently oblivious to the range of emotions I'd been wrestling with, 'I've bin looking forward to seeing you again. You look great.'

By then I was breathing normally enough to thank him for the compliment and to send a mental vote of thanks to Illy for insisting I add a few more items to my wardrobe in the intervening period, so that this time I was attired in trousers and an emerald jacket in which I did feel surprisingly good. Marlon, I noticed, had also swapped the formality of his suit and tie for a blazer and chinos.

I thought, as he drew my arm through his, and began steering me along the quayside, that we were heading for one of the floating restaurants moored nearby, was surprised to find us entering the marina. The array of cruisers took my breath away. Talk about a millionaire's playground. I'm used to seeing flashy boats of course, but usually yachts not sun-seekers, and not so many all in one place. Mooring at Mullion Quay was, I realised, like playing with your boats in the bath compared to berthing at St Katherine's dock. I was flabbergasted when I found myself propelled up a spotless gangplank onto what turned out to be Firefly's gleaming deck.

Onboard, Marlon embarked on a whirlwind verbal explanation.

'I've only had 'er a couple of months,' he said. 'Traded my old tub in for her. Was a choice between Firefly and a Lamborghini and I thought, what the hell do I need wheels like that for, when you can't do more'n seventy without attracting the old bill like a cloud of locusts.'

I said I had a boat myself, although nothing like this obviously, and he said things had been going pretty well for him over the last few years and that you can't take it with you. And I agreed that no, you couldn't, whilst privately thinking if I'd invested a bomb in a luxury like Firefly, I'd certainly try.

After a guided tour of the wheelhouse and a detailed description of any number of high tech thingamajigs, I was shown below, where a veritable feast had been laid out.

'No,' Marlon said, catching my expression, 'before you ask, it's not down to me. I use the same people for all my entertainin',' and before I could say anything, added hastily, 'not that I think of you as someone to be entertained. Only I don't cook, wouldn't know where to start, and I wanted this to be special.'

I smiled. 'Perhaps that's where I get it from,' I said. 'I don't like cooking either.'

'Don't tell me you use caterers as well?'

This time I laughed outright. 'I wish,' I said. I'm a ready-meal, take-away kind of person.'

After a couple of glasses of champagne, conversation was flowing more freely and I felt brave enough to ask him to tell me some more about the two families.

'What d'you want to know exactly?'

'Anything that helps build a picture. I guess all the years of not knowing is catching up with me now.'

'Well, like I said, I don't know much about Vicky's side, other than Jack Davenport married into money.' He went on to say that Jack Davenport had been skipper of a schooner working the top end of the charter market in the Caribbean when he'd met my grandmother, Reva Jaubert. Marlon said it was love at first sight – Jack had sighted the money and she'd seen an Errol Flynn type swashing his buckle. (The thought crossed my mind as he described Jack Davenport like this that Marlon had obviously inherited an interest in film stars from Ginger and Charlie.) He did go on to add grudgingly that he'd never heard any rumours about Davenport playing dirty, once he'd got the girl.

Regarding my grandmother's side, as I'd already established, the Jauberts had been wealthy and had a reputation for sowing their oats on the other side of the blanket. Jack and Reva had lived in the Manor House until the death of the old man when, being fonder of money than tradition, the estate had been sold off to pay the death duties, leaving the rest of the fortune intact; the rumour being that even after death duties Reva had 'wads of dosh' stacked away. Marlon knew that Reva had been only surviving child because of the gossip, rife at the time, about the size of her inheritance.

'Is that when they moved to Halnaker House?'

'Most likely. Marilyn said you're still livin' there now.'

'Mm. I love it; can't imagine living anywhere else.'

'Oh, well, that's where we do differ. I'm always on the move. Only bin in my current pad six months.'

'I do get restless,' I said thoughtfully, 'but I push off in Lady Lou rather than moving house.'

'There you go, then.' He grinned. 'It's obviously in the blood.'

'Can you remember anything else?' I asked, while I was thinking that if the only genes I'd inherited were the colour of my hair and eyes and being a bit restless, I'd be more than happy. It was the other stuff about mental illness, not to mention slavery and parricide, which gave me the creeps.

'Sure,' he said, 'so long as you realize that by and large Boyces live by their wits. Not to beat about the bush, we come from a long line of bootleggers. Charlie and Orson was still runnin' cigarettes and booze in the seventies. Might even have bin more recent than that. Only come to an end when Charlie was sent down and Orson found himself at the wrong end of a shooter. Still want to know about your relations?'

'Of course,' I said, sounding much more positive than I felt. I waited while he refilled our glasses and settled back against the cushions.

'I'll tell you a couple of tales the way I 'eard 'em from Ma. Both of 'em happened long before the council estate was built. There was two sides of the village then, divided from each other by the old road; one part was on the coast, the other inland. The pub stood on the road between the two; had stood there for two hundred year by all accounts. There were a lot of longstanding grievances on both sides and control of the pub figured pretty high on the list. Thing was, there was a tunnel that run from the shore, inland, which the smugglers used to move their contraband. It came out in the cellars of the pub. So if the wrong man was in, they couldn't get to their booty.'

'The Boyces were on the sea side,' I said.

'Yeah, Alf, Charlie's dad, was king of the castle. They called him 'Cock-Robin'. Word is that he was a real mean bastard. Time came when The Feathers was temporarily held by the yokels. There'd been a couple of skirmishes but Cock-Robin's merry band had failed to oust them. A trap was laid. One way or another the hayseeds were enticed into the tunnel. They say half a dozen men went in. None came out, alive that is. Alf's gang waited 'til they were in, then on a signal, fired the pub and blew up the seaward end of the tunnel, so the opposition was trapped inside. The story was they never meant to kill nobody, only keep 'em in there a while to teach 'em a lesson.'

Bloody Hell! More death and destruction. What was it with my family? 'What happened to Alf?' I asked.

'He was thrown to his death when his horse bolted in the mayhem. Ma said it were a judgement; I said it was one way of avoiding the hangman.'

I blanched. Who wouldn't? Another skeleton in the ancestral cupboard; it was getting rather crowded. The only consolation was it was all a long time ago. Not like Victoria's spot of trouble. I don't know what expression I was registering while all this flitted through my mind, but I suddenly realised Marlon was studying me intently.

'Another wholesome relative for the family album,' I said. 'I could do with some fresh air.'

On deck, Marlon slipped his arm round my shoulders whilst I leant against the rail and took a few deep breaths. Neither of us said anything. After a while he guided me up to the wheelhouse and pointed out the sights. I realised, as I gazed out across the Thames with Marlon sitting beside me, that I was definitely getting over-emotional, I could feel my throat tightening and my voice kept drying up when I tried to speak. Again I found myself wondering why I was reacting like this. What was it about Marlon that was getting to me?

Marlon was looking at me quizzically. 'You all right, Kiddo?'

'I put it down to too much champagne,' I said. 'What was the other story you were going to tell me about Alf?'

He looked at me doubtfully.

'I have a kind of theory that thirty years of burying my head in the sand has caught up with me in year thirty one,' I explained. 'And I've decided I'm glad it's worked out this way. What's a couple of months of grief compared to thirty years of blissful ignorance?'

'Can't say I'd do it that way, but it takes all sorts.'

'About Alf,' I prompted.

'Oh yeah, that's about another fire. Maybe a kind of omen. Alf burned down the elementary school. Apparently him and another kid over-stoked the fire during the lunch break. The chimney caught, then the thatch, then the whole thing went up. Lucky all the pupils got out but the school was burned to the ground. They never decided whether Alf done it on purpose or not.'

After that Marlon changed the subject. I guess he'd decided there'd been enough revelations for one day. He asked me about boyfriends and I told him about my life-long obsession with sailing and the heights of passion I'd experienced when I was given Lady Lou for my twenty-first, which had kind of outweighed a love-life with any mortal being.

'Where d'you keep her?' he asked.

'On a mud mooring,' I said, 'it's not as convenient as a marina, but cheaper.'

He nodded agreement. 'Very wise,' he said. 'You have to 'ave deep pockets to keep a boat in the water.'

Then we went for a spin up the river.

'Was that an experience, or what? ' I'd concluded my account to Illy of my meeting with Marlon and the latest news of my bloody awful antecedents, with the description of the trip in Firefly. 'Honestly, you wouldn't believe it. I couldn't really see anything, thrashing along in a cloud of spray, but by golly, did she go!'

'You liking this?'

'As a one off, it was exhilarating. But we must have been breaking the speed limit so I wouldn't like to do it again and anyway, what's the point? You've whizzed down one river, or up, as the case may be, what's left to do? I did like the icemaker though.'

'And how you thinking about papa now?'

'I still haven't formed an opinion. I think I like him. No, I do like him, but it's all so artificial at the moment.'

'Each is being on best behaviour?'

'Yes, but how can we get round it? We can't just drop in on each other.'

She wrinkled her forehead. 'I not knowing how to make change. Perhaps soon not going to these posh places. Maybe meet at Marlon's house instead. Where he living?'

'In London, he hasn't said where.'

'He knowing where you living?

'Yes, because he remembers the house from the old days.'

'You liking Marlon coming here maybe?'

'No, I'm not ready to bring him here. Anyway, we'll see what he comes up with next time. Now it's your turn to tell me about your day at the Tower of London. Did you see the Crown Jewels?'

An Honest Trade
June 1834

A letter, dated only 2 weeks after Sarah's, is delivered to Wells from the Captain of the schooner, Guccian that is moored in the Demerary River. The ship has made the passage from Madeira in place of the agent's vessel, Justina, which has been detained in port having been holed below the waterline.

The letter brings bad news. It states that on setting out from Madeira for the London docks the Rople Helm was caught in a storm and driven onto rocks off the coast of North Africa. Debris has been found and it is presumed that all souls have been lost.

A servant despatched from Beausejour Plantation arrives bearing Wells' son, who is described as having a fair complexion and Negroid features. The messenger also reports that Lionoria has been recaptured and is in the colony hospital as a result of being mauled by the dogs used to track her down. She is not expected to survive.

Twenty-eight

The next significant thing that happened was a call from Zsa Zsa who was back on Alderney.

'I've got a package for you,' she said. 'I'm arranging for someone to bring it over.'

Marilyn phoned next. 'I've got somethin' for you,' she said. 'Only thing is, you've gotta come and visit Ginger before I'm 'anding it over.'

I left Illy at home immersed in a bulky omnibus edition of Wilkie Collins's sensation fiction, which contained The Moonstone as well as The Woman in White, and another novel of his called Armadale that I'd never heard of. I thought that having regard to the rate at which Ileana consumed literature, she'd be engaged until about teatime. Actually I couldn't believe the speed at which she devoured books. I'd given her my library ticket and she always took out the full entitlement, but they never lasted her the full loan period. She quite often hopped on my bike and took herself off for a fresh supply when she'd run out. Which made the eccentricity of her spoken English all the more baffling. A case of long-established habit prevailing over newly acquired knowledge, I supposed.

Marilyn was hurrying down the ramp to meet me as I opened the front gate. We met in a mutual hug on the garden path, the flowers I'd bought for her squashed between us. 'These are for you,' I said, as we disengaged.

'They're lovely,' she said, burying her face in them. 'Ma loves flowers an' all; one of her greatest sorrows not bein' able to see them now. 'Course she had to give up doin' the garden years ago, when 'er legs give out.'

'Well, I can see that someone's still attending to it,' I said, 'it's beautiful.'

'I like to get out here,' Marilyn said. 'Not that I manage as often

271

as I'd like wiv lookin' after Ma.' She added that she was lucky to have a bloke come in once a week to help out, by which time we'd reached the front door. She was about to lead me inside when I laid a restraining hand on her arm.

'Just a minute,' I said, 'before we go in, you need to tell me about Ginger. What you've said to her about me.'

'Oh,' Marilyn said, looking surprised, 'I've told 'er all about you. Didn't I say?'

'No, you didn't. How is she about it?'

'Overjoyed,' Marilyn said. 'She's up, wearin' 'er best bib and tucker and she's 'ad her 'air done. Most excitin' thing happened to 'er for years.'

Ginger was waiting for me in the conservatory.

I don't know, perhaps I've grown so used to keeping the lid on my emotions I'd been able to manage my first meeting with Marlon without too many hiccups. Or maybe it's a cumulative thing because I'd definitely been wobbly on the second occasion, although that had been nothing, I now realised, compared to the trauma of meeting my grandmother. I might have wondered why this was if I'd been capable of any rational thought. As it was, from the moment I saw her, propped up in one of those special chairs, I dissolved into tears. Not delicate ladylike tears, but a great, gulping, wrenching torrent, enough to float an ark stranded on Mount Ararat. I couldn't say how it happened. One minute I was standing in front of her, this old lady, neatly dressed in a frock and cardigan, and I was looking at the red hair without a hint of grey and was picturing the blue eyes which I knew were hidden behind the dark glasses, when I found myself on my knees, my head in her lap, bawling my eyes out, her arms wrapped round me, closing me in.

It took quite a while to get things back to normal. When I'd cried myself out, Ma released her hold on me and Marilyn helped me to my feet and guided me into a chair. Dabbing my soggy features with the towel that Marilyn had stuffed into my hand at some stage of the proceedings, I made a determined effort to get myself together by imagining the ravages my outburst would have wrought on my face.

The first thing I noticed when my eyes dried and I could focus properly again, was that Ma had discarded her dark glasses and her cloudy eyes were puffy and rimmed with red. Judging by her blotchy cheeks Marilyn had evidently been crying too. What anyone coming unexpectedly upon the three of us would have made of the scene, I can't imagine.

I think we were all too choked up to speak, I know I was, but in the way of that old cliché, the silence spoke volumes: volumes about estrangement and reunion, about missing years and belonging.

'Cuppa tea or somethin' stronger?' Marilyn asked at last.

We all knew the answer to that.

I was there all afternoon although we didn't do much talking about the past. What was there to say? Each of us knew what had happened and why, and I don't think any of us thought it hadn't been for the best. Instead, I prattled on about sailing and Lady Lou and my much postponed trip to the Azores, and Marilyn talked about films and the stars Ginger and Charlie had named the kids after, and then we got Ma into the wheelchair and went out into the garden. Not having a clue about gardening myself, I was seriously impressed by the sheer profusion of plants and shrubs, but even more so by the scent that wafted up from almost every bloom.

'I can see someone's got green fingers,' I said.

'Me gel put 'em in for me,' Ginger said proudly, 'so as I could still see 'em when me eyesight went. She's a good gel, Marilyn, does 'er best for 'er old ma.'

I said I could tell she was well looked after and she said I didn't know the half of it. When I thought about it afterwards I realised that although Marilyn and I had both recovered our powers of speech after that first emotional muteness, apart from the comment about Marilyn, Ginger had hardly uttered a word the whole afternoon. She'd simply taken my hand and held onto it, only relinquishing it for short, essential tasks, before grasping it firmly again. There was nothing she could have said that would have said so much.

I didn't promise to visit Ginger and Marilyn again; there simply wasn't any need. We all knew our reunion was permanent; a relationship, which would, no doubt, have its ups and downs, but would ripen as naturally as breathing.

It wasn't until we'd said goodbye and I was getting into my car that Marilyn pressed a slim package into my hand, 'Zsa Zsa sends 'er love and says she 'opes this will make your friend's life a bit easier.'

Illy hurried over to the car as I drove into the yard. She was hoping my meeting with Ginger was good whilst I was getting out and had progressed to wondering if I had the parcel from Zsa Zsa before we'd reached the front door. 'I wishing you not thinking I thinking of self only but I really truly wondering if you have papers for me.'

'If you'd let me get a word in I'd tell you Marilyn did give me a packet for you. I haven't opened it yet. Why don't you get us a drink while I shoot upstairs, then we can look at it together.'

There was no note in the parcel, nothing to say where it had come from or to indicate its destination. What it did contain was an ID card and passport in Ileana's name. The ID card indicated Illy was a citizen of Hungary and the passport that she'd entered GB from there in 2005.

Illy went very quiet. 'I not knowing what to thinking,' she said, when I asked her if she wasn't pleased. 'Zsa Zsa has making papers for me and she not even meeting me. Why she doing this thing for me?'

'I'd say she's done it for me,' I said, 'or rather she's got Spencer to do it as a kind of statement that blood's thicker than water.'

'But I not of family blood,' Illy declared, somewhat unnecessarily.

'That's true, but I think also irrelevant. It's a statement that I'm one of them.'

There must have been something in my voice as I said this, as Illy asked, 'Why you worrying?'

'I'm not worried, I'm just aware that it's about being bound by some Boyce code of honour: an all for one, one for all kind of thing – like the three musketeers.'

'What are musketeers?'

'They're characters in a book who took an oath to protect each other. On the other hand it might be a damn sight more prosaic than that and simply be a case of Boyces sticking what I think we can safely assume to be their customary two fingers up to the world.'

Ileana looked bewildered.

'I mean like this.' I stuck my fingers up in the usual rude gesture. Illy gave way to a fit of giggles. 'I gather you get the meaning.'

She spent the next minute probing my extremely limited knowledge of Alexandre Dumas before saying abruptly, 'I thinking Spencer making me from Hungary for good reason.'

'What?' I asked, confused, my head still full of daring do and devilish plots against the French throne. 'Honestly, I can't keep up with you.'

'I saying your uncle must knowing Hungary sharing border with Romania and has coming into European Community one or two years ago. So is easy for me to say I living in that country since being child.'

'It beats me how you know these things,' I said.

'I always looking about EU when I going to library to see when Romania may joining. I seeing many old communist countries already becoming member.'

'Well then,' I said, 'if you've finished researching French literature for today and are up to speed on European politics, I think we should set about applying for a provisional driving licence for you. We'll think of it as a first step ...'

I was interrupted by Illy grabbing me by both hands and starting up a mad dance, which appeared to be based on swinging round in circles and kicking up one's legs in a kind of frantic polka, getting faster and faster, with Illy letting out a series of ear-shattering whoops, until inevitably legs and feet became fatally intertwined and we collapsed in a breathless heap on the living room floor.

Luckily, Illy had cycled over to Greg's for an English lesson when the police arrived. Considering the pace at which life had taken to flinging itself at me, I suppose I shouldn't have been surprised - at least thirty-six hours had elapsed since we'd received Illy's dodgy papers and nothing out of the ordinary had happened. This latest incident made up for it.

One might have thought, considering the events of the past few weeks, all my chickens were safely tucked up in their roost.

Unfortunately not; one very large squawking bird was still out there, waiting to come home. Subconsciously, I guess I'd been expecting it all along, but had managed to back it into a corner and throw a cloth over it, to keep it quiet until someone forced me to remove it. Now it seemed, the cover was well and truly off.

I watched from the open door as two uniformed officers got out of the car and came across the yard. I proffered an enquiring expression as they reached me. They established who they were and who I was and asked if they might come in. I wondered if they'd mind saying what their business was first.

'It's about Mr Proivil,' one said. 'Mr Floyd Joseph Proivil. We understand he's a friend of yours.'

God, I felt sick. I opened my mouth to reply but simply couldn't speak, and all the time they just stood there staring at me. 'What's happened to him?' I finally forced the words out.

'Perhaps we could come in,' one said.

I nodded, set off for the kitchen, sat at the table, indicated they should sit too. 'What's happened? I asked again.

The one who wasn't taking notes, said 'Mr Proivil's missing.'

'What d'you mean, 'missing'?' I asked, my voice shaking.

'He hasn't been seen for about two months.'

'Two months! Surely that's impossible. What about his family? His friends?' The words poured out, unconstrained. Hadn't I been constantly asking myself those very questions? 'What about work? Hasn't he been to work?' Was that how they'd make the connection to me?

'Seems Mr Proivil was on annual leave. He'd submitted his resignation and wasn't expected back. Told his colleagues he was taking a sabbatical to write a book.'

'Oh yes, he mentioned that to me. In fact he showed me part of it. And I remember he did say he'd like to give up work to concentrate on writing.' Although all this was perfectly true, I was aware that what I wasn't saying was getting the upper hand; filling my head; swelling and swelling until it seemed as though it would burst out through the layers of skull and skin, exposing the truth to the light of day.

'Did you think that was odd?'

'Pardon?' Swamped by the mess in my head, I didn't hear the

question.

The policeman smiled politely. 'I asked whether you had any thoughts about his disposition; whether you thought he was acting at all strangely.'

'Well, I suppose with hindsight it was out of character, but I didn't take him too seriously. I mean, he's not long moved into his flat and he has his mortgage to consider. And he just isn't the reckless type.'

'So what's not clear is what he was expecting to live on if he didn't go to work.'

'I don't know what to think. Perhaps he's taken another job, something less high-powered that leaves him more time. I know he's done loads of research. Maybe he's gone on a retreat or something like that, to write it up. You do hear of those kinds of places.'

'A retreat.' The one officer glanced at the other as he wrote it down. 'I suppose it's a possibility. Another avenue to explore.'

'What about his family, don't they know anything?'

'It was his sister who reported him missing.'

'Sister, I didn't know he had a sister. I've never met his family.'

'How well do you know Mr Proivil?'

'We're friends. Good friends.'

'Nothing more?'

'No, it didn't work out,' I said. Nor ever would now, I thought, wiping my eyes with the back of my hand, as much to reassure myself some fiery brand wasn't burning itself across my forehead as to brush the smarting away.

'When did you last see him?'

'In May. I went up to stay at his flat for a few days, but we had words and I came back.' Now I was on dangerous territory. Had they questioned the neighbours? Searched the flat? Had anyone noticed Illy?

'What did you fall out about?'

'I wouldn't exactly describe it as falling out, more that neither of us fully appreciated the other's finer qualities at close quarters.'

'Would you like to expand on that?'

'Not really, except to say I suppose I found him a bit highfalutin and I guess he found me flippant. It was very personal.'

I saw them glance at each other and the note-taker jotted something down. After a pause the cross-examiner said 'You haven't heard from him since?'

'Not a word. To be fair, he did think I was going away for a longish trip on my boat. He wouldn't have expected me to be around.'

'But you didn't go?'

'No. I, well, truth is,' I stammered, tried to assemble the words, 'the truth is, I was pretty cut up about Floyd, and then, out of the blue, I discovered I'd been adopted. Which was fairly traumatic, as you can imagine. Then I got embroiled with trying to find my natural parents and what with one thing and another I missed the weather slot, and well, here I am.' I despised myself for bending the facts in this way, but what else could I do?

To give my interrogators their due, they did seem fairly nonplussed by my explanation, 'I hope that's worked out for you Miss,' one murmured, after a pause.

'Oh, you know, swings and roundabouts,' I said. 'We're all finding our feet. But now, on top of all that, you're telling me Floyd's missing.' Alarmed to find the pricking in my eyes was resolving into tears, I stopped speaking and groped for a tissue, but even as I found myself wondering why it was that recently I kept giving way to these displays of emotion when I'd successfully kept things buttoned up for the previous thirty years, I was in full spate again.

The coppers gave me a very long look before evidently deciding I was a hopeless case. Saying I was to ring the local nick at once if I heard from Floyd and that they'd see themselves out, they departed as unceremoniously as they'd arrived.

Illy found a snivelling blob sitting at the kitchen table when she came back. She was toting library books and bits of shopping. 'How did you manage all that stuff on the bike?' I asked, trying to pretend there was nothing the matter.

'I hanging bags on handlebars,' she said. 'But why you asking this when something has happening? Why you crying? Is something to do with Marlon or grandma?' She swooped over me clucking and fussing like a mother hen, not giving me a chance to explain. 'You sitting on settee and putting feet up and I bringing brandy and making tea quick as a flash and soon you telling what is up.'

There didn't seem to be anything to say to that.

Actually, I did feel better when I'd done as I was told, but whether it was the ministrations or simply having her there to confide in is a moot point. Then again, I'd had to rally pretty swiftly to her assistance as when I mentioned the police had turned up, she'd gone a ghastly putty colour and slumped down beside me on the sofa. The result of this was we had to make serious inroads into the brandy before Illy allowed herself to be convinced the police hadn't come for her and I'd been almost persuaded they didn't suspect me of having anything to do with Floyd's disappearance.

'We having near shave,' Illy said, recapping the incident for about the hundredth time.

For a moment she threw me. 'Near what?'

'I saying English expression about only avoiding danger by a very little piece.'

'Oh, I see. I think that should be either 'a narrow shave' or 'a near squeak' although I'd've thought a shave would be near rather than narrow and I can't see how a squeak comes in at all.'

Illy waited thoughtfully for a further explanation.

I inspected my hand through the bottom of my glass, but failing to find the derivation of the idiom there was obliged to resume the discussion about the police. 'I got the impression they thought Floyd might have been depressed or that something was worrying him at work. And honestly, now I'm thinking about it properly, I'm wondering what on earth he was intending to live on if he did give up work. As far as I know, putting the deposit down on his flat had more or less cleaned him out and his mortgage was pretty hefty.'

'Maybe, he soon giving up flat; maybe thinking to live with family while writing book. I think maybe he having to do this thing. Is very important for him to say what has happening in old days, so world sees. I also would liking to write book to tell about hard times for people to come to this country without papers. I knowing plenty.'

'Mm. You could, you know. But I don't think you're right about Floyd. I can't see him going back to live with his folks. And

279

however disillusioned he was with the Home Office, I can't believe he'd just resign and risk losing his flat; he must have had something else up his sleeve.'

'You not remember he giving you clue?'

I shook my head. 'I can't think of a thing, but whatever he had in mind, it doesn't seem right to let people think he's walked out because he's depressed or has had a breakdown or something, when we know what really happened.'

'Is like making his name bad when he trying to do good thing.'

'Yes. It's exactly like that. Trouble is, I don't see what else we can do without implicating ourselves.'

About all we resolved that day was that we needed another bottle of brandy. Luckily we had plenty of other stuff in to tide us over but we zipped into town the following morning to stock up anyway. There was a message from Marlon on the answer phone when we got back.

'What say you come to my pad next time, kiddo? See your old dad with his slippers on. I could make Monday or Friday next week.'

'Monday would be fine,' I said, when I 'phoned back. He sounded relieved that I'd accepted the invitation, and added that he'd been nervous about meeting on his own turf but had decided we'd never consolidate our relationship until he'd bitten the bullet.

Having established that Marlon's place was located fairly close to the marina where Firefly was moored, I decided to make the most of the visit.

'We'll go up for another short break,' I decided. 'Book into a hotel for the weekend, do some sights, and dump you in a museum or art gallery, while I'm busy. Would that suit you?'

She beamed. 'You always making nice things for me. I so happy with you, Daysee. Is like a dreaming. Even when we worrying about bad things we having each other.'

'It's good for me too,' I said. 'Don't forget that. I never really had anyone to share things with before I met you.'

It occurred to me when Greg announced he'd booked us into a different hotel for this trip that he was another person I'd got used to being around, and what with Illy and my sudden influx of relatives I hadn't noticed the loss of Megan and my other sailing cronies anywhere near as much as I'd expected. I don't know what this says about my character, other than I don't imagine it's a very endearing trait to be quite so ready to substitute one set of people for another without really noticing.

I did miss Floyd though, and what was especially alarming was that I couldn't always recall the sound of his voice or see his face clearly anymore. And the awful thing was, I didn't even have a photograph of him.

We didn't waste any time after booking into our hotel on the Saturday: amongst other sights we took in the Post Office Tower, the Royal Albert Hall and Madam Tussauds before ending up on the London Eye. I have to say I was seriously impressed and Illy was practically beside herself as she clutched my arm and gazed out over the landscape. 'Is so wonderful,' she whispered. 'I never been so high before and going round and round also.'

On the Sunday, we got up early and caught a pleasure boat down the river to Southend. It was a great trip with a commentary all the way and the weather was on our side as well. I'm not sure that Southend would figure in my list of favourite holiday hot spots but we had a very silly day, like a couple teenagers out on the town. We hit all the big rides in the Adventure Island theme park, tackled the slot machines in the amusement arcades, bought candyfloss and kiss-me-quick hats on the pier and finished up with fish and chips.

Minus the commentary on the return journey, one elderly man took the opportunity to entertain us all on the accordion. With a seemingly endless supply of requests and suggestions from the passengers and the fact that the bar was open, the trip turned into a fairly rumbustious water-borne sing-a-long, and I have to say Illy and I weren't exactly sheltering below with our hands clapped over our ears. Arriving back at the pier we fell, a little the worse for wear, into a taxi and hence to our hotel. Perhaps because of the store I set by the next day's meeting with Marlon, I actually remembered to drink several glasses of water, and to remind Illy to do the same, to allay any hangover, before falling exhausted into bed.

This time, I dropped Illy off at the London Museum and, having invested in a mobile for her, was secure in the knowledge that we could reach each other if we needed to.

Marlon's address was at St Katherine's dock, close to Firefly's mooring. He'd said it was a converted Victorian warehouse and I couldn't miss it. All I had to do was retrace my steps along the quay. I really had no idea what to expect as I hurried past the coffee houses and bakeries, restaurants and bars, elegant boutiques and jewellers too select to display prices, which lined each side of the lock, but was forming a general idea. Given Firefly and the ultra trendy location it seemed unlikely that Marlon's pad would turn out to be a modest bed-sit with a gas ring, shared bathroom and a `phone on the landing.

Even so, I was unprepared for the luxury in which Marlon lived. An entry `phone allowed me through heavy oak doors into a stone-flagged lobby. Light percolated in from a string of windows high above my head. The atmosphere was cool and dim. A uniformed security guard stood behind a desk in the far distance, and behind a second man, standing miles away in a doorway to one side, I glimpsed a battery of camera screens.

I moved across the expanse of hallway towards the reception desk, thankful for the soundlessness of my posh boots on the stone floor. I wouldn't say I was over-awed but I wasn't exactly relaxed. Uniformed flunkeys always make me feel inferior. Thank heavens Marlon came down to meet me.

We went up in the lift to the top floor. 'I'll give you a quick guided tour,' Marlon said, as he unlocked his door, 'then we'll talk.'

The apartment that awaited my appraisal turned out to be an extremely smart split-level affair located on the corner of the building, so that one side overlooked the quay and the other had views across the river. It had wooden floors and beams and the original ironworks combined with luxurious modern fittings and interior design. The bedrooms on the upper floor were softly lit from low-level arched windows but the living space below was filled with light streaming in from the floor to ceiling panes set next to each other along the flank wall. I could hardly take it in.

'You're very quiet,' Marlon said as we stood side by side contemplating the river.

'I guess I'm …' What was I feeling exactly? I couldn't put my finger on it. 'Impressed,' I said, knowing that wasn't it. 'Who wouldn't be? You've got an address to die for, with absolutely stunning views, and it's all totally chic and man-about-town.'

'What's worryin' you, then?' he asked.

'Nothing, why should it be?'

'I can see something is. I had my doubts about askin' you here,' he said. 'Like it was jumpin' the gun.'

'Don't say that. I was so pleased you asked me to come.'

'What is it, then?'

'I don't know,' I said, and I didn't. I simply couldn't pinpoint what was on my mind. Noticing that Marlon was waiting for me to elaborate, I did my best. 'I want to get to know you properly, but perhaps it's the reverse of you feeling you've been too quick off the mark,' I said. 'I'm feeling I'm invading your space.'

'How could you think that? You're my daughter. My daughter. Best thing that's happened since they invented sliced bread.'

I think I blushed. I certainly felt very hot. 'I only mean that after thirty years of you doing your own thing, I'm very aware of the danger of getting under your feet.'

'Oh, come on now,' he said in a jokey voice. 'How many times have we met?' He answered his own question without giving me chance to reply. 'I make this number three in as many weeks. I think you're stretchin' a point. Let's have a drink.'

Having a drink was a good idea. Things gradually got easier between us. With a bit of prompting, after I'd said there wasn't that much to tell him about myself, I mentioned the succession of temporary jobs I'd had over the years. He asked me if I'd never wanted a career and I explained that I'd always thought of sailing as my occupation and going to work as the inconvenient backwash.

He grinned. 'So you're telling me I'm not the father of a thwarted pop singer or the next Margaret Thatcher?'

'God, no! I can't think of anything more awful than being in the limelight or being endowed with a burning desire to change the world. How about you?'

'Me. I get along minding my own business. Or perhaps I should say 'businesses'.'

'They must be quite profitable to judge by this place and your snazzy boat.'

'Yeah, I do all right.' I heard the pride in his voice. 'You've heard of that American book called, 'Rich Dad, Poor Dad'. Well, I'm the rich one.'

I hadn't, but I laughed anyway and thought I'd try to remember to ask Illy to get it for me when she next went to the library.

'Only one fly in the ointment,' he said, 'until recently I wasn't a proper dad.' He looked at me keenly. 'I'm hoping to change that now.'

Twenty-nine

In the lull that followed Marlon's declaration I mustered the courage to ask him a few questions about himself, or rather about his life as it pertained to me. 'You haven't said whether I've got any other family I don't know about,' I said, grasping the bull by the horns.

'How d'you mean?' he asked.

'Well, if I've got a step-mother, or half brothers and sisters?'

His mouth didn't actually drop open, but he was certainly taken aback. 'You're askin' if I've married and had kids?' he said, after a longish pause.

'Yes. I just thought … after all it's been thirty years … I just wondered …'

A longer pause followed. At last he said, 'I told you the first time we met that Vicky was the only one for me. Maybe I should have moved on; I dunno. Could be why I never visited her all these years; didn't want to face reality. Whatever. Fact is there's never been anyone else. Not that I'd have thought of settlin' down with, anyway.'

'What, nobody special, ever?'

'Sure, women have come and gone and some have lasted longer than others. But none of 'em ever held a candle to her.'

'You felt like that in spite of what she did?'

'Yeah, well, she never asked to be ill. Someone should have seen it comin'.'

I couldn't help thinking that he'd been closer to her than anybody but clearly he didn't include himself in the category of people who'd failed her.

'I blame the so-called authorities,' he went on. 'Them bastards that's supposed to be in charge.'

I tried not to show it, but I think he must have seen how his words jarred with me, because he added quickly, 'You gotta see it from my point of view, I lost my girl, my kid and eventually my job, and

285

all because Vicky never got the treatment she needed.'

'Heavens,' I said, 'I'm not arguing. I'd have preferred someone to intervene before my mother was driven to do away with my grandparents. It's hard enough coming to terms with it now, all these years after, I can't imagine what it would have been like then.'

'It never leaves you,' he said gruffly.

I let a minute or two lapse before I asked, 'You said you lost your job as a result of what happened, but I thought your boss spoke up for you at the trial?'

'Yeah, that's right enough. Reg Miller was a fair man, straight as a die. But he couldn't hold out against the motor mouths spreadin' the dirt about sex and drugs, like I was some sort of ponce who'd led her astray. He had no option in the end. Mind, I'll say this for him, he slipped me a ton to tide me over. I'd've been up queer-street without it.'

'I suppose a hundred pounds would have gone a long way in those days,' I said.

'Yeah, and Zsa Zsa helped out. I guess I did okay, considerin'.'

'I suppose you moved away?'

He nodded. 'Spence found me an openin' 'til I could stand on my own feet.'

It was pretty two-faced of me considering what Spencer had so recently done for Illy and me, but I didn't like the sound of such an obvious crook being involved on a rung of Marlon's career ladder, even if it had only been near the bottom.

Luckily Marlon was oblivious to the hypocritical thoughts swirling round in my head, and was explaining how it had all worked out for the best in the end. 'Jolted me out of what would have been a dead-end job. Eighteen months later I'd bought me first business.'

'Blimey,' I said, 'how did you manage that?'

'Well, kiddo, let's say I'm a quick learner. I learned who to know and what to know. You get my drift?' He tapped the side of his nose in a significant manner.

'I can see you went on from there in leaps and bounds,' I said.

He nodded. 'You got it in one. I learned to diversify my interests. I see a gap in the market; I supply it.'

'It sounds too risky to me. I like to know what I'm getting in my wage packet at the end of the week.'

He grinned. 'It takes all sorts. I like to take risks. I guess you'd say I'm a natural wheeler-dealer. I keep my finger on the pulse. Get in and get out when I see the tide turnin'. Like the chip shops, I've just sold off. Fish getting scarce and prices goin' through the roof. Time to get out.'

Buying and selling fish and chip shops! How humdrum. How wonderfully, boringly, humdrum.

I'd say this conversation was the turning point in how I felt about Marlon. My reservations seemed to disappear in the clichéd puff of smoke and something I'd been holding back jostled to the fore, so that after lunch, when we were sitting by the open windows, the Thames flowing below like a feature in an advertisement for the very latest in stylish apartments, I surprised myself by asking Marlon if he'd like to come to me next time we met.

His eyes widened. 'You mean, uh, you mean I should come to your place?'

I said yes, that was what I meant.

Abruptly he stood up, excused himself for a moment and strode briskly out of the room.

Left alone, I realised I'd overstepped the mark, had pushed too hard, been too eager. I wished I could take it back and saw, in one of those devastating insights into one's own character, what I'd lost by not saying enough to Floyd, to saying too much too soon to Marlon.

I was still slumped in the chair when Marlon came back. He stood in front of me and held out his hands. Wondering what was coming I raised mine to his. He grasped them firmly and pulled me to my feet. Holding me at arms length and looking me straight in the eyes, he said very, very quietly that he'd love to come; that he thought it was an honour and a privilege to be invited to my home and that it knocked the spots off anything that happened to him for years.

Bizarrely, considering how tearful I'd been recently, this time I wasn't in the least. I was happy and excited and was soon burbling on about the house and asking if he remembered it. He said he knew where it was well enough. He added that he'd only been inside when everyone was out, which, given Vicky's two sisters as well as her parents, he doubted had happened more than half a dozen times, and that that was before they'd moved Vicky from the room with its own outside steps to an ordinary bedroom inside.

I'd had to interrupt him then. 'That's my room,' I said. 'The converted barn. I didn't know it had been Victoria's room.'

Marlon gave me an old-fashioned look. 'You never call Vicky your ma, do you?'

'No. I, I, well, really, she never has been, you know. I mean I've only known she is my real mum for a few weeks, and I've never actually known her as a person at all. I went to see her when I found out, but she doesn't seem to know anyone now. It may sound hard but there wasn't anybody there for me to try to get to know.'

'You're saying she's away with the fairies,' he said, subdued.

'I'd like to think that's where she is, flitting around some enchanted glade, but somehow I doubt it.'

'She's totally out of it?'

'Yes. Wherever her mind is, her body is certainly trapped on earth. And I guess it doesn't put me in a very good light to say I didn't find seeing her like that very easy to take.'

'D'you want me to go and see her?'

'It's hardly up to me. Perhaps you want to remember her as she was, before she did that terrible thing. On the other hand, if you saw her as she is now, maybe you'd come to some sort of resolution. I don't know what's best.'

'Hark at me, an old geezer, asking my kid what to do.' He was obviously amused by the idea.

'Anyway,' I said, not anxious to discuss Victoria any more than absolutely necessary and not wanting to lose that initial excitement, 'apart from seeing where I live, you could look over my boat, Lady Louella. I'd love you to see her. She's not as new as Firefly of course, but she is special. Very special. I stopped abruptly when I heard what I was saying, realised what I'd nearly added about her being named after Ellen and Louise. Hoped he wouldn't ask.

Maybe he was being tactful because all he said was, 'Where do you berth her? I used to know the waters round those parts like the back of my hand.'

'I've got her in the estuary at the moment, but I don't know how long I'll keep her there. I miss the amenities I used to have at the marina.'

'Why did you move?'

That caught me on the hop. 'I'd planned a longish voyage to the Azores, but finding out about Victoria disrupted those plans, so I opted for a change of scenery instead.'

He nodded. 'And now you regret it?'

'Now and then. Plus I'm tied to the tide. I kept forgetting at first and would turn up only to find several yards of mud separating us from Lou.'

'Us?' he queried. 'I thought you said you didn't have a boyfriend.'

'I don't. Why d'you jump to that conclusion?'

'You're far too attractive to be unattached.'

'There was someone,' I heard a voice saying, 'but he died a little while ago. His name was Floyd.'

'You poor kid.' His hand touched my face.

I was saved from having to think what I wanted to add about Floyd being the man in my life without my ever acknowledging it, or indeed having to consider whether I wanted to say anything else about him at all, by the 'phone. My 'phone. The problem was that it had rung so infrequently that I failed to recognise 'What Shall We Do with the Drunken Sailor' that was issuing from the ether as in any way connected with a telephone. Thus it had rung for several seconds before Marlon asked, 'Aren't you goin' to answer it?'

'Answer what?'

'Well, it must be yours, mine doesn't play anythin' so sophisticated.'

I did feel a fool.

It was Illy. Who else could it be?

'Daysee, I just wondering if you forgetting time,' she said. 'Is nearly five o'clock and I worry just a little.'

'Oh, Illy, I'm so sorry. I didn't realise how late it was. We've been talking.'

'Is fine so long as I knowing all is well. When shall you come?'

I glanced at my watch. 'Give me an hour,' I said, 'to be on the safe side. It's rush hour and I'll have to get a cab. Will you be okay?'

'Is fine,' she said again. 'Museum not closing until eight. I see you soon.' She rang off.

'I'm so sorry,' I said to Marlon, who was looking perplexed. 'I arranged to meet my friend at four o'clock and she's been getting worried.'

'I see.'

'Oh,' I said, light dawning, 'that sounds awful. It's not like I planned to meet her as a sort of second string to seeing you, I left her there this morning.'

'I'm not with you,' he said.

'Well, she's staying with me at the moment. In fact, that was whom I was talking about a little while ago when you thought I meant a boyfriend. We came up to town on Friday so we could visit some attractions over the weekend before I came to meet you. She's foreign, you see.'

The upshot of all this was that Marlon said he'd give me a lift. The car was parked in a private underground car park a couple of streets away. It was a Jag and I was clearly expected to appreciate its finer features. Unfortunately, cars are a closed book to me. As long as they go when required and bits aren't actually dropping off, they meet my bill. I did my best but I could tell I fell a long way short of the mark in the 'being impressed by the wheels' stakes.

Marlon wasn't what I'd call a relaxed driver. He carved a route through the meanderings of his fellow road users with the kind of single-minded determination that I imagined would characterise his business dealings, his face set in a dogged scowl. Nor did he chat. Now and then he punched out a comment, which, not requiring a reply, left him free to deal with his antagonists. I looked forward to the journey's end when I expected the pre-chauffering Marlon to reappear.

Ileana was waiting for me outside the museum as we zoomed up.

'I'll give you a bell in a couple of days,' Marlon said, screeching to a halt barely long enough for me to scramble out. He pressed his fingers to his lips and flicked a kiss. 'Love you, kiddo. Take care.'

Illy and I stood and watched him go. Which didn't take very long.

'Marlon is being very fast driver,' Illy said, 'and having supadupa car.'

'Where did you come up with that expression?' I asked. 'It went out with the ark.'

She shrugged, 'I knowing plenty. I not remembering where I learn each.'

We went back to Halnaker House the following morning, by which time I'd been comprehensively cross-examined. I doubt there was a sentence that had passed between Marlon and me that I wasn't required to recount word by word. 'Honestly, Illy,' I'd said at one point, 'where'd you learn your interrogation technique? I feel as if I've been brain-washed.' She'd grinned and murmured that she wanted to be sure Marlon wasn't trifling with my affections, and I told her she'd been reading too much Victorian fiction, and that anyway that term was usually used in the context of unsuitable lovers, not recently acquired fathers.

'What we need,' I said, 'is a period of R and R.'

'What is R and R meaning?'

'Rest and relaxation, I think. Or it might be recuperation.'

'You mean, we going to Lady Lou. Hooray. Hooray. I making big cheering,' she added, unnecessarily. 'I will getting ready straightaway but maybe needing to go to shops for some few stocks for onboard. How long shall we going for?'

The stocks didn't look that few to me when they were loaded into the supermarket trolley, unloaded into the car, reloaded into the dinghy, and finally put away on Louella. 'Blimey,' I said, collapsing in a heap on a bunk, 'now all we've got to do is fill up with water and diesel and we'll be off.'

'Where we going?'

'I think it would be nice to take a trip to Alderney, don't you?'

'We go to see Zsa Zsa?' Illy's eyes were bright.

'Yes, I got her number from Marilyn, and she's expecting us. I thought you'd like to thank her personally.'

It was very straightforward trip - busy enough to keep my mind almost fully engaged with nautical matters to the exclusion of those painful thoughts about Floyd which would overtake me in

291

unguarded moments. The thought that whispered I was losing my grip on the sound of his voice, the look of him, the way he did things: the thought that to hold onto him, sooner or later I'd have to face up to reality.

We made a good five knots most of the way and did it in a little under twelve hours. I was beginning to feel as if I'd sailed with Illy for years, rather than just a few weeks. Now and then when I glanced at her I would notice the same intense awareness that I experienced myself when I was totally tuned in to Lou. It was a sensation which came up through the soles of my feet and percolated my whole system right through to the tips of my fingers, so that when I held the wheel or tweaked a sail I felt as if I were a living part of her.

Anyway, Illy took her watch without batting an eyelid and we got tide right as we approached the island, so that buoyed up with our success, picking up a floating mooring in the harbour was a cinch. We freshened up in the onshore ablutions before striking out for Zsa Zsa's.

Zsa Zsa had another of those unpretentious little pads as epitomised by Marlon. Hers was a sprawling single-storey edifice in the style of a Spanish hacienda; to call it a bungalow would be as inappropriate as describing the Brighton Dome as a beach hut. It was set on the top of the hill amongst rolling lawns and flower gardens and had dazzling views of the ocean on three sides and of the town on the other. I recalled that Alderney was a tax haven and thought that if the height of the fountains was anything to go by, Zsa Zsa's husbands must have sheltered a bob or two from the taxman's grasp.

Illy and I were slightly out of breath when we got to the top of the hill, but had recovered it by the time we'd traipsed the length of the gravel drive leading to the house.

A maid answered the door. I had to mentally pinch myself before I could believe the evidence of my own eyes. She was real. She was wearing a smart short-sleeved navy dress and a spotless white apron. She was youngish and probably from the Philippines: I was too taken aback to be absolutely certain. I would never have envisaged being greeted by a uniformed maid; not in England anyway, and certainly not in the employ of my own relatives. I glanced at Ileana out of the corner of my eye. Her face was completely expressionless. I hoped the visit wouldn't prove to be a huge error of judgement.

I needn't have worried. Even as the maid was ushering us in, Zsa Zsa appeared. She was wearing a strappy sundress, high-heeled sandals, an expensive-looking tan and a wide smile.

'Daisy, my dear, I'm so pleased to see you.' She pecked me on the cheek. 'And your friend as well. Ileana isn't it?'

Illy shuffled a bit and stared at the floor.

'There's no need to be shy. I've been dying to meet you. For one thing I wanted to see if you're as pretty in the flesh as you looked in the photos. And that wonderful hair, so long and glossy, I'm really envious. You can't do a thing with a curly red thatch like mine.' She patted her immaculately styled coiffure and snatched a breath. 'Anyway, I'm forgetting my manners, keeping you standing here in the hall. Perhaps you'd like to sit outside as it's such a nice day.'

We followed Zsa Zsa through the house over acres of pristine white carpet. I don't know about Illy, but I was certainly hoping I wasn't leaving a trail of dirty footprints behind me.

Outside an assortment of sun-loungers was grouped under the shade of the umbrellas by the brilliant blue, kidney-shaped, film star swimming pool. Illy's eyes looked as if they were about to pop out of their sockets.

'Would you like to swim?' Zsa Zsa asked her. 'Don't answer that, I can see you would. And what about you, Daisy?'

I shook my head. 'I'm still recovering from the hill. I'll watch Illy.'

'I would like to swim but not having bathing dress,' Illy said.

'You'll find costumes and towels in the changing room,' Zsa Zsa said, indicating a gazebo-type building peeking out from behind a cluster of shrubs and bushes. 'Help yourself.'

Illy glanced at me and I nodded my reassurance. She headed off in the direction of the changing room. Zsa Zsa turned to me, 'Make yourself comfortable. Gin and tonic or coffee?'

I said a G and T would go down a treat and Zsa Zsa rang a little silver bell. The maid appeared.

'A jug of you-know-what, please, Maria.'

The maid disappeared as silently as she'd appeared. Almost simultaneously Ileana emerged ready for her dip. She'd pushed her hair up into one of those silly flowery bathing caps and was wearing a one-piece number in shocking-pink. She looked extremely fit and healthy. I felt quite proud when I remembered the scrawny, pastey-faced girl I'd pulled out of that filthy attic.

Walking quickly to the edge of the pool, Illy gave us a bashful wave and dived in.

'Nice little swimmer,' Zsa Zsa commented as Illy set out to skirt the perimeter of the pool in a competent crawl.

'Yes,' I agreed, 'she's improved no end since she's been staying with me. Being by the sea helps, of course, we can slope off for a swim whenever the mood takes us. And Illy isn't the sort of person to do things by halves.'

'You seem very fond of each other. How did you meet?'

I choked, spluttered and dropped my drink. Ice and glass splintered on the tiles. Alcohol dripped down my chin. I could have died of embarrassment. However Illy, clocking up her water miles, was oblivious, and Zsa Zsa unperturbed. She rang the bell again.

The intermission that occurred whilst Maria cleared up the mess was a blessing, giving me chance to decide whether I wanted to confide in Zsa Zsa or not. On the whole I thought possibly, but not unless Illy was in complete agreement, and since she was currently intent on swimming the channel in kidney-shaped circles, any discussion on the subject would have to be postponed until she beached.

I don't know whether Zsa Zsa was clairvoyant or whether my clumsy over-reaction had been a touch of a give-away but she didn't pursue the matter. She made an innocuous remark about life on Alderney giving me an obvious opening to ask her how long she'd been living there. She said she'd come over for a couple of years with her first husband but had returned to the mainland after the divorce. She'd come back with Dennis, husband number four and had lived on the island ever since. She chatted on about the ups and downs of residing on Alderney, the life of ease being both the attraction and the downside. 'Of course it's unspoiled and relaxing; on the other hand, you could say there's not that much to do,' she said, 'not day in and day out; how could there be when the island's only five and a quarter square miles altogether?'

'I hadn't realised that,' I said.

'The main problem is we live in each other's pockets; coffee mornings, cocktails, lunches and dinner parties, charity functions and the Yacht Club. The same faces milling round in ever decreasing circles. Inevitable given the size of the place, but sometimes I feel I'm going stir crazy.'

'I'm sure there are compensations,' I said.

'Well, we have wonderful beaches and a mild climate, and of course we're a VAT free zone, but even these excitements begin to pall when you've exhausted every shop in St Anne's and can't go anywhere at more than 35 miles per hour. Which is probably just as well, as if you got up any speed you could drive straight over edge.' She paused to drain her glass. 'Refill?'

When she'd topped us up, she said, 'Hark at me going on - you'd think I hate the place. I don't at all. I've just outgrown it.'

'Why don't you move then?'

'Tell the truth, I'm trapped. Trapped by my trappings.'

She'd begun to explain the complexities of being a tax exile when Illy emerged from the pool, pulled off the bathing cap, shook out her hair, scooped up a towel and came over to join us.

'I suppose you've come to claim your medal for endurance swimming,' I said.

Her brow crinkled whilst she processed the comment, then she grinned. 'You making joke,' she announced. 'Saying I like Olympic swimmer.'

Later, when Illy had had a breather and a drink or two, Zsa Zsa and I went in for a dip with her. Or to be more accurate, I should say I joined her in the water, whereas Zsa Zsa, although in the pool, didn't actually go so far as to get wet, choosing instead to drift around looking elegant on an airbed. 'I swim in the mornings,' she explained, 'before I get my hair done.'

'If I having swimming pool,' Illy whispered, 'I only not swimming when I sailing on Lady Lou.'

Zsa Zsa was clearly upset when I said we ought to be making a move.

295

'Oh, dear,' she said. 'I didn't realise you'd have to go. I thought you'd be staying with me. I can't tell you how much I've been looking forward to getting to know you, what with Marlon going on about you being the bee's knees, and you being such a big hit with Ma and Marilyn.'

So it was settled. I said we'd need to pick up a few bits and pieces from Lou and Zsa Zsa said she'd come with us if we'd give her a minute or two to get changed into something more suitable. Then, arm in arm, the three of us tromped down the road to the harbour. There was a hint of unsteadiness about us when we came to get into the dinghy to row across to Lady Lou, which may have had something to do with the buckets of gin and tonic we'd imbibed, but that paled into insignificance when it came to the difficulty of shinning up over the side onto Louella's deck especially when one of us had an unreliable ankle.

What's that saying about where there's a will there's a way? Eventually, we made it onboard.

Worn out by the process of tossing toothbrushes and other such cumbersome articles into a bag, we had a quick drink to sustain ourselves for the journey ahead and departed whence we had come. The dinghy was very uncooperative and our efforts to row back to shore are best left to the imagination.

We popped into The Divers, my favourite pub on the quay, to brace ourselves for the hill. We left at closing time. We may have been singing.

We didn't get up very early next day, and because of what we put down to a bout of food poisoning, neither Illy nor I fancied breakfast. Which was just as well as it was practically lunchtime. Zsa Zsa eventually put in an appearance wearing dark glasses and a wrap-around robe. She hadn't had her hair done. She said she too had been struck down with the same mystery bug. The day passed in desultory conversation and the occasional chink of ice as one of us carefully tilted the jug to pour out a little more water, keeping our eyes averted from the vulgar glare of the pool. In the evening we had a peck of supper to keep our strength up, and later managed a nightcap or two.

Finding ourselves miraculously cured of whatever malady had afflicted us the day before, Zsa Zsa hired a man with a horse and trap and took us to see the sights. We did the town and the beaches and the history and then went back to her place.

In the hour or so before dinner when Zsa Zsa had gone into town to get her nails done and Illy and I had swum in the pool, I told Illy about Zsa Zsa asking where we'd met.

She went very quiet. Then she said, 'What you telling?'

'Daft goose,' I said. 'As if I'd say anything without talking it over with you first.'

'I liking Zsa Zsa very much,' she said, 'but I not knowing whether I want to telling secret.'

'I know what you mean and really we can easily cook up a story in case she asks again.'

'Mm. I must considering carefully. Is two ways to think.' She held up her fingers to be sure I got the point. 'For one, Zsa Zsa already knowing I illegal. What difference if she knowing how I coming? But number two,' she waggled her finger, 'perhaps is dangerous to tell more. Spencer has making me false passport, so he having big grip on me, which is not good, but also I having hold on him for making papers, so we kind of even.'

'I couldn't argue with that,' I said, 'even if I knew what you were talking about.'

She looked indignant. 'I explaining serious thoughts and you making joke.'

'I'm just teasing,' I said. 'It is a big decision. For one thing I'd say it was odds on that anything you tell Zsa Zsa will go straight back to Marilyn, and probably Marlon as well. And then who knows? As my aunt was fond of saying, 'you can't put the genie back in the bottle.'

'I like to know what is 'genie' but you may telling me at later time. For now we must making important decision.'

'I think I'll leave it up to you and that's what I'll say to Zsa Zsa if she asks me again. Okay?'

Zsa Zsa didn't ask again and soon we were having such a great time I hardly gave it another thought. Zsa Zsa abandoned her daily appointment with the hairdresser to join Illy and me in the pool or the sea or pottering around on Lady Lou, wherever the whim took us.

We'd been over to Guernsey in Louella for a couple of days and had stopped at the pub for a meal when we got in, so were quite late getting back to Zsa Zsa's. Maria hurried forward to meet us as we came through the front door and spoke quietly to Zsa Zsa.

'Sort us out a drink,' Zsa Zsa said over her shoulder, 'I have to ring Marilyn. Apparently she's been trying to get me. I'll take it in my bedroom.'

She didn't come back. In the end I asked Maria to go and see if everything was all right. Knowing it wasn't. My immediate thought being that something had happened to Ginger.

I found Zsa Zsa hunched up on her bed, hugging her knees, her face pressed down against them.

'What's happened?' I asked, touching her shoulder. 'Can you tell me?'

I heard a muffled sound that might have been my name.

'Yes, it's me, Daisy.'

She lifted her head to look at me.

I crouched down to be at her level. 'Has something happened to Ginger?' I asked.

'Ginger? No. Not Ginger.'

'What then? Is Marilyn okay?'

'Marlon's dead,' she said.

Thirty

Mostly I was angry. It was so unfair. First Floyd and now my father: the only two men who'd ever meant anything to me in my whole life had suddenly been snatched away from me, without a by your leave. It wasn't just unfair - it was the last bloody straw - the one that broke the camel's back.

I must have made a right spectacle of myself, falling into my regrettable habit of ranting and carrying on about fate dealing me another blow, without a thought of how Zsa Zsa and Marilyn would be feeling losing their brother, or Ma, losing her son. Nor even about Marlon losing his life. I just went on and on and on about my loss until I half registered I was being held very tightly and a hand was pushing something small and hard into my mouth.

Ileana was sitting by the bed when I came round. 'Tell me it was a bad dream,' I said.

She shook her head. 'Not dream,' she said.

'Marlon's dead.'

'Yes.'

'What happened? Do you know?'

'Has having accident in boat, I think.'

'In Firefly?'

'Yes.'

'Some bloody coincidence,' I said.

Zsa Zsa was wonderful. She wouldn't have it when I tried to apologize. She said it was she who should apologize to me for not breaking the news to me properly and for force-feeding me her sleeping pills. And when I said I'd been selfish brat, she said she took it as a credit to Marlon that I should care so much when we'd known each other for such a short time. After a while I asked what had happened. She told me that Marlon had apparently lost control of the boat and it had ploughed into one of the piers near

299

Hornchurch Marshes. She expected the full facts to be revealed at the inquest. I asked about Ma and Marilyn and she said they were bearing up. Boyces were used to bearing up.

Then Illy and I decided to go home.

Navigating the shipping lanes in fog isn't much fun. You hear the turgid boom of a foghorn and then suddenly a huge shape comes looming up out of nowhere and you're never convinced it knows you're there. The other thing is you have far too much time for thinking; thinking about your ghastly family history and thinking about death.

Illy and I stayed on deck the whole trip.

There was a heap of post on the mat when we got home.

'You having lots of letters,' Illy said scooping them up and handing them over.

'They'll all be bills,' I said.

But one wasn't.

'I'm taking my stuff upstairs to unpack,' I called through to Illy who was busy putting the kettle on in the kitchen. 'I'll come down for my tea.'

The one that wasn't a bill was from Marlon.

Kiddo,

This isn't what I wanted. I wanted my daughter. I wanted a future together, making up for the thirty years we'd lost. That's what I wanted.

But you know, it don't matter how much you want something if your luck's run out, if too much water's gone under the bridge. No excuses. I made my choices and did very well out of them.

You'll remember the last time we met. You asked about my business interests and I said I bought and sold commodities. Then you told me some things about yourself. You said your boyfriend, name of Floyd, had died recently and that you'd moved your boat Lady Louella from the marina. You also told me about the foreign friend who'd been staying with you.

There's this thing about putting two and two together. I did it when I rang Marilyn. She tells me she's met your friend who's called Ileana. She also says that Spence is sorting some papers out for her. The long and the short of it is, I give our Spence a bell and he tells me the girl's surname is Petrescu and she's about twenty years old and comes from Romania.

As it happens I know people who have dealings with girls from Eastern Europe. So I check it out with my associates and they say the name's familiar but she hasn't been around for a while. Like the black geezer who'd been sniffing about.

That's the way of it, kiddo, and I can't change it. I want to, but I can't. I can't change it and it could never be right between us because of it. You're a bright kid; you'll see that. So what I'm planning is a trip on Firefly. You won't be seeing me again.

Keep shtoom with Ma and Marilyn for their sake, not mine. Zsa Zsa's got a shoulder you could cry on if you was desperate, but I don't think you will. Take care of yourself, kiddo.

Marlon

Full circle.

You think about Floyd and Illy and all the lost women and wonder what could have driven your father to become involved in trading in abuse and misery.

You wonder why he changed from a hard worker to someone whose criminal activities even encompassed murder. The murder of the man you loved and who knows how many others.

You can't imagine how your own father could have been capable of such terrible things. You ask yourself if it was some kind of twisted revenge for what happened to your mother.

Then you remember your mother's crimes.

Then what you really, really hope is that it isn't in the genes.

After a while you fold the letter in half and slip it back in the envelope. You put the envelope in the box with the records relating to the family slaving business. It seems appropriate.

I went to the inquest with Ma and Marilyn and Zsa Zsa. They were all very subdued. I wondered what they really knew about Marlon's affairs.

A verdict of Accidental Death was recorded. There was some debate about the level of alcohol in Marlon's blood, but given the autopsy had revealed he was suffering from sclerosis of the liver, it wasn't pursued.

I told myself that Marlon's death atoned for Floyd's murder but I wasn't really convinced.

Everybody came to the funeral, even Dirk. I didn't warm to him. Spencer came with his wife Greta. Greta was blonde and younger than me. A generous description of Spencer would be that of 'rough diamond'; a thought crossed my mind and wouldn't be dispelled – what if he and Marlon were in the same line of business? What if certain associates were at that moment looking for Ileana?

The wavery promise I'd made to myself, to report what I knew to the authorities, waxed and waned.

Illy was having a driving lesson when my investment in computer tuition from Greg paid off. I was fit to burst by the time she came home.

'You won't believe what I've found.'

She glanced round the room. 'I not seeing anything exciting.'

'Here, on Floyd's computer. D'you see what it is?'

She peered at the screen. 'I not sure exactly, but I thinking maybe beginning of Floyd's story.'

'It's more than that. It's the whole thing. See.' I ran through page after page of **An Honest Trade**. 'And here, look,' I clicked on another file, 'here's a whole list of articles and papers he's already had published and the fees he's received. No wonder he felt able to give up the day job.'

'I not quite understanding.'

'I think it means that Floyd turns out to have been quite a dark horse. He's evidently been writing seriously for some time without ever saying a word, not to me at any rate.'

She nodded. 'You thinking Floyd sending book to people on list?'

'Well, not as far as I can tell. Leastways, I haven't found copies of any correspondence to indicate so, and I'm sure there'd be something given his meticulous record keeping.'

'Daysee?'

'Mm?'

'I wondering who may send Floyd's book to publisher now?'

I'm studying my charts and books about the Azores, with Illy sitting beside me so our heads are almost touching, and I'm pointing things out and she's laughing and asking when shall we be going?

And suddenly I'm thinking, why not? It might be a good idea to get away for a while. Illy's a good sailor and we have the passport now. We could go next season and with any luck Romania would be a fully-fledged member of the EU by the time we got back. In the meantime there's always the trip round the British Isles I mentioned to Megan.

So it's kind of settled and that only leaves one matter still to be cleared up.

'I coming also,' Illy says.

'No,' I say. 'I have to do this by myself.'

In the event it's nothing to write home about. The weather's damp and misty and it's dark when I arrive at the parade. Cutting it Fine is closed and the lights are out. For good, I suppose.

I lean my bike against the shop wall and stand there, wondering what I was expecting. Nothing stays the same; not that I'd have wanted it to. The Fast Tan Studio and the sex shop have made way for an estate agents specialising in commercial lettings, and a bookmakers. And the Party Place has been stripped of its novelties save for a bunch of shrivelled balloons and a faded poster advertising Harry Potter merchandise.

All of which seems to say something about society, although exactly what, I can't decide.

In fact, I can't decide about anything. Least of all why I have come.

Presently I feel a few drops of rain spotting my face and pull up the hood of my Musto. Dark and wet. Invisible. But even as I hunch up my shoulders and turn to wheel my bike away from the barber shop, I notice the fluorescent bands on my jacket reflecting back at me through the empty window.

Printed in the United Kingdom
by Lightning Source UK Ltd.
123562UK00001B/228/A

9 781847 535917